Doves in Flight

ii

Doves in Flight

Prism of Truth: Book 2

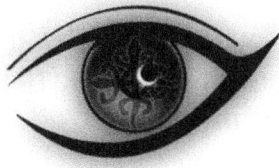

Shivon Mirza Sudesh

Cover art doves and dark moon by
Kiều Trường and Pexels respectively (Pixabay)

In memory of Suresh Chellayan,
the sweetest uncle in the world.
You were supposed to be the first one to read DIF.

Table of Contents

viii

Vishnu the Sustainer

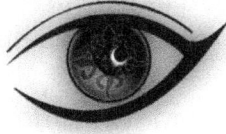

Om devi Mookambike
Vidhya kaarani Saraswathy
Naavil manassil vilangane
Kollur vazhum Njaanambike

I

Hail O'Lord Vishnu,
the Supreme Soul and Preserver
The all-pervading life's essence,
showering blessing with mere prayer

Wears the crown of supreme authority bright
and lustrous like the sun that glows
With brilliant yellow robes of earthly righteousness
that drapes his body and flows

Ears adorned by dazzling earrings
that opposites in creation balance
Happiness-unhappiness,
pleasure-pain, knowledge-ignorance

Kaustuba jewel, satisfier of genuine desires,
on his neck glistens and rustles
While the Srivasta mark, Lakshmi as a curly hair,

close to his chest nestles

Divine attributions adorn his body,
blue like the sky attracting and shimmering
On which Vanamala, the lovingly woven garland,
lies complimenting and adoring

Divinely pure and perfect lotus petals opening
under the sun, he holds
To accept knowledge and wisdom of God
so spiritual consciousness blooms and unfolds

Bears a conch whose slender contours spiral out
from the centre into eternity
Blowing and wafting his breath as 'om',
the primeval sound of creation and continuity

Handles a mighty mace, the divine power within us residing
Helping to purify and help us from demonic tendency
and material longing

Sudarshana chakra, the purified spiritualised mind,
on his finger spins
Helps discover and realise essence of God,
and returns after one's ego it destroys

II

Hail O'Lord Vishnu, the Supreme Soul,
Omnipotent and Omnipresent
With Maya, his dark energy
and the power within him resident

Great Earth Goddess Ammavaru showered blessings

by Trimurthi's conception
Brahma, Vishnu and Shiva for Creation,
Sustenance and Destruction

Vishnu, the dark matter of the Universe
and its primary intelligence
Whose front and back hands signify
his physical and spiritual providence

Stands a firm pillar establishing
earth to heaven connection
His four hands representing pleasure
and material gain, duty and liberation

As Mukunda, the supreme God and liberators
of Souls, grants ultimate salvation
A heavenly paradise to escape the cycle
of life and death by acts of sublime devotion
The Lord of truth, discards royal virtues
through his navel for Brahma to take
Accepts as his seat the twisted coils of the vices
of darkness, Sheshnaga the snake

From his feet in Vaikuntha flows the river Ganga,
gurgling and gushing with turbulence
Ultimately descending to earth to cleanse
and liberate departed souls in her benevolence

His consort Lakshmi arose from the murky ocean
seated on the heart of the lotus of purity
She as Goddess of Prosperity and Beauty
is his creation and creativity

On the milky ocean his deep slumber with his Devi

suspends creativity and creation
Leaving Shesh (remainder) Naga, swimming
like a germ in its womb awaiting conception

III

Hail O'Lord Vishnu, the Supreme Soul
and Possessor of Virtues
Splendour, energy, vigour, strength,
sovereignty and omniscience

Vaikuntha, the supreme eternal abode
beyond material Universe situated
Heavenly realm of bliss and happiness for all souls
blessed and enlightened

Reclines on timeless Adishesha, coiling and uncoiling,
creating daunting waves and ripples
His residence in material world amidst good and evil
engaged in continuous battle

As Soul of Vedas rides on fearless Garuda,
the mighty Eagle King's shoulder
Whose perpetually flapping wings disperse
Vedic wisdom and awe-inspiring power

As Trivikrama, the triple-strider, from East-West,
North-South and over heaven does leap
Creating dwellings for all creatures big and small to live,
mate and sleep

Sits beneath the thousand-headed Sheshnaga,
taunted by innumerable desires and passions
Thus showing control of mind over venom

of greed and immense temptations

Lies on a gleaming, smooth,
slithering but venomous serpent
His pose in the face of terror and worry one of calm,
divine detachment

Listens smiling to songs of his thousand names,
rejoicing on Ananta the immortal and endless
Floating and gliding on the sea of pure consciousness, vast,
immeasurable and immense

His progressive incarnations from water dweller to human form
Relates to human evolution from aquatic to land-born

IV

Hail O'Lord Vishnu, the Supreme Soul,
who with the avatars of Adishesha,
Lakshmana and Balarama, stamped out unrighteousness,
restoring dharma

Started as Matsya the fish to kill Damaka,
churning the ocean with his might
Saved mankind by bringing the ancient literatures of wisdom,
the stolen Vedas, to light
As Koorma the valiant, powerful tortoise
to the depths of the ocean he dived
Bringing up the sunken mountain for churning
on his paved back balanced

As Varaka the boar-faced, Earth Mother
to her rightful place he restored
Gently lifting, carried her on his tusks

after Hiranyaksha was slaughtered

As half-man, half-lion Narasimha
he came out of a pillar roaring
Saved devotee from Hiranyakashapu in divine anger,
claws tearing and ripping

Came as Vamana the dwarf to claim three steps of land,
to a towering giant he transformed
After taking earth and heaven he placed his third stride
on King Bali's head, immortality granted

As possessor of Shiva's axe,
Parashurama the priest-warrior
Travelled twenty-one times around the earth,
eliminating each and every evil-doer

As Rama, Prince of Ayodhya and the perfect human,
fought alongside invincible Lakshmana
To rescue wife Sita abducted by the trickery and illusion
of ten-headed Ravana

As cow-herd born, Lord Krishna of Dwaraka,
who with a flute and peacock feather he charmed
As Divine Diplomat and Statesman,
through Mahabharata and Bhagwatgita informed

Hail O'Lord Vishnu, the Supreme Soul,
as we await your ultimate Kalki arrival
Riding a white stallion, to dispel the foulness
within for a mind the clarity of crystal

Sudeshni Mirza

Behold, I send you forth as sheep in the midst of wolves: be ye therefore wise as serpents, and harmless as doves.

Matthew 10:16

"O how they cling and wrangle, some who claim
For preacher and monk the honored name!
For, quarreling, each to his view they cling.
Such folk see only one side of a thing"

Udana 68-69:
Parable of the Blind Men and the Elephant

Prologue

The fabric rustled softly as the breeze wound through the curtain, masking the shallow breathing of the three people taking refuge in the dark shadows behind it. The man stood slightly in front of the woman and the boy, so that he could shield them from approaching danger, so that he could try and protect them, even though he knew there was really no hope for any of them.

He could hear in the kitchen, not far from their hiding place, the vengeful mutterings of the stranger in their home; he could hear the monster swearing revenge on those who disturbed his peace of mind, who tortured him constantly with hurtful words. Their voices resounded so deeply in his mind that he thought they must belong to the only other people in his house, forgetting in his insanity that those people wore the faces of those he'd once loved.

The man tensed as his son paused in front of the curtain. He drew back slightly, motioning to his wife and younger son to be quiet, to not even breathe, while his much-loved eldest looked around with the eyes of a bloodthirsty hunter, a carving knife in his hand.

PART ONE

xx

Chapter One

House of Peace

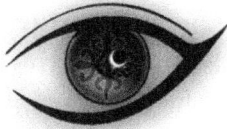

'Sathi *chechi*, Sathi chechi, Sathi chechi!'

She groaned, turning her face away from the harsh light and trying to ignore the loud buzzing in her ears.

'Sathi chechi, Sathi chechi, Sathi chechi!'

She began to shake up and down, her face banging against something soft each time. What the hell? Had the forecast for this morning included an earthquake?

'Sathi chechi, Sathi chechi, Sathi chechi!'

Finally, her sleepy mind gave in to the insistent voice and equally insistent banging. Groggily, she opened her eyes and sat up, blinking against the light in her eyes. 'Wha-?' Her enquiry turned into a yawn midway through.

'Sathi chechi!'

Someone pulled on her arm, and Sathi looked around at the small person who was still bouncing up and down on her bed. 'Zoya?'

The four-year-old had tears streaming down her cheeks. Fully awake and worried now, Sathi leaned forward and put her arms around the little girl. 'Sweetheart, what's wrong?'

Zoya buried her face in Sathi's neck. 'It's Aman,' she sobbed. 'He's mad.'

Without another word, Sathi flung off her covers and rose to her feet, scooping the girl into her arms and hurrying out of the bedroom. From there, she didn't need directions from the crying kid to follow her ears to the kitchen. The crashing sounds emanating from there said she shouldn't rule out the earthquake as a possibility, either. She burst into the kitchen and came to a sudden stop, stunned by the sight that greeted her.

Early morning sunlight streamed through the open window, the curtains rustling as the rain-sprinkled air pushed its way inside. A dark-haired man in his late twenties stood in the middle of the cosy, brightly lit room, facing the window. The floor around his feet was littered with remnants of the plates that used to be neatly stacked on the kitchen cupboards, and he held a drinking glass in his hands.

Crash!

Sathi flinched as the glass struck the floor; it splintered into a thousand pieces, the spiked shards scattering across the room in all directions.

'Aman, please, stop this.' The woman whom Sathi had not immediately noticed in the room stepped forward and rested her hand on the man's arm. She had petite features, with the top of her dark-maned head barely brushing Aman's shoulder, but she had a certain way of standing that conveyed power.

Aman flung off his mother's arm, his features pulling back into a snarl. 'They have to go!' he screamed.

For a moment, Sathi thought he was talking about her and Zoya, still standing frozen in the doorway. Then Aman threw another pan onto the floor, where it cracked against the hard ground, and jabbed a finger in the direction of the window. 'Go! Go the f*** away! Leave me alone!' he shouted. 'Go,' he repeated, his voice cracking with a desperation that sliced through Sathi's heart. With a shock, she realised that Aman was bleeding. The glass he'd thrown was now getting its revenge, and shards had pierced his feet while he paced in agitation.

Maira – Aman's mother – used his momentary distraction to shoot Zoya a hurried glance. 'Get your father,' she ordered. Before Sathi could bend to put the little girl down, Zoya had launched herself out of Sathi's arms. She took off at a run as soon as her feet touched the floor. Maira

2

then turned her gaze to Sathi, her near-black eyes resting on hers. 'Can you wake Zakiy?'

Giving Maira a quick nod, Sathi turned and sprinted the length of the short hallway, quickly cutting across to the stairs. Taking the narrow steps two or three at a time, she stopped in front of the closed door opposite the stairway and knocked sharply.

There was no answer. Sathi impatiently yelled, 'Zakiy!' and banged on the door again, restless at the thought of the woman who had been left alone downstairs with her unstable son.

Finally, a sleepy voice called, 'It's open.'

She pushed the door open, and her eyes immediately went to the single bed in the room. Eyes eyes still closed, and his words muffled by sleep, Zakiy complained, 'It should be a crime to be up this early. More importantly, it should be a crime for people who are up this early to wake up other people who *aren't* up this –'

Zakiy broke off as he finally opened his eyes and caught sight of her face. His expression immediately hardened. 'Where?' he barked as he launched out of bed and yanked a T-shirt over his head.

'The kitchen,' Sathi replied, barely managing to keep up with him as he charged past her and out of the room, down the stairs and into the kitchen.

Zakiy immediately rushed to his brother's side, and started talking to him in a low, soothing voice. Sathi hung back, not wanting to get in the way. Besides, she had no clue what she could do to help in what was apparently a recurrent family emergency in this household.

Then, a small hand slipped into her own. Sathi looked down to see Zoya standing close by her side, her small body trembling and her dark eyes fixed on her brothers. She was no longer crying, but she still looked so afraid that Sathi felt her heart clench. She squeezed Zoya's hand reassuringly, wishing she could do more.

Zoya's father had followed his daughter into the room. A dark-skinned, middle-aged man with greying hair, Narayan crossed the space to Aman with single-minded focus. 'Aman, shh, it's okay,' he said, elbowing Zakiy aside and taking his place next to his eldest son. The change in Aman was palpable; his shrill voice calmed into incoherent mumbles as he confided his fear and confusion to the man that he trusted most in the world. Aman allowed his father's assurances that it was okay, it was all okay, to lull him into compliance. Finally, Aman managed to quiet down enough for his father to lead him out of the room, carefully guiding him around the blood and glass. They left behind eerily empty silence.

Zakiy stared after the two of them, his expression unreadable. After a moment, Sathi tentatively reached out and touched his arm. He looked at her, but his unfocused eyes made her think he wasn't really seeing her.

'Zakiy?'

The sweet, questioning voice jolted him out of his preoccupation. His gaze shifted to Zoya, who held out her arms to her older brother. Zakiy leaned down and picked her up, hugging her fiercely to his chest when he saw the fear that still marked her eyes. Then he turned to face Sathi, his expression becoming wry: 'Welcome to the house of peace.'

Sathi, back in her room, pushed away from her laptop in frustration. She stood up and paced the narrow confines of her bedroom, trying to think calmly even though she felt anything but calm after what had happened that morning.

This wasn't the first time she had seen her best friend's brother in the throes of his illness since coming to stay with Zakiy, but it wasn't the kind of thing you got used to. Her eyes closed as Aman's terrified expression flashed into her head. How did his parents stand to see it? It must be horrible to see your child in that kind of pain and not be able to do anything about it. And they'd been dealing with it for fifteen years, since Aman was just a child, and had first been diagnosed with schizophrenia.

She shivered as she recalled the desperate fire in Aman's gaze as he shouted at the imaginary constructs of his mind, and the uncontrollable rage that had seemed to possess him at that moment. Those images, seared into her memory, were so different to what Sathi had come to expect from the quiet, shy man who sat in a corner of the living room all day, more often than not huddled close to his father.

Sathi's face unconsciously formed a frown as she thought of Aman's – and Zakiy's – father. She couldn't deny that the man was an expert at dealing with his mentally ill son. Narayan's infinitely patient expression when he persuaded Aman to sit down to a meal with his family, or when he tried to make his skittish son go outside for a walk, was inspiring to say the least.

When Zakiy had initially told her about his father, back when they'd first met, Sathi had immediately noted that the two men didn't always get along or see eye-to-eye. A few days into her arrival at this house, her hunch had solidified into a certainty. For an easy-going guy, Zakiy could be unbelievably brusque with his father, and it wasn't difficult to figure out where he'd got that particular character trait. She still remembered the painful friction between father and son three weeks ago, when Zakiy had arrived home after four years of attending college in Nelliampathi – a beautiful hill station in Kerala – with Sathi, a complete stranger, in tow. Because of their rapid and largely unplanned departure to Mysore, Zakiy hadn't been able to give his family any warning that he would be turning up with an extra guest.

Despite herself, Sathi chuckled, thinking back to those initial humorous moments as Zakiy's parents tried to work out the implications of their adolescent son bringing some random girl home with him – it had taken some time for Sathi to be cleared from suspicions of being his girlfriend. Urgh.

Once the initial confusion had been explained away, however, the way had been paved for a greater issue to take centre stage: the issue that arose from the fact that Narayan had never intended for his son to return to their home in Mysore.

Later, when pressed on the subject, Zakiy had admitted to her that his father had hoped his comparatively anxiety-free college life would be enough to keep Zakiy away from Mysore and the dangers that came with living with his mentally ill and highly volatile brother. Zakiy had gotten worked up over the topic, indignant that his father expected him to abandon his family. Sathi had kept her mouth shut and let him rant, knowing that Narayan's sole motive was the safety and well-being of his son, but also knowing that pointing out that fact to said son in his present mood would be far from productive.

Actually, listening to Zakiy's complaints about his father had taken her mind to her own father, her thoughts turning wistful...

A closed chapter, Sathi reminded herself, shaking herself out of her fantasies. She refocused on Narayan, and her forehead creased again as she thought about what really troubled her about Zakiy's father.

The truth was, she was pretty sure he blamed her for Zakiy's return to Mysore.

Of course, Narayan had never said anything to her about it. And he was never impolite to her, and always treated her with courtesy. Yet whenever he looked at her or talked to her Sathi got the distinct impression he wished she were elsewhere. Something in his body language spoke volumes about his displeasure at her presence. She hadn't said anything about her suspicions to Zakiy because she knew he would immediately deny it. Even if he didn't, what good would telling him do? It would only serve to worsen his relationship with his father.

Besides, that wasn't the real problem. Was Narayan right? *Was* she the reason Zakiy returned to Mysore? Was it because of her that Zakiy put himself back in a dangerous situation his father had constantly strived to keep him out of?

'Sathi?'

Zakiy stuck his head around the door, which she had left ajar. She waved him into the room, all her worries about Narayan fleeing her mind at the haggard expression on her best friend's face. He walked in and flopped into her desk-chair.

'Hey,' he said.

'Hey,' Sathi replied, perching on the edge of her bed.

There was silence for a few minutes while she tried desperately to find something to say that would, if not alleviate, then at least distract him from the despair that so obviously cloaked him. Before she could say anything, though, Zakiy broke the silence. 'We need to do something. About Aman,' he clarified.

Sathi nodded. 'I've been thinking about that. I looked up that institute in Bangalore you told me about, NIMHANS?'

The National Institute of Mental Health and Neurosciences was a research institute cum psychiatric hospital and was renowned for its expertise in dealing with mental health issues.

'I know your parents already tried taking Aman there but that was years ago and –' She broke off as she realised that Zakiy wasn't listening. He was staring at the floor, his gaze unfocused. She walked over and put her hand on his shoulder. 'Hey,' she said softly. 'It'll be okay. We'll figure this out.'

He shook his head slowly, still not looking at her. 'I don't know, Sathi. What happened this morning... I thought Aman had gotten much better. He *sounded* better on the phone, he looked better... now it's like all that never happened. He's gone back to that same state...' Zakiy trailed off, screwing his eyes shut as fresh ridges of pain broke out over his forehead.

Sathi didn't need him to finish his sentence to know what it was that haunted him so much. She thought back to the first time he'd opened up to her about his older brother, and his descriptions of how violent Aman used to be; what had started with sleeplessness and paranoia had melded into hallucinations, and his savage, unpredictable moods had caused his family to live like captives in their own house. Though Zakiy had never told her the details, Sathi could guess from his family's reaction this morning and from Zakiy's bleak expression right now that those long years had been like a living nightmare for them all.

Zakiy had told her that a few years ago there had been a big change in Aman. While he was by no means back to normal, the violent mood swings that had thus far been the most prominent markers of his disease had abated slightly. However, it had been replaced by fear – a sort of chilling, crippling fear of life itself. Aman would not go out of the house – ever – and even inside the house he was never more than a few feet away from his father. Something about Narayan's presence seemed to calm the turbulent mass of emotions lurking beneath the surface of Aman's mind.

Looking at Zakiy now, she could only imagine how agonising it must be for him to return home and find that his brother had, instead of getting better, gotten *worse*. Sathi quickly tried to think of something positive to say.

'This change in Aman is exactly why we should get an expert's opinion. Who knows, this could be an indication that his prognosis has changed.'

Zakiy looked up, incredulous surprise replacing the despair as he gaped at her. 'Sathi. Why do you sound like you've swallowed a medical textbook?'

Sathi flushed, torn between embarrassment and happiness that she had finally managed to distract him, albeit inadvertently. She nodded to the laptop still open on her desk. 'I've been researching schizophrenia,' she told him half-defiantly.

Zakiy looked between her and the laptop, and then started to slowly shake his head back and forth. Humour glinted in his brown eyes, the first she'd seen there for a long time. 'Typical Sathi response,' he teased. 'If you don't know the answer, Google it.'

Sathi glared at him, hiding the big, goofy smile that threatened to break out over her face in response to his trademark grin. 'It's better to be well-informed than ignorant,' she replied haughtily.

'But of course, m'lady.'

Hearing the familiar nickname shattered her self-control, and the smile she had been trying to contain slipped past her lips.

'So, what were you saying about NIMHANS?' Zakiy asked.

Sathi was pleased to note that his voice, while not exactly upbeat, at least sounded less hopeless. 'I was saying that we should try taking Aman there again. Your parents took him there, what, more than ten years ago?' She looked to him for confirmation and he nodded. 'It wouldn't hurt to get advice from someone more...' she trailed off, searching for the right word.

'Recent?' Zakiy suggested.

8

'Up to date. You know, with the newest medicines and stuff,' she finished.

'Same thing,' he muttered under his breath, and Sathi spared a moment to glare at him. 'Anyway,' she went on, 'I think it'll be a good idea to take Aman to one of the psychiatrists there and see what they say. What do you think?'

He nodded, looking thoughtful. 'Yeah, that makes sense. I'll call the institute and try to get an appointment. In the meantime...' He looked at her, worry shadowing his eyes once more. Sathi looked at him searchingly, and he sighed.

'In the meantime, we pray.'

'Please, no, I don't want to. Please don't make me do it again,' the boy begged, trying to break away from the iron grip he had come to loathe.

The man acted as though he could not hear the boy. 'Nurse, turn it to the next setting.' Then he turned to the boy and smiled, his eyes vacant sockets without a glimmer of warmth. 'You know what to do.'

Chapter Two

Battle of Wills

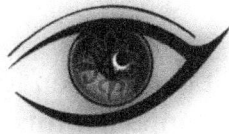

Zakiy made his way down the stairs, leaving Sathi engrossed in her laptop once more. He smiled, thinking of her Google addiction. The amusement was short-lived as he entered the kitchen to find it empty save for his father, who was sitting at the small table, drinking a cup of tea. Someone had already cleaned up. Dad looked up as Zakiy came in and jerked his head to the stove where a saucepan full of milky tea was sending up a fine sheet of steam to the ceiling. 'There's more there if you want it,' he said gruffly.

Zakiy declined and leant against the counter. 'Where's Aman?' he asked.

'Upstairs. Sleeping.'

'What about the glass?'

'Surface scratches. Fine once I cleaned up and put Band-Aids on.'

Zakiy nodded. He couldn't help but be amazed – only Dad could persuade Aman to sleep after an episode, especially one that violent. Silence descended over the kitchen, broken only by sounds of sloshing liquid as his father finished his first cup of tea and drank his way through another. Removed from Sathi's company, Zakiy found that the brief good mood she had teased out of him was rapidly evaporating.

As though he had read Zakiy's mind, Dad said, 'You shouldn't have brought her here.'

Zakiy looked up quickly. 'What?'

His father fixed his unflinching gaze on him. 'You shouldn't have brought that girl here.'

Zakiy stared back at him. 'Why not?'

'It's not safe,' Dad snapped, his patience finally running out. Zakiy had a feeling his father had been building up to this for a while now. 'It's bad enough you came back, did you have to drag a stranger into this mess as well?'

'Dad, you have no idea, if it hadn't been for her, I –'

'Have you forgotten what happened this morning?' Dad demanded, rising from the chair. 'When we already live in constant fear, how can you even *think* about letting someone outside the family get involved?'

His own temper rising, Zakiy glared at his father. 'Sathi's put enough effort into helping Aman that she can't be classified as anything *but* family! Do you know how many hours she's spent up there,' he said, jabbing a finger to the ceiling, 'trying to find a way to help Aman get better?'

This seemed to throw his dad off guard. 'What do you mean, trying to find a way to get Aman better?'

Taking deep, calming breaths, Zakiy explained their plans to take Aman to another psychiatrist. He had barely begun to describe Sathi's idea to visit NIMHANS when Dad burst out, 'What? You mean you're actually considering taking the advice of those crackpots who call themselves doctors?'

Zakiy sighed deeply. 'I know you have a prejudice against doctors because of what happened with Aman years ago, but believe it or not, not all doctors are crackpots these days. Things have changed, and we just want to explore all options –'

'We?' Dad interrupted again. 'So you're still not willing to leave that girl out of this.'

'Without "that girl",' Zakiy began angrily, but he broke off when he realised that the girl in question had just entered the kitchen and was staring at them, wide eyed.

'Er, hi,' Sathi said tentatively into the prickling silence. Her skin was flushed with embarrassment, and she seemed reluctant to look at him or his father.

Dad had his voice carefully under control when he spoke. 'Good morning, Sathi. I hope you slept well.'

As he listened to Sathi's equally polite reply, Zakiy's hands curled into fists again. His father was trying to act like nothing had happened, but Zakiy wasn't going to let him sweep this under the carpet. It was far too important. 'We want to take Aman to NIMHANS again,' he loudly interrupted the niceties.

His father's attention snapped back to him. 'No,' he said in a tone that did not lend itself to argument.

'Dad, come on!' Zakiy said, exasperated. 'Sitting at home isn't going to help Aman.'

'Neither will parading him in front of more so-called professionals!' Dad retorted.

'What if we didn't have to parade him in front of anyone?'

Both men stopped and turned their attention to Sathi. She hurried on, 'At least, not initially. Zakiy and I could go there first and talk to the doctor. That way, we get an idea of what they can do, and Aman doesn't have to come until we're sure it will help.'

She looked back and forth between their faces, looking slightly nervous. Zakiy turned to face his father triumphantly. He was sure he saw a glimmer of hope in Dad's eyes before they dimmed again.

'Would that be okay, Uncle?' Sathi asked timidly, adopting the term Indian kids used to address adults in their parents' generation.

'Yes, I suppose so,' Dad said heavily. 'I can't stop you two from wasting your own time. Excuse me.' He nodded to both of them and left the room.

Sathi moved to the stove and filled two cups with tea that was now not so much as steaming as scabbing over with milky skin. She pulled a face as she used a small sieve to get rid of the skin, but there wasn't much she could do about its tepid temperature. She put the cups on the table

13

and sat down. When Zakiy made no immediate move to follow suit, she looked up at him questioningly.

He tried to shake off his feeling of awkwardness and sat down opposite her, pulling the cup towards him. However, he did not drink. He was still watching Sathi and dreading the moment when she would ask about his father and the fight she could not have helped but overhear. However, as she crossed her ankles and sipped her tea serenely, he realised that she wasn't going to discuss it – not unless *he* did. As this dizzying fact sank into him, he recalled something else: Sathi had an even more tenuous relationship with her father. In fact, as far as he knew Sathi and her father hadn't been in contact at all since she came to India to find the pathetic excuse for a human being who had murdered her mother.

Sathi had spent most of her life in London along with her father, attributing the absence of her mother to the belief that she had died giving birth to Sathi. Then, on the day of her eighteenth birthday, Sathi had found some evidence – in the form of a letter written by her mother and some flight tickets – that suggested that her mother's death had not been so innocuous. She had been killed, murdered by someone in Kerala, south India, and Sathi had fought with her father and set out – alone – to avenge her mother.

Zakiy had met her in Nelliampathi, her mother's hometown. They had become friends almost instantly after arguing over rights to a campsite and then bonding over their shared love of Tarot cards.

The two of them had then embarked on a quest to find out more about Sathi's mother, tracking down the school and college she had attended, and even managing to get in contact with an old friend of hers. However, none of this had yielded any more information about why someone would want to kill Sathi's mother, or who that someone could be. Their last hope had been her mother's adoptive family, who had been out of town when Sathi first arrived in Nelliampathi. The night they returned, though, Sathi and Zakiy had had an awful fight. They had gone their separate ways, and Sathi had stumbled upon her long lost relatives.

14

She'd spent several months with her mother's family, and it was only three weeks ago that she and Zakiy had reunited.

Zakiy thought back to that day, a frown creasing his brow. Under the surface of her joy at seeing him again, there had been something off about Sathi. *Her eyes*, he decided after a moment of thought. Where before they had been clear and expressive, that day they had been almost... haunted. He guessed that the change had something to do with the time she spent with her mother's family, but he couldn't understand why. Judging by what they'd found out before their fight, Madhu – Sathi's mother – couldn't have been brought up by better people after her parents were killed in a car accident when she was just a toddler. Her aunt's and her husband – who ran a charity that aimed to wed off couples without dowry – had adopted Madhu, and looked after her like their own daughter.

Whatever had happened, Sathi hadn't told him anything about those months she'd spent with her mother's family. Zakiy hadn't pushed her on the subject, trusting that she would tell him in her own time, but his patience wore thin sometimes when he caught a glimpse of that haunted look in her eyes. Looking at her now, he wondered whether this was a good time to broach the topic.

'Oh, here,' Sathi said suddenly, interrupting his musings. She set the mug down and reached into her pocket, pulling out a scrap of paper. She pushed it across the table to Zakiy. 'It's the number for NIMHANS. I would've called them myself, but I don't think my Malayalam is up to it.' She grinned ruefully at him.

Zakiy felt a rush of affection and gratitude towards her, his best friend in the world. 'Nonsense,' he said, waving a hand in the air. 'There's nothing wrong with your Malayalam. You speak it like you've lived in Kerala all your life.' He paused, considering. 'Actually, I think you speak it better than even *I* do. And that's saying something. Besides, this isn't Kerala, remember? The best Malayalam will sound like perfect Greek here. You don't happen to be fluent in Kannada, do you?' he added hopefully, referring to the native language in Mysore.

'Nope, sorry.'

'Ah, well,' he sighed. 'English it is, then.'

'You've lived here for a long time, haven't you?' she asked curiously. 'Surely you know some Kannada by now?'

'Let me put it this way. I once told a woman that her moustache was red instead of saying that her house was beautiful. She, um... well, she didn't like that,' he said, wincing at the woman's retribution. 'It would have been okay if I'd only gotten one of those words wrong, but no, I had to mess up both of them.'

'You think it would've been okay if you'd said her moustache was beautiful?'

'At least that's a compliment,' Zakiy said regretfully.

Sathi's lips twitched. 'I don't think a woman would take *any* reference to her moustache as a compliment.'

He sighed. 'So difficult to please,' he said, but under his breath.

'What was that?' she asked suspiciously.

'Oh, nothing! Just saying that I should call and try to make that appointment now,' he lied cheerily.

'Yes, I think you'd better,' Sathi said, her eyes narrowed. 'If a woman answers the phone, make sure you don't tell her that her beard is yellow.'

Unlike Nelliampathi, Mysore was not a remote hill station, nor was it surrounded by thickets of lush teak trees or blanketed by beds upon beds of neatly cultivated tea plants. It was a city fully immersed in tourism and industry. Yet it did not contain the typical skyscrapers and blocky buildings that were as boring as they were identical. Instead Mysore had the feel of a city from old – as though someone had video-taped the town in the 16th century (when it had first become a kingdom under the rule of the Wadiyar royal family) and put the recording on a loop until the present day.

Sathi stared out of the window at the passing city, trying to find the right word to describe the small yet busy roads, the unusual architecture of the houses, buildings and of course, Mysore Palace itself.

For a minute she became distracted as she thought of the palace. She'd only seen it in passing as they waited for traffic to move on, but what little she'd glimpsed had struck her with its unique beauty. It was constructed of arches and gorgeous rounded domes like those of a mosque, and there was something intriguing about Mysore's old seat of power that made her eager to explore the architecture of the place properly.

Quaint, Sathi finally decided. There was no other word for it: Mysore was a quaint city. She wondered what it would be like to live in India permanently and to surround herself with the amazingly diverse architecture that was prevalent here. A smile played with her lips as she indulged in a fantasy about studying in Nelliampathi instead of going back to the UK, of just visiting and analysing as many of these ingenious constructions of India as she could...

'I miss Toothless,' Zakiy whined, breaking into her reverie.

Sathi glanced across to see him glaring distastefully down at the steering wheel of the rented Maruthi. Toothless was Zakiy's highly adored Jeep, named after the black Nightfury in the movie "How to Train Your Dragon". She still hadn't figured how he'd found a link between a Jeep and an animated reptile, but she'd long since learned not to question his baffling idiocy as it usually only served to generate even more of the aforementioned baffling idiocy. Toothless was Zakiy's pride and joy, but it – no, *he*, Sathi mentally corrected herself, knowing that referring to the Jeep as merely "it" was tantamount to blasphemy in Zakiy's book – was still in Nelliampathi since they had travelled to Mysore by train, leaving "him" behind. Zakiy was trying to get the Jeep transported here, but in the meantime they were stuck with the rental car for the three-hour drive to Bangalore. Something Zakiy was not remotely happy about.

'Stupid saloon car,' he muttered.

'You know that's an idiotic thing to say at the start of a long journey,' Sathi said conversationally. 'In my experience, cars don't take lightly to being insulted. They mysteriously stop working and leave you stranded on the middle of the road. Lovely, sweet car,' she added, patting the dash.

Zakiy shot her a look of outrage. 'How could you? How could you be so disloyal to little Toothless? Your betrayal will just break his heart.'

She stuck up for the poor Maruthi. 'This car has a heart too, you know.'

'No, it doesn't. It is a cold, heartless piece of machinery that is nothing compared to the majesty of my Toothless.'

Sathi shook her head sternly. 'Well, don't say I didn't warn you when this poor thing gets fed up with your abuse and breaks down.'

'Huh!' he huffed indignantly, giving the Maruthi yet another scathing look and revving the engine loudly so that a couple of girls crossing the road in front of them gave a start and glared at him reproachfully.

Sathi ducked her head, grinning. She knew that it was more than the car argument that was causing her such amusement. She couldn't describe the joy it gave her to watch Zakiy getting up to his old antics again; she had missed these nonsensical conversations and his general hilarity these past few weeks – at the house, his mood had always been overshadowed by his brother's illness.

The thought of Aman had her glancing down at the file sitting open in her lap. Time to stop daydreaming, she told herself as she turned the page and resumed reading. Narayan – after making his displeasure clear – had reluctantly dug out Aman's old medical file for them, which summarised his symptoms and detailed the two years of treatment he'd received at NIMHANS in the early stages of his illness.

The more she read, the sicker she felt: Aman's family had really, truly suffered. For fifteen years his parents had been living with someone so paranoid, so violent that they never knew if they were looking into the eyes of their son, or those of a bloodthirsty stranger. They had never known a moment's peace. Sathi bit her lip, hoping against hope that this new endeavour of theirs would work.

'Do you know why Dad doesn't like psychiatrists?' Zakiy asked quietly.

18

Startled, she looked across at him. He had been staring out of the windscreen, but now he glanced at her. She shook her head mutely.

He was silent for a few moments. 'Remember when I said my parents travelled all over India to find a miracle hospital that would cure Aman?'

'After NIMHANS didn't work out?' Sathi asked.

'Yeah.' He laughed bitterly. 'Well, they found a hospital all right, only it wasn't a miracle one. It was a private hospital, back in Kerala somewhere, and the doctor "treated" Aman for a few months. He gave Aman insulin shots.'

Sathi frowned. 'But insulin-'

'Will make the blood sugar level drop so low that you collapse, yeah. That's exactly what that idiotic doctor did to Aman – that was his solution to manage the violence. Then he made Aman assist with giving ECT – shock treatment – to other patients.'

'That's...' Sathi couldn't finish and had to try again. 'That's horrible.'

Zakiy shrugged, his face hard. 'I still don't understand what he was thinking when he did that. He also milked my parents for money, suggesting all these expensive treatments and drugs. My parents didn't care about the money but they couldn't forgive what he did to Aman with the insulin and the ECT. Aman became afraid of doctors after that. That's when my parents gave up with treatment and we settled in Mysore. I think Dad was afraid that going back home to Nelliampathi would just expose Aman to stupid, illiterate people who don't understand that mental illness isn't a reason to mock and bully-'

Zakiy broke off abruptly as he struggled to bring his anger under control, and Sathi thought back to the one and only time she'd seen him lose his temper. Some school children had decided to make a sport of jeering and throwing rocks at a homeless woman who had mistaken a rock for a baby in her illness. Her eyes filled as she remembered the way the woman had protected her "child", putting herself as a shield between it and those nasty boys.

She could imagine how it must have affected Zakiy, to see someone like her being targeted because of her illness. How cruel people could be when confronted with the unknown. It made her sick to think that Zakiy and his family had been driven out of their home – a beautiful mansion that now stood like an impassive shell – because of fear and ignorance.

Sathi looked back at the medical file, doubt trickling into her mind like sand in an hourglass. Were they doing the right thing? She'd never realised that Narayan had such a forceful reason for distrusting doctors. After listening to what that psychiatrist had done to Aman she didn't know what to hope for. What if she was just paving the way for more disappointment by encouraging Zakiy?

Even though she tried to convince herself that things were different now, that such behaviour wouldn't be tolerated from medical professionals, worries and doubts plagued her for the rest of the journey.

She lay awake, unable to calm her churning thoughts. Tears slid down her cheeks even as anger burned within her chest. How dare he? How dare he treat her like that? How could he have threatened her with divorce when her mother had just had a stroke? Had she really fallen in love with such a cold-hearted man?

The pain in her chest flared suddenly. No. He wasn't cold-hearted. He was the kindest, most gentle man she'd ever met. He'd won her over with that gentleness, that patient love that never faltered, never diminished, even when she pushed him away for fear of losing her heart.

Her eyes burned as the tears flooded again, and she hunched over onto her side, drawing her knees up and wrapping her arms around herself to try to fill the festering hollowness in her chest. She loved him so much, but she wasn't sure she could ever forgive him. How could she forget the look on his face when-

Her thoughts abruptly cut off as an odd feeling of heaviness crept over her body. It felt as though her mind and body had separated. Mind spinning with panic, she tried to do something, to move her arms, or raise her head, but she couldn't do anything - it was like trying to push against some invisible, invincible force holding her down. She was immobilised.

Then, slowly, the panic abated. It was replaced by a strange feeling of dullness. A part of her knew there was something very wrong, but that part of her was buried under a thick layer of dark fog. A strange blankness gleamed like a field of untouched snow on a bleak winter morning.

Smoothly, she sat up, though her mind never commanded the action. Her eyes were dry. Mechanically, she gathered her long hair into a bun at the nape of her neck. She stood and moved to the door, quietly slipping through it into the moonlit corridor outside. Her fixed gaze staring straight ahead, she walked the short distance to another door. As she reached out to turn the doorknob, a single gold bangle slid down her wrist.

The man leaning back against the headrest looked up as she entered. He smiled, though his eyes were as cold as a serpent's scales. 'Ah, you've come,' he said, rising from the bed and approaching her. 'I've been waiting.'

He reached for the sari *draped over her shoulder just as a piercing scream ripped through the air.*

Chapter Three

Prince of Darkness

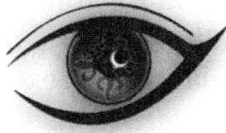

D espite Sathi's earlier prediction, they made it to Bangalore without any vehicular breakdowns, though she claimed it was because of the tender loving care she constantly bestowed upon the rental car. The reminder re-ignited a smile on Zakiy's face, and she felt optimistic again. As Zakiy said, they shouldn't lose hope just because the doctor who'd treated Aman in the past had been a vampire with no moral compass. After all, NIMHANS was a renowned institute for psychiatry.

The capital city of Karnataka had none of the ancient charm of Mysore; Bangalore was a typical modern city centre, complete with huge shopping malls and towering buildings, dusty sidewalks and chuntering buses, not to mention bumper-to-bumper traffic. In fact, the traffic was so bad that it took them nearly forty minutes to reach NIMHANS from the city centre, a distance of barely five kilometres. Finally, they pulled into the hospital grounds, passing a series of beautiful adjoining buildings built in an L shape with a vast grassy patch in front. They found a parking spot under the cover of some trees and proceeded on foot to what looked like the main entrance, a red-capped porch with wide pillars. Behind it was a large rounded glass building, with white trimming at the top.

After entering through the swinging doors, they went over to the reception desk to get directions. 'Excuse me,' Zakiy said politely to the receptionist, 'we have an appointment with-'

'Priya!' A harried-looking man strode up to the desk, dumping a cardboard box overflowing with papers on top. 'Where are they?'

The receptionist hastily pulled her shawl free from under the box. 'Sir, I-'

'I've been waiting for them for hours! When are they going to arrive?' He ran a hand through his hair in frustration, and that's when he caught sight of Zakiy. 'There you are!'

Zakiy shot him a startled glance. 'Uh, excuse me?'

The man fixed Zakiy with a stern look. 'About time!' he said, wagging a long finger. 'I've been waiting for you for hours,' he repeated. His gaze shifted to Sathi, and his dark eyebrows rose. 'So! They've sent me another one, eh? Trying to bribe me? Well!'

Sathi just stared back at him, speechless. The man suddenly started striding away, glancing back impatiently when they didn't move. 'Come along, come along, I can't waste any more of the morning. And bring the box.'

Zakiy and Sathi looked at the receptionist. 'Are you his assistants?' she asked desperately.

'Er... no,' Zakiy said apologetically. 'We have an appointment with a child psychiatrist. I think he's the head of the department.'

The receptionist's eyes widened. 'That was Professor Karuppuraja. *He's* the head of child psychiatry.'

Zakiy and Sathi exchanged startled looks. Then Zakiy sighed, grabbed the box, and they scurried after the man.

'Good thing you're both young and fit, this damn building has too many stairs... Don't know what they were thinking, giving me an office on the third floor. I just moved here from Tamil Nadu, you see,' he added conversationally. 'I've been asking for an assistant since last Friday, and *now* they finally decide to send someone. Well, it's a good thing there are two of you, I'll tell you that, there's so much left to do... Keep you out of mischief, I suppose.' He suddenly turned around and flashed them a wide grin, his eyes twinkling.

24

Before they could do much more than open their mouths in protest, the man loped over the last couple of steps and said, 'Ah, here we are. Now, where the hell is my office?' He stood in the middle of the corridor with his hands on his hips and gazed around in concentration.

Sathi used the opportunity to try again. 'Sir, we're not –'

'Aha!' the man exclaimed triumphantly, whirling around and stalking off purposefully again.

Sathi looked at Zakiy helplessly, and had no choice but to follow. They were led along another long corridor marked with more of those official-looking labels, and finally through a door right at the end which said, 'Professor Karuppuraja, Child and Adolescent Psychiatry (HOD)'. The room inside was a clutter of catastrophic proportions; a huge cardboard box sat on top of the desk, flattening a bunch of important-looking papers, and more boxes were strewn around the room, filled with books, a desk lamp, photographs and, more randomly, a beach ball. Box files overflowing with paperwork filled the rest of the space.

Karuppuraja groaned as he surveyed the room. 'Look at this mess,' he said in disgust. 'Right, you two can start by –'

'Sir!' Sathi interrupted, determined to make him listen. 'We're not your assistants.'

He stared back at her in confusion. Then he suddenly grinned again, looking from her to Zakiy. 'Oh, I see. You're joking. Well, ha ha, but if we could just get started...'

'No, sir, we're really not your assistants,' Zakiy insisted, putting the box down on the floor.

The man blinked a couple of times, and then he looked crestfallen. 'Well, why didn't you say so earlier? And why the deuce are you here anyway?'

Zakiy wisely chose not to answer his first question, and instead explained about Aman. When he finished, Karuppuraja scratched his chin, his eyes bright with interest. 'Juvenile onset schizophrenia? Hmm, I wonder... Can I have a look at that file?'

'Um, sure.' Sathi handed it to him.

Karuppuraja took it and walked to his desk, flicking through the file. He leaned against the desk and continued to read for another ten minutes, occasionally making random noises and muttering to himself. At one point, he looked up and exclaimed, 'Ten years? *Very* early onset, then...'

Then he went back to reading.

Zakiy had his hands tightly clenched at his sides, and Sathi was trying hard not to fidget. The wait was killing them.

Eventually, the professor finished reading and seemed surprised to see them still standing up. 'Sit, sit!' he said, waving his long arms at the chairs in front of his desk. Then he said the magic words: 'I'd like to meet Aman. I believe there are some relatively new drugs we can try that could help him.'

Zakiy and Sathi gasped and immediately began to thank him, but like before, he didn't seem to hear them. He still had that shrewd look in his eyes, and it appeared his listening ability switched off when he was thinking deeply about something. 'Of course, I'd like to start fresh, and not rely on these,' he continued, lifting up the file. 'It's an intriguing case, you know,' he added, grinning again in a way that made him look like a little boy. 'EOS is rare enough, I've never even dealt with VEOS...'

At their blank expressions, he explained, 'EOS is early onset schizophrenia, or juvenile onset schizophrenia, which is schizophrenia in children between thirteen and eighteen years of age. Your brother, though, has VEOS – very early onset schizophrenia – as his symptoms started when he was just ten. That's incredibly rare, and explains why he wasn't diagnosed earlier. He was treated here 10 years ago?' he asked.

Zakiy nodded, and Karuppuraja shut the file with a snap. 'Yes, he didn't present with symptoms that were typical of schizophrenia at that age, and because he was so young he was misdiagnosed. So,' he straightened up, abruptly adopting a business-like tone and reaching for a small diary on his desk, 'when would you be able to bring him here?'

Zakiy cleared his throat. 'Well, that's the problem,' he said hesitantly, 'Aman hates leaving the house, and on top of that, he has a phobia of doctors because... because of some bad experiences in the past. We live

26

in Mysore, and it'll be quite difficult to persuade him to make the trip here.'

'Hmm, yes, I see the problem,' Karuppuraja conceded, his eyes narrowed in thought. 'I might be able to make house calls for now, since it's an unusual case.'

Zakiy gazed at the professor, hope and gratitude etched in every line of his face. 'You would do that?'

'Yes, but unfortunately it can't be until next month. I've only just moved here, and I need to get this office in order first.' He gazed around in distaste at the mess.

'Let us do it,' Sathi said suddenly, making the other two glance at her like she had a brain impairment. Then Zakiy caught on, and he looked back at the professor. 'Yes. You took us on as assistants today, and assistants we shall be. Tell us what to do.'

The professor was now squinting at them like they *both* had a brain impairment. 'You realise that clearing this room isn't the only thing I need to do before I can come to see your brother?'

'Doesn't matter,' Zakiy replied, standing up. 'Where should we start?'

'Are you two sure you won't stay on a permanent basis?' Karuppuraja begged, gazing around the clean, well-organised office like he couldn't believe his eyes. 'I'll pay you double the original salary.'

Zakiy just grinned back, his expression so joyous that Sathi's breath caught. They'd spent the afternoon thoroughly decluttering the professor's office, organising his textbooks on the double shelves against one wall, clearing his desk of all the papers, emptying the cardboard boxes and arranging the desk lamp and the photo frames neatly on the desk. When Sathi asked Karuppuraja what to do with his ball, he just shrugged and told her to toss it in a corner: all without a shred of embarrassment. She found a small empty cardboard box, put in a corner of the room, threw a piece of cloth over it, and balanced the ball on top of it so it wouldn't roll away. The professor just shook his head bemusedly when he saw it.

Then they'd turned their attention to the masses of paperwork that only seemed to have expanded as the rest of the clutter was cleared away. Here, they'd had to ask Karuppuraja's help, seeing as they could hardly tell top from bottom on most of the forms. Zakiy and Sathi had then rushed back and forth all over the hospital, climbing countless flights of stairs and rushing along a hundred corridors to deliver the right set of papers to the right people.

Now, tired but unbelievably happy, they stood in front of Karuppuraja, surveying their handiwork. In Sathi's opinion, the professor's overjoyed exclamation summed it all up: 'I can find things again!'

'You are two extraordinary young people, you know that?' he said, beaming at them. He reached into his pocket and drew out his wallet. 'Now, the least I can do is pay you what I would have paid my real assistant if he'd ever turned up. Though I doubt he'd have done such a good job. Here,' he said holding out some money.

'No way,' Sathi said at the same time as Zakiy said, 'Nope.' They glanced at each other, grinned, and turned back to Karuppuraja.

He shook his head at them, then the good-humoured twinkle returned to his eyes. 'You two!' he accused, but affectionately. 'Okay, fine, I give up. Young man, write down your phone number for me and I'll give you a call as soon as I can come to Mysore. In the meantime, here's my direct number. You can contact me any time.' He handed them both a business card (a stack of which he'd delightedly re-discovered five minutes ago).

Zakiy scribbled down his number and they had just turned to leave when the professor's voice floated across to them, 'Remember, when all else fails...' They glanced back in surprise, and Karuppuraja's eyes turned incredibly gentle as he regarded them. 'Put your faith in God.'

'Phew, it's hot!'

Zakiy's exclamation pierced the quiet that had fallen over them once they'd left Karuppuraja's office. For some reason, the professor's last words had bullied their way to the forefront of Sathi's mind, and refused to give her any peace.

When all else fails, put your faith in God. Why did he say that? What did he mean? Why did it feel like a message for her?

'Let's get something cold to drink, this heat is awful,' Zakiy was saying. Sathi was vaguely aware of making some noise of assent, and of the car becoming stationary at the roadside. There was a swish of air, and then a door slammed.

When all else fails, put your faith in God.

Those words were becoming etched into her brain, opening up all sorts of fears she had pushed down for the past weeks. A cold, impersonal house, a sickening kind of love, suffocating and merciless, a pair of eyes, cold and revoltingly reptilian, sinister dreams, and a nauseating reality she wished desperately could have been part of a nightmare, too...

'Here ya go!' Zakiy opened the door and pushed a glass of crushed watermelon juice into her hands.

Sathi shrieked and jerked away from the glass in a movement so quick and primal, it was like that of a caged animal when confronted with its most feared predator.

Zakiy caught the glass before it could fall, sticky liquid sloshing over his fingers. Staring at her, he took it away. She didn't look at him as he went around to the driver side and got in, shifting around in his seat so that he faced her.

Sathi fisted her hands in her lap, trying to stop them trembling. She tried to take deep breaths, but the air seemed too dry, it kept getting caught up in her lungs, hitching and breaking. Zakiy waited while her breathing finally calmed, evening out. Her hands loosened and relaxed of their own accord as they steadied. He was silent for even longer, the car filled only with the sound of their breathing. Finally, he said, 'What's wrong?'

She shook her head, more to clear it than anything else. What was *with* her? She'd thought she was over all that, she'd thought she was fine. Why was she losing control *now*?

'Sathi, tell me.'

She had to tell him; she owed it to him. Sathi took in a deep breath. 'The night we had that fight back in Nelliampathi and I walked off... do you remember it?'

'Of course I do.'

She nodded. 'Well, I ended up in that temple near *Amma*'s old house, the one I told you about? Anyway, I saw a light in the house. My great-aunt and great-uncle were back.' Just saying those words, just acknowledging that they were related to her, to her *mother*, filled her mouth with bile. 'I was there the whole time after our fight, until... until the day we came to Mysore.'

'I know,' Zakiy said. She looked up in surprise. 'Your colleague at the resort told me,' he explained.

'You were in contact with Ravi?'

'Yeah, he's a great guy. Needs a bit of brake fluid on his tongue, but great otherwise.' Zakiy paused, suddenly hesitant. 'He tried to get you to talk to me again, you know.'

Sathi stared back mutely, too surprised for speech.

He nodded. 'You know that day he called you, and said he wanted you to meet his kid?'

Of course she remembered; that had been the day her saintly image of her great-aunt and great-uncle had begun to crack, although she had been too blind to realise it then. Zakiy continued, 'Ravi insisted on meeting you in Nelliampathi so he could orchestrate a meeting between us – but then he said you couldn't come because your great-aunt had a heart attack or something?'

Sathi snorted, her humour tinged with darkness, with bitterness. She could have seen Zakiy that day, she might have made up with him, she might not have had to go through the horrors that had ensued. She felt like such a fool. 'Yeah, my darling great-aunt – aka Drama Queen – conveniently had a heart attack just in time to prevent me meeting Ravi.'

He was silent for a moment. 'She was faking it?' he asked quietly.

'Yup, just like she faked a heart attack later when she didn't want my aunt and uncle going to visit my aunt's mother, who'd just had a stroke,

30

a real one,' she continued flippantly. She didn't know what was going on with her – she felt anything but flippant inside.

Zakiy didn't react in any way except for the fact that one of his hands formed a fist around his bunch of keys.

Somehow, that fist was more effective than probing questions. 'Then my great-uncle nearly raped my aunt.'

The fist slipped, and a tiny burst of red bloomed on his palm where the sharp teeth of a key sliced into his skin. Sathi found her gaze drawn to the minuscule droplet of blood; she couldn't look away, she was admiring the colour, the sharpness of it, the way it assaulted her eyes and demanded their attention.

The silence drudged on.

She couldn't take it anymore. 'They're truly awful people, Zakiy,' she whispered.

She sensed movement, and then he was right next to her, slipping his arm around her and squeezing her shoulders. When he spoke, though, his voice was anguished. 'Why didn't you tell me?'

Sathi leaned her head against his warm shoulder and closed her eyes, trying to hold back the tears that threatened to brim over. 'I don't know... I just felt so confused. I still am. Is that who my family is? A bunch of monsters?'

'No, Sathi, no,' he said, tightening his arms around her. 'Family isn't about blood – it's about genuine love and care and affection. If they'd been good people, they would've gained the love of an amazing granddaughter. As it is... well, it's their loss.'

She sighed and rested against him, wishing that she could let herself believe what he was saying. That it was only their loss, and not hers. She steeled herself and pulled away. There was one more thing he needed to know. 'There's something else. Something... something even worse, if you can believe that.'

He sat back as well. 'What is it?'

She took another deep breath. 'I think they – my great-aunt and great-uncle – practise black magic.'

Zakiy looked up sharply. 'What?'

She nodded miserably. 'They give *kaivisham*.' Kaivisham was a form of sorcery in which a person would give their enemy or the bearer of their grudge some sort of disgusting concoction made with their hair or fingernails, or even blood, all masked in food, and use it to gain control over them.

'How do you know?' Zakiy asked, his voice still hard and oddly business-like.

She didn't respond immediately, trying to construct an argument that was more to do with evidence and less to do with a *feeling*. 'Well, there have been a few things... one time was when my uncle and aunt were getting ready to go out for a meal with some of Aunt Maya's friends. Then just as they were about to leave Maya got really sick, with stomach cramps and a fever, and they couldn't go out after all.'

'So?'

Sathi looked up at him. 'Great-aunt gave Maya a glass of milk just before she got ill.'

'That could have been a coincidence.'

'It could have been, except Great-aunt hates Maya. So why would she suddenly decide to give her a glass of milk — out of the kindness of her heart?' She snorted. 'You should've seen her when Maya got sick; she couldn't care less. Plus, Maya was completely fine the next day, as though nothing had happened.'

'What else?' Zakiy asked.

'I also think Great-aunt gave Maya something the night... the night she went to Great-uncle's bedroom.'

'*What?*'

Sathi glared out of the window. 'Whatever she gave Maya, it made her go into some kind of trance. She only came out of it when I screamed. Otherwise... otherwise he would have done it.'

She couldn't imagine anyone getting any more messed up than that. Although to be honest, she hadn't imagined that someone could even be *that* messed up, so maybe that was something to be said about her imagination: it kept her blissfully ignorant.

Silence descended again. After all, what more was there to be said? What would further talk achieve, except to give the evil that was her mother's adoptive parents an even bigger presence in their lives?

Sathi desperately cast around for something to say, *anything* that would distract both Zakiy and herself from this morbidity. After a moment, she said, 'That was nice of Professor Karuppuraja, wasn't it, to say he'd come to see Aman in Mysore?'

Zakiy seemed to give himself a little shake. 'Mmmm,' he replied.

'I suppose his interest is because he's a child psychiatrist, and Aman has VEOS, or whatever it was,' she mused, not giving up.

'Yeah,' he agreed. His lips twitched a little. 'Lucky he mistook us for his assistants.'

Sathi smiled, and it was almost genuine. 'Remember his ball? Of all the things to bring to his new office...'

Zakiy gave a small chuckle. 'He's awesome.'

'Yup. Maybe not all doctors are vampires, huh?'

He didn't reply, just looked at her weirdly.

'What?'

'Do you know what his name means?'

Sathi shook her head, puzzled.

'Karuppuraja,' he said slowly, only the way he pronounced the word made it seem like a title: Karuppu Raja. She looked at him expectantly and he smiled widely, baring his teeth in an unnatural way as though expecting fangs to sprout from the corners of his mouth.

'He's the Prince of Darkness himself.'

Chapter Four

The Elusive Wolves

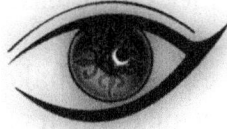

Professor Karuppuraja – or the Prince, as Zakiy insisted on calling him – kept his promise.

The first time he came to the house in Mysore, the tension had been immense with Narayan's silent fury. Then Maira had laid a calming hand on his arm, and smiled at Karuppuraja, graciously thanking him for making the long journey. Narayan took his cue from his wife and reluctantly agreed to the consultation, but only if he could stay with Aman for the duration of it. Sathi could tell that Narayan had been expecting the professor to protest. Instead, Karuppuraja just shrugged and said, 'The more the merrier.'

Yes, he actually said that.

It was fun to Narayan gradually ease up with his distrust. He continued to sit in on his meetings with Aman, but he also spent ages afterwards talking to Karuppuraja. It was amazing how dedicated Karuppuraja was; after the first few initial sessions talking to Aman, he came prepared with a pile of printed articles tucked under his arm. He explained that he'd done some background reading and found some cases of children with very early onset schizophrenia.

'There's a little girl living in London who started showing signs of schizophrenia at the age of six,' he told them. 'She had symptoms that were very similar to Aman's: violent rages, hallucinations, antisocial behaviour in general.'

Zakiy immediately picked up on the key word. 'Had?'

Karuppuraja nodded. 'Yes. Through regular medication, she now lives an almost normal life. She rarely lapses into violence anymore, and whilst her hallucinations are still firmly in place, she can mostly ignore them, whereas they used to order her to hurt her family and others.'

Narayan cleared his throat. 'And you say this was achieved through medication?' The hope in his voice was almost obscured by his distrust of drugs.

'That's right,' Karuppuraja replied, betraying no sign that he had noticed Narayan's reticence. 'In fact, I have a drug in mind that I think will benefit Aman – an antipsychotic.'

'We've tried antipsychotics before,' Narayan said wearily. 'We've tried several, in fact. The only one that seemed to make any sort of difference was... What was it called?' he asked his wife.

'Haloperidol,' Maira replied. 'It helped but the side effects were too awful – even at a low dose Aman started shaking and twitching uncontrollably. So we stopped giving it to him – he was starting to suspect us of poisoning him again, anyway,' she added almost nonchalantly, but pain was apparent in her eyes.

'I understand that you have reservations,' Karuppuraja said, 'but haloperidol belongs to an older group called typical antipsychotics. They cause muscular spasms, and the involuntary movements you've described. The medicine I'm thinking of is an atypical antipsychotic, which essentially means that it does not have the side effects associated with the typical ones. Of course, like all drugs, atypical antipsychotics have side effects – just a different set of them. However, clozapine – the antipsychotic I have in mind – has a low incidence of adverse side effects, and I think it will be worth it for Aman to try it.' He paused and added, 'Of course, ultimately it's up to Aman. But I would like your permission to talk to him about this.'

Narayan and Maira's eyes locked on each other, communicating silently as they tried to decide on the best course of action for their son.

'Let's do it,' Zakiy blurted. When his parents' gazes shot to him, he continued, 'It's worth a try. What do we have to lose?'

His parents exchanged another look, and Maira gave an almost imperceptible nod. Narayan sighed and said, 'Okay.'

And so it began.

Karuppuraja took it upon himself to talk to Aman about the new medication and persuade him to try it.

'You see,' he said to Narayan and Maira beforehand, 'in the past you've had to give him his medicine covertly, by putting it into his food or drink, and his already paranoid mind probably sensed it; his suspicions themselves would have reduced the effectiveness of the medicine. The mind is a very powerful thing, much more powerful than a few chemicals in a pill – Aman cannot get better until he believes that the medicine is something to help him, not harm him.

'I've spent the last few weeks gaining his confidence, and that involved playing along somewhat with his delusions. Right now his worst fear is that he is being monitored by intelligence agencies – he believes that his signals are being picked up by tiny detectors everywhere and he is constantly on the look-out for those detectors. So I'm going to present these pills to Aman as things that will block his signal from the detectors he fears so much.'

Maira's forehead creased. 'Won't playing along with his paranoia be bad for him in the long term?'

'That's a valid point,' Karuppuraja acknowledged. 'But the beauty of my lie is that ultimately it is the truth – the medicine will help cure the paranoia itself, which is paramount to "blocking the signals". What's most important, though, is that his mind – and hence his body – will be open to the drugs, instead of rejecting them out of hand.'

Still dubious, Maira and Narayan agreed, but all remaining doubts were vanquished when Aman not only conceded to try the new medication, but, under Karuppuraja's strict instructions, dutifully went to the medicine cabinet every night and took down his daily dosage.

After that it was a matter of waiting. Karuppuraja had warned them the first stage of the process would be dedicated to side effects, and it would be a month or so after taking the medication that the actual effects would start to show.

Despite Karuppuraja's repeated assurances that the side effects would be minimal, those initial few weeks were a minefield of stress. The family was caught between a fierce whirlwind of anticipation and a raging hellfire of fears; Sathi couldn't even imagine what it must be like for Maira, Narayan and Zakiy to have new hope after such a long time. Tempers ran high and after an inevitable outburst that ended in Zoya breaking into loud wails, Sathi took it upon herself to keep the four-year-old as occupied as possible.

The back garden was their preferred haven during those long weeks. It was an erratic mixture of gorgeous flowers in full bloom and a spattering of long, weed-like grass that tickled her calves when Sathi walked through it. Roses, hydrangeas, lilies and other familiar blossoms had a happy home in this little garden, but so did an array of weird, leafy plants that she didn't recognise. One corner was devoted to a playground, with a slide, swing set, and soft grass padding the ground underneath. This was Zoya's daily hangout, and she was content to play there as long as Sathi stayed somewhere in the vicinity.

One day – a fortnight or so after Aman had begun to take the new medication – Sathi again kept Zoya company in the garden. While Zoya made a beeline for the plastic slide, Sathi chose her favourite spot on the swing-chair that hung under the shade-giving branches of a large cherry tree. She gently rode the sweet breeze of the December afternoon, welcoming the rustle of wind that washed against her face and relieved the heat of the otherwise humid day. She was sad that the monsoon season was now over, and the crashing, sweet-smelling rains she had grown to crave wouldn't come again until June. Sathi sighed and automatically tilted her face up, as though a wistful stare might be enough to urge the heavens to open. Nope. The clouds remained perkily perfect and white, and the heavens annoyingly unresponsive.

A clatter of noise and a burst of giggling drew her attention away from the disobliging sky, and she glanced over at Zoya. The four-year-old sat chuckling to herself in a patch of bright sunshine at the bottom of the slide, having obviously just slid down and landed with a thump at the bottom. Sathi felt her lips form a smile even as her head shook in wonder; she still found it unbelievable how quickly the kid had taken to her. Even as she looked, Zoya glanced over and flashed her bright teeth at her in a wide grin.

Sathi had never been any good with kids. Maybe it was because she didn't have any siblings – younger *or* older – and she just didn't know how to interact with them. Or maybe it was because she just didn't have the knack like Zakiy did. The few times she'd had any contact with children, she'd felt awkward and hadn't known what to say or do. Anything she'd managed to blurt out sounded fake to her own ears, and the kid usually just stared back at her with large, unblinking eyes anyway.

Sathi's gaze again found Zoya, who was now trying her best to catch a butterfly that was drinking from a hibiscus blossom. She must have moved too quickly, because it suddenly took flight with a flutter of brightly coloured wings. With Zoya things were so different; Sathi grinned to herself as she remembered how apprehensive she had been when she first came to Zakiy's house. But after about twenty minutes of standing shyly behind Maira, peeking out at Sathi every so often, Zoya had bounded up and onto Sathi's lap.

Sathi chuckled, thinking back to her shocked delight at this unexpected little sister... a living, breathing sister.

Her smile faded as her thoughts abruptly slid down a different route – to the closest to an actual sibling she'd ever had. She'd known Arjun, her six year old cousin, for only a few weeks while he and his parents came to visit his grandparents. By that time, though, some part of her had been far too disgusted with life at her great-aunt and great-uncle's house to try to befriend her little cousin. She shuddered, thinking of the way Great-aunt and Great-uncle had always made a huge fuss of Arjun, and tried their best to win his favour and distance him from his parents. What kind of grandparents were they?

What kind of *humans* were they? Sathi corrected herself in disgust. She couldn't believe that she'd thought them so lovely and kind before.

How could she not have seen them for what they were? Why had she been so blind to everything when she was in their house, so happy to live inside her own fantasy of a happy family? Even when faced with proof that things were not as hunky-dory as they seemed she had still continued to make pathetic excuses for her proxy grandparents. At every turn she had tried to justify their heinous actions. Her own morals, her own strict sets of right and wrong, had gone straight out of the window.

Sathi bunched her calves under her, swinging harder, trying to swing right away from herself. The wind whistled in her ears as she swung to and fro, the garden blurring in her eyes. How could she have acted like she had? How could she have been so tolerant of their evil? By staying in their house, it was like she had drawn their evil into herself...

She suddenly dug her toes into the hard ground, bringing the swing – and herself – to an abrupt halt, paying no attention to the whine of protest from the steel hinge above her head. Ricku, the utterly loveable and utterly mad Labrador belonging to Zakiy's family, rushed at her legs and promptly started licking every bit of her he could reach, delighted that she was now stationary and hence within reach of his tongue. Sathi absently put out her hand and scratched behind his ears, her other hand reaching into her pocket to bring out the picture she always carried around with her.

The small rectangle of card was incredibly tattered, owing to the fact that it was at least twenty years old and had been torn into tiny bits and then pieced back together with clear tape. Sathi barely saw the tears and cracks in the abused paper as she looked into the beautiful, serene face that had given her courage and hope in moments when she feared she would break down.

Dressed in a rich red *sari* – traditional Indian-wear consisting of six metres of cloth – that wrapped alluringly around her body, and bedecked in golden jewellery, the goddess was a breath-taking sight. Glistening black hair rippled down and clung lovingly to her full hips, a perfect contrast to the golden coronet that graced her crown. Her many hands held a trident, conch, sword, spear, bolt of lightning, serrated discus, flaming dart, noose and goad, a scroll and a pink lotus blossom that drooped to the ground, as though aching to join the bigger, fully opened lotus that encased the goddess's petite feet.

Devi. The divine mother, who personified nature and was the supreme female deity in Hindu mythology.

Her Amma's goddess. *Her* goddess.

Sathi fingered the picture, remembering how she had found it on the day she learned the truth about her mother's death – ripped up and stuffed to the back of a box containing her father's most treasured belongings. She'd always wondered whether her father had torn it up because he resented the goddess for allowing Amma's death.

She sighed and gazed unseeingly at the darkening horizon, oblivious to the fact that the affectionate Labrador had slobbered all over her fingers. How had her mother lived in that house for so many years? How was it possible that she hadn't known her aunt and uncle's true nature?

Sathi shivered in the hot sunshine, thinking back to the night she had found Maya going into her father-in-law's bedroom. She recalled how panicked and helpless she had felt when she realised that Maya was not in her senses. She hadn't known what to do, and had frozen in absolute panic. Then somehow her mind had cried out to Devi for help, and she had managed to wake up the household and "rescue" Maya.

Her eyes closed of their own accord as she considered how she'd almost been too late. If it hadn't been for Devi, she would have been. Just like if it hadn't been for Devi, she might never have left that infernal house. She saw in her mind's eye the gorgeous meadow she'd dreamt of after her midnight adventures. She marvelled at how it had seemed as though light was infused into the place, a far cry from the dark, dusty room that had featured all her recent nightmares. Sathi saw herself looking into a huge, gilt-framed mirror, and saw her reflection change into a simple outline with pulsing black sludge appearing here and there, eventually colonising her whole body. As her horror-struck eyes lifted to her face, a third eye had suddenly opened in the middle of her forehead, a brilliant eye painted scorching blue and gold as it shot out light at the sludge: Devi's eye. It had been a terrifying experience as the goddess's righteous anger blazed around her.

When it seemed like the golden light was winning out against the stubborn muck, a book had appeared at Sathi's feet – her old book of bedtime stories that she'd left in the UK with most of her other belongings. When she opened the book, the pages had been swept back to the title page of a Cherokee legend called "Wolves Within". She could remember the words of the story as perfectly as if they had been typed, not in the book, but on the intricate pages of her mind.

An old Cherokee told his grandson, 'My son, there is a fierce battle between two great wolves within us all. One is Evil; he is anger, greed, pride, gluttony, lust, envy and laziness. The other wolf is Good; he is forgiveness, generosity, humility, love, empathy and truth.'

The boy thought about what his grandfather had said for a moment, and then asked innocently, 'Grandfather, which wolf wins?'

The old man smiled and replied quietly, 'The one you nurture.'

It had been the realisation that she had been nurturing the evil wolf that had finally spurred her to leave that house.

And yet, she thought wildly, *and yet, was that the right thing to do – the* good *thing to do?* Had stealing away in the night like that accomplished anything? Shouldn't she have at least exposed her great-uncle for the rapist he was before she left? She thought back to those cold reptilian eyes, eyes that reflected no real warmth, and shuddered. Shame filled her as she admitted to herself that she had been too scared by those eyes to even attempt to challenge him. She was a coward. Maybe she had saved her aunt for one night, but hadn't she left Maya vulnerable to another attack?

Self-hatred surged in her until she could barely swallow, and it lodged in her throat. Sathi knew her mother wouldn't have left like that. Amma would have challenged her uncle right then and there, cold eyes or no. She was not a coward. Sathi knew almost nothing about the woman who had given her life, but she knew that much.

Her breathing grew ragged as tears of humiliation sprang to her eyes. She gripped the ropes on either side of the swing chair, knowing that she had to distract herself somehow – otherwise she would break down in sorrow and self-pity.

She found herself focusing back on the story of the two wolves. Despite the fact that it had been in her favourite book of stories, she had never paid much attention to the Cherokee legend hidden among the fairytales she loved. Consequently she knew next to nothing about its context. Her breathing returned more or less to normal and she sat thinking for a while before jumping off the swing and darting into the house, calling to Zoya and her canine fan that she would be back soon.

Laptop in hand, she settled back into the chair a few minutes later. Opening her browser, she typed in "wolves within cherokee" and waited impatiently for the page to load. As she surveyed the many results that popped up on screen, Zakiy's earlier comment ran through her mind: 'If you don't know the answer, Google it.' The memory drove a small smile across her expression. *Well,* she thought as she clicked onto the first result, *a little research never hurts.*

After nearly an hour of browsing, she was just about ready to hurl the computer at the floor. Or better yet, let Ricku have his way with it. (The dog had yet to understand that a chew toy was supposed to be chewy from the beginning – not just after he'd finished with it).

Not one of the many *many* versions of the parable published on the Internet had the same wording as the one she'd read in the dream. Not *one* of them. How weird was that? Sure, some of them were similar, very similar in fact, but none of them agreed with the exact characteristics of the wolves described in the version she'd read. Sathi couldn't understand it. Surely if the story had been published in a book, then an electronic copy of it had to be on the net *somewhere*?

Okay yes the obvious solution was indeed obvious to her: she must have forgotten the exact wording.

And yet she was adamantly sure she hadn't – those words were so clear to her, they had resonated within her mind ever since the dream. It was so frustrating. Grimly, she snatched up a pen and some paper.

She would write her version down. Maybe that would make things clearer.

A couple of minutes later, she compared her version and the most popular version on the Internet side by side. In the electronic version, the parable described the evil wolf as "*anger, envy, sorrow, regret, greed, arrogance, self-pity, guilt, resentment, inferiority, lies, false pride, superiority, and ego*" and went onto depict the good wolf as "*joy, peace, love, hope, serenity, humility, kindness, benevolence, empathy, generosity, truth, compassion, and faith*".

Looking back at her own scribbles, she read that the evil wolf was "*anger, greed, pride, gluttony, lust, envy and laziness*" and that the good one was "*forgiveness, generosity, humility, love, empathy and truth*". 'Okay,' she muttered as she crossed her legs underneath herself on the swing chair. The first obvious thing to note was that both the evil wolves had anger, pride and envy in common, and that the two good wolves had humility, love, generosity, empathy and truth in common.

Thank God, she thought. At least they both mostly agreed on what constituted as "good". So it was the bad wolves that weren't so compatible. She underlined the characteristics for the evil wolf from each story. Her sharp gaze threatened to bore a hole in the paper as she tried to figure out the mystery.

'Well, okay, another really obvious thing is they're both different lengths,' she murmured to herself under her breath. The Labrador pricked up his ears and pawed at her for attention. She barely noticed as she pulled the laptop screen closer to her, and carried on muttering, 'This is one, two, three... fourteen words... And this one is...' She rustled the paper impatiently, counting. 'This one's only seven –'

Sathi stopped short, her eyes widening. 'You absolute dim-wit,' she breathed, really looking at the seven words on the paper, there in her own handwriting. Anger. Greed. Pride. Gluttony. Lust. Envy. Laziness.

The seven deadly sins.

Chapter Five

Overcast with Hope

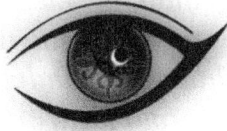

Zakiy turned away from the window, through which he'd been absent-mindedly staring for the last ten minutes and caught sight of the small box on his bedside table. He hesitated, considering. Making up his mind, he reached over and picked it up, his gaze lingering as usual on the familiar face of the serene woman wrapped in stars and planets depicted on the cover of the box of Tarot cards.

He sat down and took out the cards, fingering the clean sharp edges and tipped his hand abruptly, spilling them onto the bed in front of him. Closing his eyes, Zakiy splayed his hand over the fanned-out cards and let his fingers wander, trying to let his instincts guide him to the correct card.

Allah, please... Please.

His hand caught in the edge of one of the cards, and holding his breath, Zakiy pulled it out. He blindly held it in front of him. He exhaled sharply and finally opened his eyes. A beautiful picture imbued with yellow and gold strokes filled his gaze, showing two hands cupping a glowing sun; letters floating across the bottom of the card formed a single bittersweet word: "Hope".

I wish I had the courage to, Zakiy thought wistfully. There had been so many times when he had dared to hope, only to have those hopes dashed as each new medical endeavour failed. He didn't know if he could stand it if the same thing happened again. Yet... yet, he couldn't deny that there was actually something different about this time. It was now well into January, with Christmas and New Year flying by with only token acknowledgement, and his cynical attitude couldn't compete with the very real changes that were occurring before his eyes.

Like Karuppuraja had promised, Aman hadn't suffered any notable side effects from the new medication. But more than that, since he had started taking it Aman had not had an episode. Not one. No violence, no uncontrollable rage...

The hallucinations remained, though. Of course, it would be too good to be true if Aman didn't find foul-mouthed strangers hanging around outside the house, or if he didn't believe that all phone calls were being tapped by the CBI. But at least Aman seemed to be able to contain his hallucinations within his mind, instead of letting them take control of his body through violence.

Zakiy suddenly grinned, thinking of the way Aman joined in conversations now. Before he used to just sit quietly, sometimes with a blank expression that pained Zakiy. It seemed too good to be true, but as each day passed he was letting himself believe it more and more.

'Zakiy!' his mother called from downstairs.

'Coming!' he yelled back. He gave the Hope card one last glance before gathering it up with the rest of the cards and putting them back inside their box. Then he went downstairs and found his Amma in the living room. Aman sat on the floor next to his her, leafing through a Marvel comic. Zakiy took a double take, his eyes widening. This was the first time in fifteen years that he had seen Aman take an interest in his beloved comics. Beaming, Zakiy looked up and met Amma's eyes; even though she didn't show it, he knew she was just as overjoyed at the change in her eldest child. She gave him a secret smile to show she understood before switching to business. 'Zakiy, I think Sathi's been cooped up in the house too long. She's getting restless.'

His forehead creased. 'She hasn't said anything to me.'

Amma treated him to a look that was as exasperated as it was affectionate. 'Well of course she hasn't,' she replied, her needle going in and out steadily as it wove a bright pattern of colours across what looked like a dress for Zoya. 'She's not going to, is she, with everything that's going on?' Amma glanced pointedly at Aman.

Zakiy frowned, thinking back over the last few weeks. True, he had not seen much of Sathi because he'd been busy with Aman and Karuppuraja and generally worrying about every single thing that could go wrong, but when he *had* spent some time with her she'd seemed her usual cheerful self. Maybe Amma had seen something he hadn't.

'She's been a brick,' Amma continued. 'She's been keeping Zoya distracted, and God knows what a feat *that* is.' She grinned at him, and he smiled back automatically, marvelling at how youthful she suddenly looked. Aman wasn't the only one undergoing changes around here.

'I know. Zoya literally hangs on to her apron strings.' He paused, pretending to reconsider. 'Well, she *would*, if Sathi had any. Maybe we should get her an apron.'

Amma's eyes twinkled. 'I was going to suggest anyway that you take her out to see the sights, so you can buy her one along the way. I'm sure she'll be thrilled.'

'She might actually kill me,' he observed cheerfully, imagining Sathi's expression at being presented with an apron.

'From what I've seen, she might,' Amma agreed. 'We'll just have to take that risk. Now go and take her around before it gets too dark.'

'Well...' Zakiy began uncertainly, glancing at Aman. He didn't want to leave him. Amma guessed his thoughts; 'Don't be silly. Aman will be fine. Go.'

'Z-Man...'

Zakiy whirled around at this new voice. Sure enough, it was Aman, calling him by his old nickname, one he'd almost forgotten over the long years. He stared speechlessly at his older brother as Aman held up the comic he'd been reading. 'Will you see if they have the latest edition out yet?'

'I...' he faltered. Then he chuckled, though it was a choked sound. 'Yeah of course I will.' He hesitated. 'Why don't you come with us?'

'No.'

46

Zakiy glanced back to see that his father had entered the room. 'No,' Dad repeated. 'It's too soon.'

Zakiy ignored him and focused only on Aman. 'Would you like to come?' he asked again.

Aman shook his head, fear in his eyes, and shrank into himself again as Dad burst out angrily, 'I said no, didn't I?'

Pushing back a wave of anger and disappointment, Zakiy forced a grin at his brother. 'Next time, okay? Otherwise I might bring back the wrong one – you know how useless your Z-Man is at these things.' He winked and was gifted with a small smile in return.

Turning, his smile slipped and he left without knowing whether he should feel happy or sad.

'Oi, *makri*!' Zakiy called up to his little sister, who was seated comfortably on her perch on top of his shoulders. 'Quit wriggling around.'

In answer Zoya began to shift around even more, playfully kicking her legs against his chest. He reached up and caught hold of her short little legs and held them down. 'If you don't sit still, I'll throw you off,' he warned.

The little brat wound her fingers around his hair and replied confidently, 'Sathi chechi won't let you.'

'Oho?' Zakiy said. He glanced at Sathi, who was walking beside him with a straight face. Judging by the way she kept twisting her mouth, though, he guessed that it took a lot of effort to keep it that way. 'If you have so much faith in your Sathi chechi, why don't you go and sit on *her* shoulder?' he demanded.

There was a pause, as though Zoya was considering her options. 'No,' she decided finally. 'You're taller.'

Sathi's finely tuned control broke, and she started snorting with laughter. 'Right, that's it,' Zakiy said grimly, picking the brat up and setting her on the floor. 'From now on, you walk,' he sternly told the half-heartedly wailing Zoya.

'Great parenting skills,' Sathi murmured to him later after he handed Zoya a picture book he'd just bought for her from the second-hand bookshop that had been his and Aman's haunt back when they were kids.

'Hmm?' he said, looking up from the comic book Aman had asked for.

Sathi crooked him a smile. 'Teach her a lesson on how to be less bratty, and then give her a gift. That'll help.'

'Meh, she'll grow out of it,' he said dismissively. 'Besides, she's an angel when it really counts.'

Her expression softened. 'Yeah,' she agreed. 'She is.'

'Anyway, who're you to accuse me of being too soft on her, Miss I-Buy-Sweets-Just-To-Give-Zoya?' he teased.

Sathi looked embarrassed. 'How did you know about that?' she asked indignantly.

'I'm not blind,' he informed her. 'Or stupid.'

'That's debatable,' she muttered, glancing away. Her gaze caught on something and she moved towards one of the dusty bookshelves in the shop. 'Hey, what's this?' she asked, picking up a book and holding it up to him. Zakiy took it from her and looked down at an idol of a Hindu goddess on the cover of the book. 'It's the patron goddess of Mysore,' he told Sathi, not needing to look inside the tourism book to know. 'She's called Chamundeshwari.'

Recognition lit her eyes. 'Like on those signposts – Chamundi Hills?'

'Right,' he confirmed, impressed that she had picked up on the name so quickly. 'Chamundi Hills is sort of a hill station. Like Nelliampathi but much smaller. There's a temple at the top for Chamundeswari, the warrior goddess.'

Sathi's face took on a faraway expression. 'Can we go there?'

He put the book back on the shelf and studied her silently for a few moments. 'Sure,' he said finally. 'Let's go.'

'You should be ashamed of yourself,' Zakiy teased, shifting a sleeping Zoya in his arms. 'You should know the story of Chamundi Hills – the heroine is your namesake.' He paused. 'Unless you're actually an alien who was born millions of years ago, in which case she may have been named after you.'

'Who's she?'

'Sathi Devi, Shiva's first wife.' Lord Shiva was the god of death in the Hindu Pantheon.

Sathi frowned. 'Wait, so Parvathi is his second wife?'

'Parvathi is his consort yes, but she's actually the reincarnation of Sathi, Shiva's eternal soul mate.'

'Reincarnation? So Sathi died?'

'Yes. Her father arranged a *yagna* and invited all the gods, goddesses, sages, saints and all other VIPs except his daughter and hated son-in-law. Sathi went anyway because she felt that as his daughter, she didn't require a special invitation and she believed that she could make her father see sense. Shiva tried to persuade her not to go, that her father's dislike of Shiva transcended affection for his daughter, but Sathi vowed that she would not return to him defeated. She overestimated her father, however, and after he publically insulted Shiva, she sacrificed herself to Agni, the god of fire.'

Sathi almost tripped her over her own feet. 'She couldn't have just punched her dad in the face or something?'

Zakiy grinned ruefully. 'She was actually an incarnation of Adiparashakthi, who is literally the supreme being of the Universe, like God with a capital G. She split up into the other gods and gave them control over certain domains, like Shiva and Agni, and also Vayu, the god of air, Kama, the god of love, and a whole set of other gods and goddesses. Anyway, Sathi's parents prayed for Adiparashakthi to be born to them, and She agreed on the condition that She would leave her mortal body and take up heavenly abode again if She was ever disrespected.'

'When her father insulted Shiva, Sathi couldn't bear it, especially because she knew Shiva was only being insulted because he married her. She died uttering a plea to her beloved Shiva to forgive her, as well as a wish that next time she would be born to a father she could respect.'

'When he heard of her death, Shiva flew into a rage. He ordered everyone at yagna to be killed. Daksha was beheaded for his crime. Still not appeased, Shiva picked up Sathi's charred body and danced the rudra thaandavam – the dance that normally destroys the world so it can be rebuilt – with her in his arms.

The earth revolted; floods, earthquakes, tsunamis… the world was literally being shaken to the core. Finally the other gods intervened and stopped his rage. He gave life back to those who'd died at his command, and gave poor Daksha a goat's head. Daksha became an ardent devotee of Shiva after that.

'Chamudeshwari temple is one of the Shakthi Peetas, or holy places where parts of Sathi's body fell during Shiva's destructive dance. This is apparently where her hair fell.'

Sathi was silent, digesting her namesake's tragedy. Shiva must have loved his wife a lot, to react so violently that he was prepared to destroy the world to avenge his beloved. She knew that her father had loved her mother a lot as well. Yet his reaction to her death had been dramatically different. His instinct had been to flee to a foreign country and spurn anything that reminded him of his wife, including his own daughter…

'There,' Zakiy gestured, jerking Sathi from her brooding thoughts. He was pointing towards a huge quadrangular building constructed according to the style of Dravidian architecture, with a seven-tier pyramid-shaped entrance. They had already seen the huge statue of Mahishasura the buffalo headed demon that had tried to usurp the king of the gods, Indra. Zakiy had told her that this demon had been a symbol of ignorance and chaos, and Devi in her warrior form had ridden on her lion to slay him and rid the world of his evil.

A cool breeze with a definite chill wound through the hill, and Sathi shivered and wrapped her arms around herself. 'I like this place,' she said. 'There's something peaceful about it.'

Zakiy thought the same, but before he could say so Sathi's phone rang. 'So much for peace,' she said wryly, pulling the phone out. She glanced at the display and her expression immediately changed. 'It's Manish.'

Manish was this old tea-maker back in Nelliampathi who was about the size of a cracker. Sathi had made friends with him when she first arrived and he hyperventilated if he didn't talk to her at least once a day. And yet Sathi never seemed to mind these daily calls. Even now, she gave Zakiy an apologetic smile and moved a little distance away, the phone held to her ear.

Zakiy guessed that when your own father didn't care whether you were alive or not, you had to take what you could get.

Zoya woke up just then, yawning widely. He turned to her, a gleam in his eyes. 'Hey, sleepyhead. Shall we go scrounge for some Raspberry Ripples?'

She gazed at him, and then her lips formed a wide grin uncannily like his own.

'Here you go, Sathi chechi,' Zoya said later as Sathi walked up to them after her phone call. Zoya handed her a plastic-wrapped packet. 'I counted out the money for it myself,' she added proudly.

'Did you, you clever girl?' Sathi said, smiling. Then she looked at what she had been given. 'Um, what is it?'

'An essential part of anyone's diet,' Zakiy answered, unwrapping his own packet. 'Ice cream.'

'I should have guessed. You're obsessed with ice cream,' she told him. Then she shrugged and started to open her own packet.

'Not just *any* ice cream,' put in Zoya. 'It's Raspberry Ripple. Chechi, it's like a lolly but it has yummy vanilla ice cream inside. You'll like it,' she promised, her mouth full of her own lolly.

'Okay, Zoya. I'll take your word for it,' Sathi said gravely, 'But if I don't like it, we'll make your brother eat a hundred of them in one go. What do you say?'

Zakiy immediately set to in order to defend his honour. 'Hey I could manage –'

'*Olege eno ithe!*'

Startled, Zakiy spun around to locate the source of the voice. A moment later, he found it; standing near the temple was a man dressed in *khavi* clothes, with an orange *mundu* and shirt. He had an unkempt beard flecked with grey and he seemed to be using the outside wall of the temple for support as he leaned against it. Yet his eyes were shrewd where they focused on Sathi. Looking around, Zakiy realised that the strange man's words had attracted more than one interested gaze. Other temple visitors in earshot had come to a halt, gazing between the man and Sathi with curious and even fearful expressions. Puzzled, he glanced back at Sathi to figure out her reaction. She was staring back at the man, her face closed off and her body very still.

The man stepped forward, almost glaring at Sathi in his frustration. *'Nin olege eno ithe!'*

Sathi cringed back at the urgency in his voice, and that's when Zakiy finally took action. He stepped forward and put his hand on the guy's chest. 'Okay that's enough,' he said pleasantly, but he edged his voice with steel. 'You can leave her alone now.' Raising his voice, he addressed the rest of the crowd gathered around. 'There's nothing more to see here. Please go and ogle the monkeys – they're at least used to it.'

As a couple of those gathered gave weak, half-embarrassed chuckles at the reference to the tame primates that freely occupied the temple grounds, Zakiy ignored the khavi guy and started paving a way through the slowly dispersing crowd.

It was only when they were on the bus winding back down Chamundi Hills that Sathi spoke. 'What did that guy say?' she asked.

'I'm not sure,' Zakiy said hesitantly, wishing that his Kannada was better. 'Something about you and something there... Urgh, that's so vague! I don't know what "olege" means. Sorry.'

'It's okay,' she said automatically, but he could tell that she was still pre-occupied with trying to puzzle it out. His suspicions were confirmed a moment later when she said, 'That guy was really... intense. Like what he said was life-threatening, or something. What do you reckon that was about?'

Zakiy absently traced one of Zoya's errant curls as he stared straight ahead. He sighed and replied, 'I wish I knew.'

Chapter Six

Advice From a Monkey

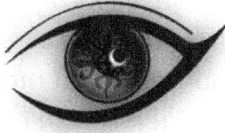

S athi's head was throbbing.

She hadn't been in the mood to go outside, so she had somehow managed to convince Zoya to stay inside today. The four-year-old was in the living room, playing with a set of miniature plastic pots and pans, while Sathi lounged on the sofa and gave in fully to her bad mood.

The events at the temple were still fresh in her mind, and the words of the weird man kept ringing in her ears. Nin olege eno ithe. What the frick had he meant? Sathi was too disgruntled to care that she had just used a word that resembled the mother of all swearwords – something she usually avoided at all cost. *Stupid Indians and their stupid languages*, she thought, knowing that she was being unfair but again, not giving a shit. *And*, she continued her mental tirade, *what is it with Indians and their bloody nosiness? Why can't they just bloody mind their own bloody business like normal people?*

The man from the temple actually reminded her of someone she had met back in Nelliampathi and dubbed "White Beard" for, well, his white beard and hair. He too had had a hard time minding his own business, giving her an unsolicited lecture on Hindu gods and their wonderfully magical and mysterious ways.

Sathi scoffed. Yeah, everything in her life had been so wonderfully magical.

Immediately, she felt guilty at that catty thought. It wasn't really fair to blame gods she didn't even know just because *she* happened to be in a bad mood. Sighing, she shifted her position on the sofa and let her head flop down onto the armrest. She seemed to be in a bad mood more often than not lately. And she didn't exactly have to strain her imagination to work out the reason why.

Let's see; a random person shouted something unintelligible at me a few days ago, I found out some useless information involving the seven deadly sins that I have no clue how to use, my best friend's brother has a chronic psychiatric condition that will make him dependent on drugs for the rest of his life, my father doesn't want to know me and my mother was murdered and I haven't done anything to try and find the person who killed her even though I now know who she is.

And there it was... The thing that had been weighing on her mind ever since she found out that awful truth. A truth she hadn't been courageous enough to face.

Sathi knew who had murdered her mother – not just once but over and over. Because that odious woman hadn't even had the nerve to expose herself as an enemy. Instead she had befriended Amma and earned her trust, all the while choking on her own jealousy and hatred. Then, probably at a moment when Amma least expected it, she had finally committing that heinous crime: she had killed her best friend.

Her mother's murderer was Vidhya Raman.

Vidhya Raman, who had been at school with Amma, who had followed Amma to college and whose absence Amma mourned when Vidhya's brother died and she had to cut short her education. Such a person didn't deserve to be called Amma's friend. She didn't deserve to live in Amma's reflected glory.

So why, Sathi asked herself, hadn't she done what she'd made her mind up to do and tracked down that worthless piece of garbage?

She thought back to the promise she'd once made to her great-uncle, back before she'd known his true nature. She'd sworn to him – and to her mother in her mind's eye – that she wouldn't go after Vidhya. But surely that didn't mean anything? Surely her every action in that house had been topsy-turvy to begin with. Why should she keep that promise in the light of all the horrors she had seen since?

'Sathi?'

She looked up to see Maira, holding a small tray with a pill and a glass of water. 'Could you do me a favour?' Maira continued.

'Sure,' Sathi said, jumping up.

'Could you take this to Zakiy's father? He should be in the *puja* room. I need to give Zoya a bath.'

Sathi hesitated, then nodded. Her apprehension stemmed from the thought of talking to Narayan, but surely anything was better than being stuck with her own thoughts? Ready for distraction, she reached out for the tray. She'd never been inside the prayer room but she knew where it was. She looked curiously at the medicine on the tray.

Maira noticed her scrutiny as she picked up her daughter. 'It's for his blood pressure.' A breath of laughter found its way into her voice. 'God knows he needs it.' She grinned at Sathi, and Sathi found herself smiling back despite her crappy mood.

Holding the tray carefully so she wouldn't spill the water, Sathi found her way to the small room behind the stairs. She peeked in through the partially open doorway, curious about what she would see in the prayer room of a Hindu-Muslim couple. It was a small but well-lit room, with most of one wall taken up by windows and the sunlight reaching into every corner. At first glance it seemed to be dominated by the rows of framed pictures of various Hindu deities, with the reflections of lamp wicks dancing across the glass of the frames. Several incense sticks had been lit, the thin streams of smoke spiralling up into the air and filling the room with a sweet, thick aroma.

Then, she noticed the small wooden ledge built into the wall in the middle of the room. Balanced on it was a huge, disintegrating copy of an ancient Hindu scripture, the Bhaghvat Gita. Beside it was an equally dog-eared copy of the Qur'an. A rolled up prayer mat sat on the floor directly below it.

Sathi moved a bit further into the room, scanning it for Narayan. She found him standing in front of a picture frame that had been set on a table to the far left of the room. His eyes were closed and his head was bowed slightly. His palms were placed together in prayer. Curious, Sathi shifted a little so she could see the picture more clearly. It showed a man half kneeling and half sitting on his haunches, scantily dressed in a sort of expensive-looking loincloth and jewellery that circled his neck, wrists and bulging biceps. A crown sat above his forehead, which itself was adorned with a red U-shaped mark that came down almost to the bridge of his nose. In what was a typical pose for Hindu deities, one palm was held up in blessing while the other lay on his knee.

Squinting, Sathi realised that what was *not* typical was the god's face; his jaw protruded in an inhuman way, and his cheeks were puffed out as though he had somehow managed to contain a large jug-full of water inside his mouth. It gave him a distinctly ape-like appearance. The long tail that rose up above his shoulder and waved in the air didn't help, either.

He seemed only vaguely familiar to Sathi, no doubt due to the vast plethora of deities in the Hindu pantheon. Tugging her gaze reluctantly away, she set the tray down silently on a nearby table and turned to leave.

'It's Hanuman.'

Startled, she glanced back. Narayan had not changed his position in any way but there was no doubt that he was talking to her. Embarrassment heated her cheeks as she thought of how she'd just been standing there, staring, but those feelings were batted aside as the name of the deity unexpectedly brushed against a memory: 'You mean from the Ramayana?' Sathi asked.

Evidently surprised, Narayan opened his eyes and glanced at her. 'Yes. Do you know the story?'

Slowly she nodded, trying to remember what she'd been told years ago. 'It's one of the Hindu epics. The one about Rama and Seetha.'

'Yes. Rama was an avatar of Lord Vishnu and was born as the eldest son of the king of Ayodhya. He and his wife Seetha were sent into exile and Seetha was abducted by Ravana, a ten-headed *rakshasa*.' Narayan nodded to the picture. 'Hanuman helped Rama to find Seetha and ultimately defeat Ravana.'

56

'Yeah, by setting fire to his own tail and leaping around Ravana's kingdom like a mad monkey,' Sathi said with a giggle, forgetting for a moment that she was talking to Narayan – aka Man Who Did Not Like Her. She sobered quickly, half-expecting him to throw her out of the room for her irreverent words. Instead Narayan did something completely unexpected: he threw back his head and laughed.

Sathi stared in amazement, realising that this was the first time she'd ever seen him laugh. His face lost its hard, cynical crust and crinkles came to life around his eyes and mouth. Still smiling, he met her eyes. 'Exactly. And that's not even the most extraordinary of his antics. When he was a child he thought the sun was a ripe mango and promptly set out to try and eat it.' Narayan chuckled.

Encouraged by this sudden friendliness, Sathi said, 'In the Ramayana, when he was sent to get a medicinal herb to save Rama's brother, didn't he come back with the whole mountain because he couldn't identify the herb?'

'Ah yes. His quest to find the *mritasanjeevani*.' Narayan looked back at the picture of Hanuman as he said it, but not before she saw the humour fade out of his eyes.

Silence fell, and Sathi wondered whether she should leave. Yet that brief rapport made her reluctant to abandon Narayan to his troubled thoughts. 'What's wrong, Uncle?' she asked hesitantly.

Narayan sighed, still not looking at her. 'Mritasanjeevani is the ultimate medicine. It is something that, in Hindu mythology, can heal any disease or injury, a draught of immortality, a substance that can bring the dead to life.'

Sathi stiffened. 'There's no such thing.'

'No, of course not,' he agreed. 'Not in the literal sense. The symbolism is what matters, and by immortality they mean life after death, when souls depart from their bodies and go to Lord Shiva's abode.'

'Shiva's the god of death?' she clarified, remembering what Zakiy had told her at Chamundi Hills.

'Not exactly. He's the conqueror of death – or more simply, the god of immortality. In Hinduism there's not so much heaven and hell as much as heaven and life. If you don't achieve heaven, then you go back to earth for another lifetime and try again for as long as necessary.'

This was all fascinating stuff, but he hadn't exactly answered her question. Uneasily wondering whether she was crossing a personal boundary, she said, 'That still doesn't explain why the thought of mritasanjeevani makes you sad.'

His lips pressed into a thin line, and she braced for an angry response. Then he just sighed and shook his head, as though in resignation. 'I should have listened more carefully when Zakiy told me about your persistence.'

Zakiy had talked to his father about her?

Narayan turned to face her, and Sathi filed the information away for later. 'Mritasanjeevani is the ultimate medicine,' he repeated. 'The ultimate but unattainable medicine.'

Finally she understood. 'It's what you want for Aman.'

Narayan shrugged in response. 'There's only so much these modern drugs can achieve – they treat symptoms. They're not a cure. Of course,' he added hurriedly, 'I didn't even think this much progress was possible. Professor Karuppuraja is a godsend. Without him – without *you* – Aman would never have had even a semblance of a normal life.'

Sathi was momentarily stunned by this unexpected praise. Surprised pleasure rose in her, and she dropped her eyes. Then all of what he'd said sunk in, something which was remarkably similar to what she'd been thinking earlier. 'But that's not enough, is it?' she asked softly.

'It's enough,' Narayan said wearily. 'But I just can't help but think of what kind of a future Aman will have.' He sighed.

Sathi was back to thinking about this miracle herb. 'Surely...' She stopped, thought some more, and tried again. 'Even if you can't take these myths literally there's usually a kernel of truth to them, isn't there? I mean, does anyone know what this mritasanjeevani is supposed to symbolise?'

'There are lots of theories. The latest one I've heard is that mritasanjeevani is green tea.' Narayan regarded her confused (and sceptical) expression with amusement, and for a moment his resemblance to Zakiy was remarkable. 'As you can see, that particular theory focuses on prevention of disease by keeping your diet and lifestyle – and hence your body – healthy. Some others insist that mritasanjeevani is a real herb, and have devised quests as fervent as those for the Holy Grail – but I don't believe they've got it right either. No, I don't think even Lord Dhanvantari knows what it is.'

'Who's that?' Sathi enquired.

'Dhanvantari is an aspect of Vishnu the Sustainer. He is the founder of *Ayurveda*.'

'Ayurveda?' she repeated, feeling completely clueless. Again.

'Ayurveda is the most ancient form of medicine in India – it literally means "the knowledge of life". It's a traditional health system, one that has its roots in the Vedas, the ancient scriptures. Ayurveda is a very complex branch of medicine, but its main characteristic is that that herbs and plants in their natural form are administered as medicine. It's about being in tune with nature, and bringing about a state of harmony between body, mind and spirit. It's been mostly overshadowed since allopathic medicine took root, though.' Narayan shrugged.

Silence fell again, but it was comfortable this time. Sathi's mind was spinning with all the new information and the beginnings of an idea were starting to take form. She excused herself and wandered up to her room without paying much attention to her surroundings.

She needed to check out some things before she repeated a monkey's quest – a quest to find the mritasanjeevani.

Chapter Seven

Under the Veil

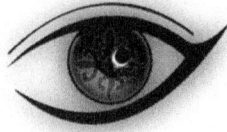

W e're going back to Kerala,' Sathi informed Zakiy, flopping into a chair beside him and thrusting a sheet of paper into his hands.

'You're sick of Mysore already?' Zakiy quipped half-heartedly. He glanced at the print-out and read, '"Ayurapy: therapy that will change your life." Huh?'

'It's an Ayurvedic clinic in Thrissur.'

'Ayur*apy*?' he repeated, this time incredulously.

'Okay, so the name's a bit lame,' Sathi admitted. 'But if it helps Aman, does it really matter?'

'Wait, back up a minute,' Zakiy said. 'What do you mean about helping Aman? Isn't that what Karuppuraja's been doing?'

She started to explain about the conversation she'd had with Narayan, but he interrupted immediately. 'Hold on. You actually had a reasonable conversation with my father? Like, the guy who's married to my mum?' He got up and crossed over to the window, flipping back the curtain and staring up at the still sky.

Sathi sighed. 'Okay, what on earth are you doing now?'

'I'm checking to see if a crow is flying upside down.' Zakiy saw her confused expression and explained, 'It's the Indian version of a flying pig.'

Before Sathi could tell him exactly what she thought of his menagerie of flying animals, Karuppuraja stuck his head inside the room. 'Ah, here are my favourite little assistants.'

She barely heard Zakiy mutter, 'Well, speak of the devil.' He started to grin his Dracula grin, caught sight of the murderous glare Sathi was giving him, and promptly rearranged his face. 'I didn't know you were coming by today, Prin– Professor,' he said, coughing to cover up his slip.

'Yes, I had planned to come tomorrow but my wife reminded me that it's our anniversary this week and that I've been promising to take her to Hyderabad for the last ten years. She also mentioned that if the trip doesn't happen this time then I will become a divorcee.' Karuppuraja shrugged, looking adorably helpless.

'Hmm,' Zakiy said thoughtfully. 'On the bright side, you wouldn't have to worry about anniversaries anymore. Ow!' he yelped a moment later as Sathi elbowed him in the ribs.

'That's true,' Karuppuraja said, brightening.

Sathi kept her groan to herself and found herself empathising with this absent wife. 'I don't think that's your best option, Professor. Just take your wife to Hyderabad. So, did you talk to Aman?' she asked hastily, changing the subject before the two men drove themselves further into the realm of insanity.

'Yes,' Karuppuraja replied. 'He seems to be responding very well to the treatment so far. Narayan and I were just talking about it.'

'Everyone else has reasonable conversations with my father,' Zakiy murmured.

Sathi's lips twitched. But the mention of Narayan reminded her...

'We were talking about that too, and I was thinking that maybe it's a good idea to explore something like Ayurveda.' She explained about Narayan's apprehension about clozapine not being a long-term solution and her own brief research on Ayurveda while Karuppuraja and Zakiy listened intently.

'And you really think this Ayurapy clinic is the answer?' Karuppuraja asked.

Sathi shrugged. 'I don't know. It just seems like we should try.'

'Well, Sathi,' Karuppuraja said, standing up, 'I can tell you that it will be a waste of a trip to go to Kerala for this. I respect Ayurveda – *real* Ayurveda – but it's all become too commercialised now. Any actual science has been stripped out of it.' He nodded to Sathi and Zakiy. 'I'll see you next week – assuming my wife hasn't murdered me by then.'

Zakiy saw him out, and then returned to find Sathi sitting with her arms crossed across her chest. He took one look at her stubborn expression and grinned. 'You're not going to give up that easily, are you?'

She looked up and gave him a reluctant smile. 'Would I be Sathi Varma if I did?'

'Nope,' he replied, picking up the print out she had given him earlier and reading it again. 'You certainly wouldn't.'

'Train journeys always make me hungry,' Zakiy announced, rifling through his bag to see if it had miraculously acquired food while it travelled the world. It was night-time, and the train thundered contently through the sleeping countryside. Most of the train's occupants had drawn the washed out curtains around their cubicles and turned their small lamps off. The faint sounds of snoring came from somewhere further along the compartment.

'You're *always* hungry,' Sathi pointed out.

'Your point?' he asked, throwing his bag aside and reaching for hers, preparing to conduct a similar search. She smacked his hand away. 'Hey!' he protested. 'My brain requires food.'

'How can something that doesn't exist require food?' she said wearily. But she reached into her bag and pulled out a packet of biscuits, which she then handed to him. 'Do you know where we are?'

Zakiy immediately ripped open the packet and stuffed a whole biscuit into his mouth. Then, chewing in a way that defied the laws of spatial physics, he turned and peered out through the rungs of the window. He couldn't make out more than vague outlines and bulging shapes that, when they passed under an occasional streetlamp, momentarily revealed themselves to be sprawling fields and thick bands of trees and a mass of vegetation. No signposts, however.

'No idea. Pretty sure we've crossed back into Kerala, though. We'll check at the next station.' This was the second train they'd travelled in, caught from Coimbatore, a city in the state of Tamil Nadu that bordered Kerala on the east. It was on its way to Thrissur, from where they would find their way to the Ayurveda clinic. 'We should be there in a couple of hours.' Zakiy sat back and crunched on another biscuit. Now that his hunger pangs had settled somewhat, he could focus on other, more important things. 'I asked my dad what "olege" means in Kannada,' he told Sathi.

Her head snapped up, her eyes sharp and focused. 'What did he say?'

'It means "inside". So the whole thing put together means "there's something inside–'

'"inside you",' Sathi finished. She snorted. 'Or rather, there's something inside *me*.' She paused to shake her head in disgust. 'Why do some people act like they know everything? I mean, could a statement be any more idiotic? And to think I spent the last week wracking my brains over something completely useless! It makes me want to march back there and throttle that guy!'

Looking at her, Zakiy noted with surprise that part of her really meant it – she was really that angry. Her hands were actually trembling, and her cheeks had become flushed with rage. 'Hey, let it go, Sathi. It's not worth it.'

'How would you know?' she snapped. 'You're not the one who's been stewing over it.'

Completely caught off guard, he didn't know how to respond. He was too shocked to even take offense. After a moment he said quietly, 'I didn't mean to trivialise it. I just meant that the guy was obviously unhinged, so his words aren't worth getting annoyed over.'

'Well, I *am* annoyed!' She crossed her arms and glared out of the window.

Zakiy continued to watch her, his sense of unease growing. This certainly wasn't the first time Sathi had lost her termper over something, but she usually didn't get this angry unless there was a good reason for it. Or, on the rare occasions there wasn't, he was usually able to simmer her down with a reasonable argument. This obstinacy was unlike her.

After some more thought he decided the best thing to do was to just distract her. There was something he had been meaning to tell her for a while, and maybe it would be enough to snap her out of this weird mood. 'When I was in Nelliampathi in October I contacted a police friend of mine.' He paused and amended, 'Well, he's my friend's older brother, but we talk sometimes. He thinks I'm amusing.' Zakiy waited, hoping to tease a smile from her. It didn't work, and she didn't look away from the window, either. He knew she was listening, though. 'He did a favour for me and pulled the records from 1996.'

Sathi stiffened. 1996 was the year her mother had died.

Zakiy continued, 'There was no mention of your mum's death at all. I asked him to search 1997 as well, but it was the same story. He was really puzzled, said I must be wrong because if she had died while she was here there would have been a record of it somewhere. There was no case or, uh, body at all.'

The train glided through several kilometres of dark countryside before Sathi spoke.

'What does that mean?' she whispered.

Zakiy hesitated before answering. 'I think it means you're right. And I think it means that whoever killed your Amma was clever enough to cover up all the evidence.'

She was quiet for another long moment. Then, in such a low tone he had to strain to hear her, she muttered, 'Sly fox.' She made a choked noise that sounded vaguely like a chuckle, though the sound was so dark there was no humour in it.

'What are you talking about? Sathi!' he said urgently when she didn't respond.

Her brown eyes fastened on him, and the look in them made him flinch. 'I know who killed her.'

'What? Who?' he demanded, straightening in his seat.

'Vidhya Raman.'

'*What?*' His voice, way too loud in the silent train, slapped against the air. Trying to control himself, he gritted out, 'How? Vidhya was Madhu's best friend.'

'She *pretended* to be her best friend,' Sathi corrected, staring down at the floor. She was quiet again for a moment, and then she sighed. She stood up and came to sit next to Zakiy, leaning her head against his shoulder. 'I'm sorry.'

Zakiy picked up her hand and squeezed it. 'Don't worry about it,' he told her, butting his head playfully against hers. 'So what's the story with Vidhya?'

Sathi's hand clenched involuntarily, fingers biting into his hand. Then she forcibly relaxed it. 'Vidhya was apparently always jealous of Amma, because she was sullen and plain and Amma was beautiful and vivacious. And apparently Vidhya had her sights set on my dad, and couldn't bear it when he married Amma instead.'

'Who told you all this?' Zakiy asked.

She hesitated, then reluctantly said, 'My great-uncle.'

Pity surged through him. 'Ah yes, the great-villain.'

Sathi laughed uncomfortably. 'Anyway, that's not all. The day my... my great-aunt had a... faked a heart-attack, I met this old nurse.' Zakiy missed her next words as he noted that same hesitation when she talked about the great-villains, as though she had to physically force the words out. '...a bit of a pain to talk to, but the nurse was there when Amma was in hospital, pregnant with me. She said Amma had visitors who came and talked to her at a time when none of the family was around.'

Understanding lit in him. 'You mean visitors like the ones your mum wrote about in her letter?'

'Exactly.' Sathi rummaged in her bag and took out a very crumpled, folded up piece of paper. She handed it to him and he opened it to see smudged handwriting spreading over every corner of the paper:

Darling Nakul,

How are you? I am counting the days until you come back to me. I hate the thought of you being all the way in London, with no one to look after you – apart from Devi, of course. I ask her every day to pay special attention to you. And yes, I will be honest; I also want you to be right next to me, not halfway across the world! I never claimed to be unselfish. As annoying as you can be when you are worried, I miss you. I feel the loss of that sense of safety you give me dearly. But then, what excuse would I not give to make you hop on the next plane home?

Anyway, talking of separation, here is another reason why you should hurry back: I have a feeling that he-she is an impatient one and will come out sooner than expected, whether we are ready or not!

There is something else. I have been blaming you for my uneasiness but that is not the real reason. They came for a visit last night. They... well, they started again with the persuasion. They should've known by now that I am not going to back down. If it had not been for this blasted hospital's policy, all this would have been over and done with by now. No matter. We have taken care of all the details and as long as our little he-she is well, I will be able to sort this out come March.

And as for them... well, maybe I am just being paranoid. When I asked them to leave, they were not the least bit ruffled. They just smiled – those cruel smiles I am becoming accustomed to – and walked out without a single sound of protest. The lack of reaction makes me think that they are up to something. And I am not in a position to find out what they are planning now, not when I am pushing eight months.

Just hurry back to me, my love, and these worries will be put into perspective in my mind. I will be able to ignore their doomed efforts and concentrate fully on the joy our child will give us.

Loving you always,
your Madhu

For a moment, Zakiy was distracted by the obvious affection in the letter – Sathi's parents had been so deeply in love when Madhu had been killed.

Sathi leaned forward so she could read the letter over his shoulder, though he imagined that she'd already memorised her mother's words. 'The nurse said it was two women, one around Amma's age and the other old enough to be her mother.'

'Weird,' Zakiy mused. 'But how do you know they were the ones to threaten your Amma? Couldn't Vidhya have just been there to visit her?'

Sathi's eyes glittered. 'Would Vidhya wear a *purdah* for a casual visit?'

Oh. 'Vidhya Raman isn't a Muslim name,' he said slowly.

'She was wearing it as a disguise –'

'So that she wouldn't be recognised,' Zakiy finished. What a horrible, deceitful creature this Vidhya is turning out to be. He looked back at the letter. 'What do you think your mum meant about persuasion? And something about backing down – backing down from what?'

Sathi shrugged, and he realised that she looked very, very tired. 'I don't know. I've been trying to figure that out for ages, and I still don't have any answers. I also don't know what Amma was going to do in March –'

Her words trailed off as a static-filled voice rumbled through the train: 'Attention all passengers. This train will terminate at the next station. This is due to a train fault.'

Zakiy jumped up and peered through the window again as the train pulled into the station. Pinpricks of light were the only indication of civilisation. He could see other heads hanging out of doors further along the train as they came to the same grim conclusion that he had. The announcement continued. 'I repeat, this train will terminate at the next station. All passengers please disembark. We apologise for the inconvenience caused and thank you for your patience.'

Zakiy turned and met Sathi's eyes, which were filled with dismay. He crooked her a resigned grin. 'I always think it's presumptuous of them to thank us for patience we haven't yet exhibited, don't you?'

Chapter Eight

Derailed

This sucks, Sathi thought as she went in search of a less crowded restroom further along the platform in the tiny station. The train had long since lumbered off to wherever it would go to get checked out by engineers, and an angry horde of passengers had circled the sleepy-looking station manager, demanding information about their disrupted journeys. She and Zakiy had joined the crowd long enough to find out that there wasn't another train to Thrissur until the next morning.

Which, repeating her earlier sentiment, sucked.

Sathi sighed and pushed open the door to the restroom, and gingerly, using the tip of a fingernail, nudged open one of the cubicle doors. The closet was an Indian one.

'Yes!' she exclaimed, punching her fist in the air. Then, she hastily lowered her arm and looked around sheepishly at the empty room.

Okay so maybe it wasn't normal to get so excited about a type of closer that you have to squat over on the floor, but during long-distance journeys she had learned to count it as a blessing since it meant she wouldn't have to sit on unidentifiable liquid – especially in unisex toilets. As she slid the bolt across the door, she made a mental note to herself: *If I ever have male children, teach them to aim.*

Washing her hands using what had to be the most diluted form of liquid soap in history, she couldn't help but wrinkle her nose. The smell was an inescapable phenomenon in any public toilet.

The door to the bathroom suddenly slammed open, diverting Sathi's attention away from the smell. A woman who looked to be in her twenties marched in, a phone held to her ear and her expression stormy. 'I'm sick of this. I'm coming back,' she growled into the phone, striding into a cubicle and slamming the door shut.

Sathi turned off the tap and plucked a few paper tissues from the box on the counter. She couldn't help but overhear more of the woman's words in the virtually empty room. 'What they're doing is against every code of ethics in the book. I can't work for them anymore.' There was a pause as she listened to whatever the person on the other end of the phone was saying. 'I don't care,' the woman declared hotly. The noise of a flush sounded, and then the woman stalked over to the sink, not even seeming to notice Sathi where she stood drying her hands. 'They can't put steroids into so called "pure" Ayurvedic medicines and get away with it!'

Sathi froze.

The incensed woman pushed her hair behind her ears in a gesture of irritation, and continued, 'Yes, I actually *saw* them. When I caught them, they even tried to justify it to me. Said that's the only way to get quick results and draw in customers. I've studied Ayurveda for five years, and I *know* that's not true. So should they. Shouldn't they at least respect the integrity of the profession?' As she listened to the response, she tossed the clump of wet tissue into the overflowing bin and left the room.

Only a faint echo of her words was left behind as Sathi stared after the woman, still unable to believe her ears. Abruptly making a decision, she yanked open the door to the bathroom and hurried after the woman as she strode along the platform. Sathi caught up to her just as she said, 'Yeah, I think that's the best thing to do. At least that will be *real*.' She paused to listen for a moment, and sighed. 'Okay. I will. Love you too. Bye.'

She tucked the phone away and turned, coming face to face with Sathi. She raised her eyebrows at the younger girl. 'Yes?'

'Er...' Sathi opened and closed her mouth like a goldfish. Then, when the woman's eyebrows climbed even further up her smooth forehead, she blurted, 'Is Ayurveda really that bad?'

Now the woman's eyebrows pulled together in confusion. Then she glanced down at the pocket in her jeans where she had stuffed her phone, and seemed to understand. She looked back up at Sathi. 'You heard my phone call.'

It wasn't a question, but Sathi nodded sheepishly. 'I'm sorry, I didn't mean to eavesdrop – I just couldn't help hearing.' She hesitated, then asked, 'Is it true, about Ayurveda, er...' – she faltered, not knowing whether to call them "doctors" or "therapists"; she decided vagueness was best – 'people using steroids in their medicines?'

The woman sighed and crossed her arms over her chest. 'Not all of them,' she told Sathi. 'Just people like my *ex*-employers.' She stressed the "ex" part with vehemence. She regarded Sathi with curiosity. 'Why do you want to know?'

Sathi bit her lip, considering. She examined the woman, taking in her strong-jawed face, the straight black hair that framed it and spilled over onto her shoulders, and the sharpness of her clear gaze. With a start, she realised that she trusted her. Impulsively, she stuck her hand out. 'I'm Sathi.'

Surprise clearly imprinted across her expression, the woman nevertheless gripped Sathi's hand in hers and shook it. 'Anna,' she said.

Sathi blinked. It was a Christian name, obviously, but it was pronounced differently, with more of an emphasis on the double n and a shorter "ah" sound at the beginning. Pushing aside the mystery for now, she smiled at Anna. 'Pleased to meet you.'

Anna opened her mouth to reply, but before she could say anything there came an interruption in the form of a tall, lanky guy with crazy brown hair that stuck up all over his head. Zakiy walked up to Sathi and exclaimed, 'There you are. What happened?' Then he noticed Anna. 'Oh. Hello.'

'Anna, this is my friend, Zakiy,' Sathi said. 'Zakiy, this is Anna. She, um, used to work at an Ayurveda place.'

Zakiy's eyes widened. '*Oh,*' he said again.

Anna raised her hands, palms out like she was trying to keep them at bay. 'Okay, what the hell is going on here?' she demanded. 'First you,' she said, pointing at Sathi, 'eavesdrop on my phone conversation and keep going on about Ayurveda. Then, if that wasn't bad enough,' she continued, her voice rising as she built up steam, '*this* broccoli-head is looking at me like I have an extra head sprouting out of my neck.'

A moment of complete and utter silence, quiet enough to hear a pin drop.

Sathi burst out laughing.

She couldn't help herself; laughter broke through her chest like exuberant firecrackers, and her mirth only grew at the sight of Anna's dumbfounded expression. She looked at Zakiy, who was gingerly feeling his hair, and she doubled up with renewed giggles.

Finally, smiling widely, she met Anna's eyes. 'We're going to get along just fine.'

Anna stared back at her for a moment, and then her lips quirked up into a wry smile. 'You guys are crazy,' she said, shaking her head.

She grinned back at her. 'You have no idea.'

They ended up getting coffee, and Sathi filled Anna in about their interest in Ayurveda without mentioning Aman.

'This Ayurapy clinic is crap,' Anna informed them flatly. 'You might as well wad up your money and use it to style *his* hair.' She jerked her chin towards Zakiy and took a sip of her coffee.

'Hey, stop with the hair jokes already,' Zakiy protested. He paused and added, 'And I have a name, you know.'

'I know,' Anna answered coolly. 'Broccoli-head.'

Sathi interrupted before he could retaliate. 'You know the clinic, then?' she asked in dismay.

'Don't need to. It's made from the same mould as the one I worked in. You're not going to find any real Ayurveda there.' Anna looked over at Sathi as she silently played with her own cup, and her expression softened. 'Look, one thing you need to understand is that in Kerala Ayurveda has become a major tourism racket. These so called clinics are designed as a service for foreigners – and snobby Indian upper class wannabe foreigners – to come and have a relaxing holiday where they are pampered and treated like royalty – all at exorbitant rates, of course. Throw in hot oil massages, mud baths, yoga and weird herbal mixtures, and you get the ultimate "relaxation" package,' she concluded sarcastically.

Silence descended into their midst for a minute while the trio drank their coffee, each lost in their own thoughts. Then Zakiy sighed and said, 'It's just like the Prince said, isn't?'

Sathi nodded mournfully as she remembered the professor's words. 'What a waste of time.'

Anna looked back and forth between their faces, expectant. Sathi stayed silent, knowing that this was Zakiy's decision to make. She would back him up whether he chose to lie or tell the truth. Thinking of his track record, she would guess the former. Indeed, Zakiy started to open his mouth confidently, obviously about to deliver a well-prepared story. Then, abruptly, he stopped and regarded Anna thoughtfully. Almost as though she could read his mind, Sathi watched him come to the same conclusion she had about being able to trust this new friend of theirs.

Zakiy took a deep breath. 'My brother has schizophrenia. We were exploring Ayurveda for him.'

Anna was very still, her expression giving nothing away. 'I'm sorry.'

Zakiy acknowledged her with a nod. He got up and stretched. 'I guess there's no point waiting for the Thrissur train tomorrow. I'll go and see if there's a train back to Mysore.'

'Wait,' Anna said.

Zakiy and Sathi regarded her curiously. 'Just because there isn't any real Ayurveda in those clinics, that doesn't mean it doesn't exist.' She drained the last drops of her coffee and crossed her legs. 'I know a place where Ayurveda is practised the way it's supposed to be practised. By someone who's learnt it from the real teachers – from tribals whose lifestyle is completely in tune with nature.' Anna paused, seeming to become lost in thought. Finally she looked up. 'I'll take you there,' she said decisively.

'Oh no,' Sathi protested, just as Zakiy said, 'You don't need to go out of your way – if you give us the address –'

'Just sit your butts down and listen to me,' Anna ordered.

They sat.

Anna leaned forward. 'Look, I'm going whether or not you two come with me. If you want to, you can tag along. If not, get lost.'

They looked at each other, and then back at Anna. 'We're in,' they said simultaneously.

'Keep up, you two,' Anna called as she drove herself forward with a long stride that even Zakiy couldn't match with his insanely elongated legs. Sathi and Zakiy huffed and puffed along behind her as they clambered up the steep, protracted hill.

Anna looked back once, took in their pathetic states, muttered something unintelligible and quickened her pace even further.

'Did you know,' Zakiy gasped, 'that Anna means "one who is merciful"? What were her parents thinking?'

Sathi, too tired to muster even a smile, focused all her energy on simply putting one foot in front of the other. After about ten more minutes of this extended torture, they finally reached the top and promptly collapsed right there in the road while Anna stood over them like a drill sergeant.

'Are you guys for real?' she demanded as they rolled around, groaning.

'Um, not sure,' Zakiy wheezed, clutching his side. 'Ask me again tomorrow.'

Anna made a sound of disgust and strode off, leaving them to scramble to their feet and hobble as best as they could after her along thankfully level ground.

'Who is she? Superwoman?' Zakiy muttered, appraising Anna suspiciously as she moved forward steadily, not even out of breath. 'Or maybe she's an alien sent to destroy us with physical exercise.'

'"She" can hear you perfectly,' Anna said suddenly, causing Sathi to choke on a giggle.

'See!' Zakiy whispered triumphantly. 'Superhuman hearing.'

'Shut up, Broccoli-head.'

He silently wagged his eyebrows at Sathi. 'Yes ma'am!'

Sathi swallowed another giggle and called up to Anna. 'Where does using steroids fit in with those Ayurvedic clinics?'

Anna didn't respond immediately, and her pace slowed. Zakiy shot Sathi a look of gratitude. 'Like I said earlier, it's something some idiots do to get quick results and fatten their bank accounts. They add steroids or marijuana to the herbal mixtures so that the "client" experiences an instantaneous effect. Stupid fools,' she muttered, more to herself. 'Tarnishing the name of Ayurveda doctors everywhere.' She kicked moodily at a small rock. It flew forward and ricocheted off a tree trunk, boomeranging back to hit Zakiy's toe with a *thunk*. This was followed by a yell of agony. Sathi decided to leave Anna alone after that.

They trudged through more countryside with only vast paddy fields and lots of gorgeous rivers and ponds for company, and finally entered a small village that seemed to be half-asleep. There were maybe a handful of tiny shops, and the narrow roads snaked through more vegetation. They soon left the main "town" area and passed into the residential area, which had a range of houses from thatched-roof ones to the more commercial buildings, all inhabited by people who seemed very curious about the trio. Sathi handled the stares a lot better now than she had when she first arrived in Kerala; back then she'd even had this silly tactic of staring right back to make them realise how annoying the habit was. Now she paid no attention, just like Anna and Zakiy did.

A few minutes later, they came to a small house with a board that read, *Vinod Kani, Vaidhyan*, set on top of the gate.

'What does *vaidhyan* mean?' Sathi asked.

Anna glanced at the board. 'A doctor or physician. That's what Ayurveda practitioners were called in the days before Allopathy took over.' She strode over to the gate and put a hand on it, then stopped and turned to face Sathi and Zakiy. 'Before we go in, there's one thing I want to make very clear.' Anna stared at them fiercely and jerked her head at the board. 'This man is not a joke. A lot of people waltz in here and make fun of him because he lived with the *aadivasees* for a while – the local tribal people,' she explained when Sathi opened her mouth to ask. 'He learnt Ayurveda from them and even though he's been officially accredited with the Bachelor of Ayurvedic Medicine and Surgery degree, people still give him a lot of flak. So I'm only taking you to him if you swear to me that you can mind your manners.' Anna's eyes bored first into Sathi's and then shifted to Zakiy for his share of the glaring.

Sathi managed to find her voice first. 'Of course we won't make fun of him!'

'Of course not,' Zakiy echoed. Once Anna had given them a grim nod and pushed open the gate, he sidled closer to Sathi and whispered, 'That's one scary dudette.'

When Anna glanced back and told them to hurry up, Sathi could've sworn there was the faintest trace of a smile on her face.

Anna led them through the small front yard, but instead of going into the house like Sathi had expected, they instead kept walking past around the back of the house where there was another, smaller, building. It looked like it only had room for maybe one room, with a small waiting area in front. Anna ignored the benches there and marched straight into the building, which had to be an office.

The man who was sitting back in a chair in the small room inside looked up, his expression changing in no way at the sight of this girl striding into his office uninvited. He looked at Anna for a moment, then closed the book he had been writing in with a snap. 'Well, well, BAMS,' he said, 'you *do* keep turning up like a bad penny, don't you?'

When Anna stalked over to the vaidhyan guy, Zakiy was fully expecting her to smack him for the comment. Instead, she rendered Zakiy speechless for the second time in as many days by laughing and throwing her arms around the guy. 'Nice to see you too,' she retorted, pulling back and grinning.

The vaidhyan cracked a smile. 'Well, what are you doing here' he asked Anna.

She gestured to Sathi and Zakiy. 'Well, that's kind of their fault.'

He turned to face them, and Zakiy saw that he was actually a short, remarkably unremarkable man considering all the theatrics. His thinning hair tapered to show a shiny bald patch at the top, in stark contrast to his rather bushy eyebrows. Zakiy lost track of the introductions Anna was making as he briefly considered possible nicknames. *Baldy or Bushy?* he wondered.

'Zakiy.' When he looked up, he got the feeling that it wasn't the first time Sathi had said his name. 'We came to get treatment for Zakiy's brother Aman,' she explained to Bushy while giving Zakiy a look that said, *I know what you're up to and I don't like it.*

Zakiy gave her a brazen smile that exuded the *I'm sure I have no idea what you're talking about* vibe and turned to nod at Bushy. Calling him Baldy just seemed mean.

'And where is this Aman?' Bushy asked.

'We just came today to... um, I guess gather information. I have no clue about how Ayurveda works,' Sathi admitted.

'Aman is a schizophrenic,' Anna explained. 'They wanted to find out how Ayurveda can help him before making him travel all the way here.'

Zakiy blinked in surprise. That was exactly the reason he and Sathi had come alone, but how did Anna know that? He wondered whether Sathi had told her, but one glance at her equally surprised expression said otherwise. Anna must have just guessed.

Looking back at her and Bushy, he caught them exchanging a meaningful look before Anna broke eye contact, her expression almost... pained?

'So *unmaadham* is the issue,' Bushy said thoughtfully, steepling his fingers together and gazing down at them. Zakiy tried not to bristle at the Malayalam blanket term for insanity. 'If someone has a fever you could give them the juice squeezed from a mixture of *thulasi*, ginger and *kumkumam*. Or you can grind together *muringa* leaves and apply them to a wound to reduce swelling. But unmaadham... that's not so easily fixed.' He cleared his throat. 'There are a lot of medicinal plants you can use; there is *gudgunu, jadamanji, karimbadam, kannumkombu*,' he said, listing them off. 'You can gather all of these and grind them together.'

Bushy paused and glanced at Anna, his eyebrows slightly raised. She nodded almost imperceptibly. He exhaled in a soft sigh and met Zakiy's eyes. 'Medicine is not enough by itself to cure insanity – you need another component to counteract the *manthram*. For that you take out the guts of a chicken that's up to three years old and wrap it and the herbs in mustard seeds before tying it all up with palm fibre.'

In shock at the guy's words, Zakiy looked blankly across at Sathi; she was gazing at Bushy with her mouth gaping open. Well, that ruled out ear malfunction on his part.

Bushy continued, 'You burn the whole mixture with the spadix of a palm and feed the patient the drops of liquid that is made from it. This is effective for insanity, delusions and hallucinations, mental illness, mental tension... For these you need magic as well as medicine.'

Chapter Nine

Einstein & the Elephant

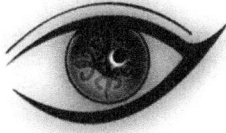

That guy is freaking insane,' Zakiy growled as he paced back and forth, kicking up clouds of dust with every furious step.

Anna stepped forward, though even she had enough sense to keep out of his path. 'Look, I know you're upset but he really does know what he's talking about. It sounds a bit weird but –'

'A *bit* weird?' Zakiy repeated incredulously, turning to glare at her. 'Are you serious? With all that talk of chickens and magic no wonder people think he's a joke!'

Anger glinted in Anna's eyes. 'Don't talk about things you don't understand,' she said harshly. 'He's helped countless people recover their health and happiness – people like your brother. If you could only get past being so close-minded –'

'Zakiy isn't close-minded,' Sathi broke in quietly, speaking for the first time since they left Bushy's office. She lifted her chin and met Anna's angry gaze. 'He's just surprised, and so am I. This isn't exactly what we were expecting.'

At her words Anna seemed to simmer down slightly. 'You're right. I should have warned you.' She stared at the floor for a moment, before sighing and looking back up at them. 'Do you know the story of the elephant and the blind men?'

'What, you're going to tell us a bedtime story now?' Zakiy demanded.

Anna shot him a glare. 'In the story a group of blind men touch different parts of an elephant and claim that they're different things. For example, one feels its tusk and thinks it's a pipe, while another declares that it's a wall after leaning against its side. Yet another one mistakes its ear for a hand fan. The point is, even though they're all right in their own ways they're also wrong because they can't see the big picture. They argue and bicker among themselves because they all think they're right and everyone else is wrong – the only way they can see the big picture is if they work together and put all the individual pieces together. But they don't do that because they're all too busy caught up in their own belief, in their own pig-headedness.'

'So...' Zakiy said slowly, 'basically you're saying that we're being pig-headed.'

Her eyes rolled heavenward for a moment, as though she was thinking, *God, give me patience!*

Zakiy nearly cracked a smile in spite of his agitation; he truly loved the art of aggravation.

Anna returned to glaring at him. 'No, you dolt, what I'm saying is that there are a lot of different ways of looking at one thing. Modern medicine works with the principle that the human body is a complex mixture of chemicals – that is their definition of science. But that's only *one* definition, one that some people can't see beyond because they're only holding one part of the elephant.'

'This elephant is turning into a major pain in the butt.'

Anna ignored him. 'The problem with science is that a lot of people try to put it into neat little boxes that will sit there comfortably and not cause confusion or any sort of disturbance. But it doesn't work like that. Just take the wave-particle duality in physics – light can exist as both particles and as waves, which is in itself a contradiction. Scientists don't like contradicting pieces of information. Even Einstein said something like, "Yeah we don't like it, but without both we wouldn't know what light is". And those are just two possibilities – who knows how many parts there are to the whole?'

For once his brain's quip-generating centre failed Zakiy, and he could only blink at her. He had been counting on Sathi having the same reaction, so he was beyond stunned when she suddenly said, 'That actually makes a lot of sense. The fact that you can analyse one thing using the...' – she paused, searching for the right word – 'the paradigms of something completely different. It's kind of like what you told me once,' she added to Zakiy.

He stared blankly back at her as his brain assured him with a hundred percent certainty that he'd never conducted a conversation that involved paradigms and Einstein and a pachyderm with an identity crisis.

'You know,' Sathi prompted when he didn't say anything, 'when you used a basic law of physics to explain something spiritual. You said if there's a God then there has to be a negative counterpart as well because energy has to be in balance. Where there's positive energy there has to be an equal and opposite energy to counteract it.'

'*You* said that?' Anna asked him, one eyebrow quirking up.

Zakiy chose to ignore the sceptical tone. 'Yeah, but that's not the same,' he told Sathi.

'I don't see why,' Anna said. 'It's actually what I've been leading up to tell you. Vinod Kani mentioned the use of manthram – magic. The truth is, in the old days insanity – or any kind of mental illness,' she added quickly at the dangerous look Zakiy directed at her, 'was believed to be caused by evil spirits possessing the body. Now of course that's all dismissed as superstition – doctors say they didn't know any better, they were ignorant idiots... blah, blah, blah. Everything is explained away using chemicals, but tell me, have chemicals in an antipsychotic pill ever *cured* a disease? Has it cured your brother's disease?'

There was no need to answer because if it had, they wouldn't be here in the first place. Anna continued, 'It all just circles back to one thing: no one knows everything. And I think, instead of clutching at what works and sweeping what doesn't under a carpet, a better attitude is to keep an open mind and embrace different possibilities. Vinod Kani uses the herbs for the chemicals, and the spell for the manthram.'

'Spell?' Zakiy echoed.

Anna looked straight at him. 'Yes, spell. A spell to counteract whatever negative energy accompanies your brother's illness.'

He was backing away and shaking his head before she even finished speaking. 'No, absolutely not! I won't have Aman treated like he has some kind of evil spirit inside him.'

She stared back at him, frustration clear in her eyes. Then her expression softened with understanding and her voice was gentle as she said, 'It's not like that. He would never hurt Aman.'

Sathi looked back and forth between them, evidently confused. 'What's going on? What are you talking about?'

Zakiy's fists clenched and unclenched. 'Years ago, the way a magician tried to exorcise a negative spirit that was possessing a human was by hitting him repeatedly with a stick, because they believed the magician's manthram meant that the spirit would be the one to feel the blows, not the human.' He gave a humourless chuckle. 'Only, it didn't really work like that. The spirit – if it even existed in the first place – probably couldn't care less and the human came away with red marks covering every inch of his body.'

Sathi's voice was choked when she finally managed to speak a minute later. 'That's *awful*.'

Anna put her hand on Zakiy's shoulder. 'Look, I know you're scared. But please trust me when I say that Vinod Kani would *never* do something like that – he's not a barbarian, he's not going to perform black magic or anything like that. He would never hurt your brother.'

Zakiy rubbed his arm across his eyes, suddenly feeling exhausted. 'I'm sorry. I really, really appreciate everything you've done for us, for Aman. But I'd rather Aman spend his whole life as a schizophrenic than take the risk of him being abused like that. Besides,' he said, his voice cracking a little, 'there's no guarantee that this will help him. I just can't put him at risk like this.'

Anna leaned back and crossed her arms, her expression suddenly closed off and unreadable. 'What if I gave you proof?'

Zakiy stared at her, trying to figure out what was going on. 'Proof for what? That it will work, or that it won't hurt him?'

'Both.'

He and Sathi exchanged glances. 'What proof?' she asked.

Anna stared out at the leafy green heads of the coconut trees high above them, where the branches stood out starkly against the light blue of the sky as though unsure whether they belonged to the sky or the earth. 'Vinod Kani treated my mother several years ago for early onset dementia. Dad and I had pretty much given up hope when someone told us about him. He brought her – he brought *us* back. We enjoy life again, instead of just getting by.' Her eyes flicked to Zakiy. 'And he never harmed even a single strand of her hair.'

She didn't say anything else. Finally Zakiy averted his eyes from her steady gaze and sighed. 'Fine. Let's go find a chicken.'

'Here,' Bushy said the next day as he handed Zakiy a small bottle full of clear liquid. 'Give this to your brother – two or three drops every day.'

Zakiy took it reluctantly and looked at Bushy, half expecting him to sprout a long beard and start chanting and leaping around manically like magicians always did in movies.

Bushy smiled sardonically at him as though he could guess what he was thinking. 'I know you have your reservations. But remember, we can't prove the power of something until we see its effects, and it's not always possible to measure those effects in a scientific way.'

Well, that cleared things up. Not.

Bushy reached behind his desk and pulled out a scrap of paper. He set it on the smooth surface of his desk and the breeze from the open window made it rustle slightly. Bushy pointed at it. 'I put a paper there and it moved. We call the phenomenon that moves it "wind". We've given it a name but has anyone seen wind? Neither those who practise allopathy nor those who practise Ayurveda have seen it. We can feel its effects but if asked to point out its path or what it looks like both parties would be stumped. Wind is something that fills the whole cosmos. Wherever the air's vibrations travel there will be movement. It fills our lungs, we breathe it every day but we don't really know it. We can't see it, we can't touch it, we can't taste it... but without it we wouldn't be alive.'

He picked up the paper and weighed it in his hands. 'Unmaadham is caused by problems in the nerves of the brain, disruptions that occur due to irregular vibrations. Whatever your beliefs are, this medicine will not harm your brother in any way. Give it to him and see if it makes a difference.' He looked up at Zakiy. 'You can decide whether or not you believe me then.'

'Okay. Thank you,' Zakiy added. After all, that was fair.

'When you decide that I'm right,' Bushy continued, 'I'd like you to bring Aman here. How many years has he had this illness?'

Zakiy shook his head in defeat at the presumption. 'Nearly fifteen years.'

Bushy nodded. 'Yes, I thought so. It would be good for him to have some sessions in the steam room.'

Zakiy had a sudden vision of Bushy, Aman and himself sitting back in a sauna wearing bright swimwear. Trying to contain his shudder, he directed a questioning glance at Bushy.

'We boil together sixty five different medicinal herbs and feed the steam arising from it into a small enclosed room,' he explained. 'It's a way of purging toxins from your body, and it would be beneficial for Aman to go through that process.'

'Toxins?' Sathi repeated, her voice a bit off as though she was trying too hard to keep it casual.

Bushy nodded. 'Yes, the body accumulates toxins on a regular basis and the steam of medicinal herbs is an extremely effective method for getting rid of them.'

'Oh.'

'Also,' Bushy continued, peering out at her from under those caterpillar eyebrows that gave him his nickname, 'if you have ingested anything toxic steam baths can help clear those out of your system as well.'

Sathi's lips pressed into a flat line, but she said nothing in reply.

Zakiy said, 'I'll let you know about bringing Aman. I'm not sure if I'll be able to, even if this stuff works.' He shook the bottle, thinking of his father's over-protectiveness when it came to Aman.

84

Bushy nodded in response, and they left after saying their goodbyes. As they neared the end of their trek back to the train station, Sathi asked, 'What now?'

'I'm going to make a quick trip home and then come back here,' Anna said. When she saw their surprised expressions she explained, 'I'm going to work under Vinod Kani as his apprentice or assistant or whatever you want to call it. I need some real experience with Ayurveda, and he's the best person to learn from. Plus, anything has to be better than learning to crush up steroids,' she added with a scowl.

'So you'll be here if we decide to come back?' Zakiy asked, more relieved than he would ever admit to her at the thought of having an interpreter when dealing with Bushy.

Anna stretched her arms out in front of her and cracked her knuckles. 'Yeah, I should be a permanent fixture here for a year at least. What are you two going to do – go straight to Mysore?'

'Actually,' Zakiy said to Sathi, 'if you don't mind I'd like to swing by Nelliampathi since we're pretty close, and drive back with Toothless.'

'Toothless?' Anna asked.

'My Jeep,' he clarified matter-of-factly.

Anna opened her mouth, caught Sathi's eye, and shut it again. She gave Sathi a look like, *So this is what you have to endure on a regular basis, huh?*

'Is that okay?' he enquired before the situation could deteriorate into a girls versus one-lone-defenceless-boy ribbing session.

'Fine by me. I miss Toothless, too,' Sathi said, smiling.

They stopped outside the train station and regarded each other. Anna crossed her arms. 'Well, I guess this is where we say goodbye.'

Sathi stepped forward and hugged her tightly around the waist. 'Keep in touch.'

'Won't have to if Broccoli-head over there gets his brain screwed on right and decides to come back to Vinod Kani,' Anna replied, reaching out to ruffle her hair. Then she glanced over at him. 'You heard me, Broccoli-head. You better get your butt back here soon.'

'Yes ma'am.' Zakiy saluted.

Anna cracked a grin. 'Take care of yourselves.'

They nodded and had turned to go when she called out, 'Zakiy?'

He glanced back. 'Look after your brother,' Anna told him, concern in her eyes.

Sudden emotion paralysed his tongue, and he could only nod before they parted ways.

Chapter Ten

The Merits of a Half-Sari

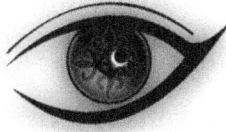

S hall we swing by the school in Nemmara?'

Sathi glanced at Zakiy, surprised. 'What school?'

'Your mum's school. Kendriya Vidyalaya.'

Her forehead crinkled. 'Um, why?'

'Well, it was Vidhya's school as well, wasn't it?'

Sathi stiffened at the mention of Vidhya and waited for him to elaborate. When he didn't, she said, 'So?'

'We might find a lead to finding her. We could talk to the mad maths prof again,' he said with a chuckle, referring to her Amma's favourite teacher.

'You know we tried that last time – he has an abysmal memory.'

Zakiy stroked his chin. 'True. But maybe there's someone else there who remembers Vidhya.'

'Who, like that disgusting headmistress?' she shot back, angry for reasons she couldn't fully explain, not even to herself.

He looked over at her in surprise. 'Well no, not her but maybe someone who remembers Vidhya.'

'Why the sudden interest in visiting the school, anyway?' she snapped.

He was quiet for so long that she thought he was going to let the subject drop. Then he said, 'I thought you wanted to find Vidhya.'

Sathi didn't answer, and he added, 'I just assumed –'

'I wish you'd stop assuming things,' she burst out, her voice shaking. 'Of course I want to find Vidhya, but I don't see how going back to that school will help! We already know she went to the same college as Amma – Mar Ivanios. That doesn't really help us.'

Zakiy's fingers tightened on the wheel. 'The reason I wanted to come get the Jeep is so we could go to your mum's school,' he said evenly. 'But going all the way to Thiruvananthapuram right now is going to be difficult.'

'I didn't say we had to go back there!' Sathi exclaimed. 'Just... let's just focus on getting back to Mysore for now.'

He apparently took her at her word, because they made the long drive back to his house in silence.

'Great,' Maira groaned, her eyes wearily scanning the letter in her hand. 'It's from Fadilah – Aisha is getting engaged next week, and she's sent an invitation.'

'Aisha's getting married?' Zakiy asked, sounding stunned. 'But she's only a year older than I am!'

Narayan sighed. 'A year too much, in your aunt's book.'

'Fadilah is my sister-in-law,' Maira explained to Sathi. 'Aisha is her eldest daughter, Zakiy's cousin.'

'Let's not go,' Narayan said. 'That woman gets on my nerves.'

'We can say we've moved,' Zakiy mused in a rare show of camaraderie with his father. 'We'll say we moved to Mars!'

Maira threw them both an exasperated look. 'We have to go. No matter how much Fadilah *gets on our nerves*,' she emphasised, shooting her husband a glare, 'she's the only one from my side of the family who still speaks to us.'

The reminder paused the protestations, and Sathi thought back to what Zakiy had told her a long time ago, how Maira's family had disowned her because she fell in love with a Hindu man.

'When is this thing, anyway?' Narayan grumbled resignedly, taking the letter from Maira.

'Wait!' Zakiy broke in. 'I have a better idea.' His parents regarded him expectantly, and he spread his arms in victory. 'Let's *actually* move to Mars!'

Sathi pawed through her wardrobe, wondering what exactly she was supposed to wear to an Indian engagement. Hell, she had no clue what an Indian engagement even involved. Was the groom expected to get down on one knee and propose in front of a room full of people? She shuddered in sympathy.

Sighing, she finally pulled out the only skirt she owned, hidden behind the T-shirts and comfortable jeans that made up most of her wardrobe. She'd already told Maira – multiple times – that she would be happy to stay at home while the family attended the function, but Maira wouldn't hear of it. She'd insisted Sathi join them. Sathi dug among her tops until she found one that was most likely to disguise its true identity – that of a T-shirt. At least it was plain, and had a slight ruffle to the sleeves. It would have to do. She laid both it and the skirt over her desk chair, ready for tomorrow, and got into bed.

Her eyelids were so tired and heavy that she couldn't hold them open but, like the past few nights, sleep refused to claim her. Her mind, despite her efforts to shut it up and undaunted by lack of sleep, still spun with thoughts, worries and self-disgust.

She still hadn't apologised to Zakiy for snapping at him the other day. He hadn't brought it up, either, though that was probably because he'd been too busy – his parents had been keen to hear all about the Ayurvedic doctor and the things he and Anna had told them. The thought of Anna brought a small smile to Sathi's face: she was so cool. Sathi hoped that they would be able to keep in contact even if they didn't return for more treatment.

Her hands clenched automatically as she remembered what the vaidhyan had said about steam baths flushing out toxins in the body – including toxins that had been ingested. It had hit a little too close to home after her experience at her great-aunt and great-uncle's house.

A teardrop leaked out of her burning eyes at the sudden pain that lanced though her chest. All that affection and joy those two had shown when they first saw her, the months afterwards that had been so idyllically perfect... all fake, all lies, lies to cover up their true, monstrous natures.

And with each passing day, Sathi had become more and more like them.

She let out a ragged breath and pulled her knees up to her chest, wrapping her arms around them. Her forehead pressed against the merciless sharpness of her kneecaps, she tried to calm her breathing. *There's no point in thinking like this. They are what they are*, she told herself firmly, but she didn't believe her own words. Hopelessness settled into her again at the shattering of a long cherished dream of being part of a happy family. Her mother was gone, her father was as good as, but her grandparents... that was one thing she had never seen coming. All the love they'd shown had only been a tactic to keep her docile and unquestioning. They had discovered her weakness and used it against her – and she had let them. *She* was responsible, *she* was the one who had been so blind, like a desperate, love-starved junkie.

She groaned to herself and rolled over onto her other side, wishing that she could fall asleep and get away from her recycled thoughts, even if for a few hours. Although if the last few days were any indication, she would wake up in the morning only to carry on straight from where she left off. It was like her brain continued with its internal rumination even while she slept. She was really sick of it, sick of feeling trapped inside her own mind. Sometimes she wished there was a way to induce amnesia at will, to erase some memories forever.

Sathi couldn't forget the expression on her father's face just before she left for India. So much hate and anger, anguish and an odd vulnerability she couldn't entirely fathom, not in her father, and certainly not with anything related to *her*. Her heart flared in pain with the power of her longing – a longing for her father to take care of her and comfort her. She gripped her arms more tightly around herself, as though she could keep the pain away by squeezing it out.

90

Always a glutton for punishment, Sathi stretched out her arm so she could reach her phone and refresh her email. The cursor swung cheerfully round and round, flashing different colours, and finally became still: No new mail.

Dark humour struck her; what a fool she was. She remembered how, after finding that none of the internet versions of the Cherokee parable listed the seven deadly sins, she had wished she could get her hands on her own copy of the book, the one that had appeared in her dream. She chuckled humourlessly now as she thought of how tempting it was to contact her father and ask him to send the book to her. How, even now, her fingers itched to email her father, to use the book as an excuse to feel like she had some sort of relationship with her father, to believe that he loved her.

She kept laughing at herself, even though her hands were shaking, even though the pain in her chest was migrating its way up into her throat, she just kept laughing through it all. Once her chuckles subsided, she lay in bed and gazed out at the night unfurled outside her window, the silence humming in her ears. Yet, even that perfect slice of sky she could see could not quieten her mind's hamster wheel. It was as she tried to work out what phase the moon was in currently in order to distract herself that she first heard it. It was faint, so faint that she hadn't heard it over the clutter inside her mind, but it was definitely there, growing louder the more intently she listened; the sweetest, most melodious music she had ever heard, carried along by the adoring air, enchanting all that those who were fortunate enough to hear it.

Enraptured, Sathi rose and pulled open her bedroom door. Instantly the notes became clearer, louder, intermingled with a sweet feminine voice that crested and fell with the rhythm of the music. Her body moved forward even as her mind swayed with the melody. She glided down the stairs and into the puja room. Some part of her identified a speaker as the source of the music, even as the rest of her exulted in the fact that the music was loud enough to completely replace any remaining chatter in her mind. She sank onto the floor and closed her eyes, soaking in the music.

Sathi had always enjoyed listening to music, but there had never been a song she worshipped like this one – when she listened to it, she *was* the music. After several moments she realised that the words, while she didn't recognise them, were sung in a pattern. She listened intently and worked out that the same four lines or so were being repeated over and over. And yet the repetition didn't make the song monotonous – quite the opposite.

She wasn't sure how long she sat there, listening, but when she finally wandered back up to her bed, she fell into a deep, blissful sleep.

'Sathi?' a soft voice called through the closed door. Sathi stirred and squinted blearily at the clock. Crap! She lurched upright as she realised that she'd overslept – no doubt due to weeks of inadequate sleep and her little midnight adventure last night.

Someone knocked. 'Are you awake?'

'Yeah, just a sec,' she yelled back, leaping out of bed and pulling open the door to admit Maira, who smiled at her over the pile of bright clothes in her arms. 'What's all this?' Sathi asked, trailing after her as Maira walked into the room and dumped the clothes onto the bed.

'Here, try this on,' Maira said briskly, handing her a deep turquoise cropped top that looked like a lot like a sari blouse. 'I couldn't get one stitched to your measurements in time, but this should be a good fit,' Maira continued.

'Uh, what– huh?' Sathi spluttered brilliantly.

'For you to wear to the engagement,' Maira clarified matter-of-factly.

'But I –' She stopped and shook her head. 'You didn't have to – you didn't need to do all this,' she said, waving her hands in the general direction of the clothes.

'No, but I wanted to,' Maira replied, throwing her a grin. 'Now try this on and let me see if it'll work.'

Touched, Sathi took the top and pulled it over her head. It came down to just below her ribcage and hugged her torso like a second skin.

'There, that's perfect,' Maira said, lifting Sathi's hair out from under the collar and tugging the edge of the blouse straight.

'It's gorgeous,' Sathi admitted, fingering the silky material and admiring the richness of the colour. Then she looked up as something occurred to her. 'Wait, I don't know how to wear a sari!' Just the thought of walking around in six metres of cloth wrapped around her without any guarantee of staying up made her balk.

'You don't have to.' Maira's mischievous smile grew wider as she reached for another folded up piece of clothing from the bed and shook it out; it was a long, pleated skirt of the same blue-green colour as the blouse. 'This is a half-sari,' she explained. She motioned for Sathi to put the skirt on and then turned up the hem a few times to compensate for her 5'2" frame. Then she picked up a long, cream coloured shawl that had gold and turquoise embroidered through it in an intricate pattern along the edges. Maira tucked one corner of it into the skirt at Sathi's waist and then draped the material around her back before bringing it back across the front to lie over her left shoulder.

'This is what girls used to wear before *churidars* became the fashion,' Maira mumbled around the safety pins in her mouth, referring to the long tunic with matching trousers and shawl that many Indian women wore instead of saris. 'All the grace of an actual sari, but a lot less complicated and with a lot more manoeuvrability,' Maira added. She finished pinning the shawl to the top at Sathi's shoulder, and then turned her around to face the full-length mirror. When she spoke again, Sathi could hear the smile in her voice. 'Beautiful.'

Gazing at her reflection, Sathi couldn't help but agree. The long skirt of the half-sari shimmered down to the floor, the full pleats swirling around her ankles, and the bright colours made her dark brown, almond-shaped eyes look huge in her face, the skin of which was smooth and coffee coloured and framed by dark hair that cascaded down to circle her waist. The soft, gauzy shawl was a perfect match for the streaks of gold lining the turquoise material of the skirt and blouse, and lay in graceful folds over her chest and shoulder, tumbling down her back in a waterfall of fabric.

Eyes shining, Sathi met the Maira's eyes in the mirror. 'Thank you,' she whispered.

The older woman beamed at her. 'My pleasure.'

'Hey, Dad wants to make a move, are you ready to –?' Zakiy broke off and his eyes widened when he saw her. 'Wow. You look amazing.'

'Thanks.' A bit flustered by the praise, Sathi hurried on before she could lose her nerve. 'Look, I'm sorry about the other day –'

'It's fine,' he said, cutting her off with a small smile. 'I understand.'

'You do?' she asked, bewildered. How could he understand when even she didn't understand her erratic behaviour?

'I shouldn't have pushed you with the Vidhya thing. You need time – I get it.' Zakiy flashed her his usual carefree grin. 'Now let's get going before Dad does what he's already threatened to do and leave without us.' He paused. 'Wait, why exactly would that be such a bad thing?'

Sathi managed a laugh and dragged him down to the car with her, relieved that Zakiy wasn't upset with her, but not entirely sure that she deserved his forgiveness.

Her earlier question was answered not too long after they arrived at the overcrowded home of Zakiy's aunt. The engagement was in fact something done before the scores of people who were stuffed into the medium sized living room, but thankfully the groom – a shy-looking guy who looked to be around Zakiy's age, maybe a couple of years older – didn't have to actually get down on one knee. He and Aisha sat side by side on the sofa while their parents beamed at each other and at their respective child. Then it was a relatively short affair as the prospective bride and groom both exchanged rings and were formally announced as betrothed.

A buffet lunch followed, consisting mainly of the specialty dish, chicken *biryani*; it was a mixture of long basmati rice and chicken spiced with chilli, coriander and other Indian flavourings. One delicious, mouth-watering bite later, Sathi vowed that she would learn to cook it, no matter what. Standing in an inconspicuous corner as she ate, she let her eyes wander over the other guests. Unlike any of the parties in UK, where black clothing was really the predominant feature for males and

94

females alike, here people wore all the colours of the rainbow and then some. Even men wore shirts of bright, strong shades, while women draped themselves with saris and churidars of every type and colour.

The room wasn't totally devoid of black, however; dotted about the room were Muslim women dressed in black from head to toe, their purdahs covering their hair and everything except for a small circle of their face. The cloak-like material hung to the floor, obscuring all curves in a shapeless curtain of clothing.

A group of women drifted close to where Sathi was standing, with Zakiy's aunt in their midst wearing a brightly glittering purdah, the silky fabric heavy with silver sequins. 'We gave 50 *lakhsham* and 1 kilo of gold as dowry, you know,' Fadilah was saying, plucking at a chunky gold necklace so it stood out prominently against the black folds of her purdah. Come to think of it, all the women in the group seemed to be wearing their weight in gold.

The woman in the fuchsia sari gasped. 'That much?'

'Yes,' Fadilah replied smugly. 'He *is* a doctor, after all.'

'Well, if you play your cards right you'll get it all back *and* more,' the one in the dark green purdah said knowingly. Her searching eyes roamed over the crowd until they found Zakiy, who stood laughing with Aman and a couple of other guys in the opposite end of the room.

Fadilah followed her gaze and smiled. 'Oh, don't be silly, Suhara,' she admonished even as her beam grew wider.

'We all know you have your eye on him for your Ruhaan,' Yellow Sari teased. 'You'd better catch him before someone else swoops him away.'

'Unless you're already too late,' Green Purdah interjected, looking like her mouth had an altercation with a sour lemon. 'Remember that girl that was with him?' she continued, turning to scan the room again with her beady eyes.

Realisation came too late, and Sathi dropped her gaze as she pretended sudden interest in the biryani that now tasted like mud in her mouth. She could feel the stares of the women boring into her like hot lasers. From her peripheral vision, she watched as the black figure detached itself from the group and advanced towards her. 'How are you, er-?'

'Sathi,' she supplied, forcing herself to look up and smile normally. 'I'm fine, thank you, Aunty. Congratulations on your daughter's engagement.'

'Thank you.' Fadilah smiled icily. 'So you are staying with Maira, I hear?'

'Yes. Maira aunty and Narayan uncle have been very kind. Zakiy and I are friends,' Sathi blurted, trying and failing not to emphasise the word "friends".

Fadilah's eyes narrowed. 'How lovely. Where did the two of you meet, may I ask?'

Sathi swallowed. 'In Nelliampathi. We bumped into each other a few weeks after I arrived in India.' No need for her to know that they had, quite literally, bumped into each other in the dark. And then fallen into a river together.

'And – do correct me if I'm wrong – you came here from the United Kingdom?'

'Yes, that's right.'

Fadilah's smile slipped, and her arms crossed over her chest. 'And when will you be leaving?'

Sathi's jaw dropped. Maybe in a different tone the question wouldn't have been so bad, but the way Fadilah said it was a clear "get out" signal, only missing a blazing red arrow pointing the way out. Before she could even compose herself, a saviour arrived in the form of Maira.

'Fadilah!' she exclaimed, embracing her sister-in-law. 'Congratulations! Aisha looks so beautiful – I can't believe how time has flown. It seems like only yesterday that she and Aman were playing house together.'

Maira smiled fondly at the memories while Fadilah's face assumed an expression you'd have at someone's deathbed. 'Yes, well, times have changed since then. Aisha studied and got her MBBS, and Aman... well, with his devastating illness...' She sighed heavily, the motion slightly exaggerated.

96

A flicker of pain streaked across Maira's expression, but she fought to maintain her smile. 'And how's Ruhaan? I haven't seen her around.'

'Oh, she hasn't come back from college – she has exams this week.' Did Sathi imagine it, or did Fadilah's eyes dart to her for a moment? 'She's in her fourth year now, you know. One more year and she'll be a doctor. Then we can get her and Zakiy married.'

Sathi choked on her spoonful of rice, while Maira looked uncomfortable. 'Oh, I don't think so, Fadilah. He's too young to get married.'

Fadilah scoffed and rearranged the scarf of the purdah around her head. 'Too young? I got married when I was sixteen, and I haven't missed out on anything! What are you waiting for, for the boy to get grey hair?'

'We should let kids make their own decisions on these things,' Maira said firmly. 'Besides, how can I ask Zakiy to get married when Aman is still... still not well?'

'Oh for heaven's sake, Maira,' Fadilah snapped, her façade finally shattering. 'That's a lost cause, and you know it. I don't understand why you even brought him here today – couldn't you just have left him at home?'

Anger flared in Maira's eyes. 'Just because you've given up on my son doesn't mean I have, Fadilah,' she replied evenly. 'Come, Sathi. If we don't start the journey back we won't reach home before dark.'

Fadilah huffed. 'All right, but don't think you can replace Ruhaan with some nobody from nowhere. Good to meet you, *molé*,' she added scathingly to Sathi.

Sathi's spine stiffened at hearing the endearment she had grown to hate after Great-aunt and Great-uncle smothered her with the false love it carried. As if she needed another reason to dislike this horrible woman.

Fadilah turned and strode away; ruining her exit, however, was the lemon yellow sari she must have been wearing under her purdah. It had become partly undone and was trailing along the floor behind her. As Sathi watched, it was unwittingly dragged through some spilled curry, splotches of ugly brown appearing in the pristine cloth. Instinctively, Sathi stepped forward, her mouth open to call out, when a cool hand closed around her wrist. She looked back at Maira's expressionless face. Then, simultaneously, they smiled and turned to walk in the opposite direction.

Maybe there was more merit to half-saris than she'd originally thought.

Chapter Eleven

Garam Cake

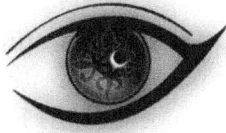

'S athi?' Narayan's eyebrows rose. 'What are you doing here?'

She pushed herself to her feet and tried not to look guilty. She'd snuck down to the puja room after coming back from the engagement and failing miserably to fall asleep – again. She hadn't expected anyone else to be awake, though.

'Sorry if I woke you, Uncle. I couldn't sleep, and listening to this music helps a little,' she admitted, gesturing to the speakers playing the same song as the night before.

Narayan nodded in understanding and walked over to a shelf, rustling for a few moments before pulling down a CD. He glanced at the front of the case and then handed it to her. 'The Gayathri Manthram.'

Her expression must have been a total question mark, because Narayan smiled slightly and continued, 'While some use it as a way to worship the sun and light, others have translated it simply as, "O Divine Mother, our hearts are filled with darkness. Please keep this darkness distant from us and promote illumination within us."'

He fell quiet, letting the melodious music fill the silence as Sathi mused over the translation and its reference to Devi. There was a slight break from the words as a few moments of instrumental music played, and then the lyrics started up again in a loop.

'What are the actual words?' Sathi asked.

'"Om bhur bhuvah svah
Tat savitur vareniyam

Bhargo devasya dhimahi

Dhiyo yo nah prachodayat.'" Narayan recited, his words intermingling with their female counterparts in the song. 'There are only twenty four syllables in this manthram, but in this song it is repeated one hundred and eight times. I keep it on a loop at night because it's just such a calming melody – the gods probably think so too, listening to it.' He glanced at the pictures on the walls and then smiled at her before lowering himself into an armchair. He steepled his fingers together. 'Maira told me about what happened with Fadilah today. I apologise for her behaviour.'

'It's okay.' Sathi hesitated, and then blurted out the question she'd been dying to ask since they left the engagement party. 'Who's Ruhaan?'

'She is Fadilah's younger daughter. Back when they were all children, Aman, Zakiy, Aisha and Ruhaan were always playing together – they used to destroy any room they played in to the point of no repair.' He chuckled, and then shook his head. 'Fadilah is still caught up in a different century. She thinks friendship can be forced into marriage, and she's filled Ruhaan's head with the same nonsense as well.'

'But she's his cousin,' Sathi objected.

'In the past it was a common practice for cousins to be betrothed to each other. It's ridiculous.' Narayan's focus shifted back to her. 'I know Fadilah said some less than kind things to you, and I hope you won't take it to heart.'

'I thought what she was saying was too ridiculous to take to heart,' Sathi said honestly, and was rewarded with a guffaw of laughter from Narayan. She grinned at him, and said, 'Seriously, Uncle, don't worry about it.'

Narayan looked wryly at her. 'You don't need to call me Uncle. I know you must be used to calling people older than you by their name.'

Sathi frowned, knowing he referred to the fact that she had lived in UK for most of her life. 'Yeah,' she said slowly, 'but that doesn't mean that I'm completely ignorant of Indian customs. Calling you Uncle is a sign of respect – and I think it's a nice thing. It's like you make everyone you meet your family by calling them Aunty or Uncle.' Though maybe

Fadilah was one person she didn't want to include in her extended family.

Narayan gave her a considering look. 'That's a very refreshing attitude,' he remarked. 'Especially in an age when youngsters think it's perfectly acceptable to call their parents by their name.'

'Well, I don't think that's completely true. I mean, I know some teenagers go all rebellious and act like they're above everyone else but I know some people who treat their parents in a more casual way not because they don't respect them, but because they're more like friends. That's nice in its own way,' she added, a wistful tone entering her voice. She also realised, belatedly, that she was still technically a "teenager".

Something in Narayan's expression made her think that he was thinking along those lines as well, but he didn't laugh at her. 'You're right,' he admitted, giving her a grudging smile. 'Aman is three years older than Zakiy, but we never insisted that Zakiy call him *chetan*. They were always more than just brothers – they were best friends.'

Sathi sat down on the floor again, leaning back against the chest of drawers. 'They do seem very close.'

'Aman was always the quiet one, while Zakiy was more outgoing and eager for a challenge. He hero-worshipped his brother, though. And Aman depended on Zakiy, too, in some ways, so they were pretty much inseparable. Although, Maira and I could never relax when those two were alone together because there was no telling what they'd get up to.' He grinned, and then sighed for those lost times. 'This illness hasn't just destroyed Aman's life – it's destroyed Zakiy, too.'

'I don't think that's true,' Sathi said. 'And even if it is, I don't think there's any damage that can't be repaired. As Aman gets better Zakiy is healing too. I can see it in him – he's filled with hope and happiness, and a lot of that happiness comes from the fact that he's been able to do something to help Aman. Already Aman is so much better, and now he can go back to *living* – instead of just getting by.'

'Yes, but he has spent too long simply *getting by*, as you say. For fifteen years he's been stuck in this... in this stasis. He has grown in body, but not in mind. He is still a child in everyday matters, and he won't survive in the outside world. I'm trying to do everything I can, but I'm afraid that everything I can do won't be enough.'

Narayan bowed his head, his fingers clenched in his lap. She shifted over so that she was kneeling next to his chair, and took his hand in both of hers. 'So let Zakiy help,' she said softy. 'You just told me how close they are. Allow your other son to take some of the responsibility.'

He shook his head without looking up. 'No. No, I can't let this spoil Zakiy's life anymore.'

Sathi bit her lip, thinking that what she was about to say was probably going to undo all the progress she'd made with Narayan. But it was far too important to be left unsaid. 'When Aman was still having violent episodes it made sense to keep Zakiy away, to send him to college far away to keep him out of harm's way. I can understand that. But now things are different.' She paused, trying to choose her words carefully. 'I can tell that it... frustrates Zakiy sometimes when you push him away for his own good, especially now when it's not really necessary.' Narayan had raised his head and was staring at her, not quite glaring but not exactly smiling, either. Sathi pushed down her apprehension and continued, 'You want Aman to grow up, to be a man in his own right, but he won't be able to do that while' – she mentally deleted the words "he uses you as a crutch" – 'you protect him so much. Your fear for Aman as a parent gives you the tendency to want to protect him at all costs, despite the bigger picture. As his brother, Zakiy might have more luck keeping his objectivity.'

She held her breath, bracing for the outburst that was sure to follow. Instead, Narayan said, very quietly and steadily, 'I'm very grateful to you for all the help you've given us, but I would very much appreciate it if you could kindly stop yourself from advising me on how to raise my own children. Now, it's very late and I am going to bed. Have a good night.'

He rose without another word and stalked away from the room.

Sathi's shoulders slumped. *Guess I don't have a future in therapy. Giving it, at least*, she clarified to herself.

It had been nearly a week since Aman had started taking Bushy the vaidhyan's medicine along with his regular meds, but Zakiy hadn't seen any change so far. It looked like his show of expertise was just that: a show. Although, Zakiy wasn't sure how he'd even know whether it was effective or not, seeing as Aman was taking the clozapine already. And he definitely didn't have enough faith in Bushy and his chicken to even suggest that they stop Aman's meds.

What a waste of a perfectly good chicken, he mourned.

Zakiy spent another moment in silent respect for the poultry before refocusing on an old Malayalam movie that was running on TV. As the drunken sidekick tried to convince the equally drunken hero that it would be more fun to vault over the wall of a house instead of walking in through the open gate, Zakiy heard Aman ask in a quiet voice, 'Dad, can you make me something to eat? I'm hungry.'

Dad said without looking up from his book, 'Zakiy, help your brother make something to eat.'

He gaped at his father, sure he couldn't have heard him properly. Just to be sure, he glanced askance at his mother. Her eyes were on the movie, but there was a small, content smile on her face that had nothing to do with the antics of the actors onscreen. Disbelieving, his eyes travelled to Sathi, who was staring at his father with an expression of joyous amazement. Zakiy was about to jump up and demand who he was and what he'd done with his dad when Aman turned to him, equal parts confused and expectant.

Zakiy swallowed his questions and stood up. 'Sure. Come, O Big Brother of mine.'

As he ambled along to the kitchen with Aman in tow, Zakiy contemplated possible reasons behind his father's abrupt relinquishment of his usual control over every little detail pertaining to Aman. By the time they stood in front of the stove Zakiy had shortlisted the following possible scenarios: 1) Dad had gone mad; 2) He'd been kidnapped by aliens in the name of research and they'd send a clone to take his place, and 3) He'd had a change of heart (and personality).

Zakiy shook his head. 'Nope, I'm going with option number 2,' he muttered.

'Hmmm?' Aman enquired.

He felt a shock go through him; the old Aman wouldn't have even noticed, much less responded to, something small like him muttering to himself. Taking in the way Aman maintained eye contact – his gaze bright and clear – Zakiy decided to take a chance. After all, they did say nothing ventured, nothing gained. 'I was just wondering why Dad was letting me do something for you for once. He couldn't have had a change of heart, so I was deciding that he's actually a clone sent to keep us fooled while aliens conduct experiments on him. Oh, and my other guess was that he'd gone mad.'

'Why did you go with the alien one?' Aman asked, staring at the floor now.

Zakiy shrugged and leaned against the counter. 'Because it's so much more dramatic. *And* it sounds so cool – can you imagine how much fun we could have with a clone of Dad? Plus I can reuse all my jokes.' He smiled blissfully. 'It's a win-win situation.'

Aman looked back at him then, and a smile broke out over his face and up into his eyes. Seeing it was like a punch to the chest – the warmth, the wide crescent shape his mouth made when he grinned... It brought back a thousand memories from their childhood. Blinking back tears, he hurriedly changed the subject. 'So what do you feel like eating, Almighty Brother?'

'Shut it, Z-man,' Aman retorted automatically, making Zakiy smile at the familiar admonishment. 'I don't know what I want,' he added, staring around the kitchen as though hoping for food to jump up and yell, *Pick me! Pick me!*

'How about an omelette?' Zakiy suggested, pulling out a frying pan from a cupboard overhead and grabbing a mixing bowl. 'Hand me a couple of eggs, would ya?' Aman dutifully passed the eggs to him, and he cracked them into the bowl. He was pleased when Aman handed him a fork without him having to ask for it. He whisked the eggs and added some salt and ground black pepper to the mixture, and was about to set it aside when Aman stopped him. 'Wait,' he said before rushing to the fridge and returning with some milk. He swished a small amount of it onto the eggs and whisked briskly until the white disappeared into the yellow.

Zakiy stared at his brother in amazement. 'Why, you sly thing, I didn't know you could cook!'

Aman actually rolled his eyes at him. 'I don't think adding some milk will win me the Chef of the Year award.'

'It will if I have anything to do about it,' Zakiy responded, reaching for the matchbox and turning the gas on. 'Maybe we can work as a team, you know, become Master Chefs extraordinaire...' He glanced over his shoulder to see Aman's reaction to this new plan, and... he wasn't there. Worried, Zakiy spun around and scanned the room. He breathed out a relieved sigh when he finally spotted Aman standing by the fridge, as far from the stove as possible.

The relief quickly drained as Zakiy took in the terrified way Aman was staring at the small blue fire that was still lit. He immediately reached over and turned off the gas before moving to his brother's side. 'Hey, it's okay,' he said soothingly. 'Now, come on, we're going to make this omelette *together*.' He led Aman back to the stove and rustled around for a gas lighter with a long handle. 'Here, use this. There's no way that fire's going to come anywhere near you, okay?'

'No, please, I can't! Can't you do it?' Aman begged, squirming against the hold Zakiy had on his wrist.

'You're going to do it,' Zakiy said firmly. 'You're the one coming home with that cooking award, remember?' When Aman still shook his head fearfully, Zakiy lit the stove again, which made Aman yell and try to pull away. 'No, look,' Zakiy urged, holding his free hand up to the flame, hovering just at that point of intense but not painful heat. 'See? It's not hurting me. It won't hurt you either. Give me your hand.' Aman just stared at him, his eyes wide with fear and anxiety. Zakiy looked back steadily. 'I'm your brother. Your Z-man. Would I ever do anything to hurt you?'

After several minutes Aman stopped straining against Zakiy's restraining fingers. Slowly, carefully, Zakiy lifted Aman's hand and brought it near the flame, stopping at the very outskirts of the rings of heat. Aman flinched as he felt the slight warmth on his fingers, but he didn't pull away. 'There. That's not so bad, is it?' Zakiy asked as he released Aman's hand, no longer needing to keep in place because Aman was doing it himself.

Aman looked at the fire and then at his warming hand. 'No. It isn't.'

Looking at him, Zakiy felt as though his heart would burst from pride. Instead of doing something stupid, he switched off the gas again, killing the flame. Aman glanced at him in surprise.

'Now,' Zakiy said as he handed his brother the lighter again, 'it's your turn.'

'If you're making dinner, then *we're* making dessert!' Zakiy proclaimed haughtily, yanking Aman up by the arm to stand next to him in a show of solidarity. Not easy to pull off when said brother is looking at you like you've gone totally and utterly mad.

Sathi, who had just moments ago offered to cook dinner for the family, looked like she was torn between bewilderment and amusement. The latter emotion won out as she crossed her arms and fought back a grin. 'Deal. At the end of the meal we'll ask everyone else to vote what they thought was better – dinner or dessert. Loser cleans up.'

'Deal,' Zakiy agreed. He turned to his still confused brother. 'Let's do this.'

Five minutes later, Aman pulled him into a corner. 'Are you insane?' he hissed.

Zakiy gave him a look like, *You really should know the answer to that by now.*

'Do you even know how to cook?' Aman demanded, clearly not giving up.

'Nope,' he replied. He grinned and manoeuvred him into the kitchen, where Sathi had already started laying out vegetables and was chopping them at top speed. 'But you, apparently, *do.*'

106

Aman gave him another exasperated look, and then headed over to the fridge to forage for ingredients, muttering under his breath about annoying little brothers.

Zakiy and Aman were both elbow deep in cake batter when their father poked his head in and took in the scene. 'Smells good,' he commented.

'Of course it does, Dad,' Zakiy said, 'we're the ones making the best dessert ever!'

Dad's lips twitched. 'Actually, I was talking about whatever Sathi is making.'

Sathi looked up and grinned broadly at him. 'Thanks, Uncle.'

He winked at her before leaving.

Watching their exchange, several things fell into place in Zakiy's mind; his father's abrupt willingness to let him help with Aman, the way Sathi had stared at Dad in joy that other day, and then this strange exchange today with huge smiles and winking... As though they were in on some sort of secret together.

'Aman,' he said grimly, wiping off the sticky mixture from his hands, 'hold down the fort for a minute.'

Zakiy walked over to where Sathi was shredding some poached chicken using a couple of forks. 'Hey,' she greeted him. 'Are you trying to cheat?'

He put his hands up in a gesture of peace. 'I don't need to cheat – we've got this in the bag. So,' he continued, crossing his arms casually and watching as Sathi threw the chicken into a pan of hot oil, 'is there something you need to tell me?'

Sathi looked up in surprise, brushing wisps of hair away from her face. 'What do you mean?'

'My father,' he said heavily, 'is in no way or shape a reasonable man. Trust me, I've had a lot of experience – he never lets me help with Aman. So why has he suddenly acquired a new personality?'

She suddenly seemed to need to concentrate really hard on tossing the chicken around. 'He hasn't acquired a new personality. He was just scared before, scared for *you*.' If he wasn't mistaken, there was the slightest hint of accusation in her tone.

'Okay, have it your way then. What made him stop being scared?'

Sathi shrugged. 'I guess he just got over it.'

He glared at her even though she pretended not to notice by looking oh so busy adding diced onion to the pan and mixing it with the chicken. 'I know he didn't suddenly wake up one morning and think to himself, *You know what, I think I'll stop being afraid that my son would end up killing his younger brother if they're left alone together*!'

She flinched at his words, but didn't say anything in reply.

He growled in frustration and pulled her around to face him. 'You said something to him, didn't you?'

Sathi met his eyes and sighed. 'Yes. After we got back from your cousin's engagement your dad and I talked, and I told him that it frustrates you when he pushes you away, and that it would be good for Aman if he let you help him, but then Uncle got angry and he stalked off and I thought I'd completely blown it, but I don't know, I mean that day he told you to help Aman make something to eat, and I don't even know if it has anything to do with what I said but –'

Her babbling got cut off as the breath whooshed out of her lungs, the result of the crushing hug Zakiy was bestowing on her. 'Thank you,' he whispered, his voice betraying the fact that he was on the edge of tears. 'I... Thank you.'

Sathi patted his back awkwardly until Zakiy pulled back, his gratitude and awe making his cheeks ache with the grin he couldn't seem to control.

'You do realise you look a bit crazed, right? More than usual, I mean.'

Zakiy ignored her and kept beaming at her like a hundred watt light bulb that had lost its off switch. 'You're the *best* best friend ever, you know that?' he demanded.

She smiled. 'Of course I am. Now go away and stop trying to sabotage my enchiladas.'

He gave her one more blinding grin, turned to walk away, and then wheeled back. 'Oh, Aman told me to grab some cinnamon.' Sathi turned back to her onion-and-chicken mixture and tipped in some shredded cheese and sour cream while Zakiy searched the cupboards, muttering, 'Cinnamon, cinnamon... ah, here it is!' Clutching a bottle of the powdered stuff, he nodded at Sathi. 'See you on the battlefield, soldier.'

Even as he turned and walked away, he could almost feel her rolling her eyes.

'The time has come to choose. On the one hand there is this rather ordinary, commonplace, cheesy meal of rolled up tortillas. The main ingredient? Tomatoes. Tomatoes upon tomatoes upon tomatoes. The most unoriginal of vegetables.'

'Er, you do know tomato is a fruit, right?' Sathi interrupted, amused.

'On the *other* hand, there is this simply amazing, wonderful, extraordinary, awe-inspiring, mouth-watering –'

'Zakiy?'

'Yes, Amma?'

'Stop talking,' she begged.

'Okay,' he said agreeably.

Maira turned to Sathi. 'This is amazing,' she said, gesturing to the enchiladas. 'You're a great cook.'

She was met with murmurs of agreement from everyone else. Sathi smiled. 'Thank you. I wanted to add some *garam masala* as well, but I couldn't find any.' Garam masala was a mixture of hot (hence "garam") Indian spices like nutmeg, cardamom, black pepper, mace and cloves.

Maira frowned. 'That's odd. I definitely had some in one of the cupboards.'

Sathi shrugged. 'Maybe I just missed it. Anyway, it doesn't really matter. I just like adding an Indian twist to the meals I make.'

'Really?' Maira leaned forward, intrigued. 'How?'

'She adds green chilli to everything,' Zakiy put in, talking around a mouthful of enchilada.

Sathi nodded. 'Yeah, and I add extra onion, garlic and ginger.'

'They're all very healthy – and tasty, when you cook it like this,' Maira approved. 'The trick is to mince garlic and ginger into tiny pieces so it all goes in without anyone having to bite and get a mouthful of the pungent flavour. At the same time they will release more juice so it subtly infuses the dish and enhances the flavour.'

Zakiy stared at his mother like he'd never seen her before. 'I never knew there were so many technicalities to cooking.'

'That's because you were always far more interested in eating than cooking,' Maira teased.

'That,' Zakiy began importantly, 'is very true. However, you will soon be eating your words because' – he exchanged glances with Aman – 'ladies and gentlemen, dessert is served!'

Aman got up to retrieve a cake with gorgeous cream cheese icing from a side table. 'It's carrot cake.' Though his voice was quiet, there was an unmistakeable note of pride in it – pride over his creation.

Maira and Narayan beamed at each other while Aman cut pieces of the cake for everyone. Grabbing a fork, Sathi dug out a large chunk and popped it into her mouth.

And fought to control her gag reflex as an entirely different flavour to what she was expecting short-circuited her taste buds. She coughed, trying her best to swallow rather than spitting her mouthful out like Zoya had.

'Yuck! What *is* that?' Zoya exclaimed, voicing what no one else was brave enough to say as they snuck peeks at Aman's disgusted and disappointed expression.

Narayan immediately launched into damage control. 'It's okay, Aman, it was your first time, it doesn't matter –'

'Wait, Narayan.' Maira was sniffing the piece of cake on her plate. 'Is this... is this garam masala?' she asked, sounding bewildered.

Sathi groaned as she put two and two together. 'Zakiy, when you were looking for cinnamon... did you take the garam masala instead?'

'What? No! I –' Everyone's eyes were on him as his expression slowly changed from denial to disbelief to pure horror. His gaze pleaded with everyone before finding his brother; Aman had his hand over his face, elbows resting on the table. His shoulders were shaking.

'Aman,' Zakiy whispered, his voice broken. 'I am so, so sorry. I can't believe what an idiot I am! Look, we'll mix it all up again, and this time you can triple check everything so I don't mess up and -'

Aman finally looked up, but he wasn't angry or upset. Instead, he was laughing so hard that he had tears running down his face. Between peals of laughter he managed to say, 'I can't' – gasp – 'believe you put in garam masala' – chuckle – 'instead of cinnamon. You're' – snort – 'such an' – chortle – 'idiot.'

He got up and clapped a dumbstruck Zakiy on the back, still doubling up with uncontrollable laughter.

Guess a few mixed up Indian spices can't break the bonds of brotherhood.

When Sathi went up to bed that night, she found a note on her desk. The CD Narayan had shown her the other night, of the Gayathri Manthram, was on top of it. The note said,

Play this in your room when you go to bed – perhaps it will help you to fall asleep.

Narayan

P.S. Thank you. For everything.

Sathi smiled and plugged in the CD player.

Doctor Rappaccini watched his daughter through the shadow-filled glass that looked out onto his prized gardens. A beauty that rivaled the glittering display of his copiously blooming flowers, Beatrice moved among the blossoms with a grace that was more than human. Rappaccini smiled in pride. And how could it not be so? She was far more than what Nature had intended, and he was the one who had, through his mastery of science, made her into something... more.

Chapter Twelve

Poison or Medicine?

'You're wrong,' Aman insisted, shaking his head. 'It's impossible to keep chemicals in their natural form when you're trying to administer them as medicine.'

'Extracting just the chemical compound for ease of mass-production just creates complications,' Anna contradicted him with equal vehemence.

Aman quirked an eyebrow, obviously not convinced. 'Like what?'

'Okay, take salicylic acid for example.' – Bushy mouthed 'Aspirin' to Sathi and Zakiy since Anna didn't seem likely to interrupt her flow to explain. 'When they discovered that chewing on willow bark helped ease pain, the first thing scientists did was isolate the active extract and put it into a concentrated, synthetic tablet form. Then when people started using them, it turned out that they caused bleeding and even death. Do you think that would have happened if they'd stuck to the original form?'

There was a pause. Then: 'It was salicylic acid extracted from meadowsweet that had that problem, not willow bark.'

Even Anna seemed taken aback at that. She directed a questioning glance at Bushy, who shook his head. 'Aman's right. It was meadowsweet.'

Aman leaned forward, caught up in the argument. 'Besides, how much tree bark can people be expected to chew when they have a headache? A handful? A bucketful? It doesn't make sense.'

'Neither does mass-producing it in a way that actually ends up harming people! Even if salicylic acid from willow bark didn't cause other issues, that doesn't mean they could just use it in its pure form. They had to add chemicals to it to make it into aspirin, whereas willow bark in its pure form doesn't need anything else added to it. *And* I bet you wouldn't have such a risk of addiction if it meant they had to chew tree bark to satiate it.'

'Okay, okay,' Bushy quickly intervened before Anna could steamroll on. 'You both make valid points. Aman, you're right that Ayurvedic medicines cannot be easily mass-produced. Anna, you're also right, and the focus has shifted with regard to medicine and its commercial practicality has a lot more bearing nowadays.' He cleared his throat. 'Aman, the steam room should be just about ready for you now. Off you go.'

Once Aman had left, Bushy said to Anna, 'Thank you for drawing him out.'

She smiled. 'It was my pleasure. I'm impressed by just how much he knows, though. Even I didn't know about meadowsweet.'

'He was always really bright, even as a kid,' Zakiy put in. 'Top of the class, and a walking encyclopaedia. Of course, that changed when...' He sighed. 'Anyway, thanks Anna. That's the most I've heard him talk in years.'

Anna shook her head. 'No really, I don't mind. It's amazing to see that change after these past few months of treatment, and besides, I enjoy talking to him.'

'You mean you enjoy arguing with him.' Zakiy corrected.

'That too,' she admitted, and they all laughed. She pushed her hair behind her ears. 'Right, I've got a truckload of plants out there that have my name on it. Want to make yourself useful and give me a hand?' she asked Zakiy.

'I'm always useful!' he protested, following her out, and Sathi went back to helping Bushy sort through the medicinal textbooks that filled his office shelves. He was trying to make space by throwing out what he no longer used. Some of them were so old that the dusty pages were practically coming apart in her hands, and some even looked to have been written in the ancient language of Sanskrit. Two of the books gave her pause; one was called *Poisonous Plants of India* and the other *Medicinal and Poisonous Plants of India*. The books didn't even share the same author, but the distinction between the titles bothered her.

With Bushy and Anna these past couple of months she'd seen how they used the leaves, fruits, seeds and even roots of various plants and mixed them up to administer as medicine. Botany not being her strong suit, most of the names had all gone straight over her head, but the other day she had seen them grinding up something that definitely bore more than a passing resemblance to nightshade.

Bushy must have noticed her preoccupation, because he came to stand behind her where she was still frowning at the books. 'What's wrong?' he asked.

'It's just... Well, a lot of the time you seem to use poisonous plants as medicine. I don't really understand that.'

He nodded thoughtfully. 'You're right. The truth is, poison and medicine are like love and hate; they're essentially the same, expect they're at opposite ends of a spectrum. There's a very fine balance between the two, and that's the line you dance on when you take something poisonous and turn it into something medicinal. Homeopathy works on a similar principal; you hear of remedies like arsenic, which is extremely toxic at high levels, but can actually be medicinal when used in very low dosage. Even if you don't put much stock in homeopathy, just think of our bodies. It's a delicate balance between all sorts of chemicals, and if the concentration of even one of those chemicals varies by a tiny degree it can throw the whole body into chaos.

'One of the beliefs I picked up while I was with the mountain tribe is that a plant that contains toxins in one part often has the antidote to that toxin in another part. This might not be true in a literal sense, but I think the point is that nature doesn't create a poison without creating its antidote as well. When something is made, its opposite also takes form to maintain balance. Just think, for example, of the elements. Earth and air, fire and water – all created in balance with each other. Ether, the fifth element, is of course all encompassing and so does not require a counterpart.'

Sathi bit her lip, her eyes still on the books. 'What if the plants are used to harm, and not to heal?' she asked finally.

Bushy shrugged, looking grave. 'That's inevitable with the way we all have good and evil inside us. Our actions and decisions determine which side overcomes the other, and how we use the things that nature provides.'

What he was saying made sense, but Sathi couldn't shake the weirdness of the medicine he had initially given Aman, the one that involved using a chicken. It reminded her uneasily of nightmares she'd had of those who practised kaivisham – like her great-aunt. She looked around, making sure that they were alone, and decided she couldn't give up this opportunity to get some of the answers she'd wanted for a long time.

'So you're saying that the, uh, magic you used to make Aman's medicine is different from something like kaivisham?'

He didn't answer for several moments, during which he kept his piercing gaze fixed on her. It felt a lot like the way he'd looked when she first mentioned toxins to him. 'Yes,' he said heavily. 'Kaivisham is the very opposite of what I do, because the intent behind it is completely different. Kaivisham is black magic, it is the twisting of what is natural to further selfish human wants and desires. What I do is intended to heal, to target anything that is not natural or benign, and remove it so it no longer prevents good health. Black magic often has the purpose of destroying another's peace of mind, often through the destruction of health.'

Bushy's gaze had become unfocused as he spoke, but now it returned to Sathi. 'The old adage "health is wealth" isn't just a cliché. There is this famous devotional poem in Hinduism, and one line is "on the shoulder of the king who climbs to the top of the palace, You are He who thrusts the irremovable burden". Lack of good health can destroy what nothing else can.'

Sathi thought of Narayan and Maira, who had lived a happy life in their magnificent house in Nelliampathi until Aman became ill – a house that did in fact resemble a palace. A house that was now empty and unused, the love and happiness sucked out of it. She thought of Zakiy, who was even now outside in the scorching sun helping to unload a truck-full of supplies out of gratitude to Anna and Bushy for helping his brother.

'Kaivisham taken over time, even if you find ways to counteract it, can build up toxins in your body,' Bushy continued, oblivious to her thoughts. He walked over to a shelf that they hadn't yet gotten to in their sorting and, after a few minutes of searching, pulled out a hardcover book. He brought it over to her, and she managed to read the words on the dark orange cover before he flipped it open: *Tribal Ethnomedicine.*

'The author attempts to apply science to kaivisham in this book... ah, here it is. "Some sticky substances like pieces of finger nail, chaff, hair, small ants, etc., will be included in the magical poison. These things will stick on the inner wall of the human intestine. The vicious magical power of a sorcerer can stay on the body of a person through these articles and he can also influence the mind of the patient through them."' Bushy snapped the book shut. 'So you see, the components of these spells remain as toxins in the body.'

Sathi opened her mouth, about to ask more, but Zakiy suddenly came rushing in, beaming all over his face. 'Come with me,' he urged, pulling her up by the arm. 'You won't believe who's here.'

He all but dragged her outside, where she saw Maira in conversation with Anna and someone else who had her back to Sathi. Nearby, Narayan stood talking to Aman, who had evidently just come out of the steam room since he was dressed only in an old *mundu* and was covered in sweat. There was another guy she didn't know with them. Sathi was pleased to see Zakiy's parents, but their visit wasn't exactly a novelty; this was about the seventh time they'd come over since Aman started having regular treatment with Bushy.

Nevertheless, Zakiy kept pulling her forward with the enthusiasm of a child on Christmas morning. At their approach Maira and Anna looked up, and the girl who'd had their back to them turned around. The stick-straight mane of hair that fell to the bottom of her shoulder blades and brown eyes that were like dark pools of honey looked striking against her unusually fair skin.

'Sathi,' Zakiy said, gesturing to the girl with flourish, 'meet Ruhaan.'

For a few moments Sathi couldn't respond; she could only gape like a moron. Ruhaan. As in Zakiy's cousin. Who wanted to marry him.

Ruhaan didn't react to Zakiy's introduction in any way except to fix Sathi with an expression that could only be described as... disdainful. Her sharp gaze travelled down to where Zakiy's hand was still curled around hers, and Sathi quickly pulled her hand free. She forced a smile on her face. 'Hi Ruhaan.'

'Hi.' Ruhaan had a low voice, one that almost purred with power. Her face was now flat and expressionless as she stared at Sathi.

Thankfully, distraction came before the situation could get any more awkward. The guy who had been chatting to Narayan and Aman earlier came over and clapped Zakiy on the back. 'Hey, aren't you going to introduce me?'

Zakiy affected a pained look. 'I was hoping it wouldn't come to that. Sathi, Anna, meet Dhameer, one of my more crazy friends.'

'My *name* is D,' he retorted. He nodded to Anna and then looked Sathi up and down. 'And it's always a pleasure to meet this idiot's beautiful friends. In fact —'

Ruhaan cut him off. 'So what have you been up to, Zakiy?'

D didn't look happy about the interruption. 'That's a pointless question. He's been up to no good, as always.'

Zakiy frowned at him, but Ruhaan just smiled sweetly. 'No, I think you're confusing Zakiy with yourself, D. *You're* the slob that hangs around with nothing to do all day.'

'And that makes you what, exactly?' D shot back. 'Drama queen extraordinaire?

Ruhaan growled and began to lunge forward, but Zakiy quickly threw himself between them. 'I see there's been no change in your relationship.

How on earth did you two make the journey here without going at each other's throats?'

'Who said we did?' D muttered.

Anna just looked amused by the whole sideshow, but Maira met Sathi's eyes and something in her gaze made Sathi think she hadn't forgotten Ruhaan's earlier animosity. For some reason, she suddenly felt like blushing. Hastily, she looked away.

Sathi had a feeling that the last few months' peace was about to be shattered.

'Wow,' Anna said several days later, her eyes widening. 'Your face looks like thunder. Who're you about to punch?' she joked.

Sathi just made an unintelligible grunting noise and stalked away. She was scared that if she opened her mouth all that would come out would be swear words. She set off towards the hotel where she and Zakiy were staying at a furious march that would've made Anna proud. All she wanted to do was throw herself on her bed and stew. As Sathi crossed the small reception area and approached her room, she saw that the door to Zakiy's room was partially open. And there was a sultry, feminine laugh ringing out into the corridor.

Sathi felt her lips twist in disgust and anger, and only just managed to contain a groan. The sound was the most grating she'd heard in her whole life and she'd already endured a lot of it this past week. No way was she staying to listen to more of *that*. Sathi turned around and walked straight out again, trying and failing to keep a lid on her irritation.

Cutting across to the virtually unused park in the hopes of calming down, she decided some fresh air and lack of people around for collateral damage were exactly what she needed.

Maira and Narayan had left long ago, and now she fervently wished they'd taken Ruhaan with them. Zakiy's cousin reminded Sathi of those popular, jealous types that couldn't handle any girl talking to her boyfriend (*not* that Zakiy was her boyfriend) without asserting her claim and acting like a total...

No, Sathi decided, *she's* not *going to make me swear.* She thought back to how Ruhaan went out of her way to exclude Sathi and make her feel unwanted. Ruhaan could flip quickly between angel and demon depending on who was there to witness it, and dark feelings churned inside Sathi again as she ruminated over the unfairness of it all. It wasn't like she had done anything to deserve that kind of animosity.

Even though she didn't want to admit it, what annoyed her most was that Zakiy didn't seem to recognise just how much venom Ruhaan had in her. Though normally quite astute when it came to reading people, he seemed to have a blind spot where Ruhaan was concerned. She supposed that it was because they'd known each other since they were kids, but that didn't really make her feel better.

'Or maybe it's because around him she acts like butter wouldn't melt in her mouth,' she mumbled to herself, causing a woman who had been walking opposite her to give her a startled look. The woman shifted the toddler in her arms, shielding it with her sari, and picked up her pace until she'd hurried past Sathi.

The sight made Sathi want to laugh and cry at the same time. She felt pain flare in her chest as that old longing come back, the longing to have her mother here beside her, to comfort her and listen patiently while she vented her frustration. Hot tears began to well up in her eyes, and Sathi brushed them away fiercely. She tried to hold onto her anger rather than slip into despair – the anger was so much easier to deal with.

Her thoughts were all over the place, swinging from Ruhaan to her mother to Zakiy, and then back to Ruhaan and how angry she was at her. Consumed by frustrated feelings, she barely noticed as her feet led her out of the park and into a small side-road. It was packed, and people kept bumping into her. Annoyed, she looked up and saw that the crowd was due to a small temple – it was *deeparadhana* time. It was when earthen pots and lamps filled with oil were lit and offerings were presented to the deity to be blessed. It occurred twice a day at dawn and dusk, and the sun had just set, making the wicks of naked flame that much more beautiful against the darkening sky. Devotees stood around in every available space and craned their necks for a glimpse of the deity, who was...

Sathi scanned the small building for a signboard and finally found it: Sree Narasimha Swamy. Despite herself, a shiver went through her. Narasimha was an avatar of Vishnu, and while she'd always thought the god of life was quite mild and easy-going, in Narasimha form he was anything but. He was half-man and half-lion, with a mane of hair and sharp canines terrible to behold. In pictures it was common to find him sitting with his long claws disembowelling an asura. Myth said that the asura was a cruel demon who had received a boon that he could be killed by neither man nor animal, not on the ground nor in the air, not inside nor outside a residence, not at night nor in daytime and not by any weapon.

And so Narasimha the half-man half-lion avatar had killed the asura on his lap on a porch at dusk using only his hands and claws.

Even though the asura had been beyond cruel and on the verge of killing his own son, a boy of great faith, this particular avatar of Vishnu had always made her uneasy. There was something savage and terrible about him, completely at odds with the benign Vishnu the Sustainer.

As she mused Sathi's gaze had been roving over the crowd absently, but then she suddenly focused on a man who was standing on the outskirts. He wore the orange coloured clothes that many hard-core temple-goers often wore, and had a thin, frail frame. He was also familiar.

She couldn't believe her eyes. It was *him*. The guy from Chamundi Hills who'd yelled at her in Kannada. Fury shot through her at the memory, and she decided that she wasn't going to let him go without giving him a piece of her mind about what she thought of his "advice". Determinedly, she started pushing through the throng of people, not caring who she was jostling in the process. Somehow she managed to fight her way to where she'd seen the guy, only to discover that he was nowhere in sight.

She whipped her head around in disbelief, hoping to catch sight of him but there was no use. She couldn't see him anywhere. She ran a hand through her hair in frustration. How could he have disappeared so quickly? He'd been right here!

Sathi reached out and tapped a nearby man on his shoulder, hoping maybe that he'd seen the Kannada guy and knew where he'd gone. 'Excuse me sir,' she said to the man, still looking around for the other guy, 'I was wondering if you could help m –'

The words got choked in her throat as the man turned around to face her. He had bushy white hair and beard that seemed to have life of their own, unusual blue-green eyes that twinkled at her and a wide smile that tipped her off to the fact that he was enjoying her shock immensely.

'Why, certainly, my dear,' he replied graciously. 'How may I be of assistance?'

Sathi could only blink back at him in confusion and mutter faintly, 'White Beard?'

Chapter Thirteen

Unite & Surrender

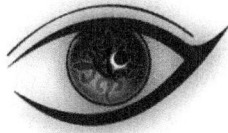

White Beard frowned mildly and leaned down towards her, putting a hand behind his ear. 'I'm afraid I didn't quite catch that, Sathi. The ears aren't really as good as they used to be, you know. I'm sure it's just wax,' he added.

Sathi pressed her eyes closed and started counting. When she thought she could speak without screaming she opened them again. White Beard's mischievous smile beamed back at her. Damn. He hadn't been a hallucination, then.

'What are you doing here?' she demanded. The first time she'd seen him had been back in Nelliampathi, in the Devi temple near her great-aunt and uncle's house. He'd given her a lot of mysterious advice about gods, and then led her to an astrologer before disappearing on her.

White Beard spread his arms magnanimously. 'I go where I'm needed. My job is to challenge people and guide them on their individual journeys.'

'In other words, you annoy the hell out of people,' Sathi muttered.

The corners of his mouth twitched, making all that hair vibrate like a Mexican wave down his chin. 'I must admit, with some people it is more entertaining than with others.' Something in his twinkling eyes made her think that the "some people" was intended for her. Then the humour in his expression dimmed slightly. 'I believe you have some questions for me.'

Sathi jumped. She had actually been thinking of her visit to the astrologer and what he'd said about her task to find her mother's killer. 'Yeah... yeah, I do. That guy you told me to go see, the astrologer? Well, he said that I wouldn't be able find my mother's murderer without help. He said –'

'"You will fail in your purpose if you attempt it alone. There is another who has as much right to justice as you do",' he quoted.

Sathi fell silent in astonishment. How could he have known that? She waited for him to say something else, but he was just gazing at her with those annoyingly bright eyes. Her surprise quickly flipped to impatience. 'Well?' she asked. 'What did he mean?'

'Exactly what he said, I assume.'

Sathi nearly growled. 'Do you get some sort of sick satisfaction from annoying me? Who else can have as much right to revenge as I do? My *father*?' she asked sarcastically, giving a derisive snort. 'If he cared so bloody much he would've done something before now. I don't need his help –'

'The astrologer was not talking about your father,' White Beard told her. There was no trace of humour in his expression now.

'Who else, then?'

'I cannot say.' He shrugged, but there was a trace of expectation in his voice. As though she should already know.

Somehow that irritated her more than his vague answers had. 'Whatever,' she said, shaking her head in resignation. She suddenly felt drained of energy and was no longer in the mood to hear any more of his cryptic nonsense. She'd turned away when he spoke again.

'Wait.' Reluctantly, Sathi glanced back. 'He was right, you know.'

'Who was right?'

Those blue-green eyes bored into her. 'There is something inside you. You need to get it out before you confront them.'

Her heart sped up. 'What's inside me? Confront who?'

White Beard was already starting to fade into the crowd. 'Remember what I said,' he called. 'You have to get it out.'

Sathi rushed forward. 'No, don't go! Wait!' A particularly beefy man blocked her way, and by the time she managed to get past him White Beard had disappeared into the crowd.

'Damn it!' she yelled at the unperturbed sky, collapsing onto her knees.

On the walk back to the hotel Sathi was so pre-occupied that it took her a while to notice that someone had fallen into step beside her. She glanced over.

'Hi, D.'

He gave her a blinding grin that she was in too much of a bad mood to return. 'Hey, there. Mind if I join you?'

She shrugged. 'It's a free country.'

D chuckled. 'At the rate you're stomping there won't be much country left.'

Sathi's scowl deepened. 'You shouldn't risk walking near me, then, in case the ground decides to break with the force of my "stomps".'

He didn't take the hint and seemed to find her response hilarious. Once those stupid snickers subsided, he said knowingly, 'Don't worry. Ruhaan has this effect on most people.'

She glanced at him in surprise. Despite the near-constant bickering Ruhaan and D engaged in, it had always seemed to her that they and Zakiy were tightly bound in the bonds of friendship. Consequently she'd worked hard to hide her irritation for the past few days. All right, she'd vented a little to Anna, but in front of those three she'd been the picture of serenity.

Or so she'd thought.

'She has her claws into you,' D stated matter-of-factly.

'I don't know what you're talking me about.'

He just laughed. Again. 'Look, you don't have to act coy. We all know how Ruhaan is. Whenever she's around Zakiy she acts like a magnetic force field that repels any other girl from talking, laughing or even breathing near him.'

It was a repeat of the Fadilah incident. 'We're just friends, though.'

'Doesn't matter,' D replied, hooking his thumbs into his jeans pocket. 'Like I said, no girl is safe. God knows what she'd do if he was actually interested in a girl.' Was it her imagination or did he give her a sidelong glance when he said that?

Before she could react, though, he grinned and playfully jabbed his elbow into her ribs. She jerked away, glaring. 'Aww, come on, I have a plan. It's kind of like the opposite of divide and conquer.'

'What, unite and surrender?' she shot back.

D burst out laughing. Once he'd finished wiping pretend tears from his eyes, he said, 'Oh, we're going to have fun, you and I.'

More confused than ever, she asked, 'What are you talking about?'

'Well, Ruhaan objects to you spending time with Zakiy – which means she goes out of her way to exclude you when you're together – but she won't care if you hang around with someone else.'

'Like who?'

D casually slung an arm around her shoulder. 'Why, yours truly of course.'

D and Sathi burst into the lobby of the movie theatre in fits of laughter. Zakiy and Ruhaan, who'd been anxiously scanning the crowd, quickly made their way over to them. 'Where've you two been?' Zakiy demanded. 'You were supposed to meet us here an hour ago!'

'Sorry, man,' D said, still breathless and holding his side like he had a stitch. 'We got delayed because this one' – he reached out to mock-punch Sathi's arm – 'got completely side tracked when we went past this decrepit old building –'

Sathi shoved him and interrupted, 'It was *not* a decrepit old building! It was this really cool place with vaulted ceilings and those huge stained glass windows. I think it used to be a church.'

'Anyway,' D continued, 'Sathi decided we had to have a detailed tour, and we lost track of time. Then, when we realised how late we were, we started racing across town like crazy people to get here.'

Ruhaan appeared only a token interested, but Zakiy immediately turned to Sathi. 'Why didn't you call me? We could have joined you there.'

Sathi felt her humour dry up at his accusing tone. She shrugged, glancing around the busy theatre. 'Like D said, we just lost track of time.' She allowed her eyes to flick to Zakiy. 'Besides, I figured you were busy.'

He frowned but she didn't give him a chance to respond. 'Are we going to watch this movie or not?' she said, leading the way to the ticket counter.

The Malayalam movie starred an actor who was very popular with the masses, and there was a lot of cheering and clapping going on that sometimes drowned out most of the dialogue. Sathi wasn't really paying attention, anyway. She was still seething over the way Ruhaan had gone out of her way to make sure that Sathi didn't sit next to Zakiy, and was even now stuck like a limpet to his side. What did she think? That Sathi was going to jump him the minute her attention was diverted?

Sathi shook her head in disgust, and tried to focus on the movie. D thrust the popcorn under her nose, his attention totally fixed on the screen where a single hero was beating up ten people at the same time. She took a handful of the buttery goodness, her mood lightening slightly. Despite her initial reservations, D had turned out to be a lot of fun. His company was probably the only reason she had remained sane in the face of Ruhaan's tendency to act like Zakiy was her own private property.

Sathi idly wondered what Ruhaan thought of all the time D and she were spending together lately. Mostly she had a pained expression whenever she looked at the two of them; still, Sathi supposed it was an upgrade from the murderous looks she received if she so much as spoke to Zakiy.

Later when they were leaving the movie theatre D weaved his way around Zakiy and Ruhaan and turned so he was walking backwards in front of Sathi, facing her. 'What did you think of the movie?' he asked.

Sathi shrugged. 'It was okay. Didn't like the hero much, though.'

D's eyes threatened to fall out of his face. '*What*? Lalettan is the best! He's not just a hero on the big screen, he's a hero in real life to some of us, you know.'

'He just seems so full of himself. And what's up with that long, circuitous speech he made at the end, just going on and on about how amazing he is?'

Speechless, D seemed to stumble from sheer incredulity. Sathi quickly grabbed a hold of his arm to steady him.

'*A re*, turn around and walk properly, *yaar*!' Zakiy called out from behind, and she glanced back to see that his eyes were tight with irritation. Then his gaze met hers, and the annoyance drained out of his expression. She turned away.

D ignored his friend, still walking backwards even though they were now out in the busy street. 'I have two words for you: Not. Cool.'

'Whatever, D, I don't- Whoops, sorry!' Sathi had been concentrating so much on D and making sure that he didn't bump into anyone that she hadn't paid nearly as much attention to where she was going.

'Hey, no problem.'

She glanced up at the couple she'd walked into and took a double take when she realised that they were foreigners – blond haired and blue eyed, no less. Well, the guy's hair was dirty blond, while the girl's pixie cut leaned more towards platinum. She met Sathi's eyes and smiled. 'Sorry, we weren't looking where we were going.' She gestured sheepishly to the map that was clutched in the guy's hands. 'Kerala is wonderful, but very confusing to get around sometimes.'

'Where are you from?' Sathi realised, belatedly, that she should have guessed from the accent. Sure enough, the guy replied, 'London. We're here for three weeks' holiday.'

'I'm from London too,' she said. She couldn't get over the shock of seeing someone from UK here – it was a bit surreal.

'Really? That's great!' the girl enthused. 'Oh, I'm Beth. And this is Luke.'

'I'm Sathi, and this is D, Zakiy and Ruhaan,' she said, pointing to each of them in turn. D and Zakiy smiled politely, but Ruhaan's expression was a competition between disinterest and contempt. No surprise there.

'It's great to meet all of you,' Beth responded, smiling around. 'Hey, maybe you guys could show us around a little – if it's not too much trouble, that is?'

D's expression brightened. 'Of course! Let's go paint this town red!'

Sathi was about to decline, feeling entirely too tired mentally, when Ruhaan's annoyingly husky voice beat her to it: 'Actually, I'm quite tired.'

Yeah, it must've been so exhausting to make sure no one with a double x chromosome came within 20 feet of her darling fiancé, Sathi thought acerbically as Ruhaan continued, 'Come back with me, Zakiy?'

Zakiy hesitated. His eyes automatically went to Sathi. 'Sure. What about you?' he asked her hesitantly.

He sounded like a faded shadow of himself, nothing like the person she had so instantly bonded with and befriended. She brutally silenced the small core of pity that started to blossom within her, attacking the part of her that wanted to forgive him with the memories of her frustration and hurt for the last few weeks.

Sathi looked away and gave the two Londoners a smile choked with false enthusiasm. 'I'm in.'

'What a great place this is,' Beth said, pushing her spiky hair behind her ears and looking around with interest. The six of them were crowded around a table in a restaurant that was well known for their cuisine. Beth picked up her knife and fork again and started trying to cut the thick *naan* on her plate into smaller pieces.

After watching her struggle with the tough bread for a while, Sathi took pity on her. 'Use your fingers,' she advised.

Beth glanced down at her hands rather blankly, and then around at the busy restaurant where everyone else was digging into their meal using their right hand. Sathi fought back a smile. 'It took me a while to get used to it, too. It's really not that weird once you get used to it.'

'I know... but it still feels odd,' she said.

Ruhaan, who'd actually deigned to join them for once, tossed her hair back and demanded, 'You wouldn't eat a burger with your fork and knife, would you?'

Beth didn't look enthused by the reminder, but she did put the cutlery down and then rip off a small piece of the buttery naan. She lifted it to her mouth and groaned like only a true food lover would. 'Wow. This stuff is fabulous,' she slurred through a full mouth. 'Isn't it, Luke?'

Luke briefly glanced up from his own plate to nod in agreement. Even in the few days they'd known the couple it had become apparent that Beth was the mouthpiece in that relationship. Sathi noticed that he was still using his knife and fork.

'For example,' Beth continued, pointing to a steaming dish in front of them, 'what is *this*? It looks sublime!'

Ruhaan snorted. 'It's a little something we Indians call food.'

'Ruhaan,' Zakiy said, his voice low with warning.

D leaned forward across the table. 'Ignore her, Beth. It's called mushroom pepper fry – mushroom and onion fried with black pepper. It goes really well with this,' he added, pushing another small plate towards her.

Sathi smacked his hand away, and Zakiy laughed despite himself. Even Ruhaan cracked a smile.

Beth and Luke looked from face to face, confused. 'It's green chilly cut into small pieces and soaked in salt water – like pickle,' Sathi explained.

'It would probably burn a hole through the roof of your mouth,' Ruhaan put in.

'Oh.' Beth eyed the offending plate. 'Maybe we shouldn't try that one quite yet.'

'Good move,' D agreed, winking at Sathi.

She shook her head at him, exasperated, and glanced away. As she did, she realised that Zakiy was staring at her – and he looked pissed off.

Just like that the relatively good mood she had managed to muster came crashing down. What was his problem? All these weeks he'd pretty much ignored her, and now that she was actually enjoying herself he was looking at her like she was annoying him on purpose. Well, she wasn't having it.

She lifted her chin and hardened her gaze. She stared back at him until, fists clenched, he looked down. Then she purposefully put her hand on D's arm and said, 'Let's all go for a walk into the city afterwards. They should have the lights up by now.'

D smiled. 'That's an awesome idea! They may even have some fireworks going at midnight – you know, because of Vishu.'

He was referring to the first day of the year according to the Malayalam calendar, which fell in April. It was supposed to be quite an occasion.

Beth perked up. 'Fireworks?'

As Sathi had hoped, Ruhaan chose that moment to make her excuse: 'You guys go ahead. Zakiy and I are going to head back.'

Sathi felt grim triumph creep over her. Mission accomplished.

Chapter Fourteen

Broken

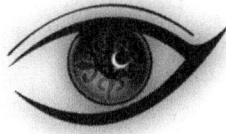

Zakiy couldn't believe it: he had his brother back!

Despite all his misgivings Bushy had really come through, and Zakiy would never look at a chicken in the same way again. All kidding aside, he could hardly take in the enormity of what it meant to have Aman sitting here next to him, not yelling at the voices in his head, but speaking normally to Anna – as though he'd never prowled through the house carrying a huge carving knife while Zakiy and his parents cowered behind curtains and doorways, hiding from his blind rage.

He shuddered and closed his eyes briefly. Then he opened them in glee as he thought of the secret he had been hugging to himself for a few weeks now. After a lot of coaxing Karuppuraja had agreed to come down and see Aman. He'd been amazed by the changes Bushy's treatment had wrought, so much so he'd been keen to stay on and witness Bushy's expertise first-hand. Unfortunately, he soon had to return to his work and a very irate wife back in Bangalore. Before leaving however, he had reluctantly agreed to let Aman try to a lower dose of the antipsychotic – under tight monitoring, of course. He might even eventually be able to stop using them altogether, though Karuppuraja had drilled into Zakiy that this would take a long time and wasn't a process that could be rushed.

Zakiy laughed to himself, in a short burst of amazement that no one noticed. How weird it was to think like this, after spending years and years in despair of Aman even becoming a shade closer to his normal self. Now he was thinking in terms of being past this terrible illness that had nearly destroyed his brother and choked the life out of his family. Even now he couldn't fully accept what this cure meant – couldn't even begin to believe that his long-cherished dream was coming true.

Which was why he hadn't even told his parents this amazing news. Maybe it was silly to keep something like this from them, but he wanted to surprise them when they came for another visit in a few days' time. He wanted them to see for themselves the changes in Aman and be amazed. He wanted to be able to tell them of the hope Karuppuraja and Bushy had presented.

He wanted to tell them that their son now had a future.

Zakiy's blissful smile faded as he spotted D and Ruhaan strolling up to where they were sprawled on the benches outside Bushy's office – along with Sathi.

He hadn't even told her, his supposed best friend, this wonderful news about Aman. She hadn't exactly been in the most receptive of moods recently. His brow furrowed and he found himself avoiding her gaze as she and D sat down on the other side of where Aman and Anna were sitting. Ruhaan dropped into the seat next to him and scanned his expression. 'What's wrong?' she asked.

Out of the corner of his vision he saw Sathi glance up at them. Zakiy put on his cheerful face and leaned back casually. 'What makes you think anything's wrong?' he said as breezily as he could.

Ruhaan regarded him shrewdly for a moment before deciding to let it go. She turned to Aman. 'How are you feeling?'

'I'm fine, *choti*,' he replied, making her smile at his old nickname for her. Then he continued eagerly, 'Anna was just telling me about the new solar panels Vinod Kani had installed. Apparently their photovoltaic system means each panel generates up to 250 kilowatt-hours annually...'

Zakiy had to duck his head to hide his delighted grin. Forgetting their recent animosity he automatically glanced at Sathi. Her expression quickly dragged his faulty memory back into reality, because she was, instead of reflecting his look of delight at Aman's enthusiastic conversation, glaring at Aman and Ruhaan with a look of disbelief, anger and hurt on her face.

What on earth was going on with her? Zakiy wondered. For months now she'd been this angry, touchy, jealous little version of herself. She wouldn't talk to him or even look at him now if she could help it. He couldn't understand it. Troubled by her expression, he watched as she seemed to tear her gaze away. She closed her eyes and took deep breaths, slowly in and out, like she was trying to calm herself. Her hands were curled into fists in her lap and – were they actually trembling?

He must have made some unconscious movement to go to her, to comfort her, because she suddenly looked up at him, and the look of hatred in her gaze speared him where he sat.

At that moment Zakiy felt fear slice through him. He was scared that he'd lost his friend, because if there was one thing he'd learned about Sathi it was that she would never look at someone she loved with hatred in her eyes – anger, yes, but never hatred. He wasn't sure what had happened, but he knew that this wasn't the Sathi he knew. This was someone else.

He was trapped in that dark-eyed gaze, in those eyes that were cold and hard and lost to him. He couldn't look away, even though that's all he wanted to do.

'Hey guys!'

Zakiy sent up a fervent prayer of thanks for the distraction that had arrived in the form of the Londoners. Beth and Luke perched on the edge of another bench and Sathi turned her body so she was facing them fully – putting her back to him.

'How are you two? Getting tired of Kerala yet?' D asked them.

'Oh no, of course not!' Beth exclaimed. Then she hesitated. 'Although... I do hate the way everyone stares.'

Luke grunted in agreement, and for a few moments everyone looked at him expectantly as they waited for him to elaborate. He didn't.

Zakiy heard Ruhaan's quiet snort and could guess what she was thinking; the couple had on shorts and sleeveless t-shirts suited to the hot weather – Beth's shorts lived up to their name and were very, um, short, and her top revealed a lot of cleavage. All in all perfect for a hot summer day back in London but, when coupled with the pale skin and hair that marked them as foreigners, a reason to gawk in Kerala, especially in rural parts such as these.

Of course that didn't justify the staring, but the truth was that it was a part of the culture here – the culture that they'd come to experience in the first place.

'Forget it, guys' was D's advice, while Sathi grimaced and nodded in understanding.

Something about that gesture made Zakiy's confusion and hurt at her behaviour change into slow, simmering anger. It started pissing him off that she was taking their side – that she was acting like such a brat for absolutely no good reason. Which was why he opened his mouth and struck the match to an argument that he would later regret.

'Wouldn't you stare if you saw an Indian guy wearing a *lungi* back home?' he asked, referring to the long skirt-like piece of cloth that men wore wrapped and tucked around their waist. 'Or if you saw a woman fully decked out in a sari?'

Beth gaped for a moment and spluttered, 'Of course not!'

'Of course you would!' Ruhaan retorted in the same tone as Beth, mocking her. 'Be honest: you'd at least do a double take. How is that different from people staring at you here?'

'But... it's.... it's not the same! If we did stare it'd be because we're admiring them, not anything else.'

Ruhaan was swift in her rebuttal. 'Who says people here aren't staring in admiration?'

'What's there to admire?' Luke wondered, sounding bewildered.

Zakiy intervened before Ruhaan blurted out something offensive, which he could tell she was on the verge of doing. 'The fact that you're *sayippu* – foreigners – makes you a novelty, especially the fair skin. You may not have noticed it, but a lot of Indians are obsessed with their skin colour.'

'What do you mean?' Beth asked.

'Some people tend to value lighter complexions over dark ones. And sometimes children born with exceptionally fair skin are all but worshipped, while darker kids are shunned – not everyone does this, but even one is too many, I think.'

'That's horrible,' Beth murmured.

'Not much different to the racial prejudice against black people in western societies,' Ruhaan replied, fixing her with a hard look. 'It may have lessened but it hasn't completely gone away.'

'Anyway,' Zakiy barrelled on, 'the point is, they don't stare because of anything personal – it's just simple curiosity for the novelty you present.'

At last the low, clear voice he was expecting rang out, 'What about me?' Sathi stood up, stone-faced, and held out her arms. 'My skin is brown and so is my hair. I look as Indian as the rest of you. So what justification is there for them to stare at me – or even at you?'

'I didn't say there was a justification for the staring – I just said that there's a reason Beth and Luke *especially* are stared at. In London maybe they don't stare, but from what I remember most of them also couldn't care less. They're too wrapped up in their own lives to pay much attention to other people, especially in the central parts.'

Sathi frowned. 'Wait a minute, you were in London?'

'We were all there for a couple of years – you know, for Aman.' He didn't really want to elaborate in front of Beth and Luke, but Sathi's expression said she understood that he meant that they'd been there for Aman's treatment. She also looked a bit stunned by the knowledge.

Zakiy continued, 'The staring is a part of our culture, and annoying or not that's just how it is.'

That snapped Sathi out of her daze. 'It seems like a bit of a cop-out to dismiss something annoying just because it's part of the culture. Maybe the culture needs to change.'

He felt anger shoot through him. 'Maybe it's not the culture that needs to change,' he said evenly. He paused and met her eyes coolly. 'Maybe it's the attitude.'

The door hinges creaked in complaint at the force with which they had been thrown into motion, and the door banged against the wall and then bounced off.

Sathi wished she could bang his head in the same way.

Fuming, she stalked over to her bed and flung herself down on it. She couldn't believe that Zakiy had been so rude to her, especially in front of everyone. What right did he have to talk to her like that? The thought made her hands form fists around the bed sheet, causing the fabric strain as though to escape the pressure. Staring. She huffed. Of all the things to argue about!

Some part of her knew she was being childish. Very, very childish. All these weeks she'd been horrible to him, ignored him and avoided him. Why should she feel so indignant now that he had decided not to take any more crap from her? Why should he continue to put up with it?

What about how he treated me? she reminded herself, viciously beating back the shame that had begun to fill her as she thought back over her behaviour. The heaviness of guilt began to lift as anger replaced it again. She thought back to all those times when Zakiy and Ruhaan had excluded her, made her feel like the third wheel. Her eyes pricked and overflowed, and she wiped furiously at the tears that seeped down her cheeks.

Damn them. Damn them both, especially *him*.

She pressed her eyes closed against more hot tears, and curled up on the bed even though she didn't feel remotely sleepy.

She chuckled once at the thought. If only she could feel sleepy.

Against the blackness that was the inside of her eyelids an image stabbed at her: Zakiy's brother smiling affectionately at Ruhaan; his voice rang in her ears as he called her "choti", which roughly translated to "little one". When had Aman ever spoken to her in that warm tone? When had he ever even had a proper conversation with her, despite all that she'd done to help him?

A small, reasonable voice in her told her that Aman had known Ruhaan since they were kids, and must have been used to looking after her when the cousins were all together. It was really no surprise that they were on such easy, familiar terms.

Just like Zakiy, she thought bitterly.

Turning over in the hopes of getting more comfortable and falling asleep, she instead found herself lying there staring at the wall, her eyes wide open. She couldn't believe that Zakiy and his family had lived in London. Why hadn't he told her? How was it possible that she hadn't known? She knew it wasn't a particularly important detail but considering that she'd also lived there for almost all of her life, the fact that he hadn't told her stung.

I bet Ruhaan knew.

Urgh! She hated this, she hated feeling like this. She couldn't get away from her emotions, and the tight feeling in her chest was unbearable. It made it easy to believe that she'd never feel happy again, and that feeling reminded her too much of those horrible years she'd spent alone in her father's house. Those miserable years she'd spent believing that her birth had been the cause of her mother's death.

Of course, now she knew better. She knew she hadn't been responsible for her mother's death. Her mother's supposed best friend had been responsible for that.

Her fingernails began to dig into the fleshy pad of her palms. How could someone do that? How could someone act like a friend to someone they hated, someone for whom they carried nothing but jealousy and bitterness inside? How could Vidhya have done what she had?

How could Sathi not have done anything to avenge her mother, like she had vowed to do on the day she realised that she had been murdered? Why had knowing the identity of the woman who had killed Amma extinguished the wind beneath her sails? Was she all talk and no action? Was that why she had turned into this weak, indecisive mess, because when push came to shove she just didn't have it in her to take action?

Sathi yanked the thin sheet up over her head. Then threw it off again as the rough material irritated her skin.

138

Unexpectedly, her breath caught in a sob and she pushed her face into her pillow. It became soaked with tears as she felt despair press in on her and burn its way through her throat and chest.

Why can't I have a mother like everyone else? she sobbed in her mind, years of pain and grief pouring out with a weight that she couldn't hold up. *I want my mother. I want her here, I want her to hold me and comfort me and tell me everything's going to be okay.*

She was gasping for breath now, she was crying so hard. The tight, leaden ball of pain in her chest seemed, impossibly, to become even more compressed and heavy, until the pain grew so strong it began to consume her. Almost unconsciously, Sathi reached out and clutched her left hand in her right. Gripping the soft flesh at the base of her little finger she sank the nails of her right hand into the skin. She increased the pressure until the throbbing there distracted her from the one in her chest. Her breathing grew slightly easier even as the stinging in her hand become so intense it was almost beyond pain. However, it was an agony she could think around, as opposed the one that had been in her chest, the one that never truly went away, just varied in intensity.

What's the point in living like this? she asked herself, whimpering, hating her weakness but not knowing how to stop it. What would it be like, she wondered, just to escape, escape this existence and just have... darkness? Nothingness. A vacuum, instead of being trapped inside a body with a mind that thought too much, imagined too much... hurt too much. Being alive seemed like too much effort.

As soon as she had the thought she felt ashamed of herself. She felt horrible and guilty, and she despised herself for thinking in such an ungrateful, immature way. There were so many people in the world who were much worse off than she was, and they still managed to live on. People caught in the barbed wires of poverty, illness, slavery... Only a weak person would think of giving up so easily.

Even as she scolded herself though, a part of her began to think of the things she didn't have once again: *No mother. No father. No family. No friends.*

The thought of Zakiy was now just a pinprick amongst the vast hurt that was everything else. What did it matter? What did it matter if he didn't talk to her, or if Aman talked to Ruhaan in that loving tone, or if Ruhaan looked at her like she was dirt? What did any of it matter when she had no family? When she had no one?

Enough!

Sathi abruptly sat up and brushed away the moisture on her cheeks. She had had enough of her self-pity and tears. Enough was enough, she decided. Her eyes were dry now, and the lump in her chest was still there, but as a dull ache. She could deal with that. What she couldn't deal with, however, was the way she was crying into her pillow like a miserable wretch. There was only so much a person could cry in one day, and she'd just about reached her quota.

Sleep was still a laughably impossible prospect, so she stood up and began pacing around the room, her familiar stride lending her comfort. She felt her breathing calm and even out, and her hands stopped trembling. She refused to feel the gouges she knew were still there along the side of her palm.

She marvelled at how cold and emotionless she felt inside, especially after the heart-bleeding session she had just had only moments ago. It was like everything that had been weighing on her had been shoved into a tiny corner of her brain, and the rest of her was content to ignore it, and it was content to be ignored. Yes, she was still miserable but it didn't bother her too much at the moment. She still hated and despised herself for being so weak, but right now it seemed like too much effort to entertain those emotions in the main part of her mind.

From being overcrowded, her brain had expanded so much that while one part swirled with the jumbled emotions that had, just moments ago, destroyed her peace, another absently wondered what she was going to have for breakfast in the morning. It was amazing.

She was still turning this over in her suddenly vast mind when someone knocked on her door.

Sathi came to a stop and her head jerked automatically in the direction of the sound. She went over to the door and cursed at the fact that there was no peephole. She wasn't brave (or stupid) enough to open the door in the middle of the night when it could be anyone outside in the hotel's dimly lit corridor. The knock came again, and she made up her mind. Hoping her voice wouldn't squeak, she called, 'Who is it?'

There was a pause. Then a very familiar voice replied, 'It's me.'

Her breath rushed out of her. Until then she hadn't realised just how scared she'd been. Her hand shaking from the unused adrenaline, she managed to unbolt the door and pulled it open to reveal a chagrined Zakiy.

'Hey,' she said weakly.

'Hey.'

It took him a while to meet her eyes, and when he did he took a double take. Too late, she realised that even in the questionable light from the single bulb outside her room it would be obvious to him that she had been crying.

Anger born out of embarrassment sharpened her tone. 'Did you want something?'

He shuffled his feet and coughed. 'Um, I heard, that is, I thought I heard something from your room.' He nodded towards the room right next door to hers. 'The walls here are thin, and I thought you might be...' he trailed off, glancing up at her and then away just as quickly. He cleared his throat and didn't say anything else.

Her humiliation grew. 'I'm fine,' she said, her words clipped.

Zakiy nodded, though he could see perfectly well that she was far from fine. *Why does he have to do that? Why does he have to act so damn... considerate?* It made her feel even worse by comparison. Especially after the way she had been treating him, she couldn't take any more of him being nice to her. She didn't want nice. She didn't want to feel so horrible about herself. She wanted to hate him: when he gave her a reason to hate him she felt justified in her anger.

Because if he was nice to her, and she still hated him, then how could she justify that to herself?

Zakiy took a small step closer to her and she made the mistake of looking up. His chocolate brown eyes were filled with concern, and they were fixed intently on her. 'Sathi, please tell me what's going on. I'm worried about you.'

'Nothing's going on.'

His expression turned impatient. 'Don't give me that bull. You've been acting weird for ages now.'

Her conflict over being angry with him vanished in the wake of the rising thermometer that was her temper. 'Oh, really? Well, I'm not the one who insulted you in front of everyone!'

Zakiy dropped his gaze to the floor. 'I'm not proud of that. But you have to admit that you were being quite unreasonable –'

Sathi slammed the door in his face

He held out a lit match to the wick; the flamed reared and then faded to a dull glow that flickered across his deity's grim features. He thought of his objective: the disgusting thief that had dared to steal coconuts from his backyard. How dare he? Didn't he know who he was? How dare he steal from someone like him, beloved of the gods? 'Go!' he shouted. 'I've given you what you want. Now go, and don't come back until you've spilled his blood!'

Chapter Fifteen

The Water's Call

Sathi dipped her hand into the cool water and gently trailed her fingers through its liquid weight, swirling them and creating tiny eddies. Her legs were already immersed up to her calves in the natural pool and she swished her feet back and forth, feeling little pieces of debris and plant material wedge into and then free themselves from the crevices in between her toes. It was an oddly comforting motion. In and out, never static, always moving, shifting, changing... it suggested that nothing was permanent. Nothing lasted forever.

And right now that was almost a cheerful thought.

Her eyes roamed over the dark mass; it was seven-and-a-half feet deep, she'd been told. The lip of the pond was high enough above the water that it would be a struggle to pull oneself out of it. She swung her legs out again, this time paying close attention to the way the water teased the edges of her rolled-up trousers. It rippled restlessly just below her knees, as though hungry to reach more of her.

Seven-and-a-half feet. It was taller, much taller than she was. What if she were to slacken her body's posture, let go of the unconscious cords that kept her sitting on the edge of the pool, as opposed to sinking down there into the water's dark embrace? What if she were to just... let go?

Her gaze burned into the silent water. What would it be like, she wondered, to completely submerge herself under there? To have the water form an impenetrable barrier around her, where all she could see would be the blackness of the pond, and all she could hear would be the grim music of the lakes and rivers of the world? In her mind's eye, she saw herself loosen the rigid tension that radiated out from her body. Her back bowed and limbs hung loosely. Her head fell onto her chest, and she began to tip forward...

A sudden noise yanked her mind back from the water's edge, and her body followed suit as she scrambled to her feet in panic, horrified at what she'd been considering doing. What had happened to her? Why was she acting so... so unhinged?

Someone cleared their throat, and Sathi realised that the earlier noise hadn't been divine intervention. It had been Ruhaan trying to get her attention: when their eyes met, Ruhaan said stiffly, 'The vaidhyan wants to see you.'

She didn't say anything else, and seemed to be waiting for a response. Still reeling, Sathi managed to nod and followed her down to where Bushy's house and office was. He wasn't anywhere to be found, though, and Ruhaan walked off without another word. After a fruitless search inside the house, Sathi deduced that he must be in his office and went in. He was there, but he wasn't alone. There a woman and a boy who looked to be around twelve years old in there with him – he was obviously in the middle of a consultation. She quickly muttered an apology and started to back out of the room, but Bushy caught her eye and motioned for her to sit down.

The women, after a cursory glance at her, went back to listing symptoms like there had never been an interruption: 'He's just come out with these horrible boils everywhere, on his arms, legs, and you know' – she leaned forward and mouthed the words – 'private parts.' She resumed in a normal voice, 'I don't know what to do. He hasn't had a full night of sleep for over a month – he spends half the night scratching. Show him,' she told her son, and he dutifully rolled up the legs of his trousers to reveal more of the pustules, expect these were red and angry-looking. Some were scabbing over, but others looked fresh and glistened with something wet.

Bushy crouched down in front of the boy and began to examine the boils, directing questions over his shoulder to the mother asking about when the symptoms started, what made the itching worse, what made it better, whether this had happened before, whether there had been any recent changes in his diet...

'No,' the woman replied to that last question, watching anxiously as Bushy drew a cotton bud from a drawer behind him and lightly touched it to a sore that was red and irritated and seeping that strange clear liquid. Bushy lifted the swab to his nose and sniffed it. His expression became introspective. The mother continued, 'Though the day before I noticed the first of those things on his arm we visited my mother-in-law's house. She gave him something, I know she did!'

Bushy made no reply to this extraordinary statement, and she seemed to find his lack of response almost offensive. 'I told you, that whole family spends their time going around temples and bringing back offerings cursed by their unholy gods!'

Sathi felt herself go very still. Bushy looked up and met her eyes briefly, and she realised this was why he'd asked her to sit in on this seemingly routine doctor's consultation.

The mother hadn't noticed their reaction. 'They've always been jealous of my Jithin's fair skin, and now they've done their best to spoil it,' she sighed, reaching out and running her hand through the kid's hair. He squirmed away and looked uncomfortable. She turned back to Bushy and said vehemently, 'They gave him kaivisham, I know it!'

Bushy slipped the cotton swab into a clear plastic envelope and then scribbled something on a scrap of paper. He handed it to the mother and told her to give it to the receptionist in exchange for a medicinal paste he told her to apply directly to the pustules.

'I've also giving him a *kashayam* to drink, three tablespoons twice a day.'

The kid made a disgusted face, and Sathi could understand why: while it was true that kashayam was an extremely medicinal mixture of herbs suspended in water, tasty it was not. She shook off the lingering shock from hearing kaivisham mentioned again and grinned at him. 'Don't worry, just eat some chocolate after you drink it to get the taste out of your mouth.'

The kid started in surprise, and then smiled back tentatively.

'Yes, well, I don't allow him to have sweet things more than once a week,' the mother sniffed, not even bothering to look at Sathi.

'That's a shame,' Bushy said glibly, 'having something sweet to look forward to is what keeps me going through the day.' He paused to wink at the boy. 'I swear it just makes people nicer! Now if you'll just see yourself out, madam, and make sure to come back if the boils persist.'

'So,' Bushy said, closing the door behind the mother and son, 'What did you think?'

'She's stingy with her chocolate?'

He smiled. 'You know that's not what I meant.'

'I know. Do you believe her? What she said about kaivisham?'

'Do *you* believe her?'

Sathi gave him a look meant to convey how much she appreciated him answering her question with another question. Then she considered. 'I'm not sure. She wasn't exactly... nice.'

'Her niceness – or lack thereof – doesn't mean she doesn't know what she's talking about,' Bushy pointed out.

She thought back to what the mother had said about her kid's fair skin. 'Seems like a pretty petty thing to give kaivisham for.'

He chuckled. 'You'd be surprised. I get people in here all the time claiming kaivisham is the cause of all their sorrows. Their daughter's marriage hasn't been fixed – so someone must have performed kaivisham. Their roof was damaged in a storm – so someone must have cast the evil eye on them. I've heard many versions of that women's story, by many different people and usually it's nothing more than superstitious paranoia.' Bushy paused. 'But on this occasion I think she's right.'

Sathi, who'd begun to relax at his words, jerked. 'What? Why?'

'Because of this,' he said, picking up the envelope containing the cotton swab and waving it at her, 'this strange liquid that is seeping from the boy's sores. It's not normal and the smell coming off it... it's not natural. I need to run some tests on it to be sure, but I'm sure something plant-based was given to the boy that his body is rejecting. It's trying to purge itself through the skin.

'There are three main ways in which something as toxic as kaivisham can affect a human body; it can affect the skin, it can affect the nerves and neurons or it can affect the brain. The nervous system and the brain... well, I don't need to tell you how dangerous damage to either of those can be. They say damage to the skin is the lesser evil of the lot, but often you see that damage to the skin affects the brain and vice versa.'

Sathi frowned in thought, 'How come? They seem like opposites – one is on the outside and one is on the inside.'

'When an embryo – which grows to become a baby – is first formed there are three layers of tissue called the germ layers. The ectoderm is the outermost layer of the germ layers and our nervous system, which includes the brain, and the outer layer of our skin – the epidermis – are made from the ectoderm. The skin, the brain and the whole of the nervous system are made out of the same tissue, essentially.' Bushy paused to steeple his fingers together. 'That's part of the reason I'm asking Aman to have daily sessions in the steam room. The herbal steam helps to purify the skin and body by flushing out toxins that have built up in the body.'

She puzzled this information over for a few moments, fascinated. 'So do you think that kid's skin problems are related to his mind?' she asked.

'I can't be sure of course, but I don't think so. No, I don't think it's that complicated a case. Now what I need to do is find out what this liquid is – then I can start to put together a more precise combination of herbs than the one in the kashayam I gave him to drink.'

'So why did you give him it today, instead of waiting till you've got it exactly right?'

'It will provide some symptomatic relief – you know, it will help with the itching but not the cause of it.'

'Do you really think someone gave that poor kid kaivisham?' she asked, feeling sick.

'I'm afraid so,' Bushy replied gravely, his expression inscrutable as he looked down at her. 'People say and do very strange things at times.'

Sathi's eyebrows drew together. Yes, people could do strange things. Like having weird, uncontrollable mood swings, acting like a pressure cooker ready to explode at any given moment, alienating your best friend for no particular reason, and worst of all, contemplating throwing yourself into a cold, dark pool where you know your feet won't touch the ground...

The sick feeling in her stomach grew. She didn't know why she had done any of those things. But a small voice at the back of her mind wondered how long she could go on doing them before she totally lost control.

Sathi left Bushy to his tests and wandered out over the grounds to sit under the abundant branches of a mango tree, out of the harsh sunlight flung down by the mid-morning sky. She purposefully ignored the vague outline of the pond she could glimpse at the corner of her eye. Feeling the humid heat that passed for summer in most of Kerala suffocate her from all sides, she felt a sudden wave of nostalgia for the refreshing coolness of Nelliampathi. Her mother's homeland. Of course, it was also her great-aunt and great-uncle's homeland, which was what had made Sathi want to flee it the moment she recognised them for the monsters they were.

A core of anger began to grow beyond the despair that thinking about them usually brought about. Why should they have the power to drive her out of the place she loved? After all, Nelliampathi didn't just represent the horrors they presented. It also represented the precious few friends she'd made while she was there – Manish, Ravi... and most of all, Nelliampathi contained memories of her mother, memories she'd yearned for most of her life, from the time when she realised *she* was the reason for her father's grief, *she* was the one who killed her mother...

No, no, no! Sathi screeched at herself. She took a deep breath to try and bring back a semblance of calm. She. Did. Not. Kill. Her. Mother. It wasn't her fault. She did not kill her mother. It wasn't her fault. She did not kill her mother. It wasn't her fault.

Her litany came to a halt when Ruhaan, D, Beth and Luke wandered up to where she was sitting. She wondered briefly where Zakiy was before remembering that he'd gone to meet his parents and Zoya, who'd come down for another visit. She thought of them with a pang – she would have loved to meet them at the train station and hug a delighted Zoya tightly to her chest. She had missed the little thing.

Sathi hastily wiped a hand over her eyes, and was surprised to find that they were completely dry. *Maybe the well's finally dried up*, she thought just as Ruhaan strolled up ahead of the others. She flipped that shiny mane of hair back and put a hand on her hip. 'Why do I keep finding you in the weirdest places?' she demanded, glancing back at her audience.

Sathi found it mildly amusing – as well as irritating – that Ruhaan, who wouldn't utter more than one word more than she had to when they were alone was apparently confident enough to taunt Sathi with an audience present.

'First the pond, and now this old tree,' Ruhaan sneered as the rest of the group joined them.

Sathi stiffened at the mention of the pond and gritted out, 'Maybe I like being *alone*.' Pointedly.

'I know what you mean,' Luke said, unexpectedly joining the conversation. He searched the ground for a good-sized tree root to sit on, first dusting it off thoroughly. Frowning down at his dusty hands, 'I find it helps to get away sometimes.'

Beth nodded vigorously, choosing not to sit down like the rest. 'Especially after we're with those poor kids all day.'

'What kids?' D asked enquiringly.

'Didn't we say?' Beth said, brightening. 'One of the main things Luke and I planned to do when we visit India is help out at some sort of charitable organisation. We've been volunteering at a local orphanage here for a couple of mornings a week.'

'That's great,' D said. He stretched an arm up above his head and plucked a mango leaf from one of the branches above. He crushed it between his fingers, sniffed it appreciatively and then thrust it under

Sathi's nose. She swatted his arm away despite the delicious aroma coming from the mangled leaf. 'It must be fun, working with kids.'

Beth beamed. 'It is! They're lovely. And it just feels so good, you know? To help out, like, when there's no one else to look after the poor things.'

Ruhaan made a sound like she was choking. 'What, is the orphanage run by the *poor, poor* kids as well?

Beth's lips flattened and then pursed into a look of contempt. 'No, but they don't have parents do they?' she bit out.

'So you're both enjoying yourselves?' D asked quickly, trying to make peace.

Beth, still scowling at Ruhaan, reluctantly turned to him and rearranged her expression. 'Yeah, we are. Although it makes me cringe to see the all these poor people here – I mean the houses some of them live in! I saw one yesterday with walls made out of pieces of scrap cardboard. It's awful! I just wish we could help them somehow. They wouldn't be left to suffer like this in the UK,' she added, her tone gaining a touch of condescension.

Sathi, who'd been silent thus far, felt something snap inside her. It was like a dam that had finally burst as all the frustration and anger and irritation that had been held inside her gathered too much force and momentum. Right in front of her was an opportunity to relieve some of her pent-up emotions, and she gladly took it.

'No,' she said quietly, 'in the UK people can just sit and claim benefits for everything, where they live in three bedroom houses that couples working full time can't afford. Instead of being resourceful and hardworking, they sit on the side of the street with plastic cups filled with coins from well-meaning people.'

'But,' Beth began in protest, but Sathi was on a roll now. 'India isn't perfect, but neither is a so-called "developed" country like the UK. There's no such thing as a perfect system. Before you decide to trek out to a poor, poor country to help out us underlings maybe you should look a little closer to home and try to resolve poverty on your own doorstep before rushing to the rescue elsewhere.'

Apparently lost for words, Beth and Luke simply gaped at her for a few moments. Then they stood up and stalked off without another word.'

Good riddance, Sathi thought as she watched them walk away. A tiny portion of the heaviness in her chest seemed to lift.

She could feel D and Ruhaan staring at her, which was precisely why she was avoiding looking at them. With a mental sigh she finally turned to face the inevitable: D grinned when he caught her eye, clasping his hands together in an exaggerated gesture of thanks.

She grinned back briefly, and then her eyes flicked to Ruhaan. Her expression was careful, controlled, obviously trying not to give away much. Despite that, though, her surprise was obvious – as was the grudging approval in her dark gaze.

Chapter Sixteen

Family – or Not?

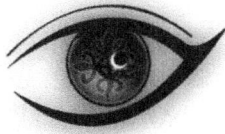

Sathi.'

She looked up slowly, unwilling to face the owner of that stilted, carefully controlled voice.

Zakiy directed his gaze at a spot just above her shoulder. 'My parents are here.'

Sathi nodded woodenly.

He left.

When she ventured outside a few minutes later Maira immediately engulfed her in a warm hug that caused the scent of lilacs to waft around her and made her eyes prickle. 'Thank you,' Maira whispered, her voice sounding like it was breaking. Over Maira's shoulder, Sathi saw Ruhaan watching them with an unreadable expression.

Narayan joined them, putting one arm around his wife. Then he rested his other hand on Sathi's head, and she was shocked to see that he too had tears gathering in his eyes.

'Guys, what's going on?' she asked, utterly at a loss. She'd never seen the two of them get so emotional before. They seemed unable to respond.

'They've just spoken to Aman,' Zakiy supplied.

Understanding hit. Yes, of course. It had been a while since the last time they'd come down, and it must have been unreal for them to see Aman more or less back to his old self.

'You've given us back our whole world,' Narayan told her, his voice rough with emotion.

Sathi shook her head, embarrassed. 'No, Uncle, it was Professor Karuppuraja and Bush— I mean Vinod Kani who did that.'

Maira finally pulled back, looking confused. 'But didn't Zakiy tell you?'

'Tell me what?'

Maira glanced uncertainly between her and Zakiy. 'Aman has started taking a lower dose of the clozapine. The professor said he may eventually be able to stop using the meds altogether.'

Sathi's head whipped around and her eyes bore into Zakiy's. '*What?*'

'I asked him about it the last time he visited.' He shrugged, but the coldness in his voice spoke legions.

She felt something compressing her chest. 'I see.'

Maira's worried eyes were fixed on Sathi. 'What's going on wi–'

'Ruhaa!'

This delighted yell came from the small form of Zoya, who had waddled up on her short chubby legs and had apparently only just caught sight of Ruhaan.

Ruhaan turned, and her face split in the first genuine smile Sathi had seen on her. 'Hey squirt!' she cooed, holding out her arms.

In what was obviously a motion practised over years, Zoya leaped into Ruhaan's arms.

'Excuse me,' Sathi muttered to Zakiy's parents and got out of there before her chest imploded.

Sathi headed straight for her room. At least there no one could barge into her personal space.

Fuck them! she thought angrily. She flounced into a chair, inadvertently shoving it into the wall as she did so.

She didn't need them. She didn't need any of them. They could all just go to hell as far as she was concerned.

Actually, no, Zakiy and his whole bloody entourage could all go to heaven and leave her alone in peace – because she'd obviously be going to hell... where her great-aunt and great-uncle would undoubtedly end up.

Sathi buried her head in her hands, groaning at the stupidity of her own thoughts. How had she been so wrong? How had she deluded herself that her mother's family would accept her as their own just as they'd once accepted her orphaned mother? That they would welcome her with open arms?

The worst part of it all was that they initially *had* done just that – or pretended to, at least. They'd fit her seamlessly into the family, as though she had belonged, as though this had been a homecoming everyone had been eagerly awaiting.

She had been such a fool.

Sathi couldn't prevent her eyes from straying to her backpack. Forcing her hands away from her face, she stood up and reached into the bag, pulling out a sheaf of papers she'd tucked away safely months ago, before she had any idea of the shock that was waiting for her. Hugging them to her chest, she retreated to the bed and spread the papers out so she could see them all at once.

They were photocopied newspaper articles she'd carefully gathered – articles about her mother and her adoptive aunt and uncle. Gingerly, Sathi picked up one that was the oldest of the lot. It described how, after a toddler was orphaned by a devastating car accident, she was adopted by her maternal aunt. The rest were about the various charitable organisations run by her great-uncle and the family, including one that conducted community marriages for those who couldn't afford the expenses of a wedding otherwise.

How was it possible, Sathi wondered, that people who seemed like such upstanding members of the family could mask such deep evil? She'd spoken to so many people about them before actually meeting them, and they'd all had a unanimously high opinion of them. No one had seemed to even have a hint of their cruel natures.

She traced her finger over Amma's name in the first article. Was it possible Amma truly hadn't known what her aunt and uncle were like?

She couldn't have known, Sathi quickly assured herself. She hadn't been like them. She'd been too *good* a person.

Of course that's exactly what she'd thought of her great-aunt and great-uncle at first, too.

Don't think like that! she ordered herself. *Just don't.*

When the knock came at her door she was actually relieved despite her earlier wish for privacy.

Until she found that it was Zakiy dithering on the doorstep.

Betrayal shot fire through her chest. Then she told herself that she didn't care. Making her voice as cold as possible, she said, 'Yes?'

He looked at her, and she saw no change in the hard set of his jaw. He hadn't come to forgive her, then.

As soon as she thought that an angry part of her reared up in indignation. *Forgive me? What've I done that needs forgiving?*

She was taken aback at the vicious force behind the thought. At the same time she approved of it. She kept hearing Maira's voice in her mind: *Didn't Zakiy tell you?*

'I came to apologise,' he said, sounding like he was gritting his teeth.

Sathi raised an eyebrow, not missing that he'd said that he'd come to apologise – not that he was apologising. 'You mean Maira sent you to apologise,' she said shrewdly.

He leaned one shoulder against the door hinge. 'She seemed to think I was being rude.'

She didn't reply to that, and the two of them stared at the floor for a few moments.

He broke the silence eventually. 'So can I come in or what?'

Sathi moved aside wordlessly, and he came inside. The room seemed ridiculously small with his elongated limbs taking up all the space. He wandered aimlessly around the room for a moment before turning to face her. 'You had a right to know about Aman.'

She nodded once. 'I did.'

'I wanted to tell you.'

'So why didn't you?' *Didn't Zakiy tell you?*

156

He made a frustrated noise and ran a hand through his hair, making it stick up even more. 'You tell me, Sathi. We haven't exactly been on the best of terms lately.'

She looked away.

Zakiy continued, 'I haven't exactly had the chance to have a heart-to-heart with you–'

He broke off, and Sathi glanced up to see what had caught his attention. His gaze was fixed on the newspaper articles that were still fanned out on the bed. He walked over and picked them up, his eyes roving over the headlines. When he turned back to her she flinched. The normal laugh lines were gone, and his eyes and lips were hard and flat. She'd only once seen him filled with such fury, and even then the anger hadn't been directed at her, not like this. He looked like he wanted to punch her.

'Why do you do this to yourself?' he demanded, shaking the papers at her. 'What happiness does reading this rubbish give you?'

Sathi found she couldn't meet that furious gaze. 'You don't understand,' she said quietly.

'So explain it to me.'

'It's not that easy for me to... dismiss them.'

'Why not?'

'Because they're all I have left!' she snapped. Loudly. 'Because they're my only family!' She thrust her knuckles into her eyes and pushed down the sobs that started trying to force their way up through her chest.

Zakiy strode forward until he was right in front of her. Surprising her, he took hold of her arms and wrenched them away from her face. A vein pulsed on his forehead as he leaned in close and said, 'They. Are. Not. Your. Family.'

'You don't understand,' she repeated dully, whispering.

His grip on her wrists tightened. 'No, you're right. I *don't* understand. I don't understand how you can still consider those sick bastards your family.'

'They're my great-aunt and great-uncle!'

Zakiy snorted. 'Great-villains, more like.'

Sathi felt anger shoot up through her in an arc of electricity. 'Don't act so clever with your stupid nicknames. You have no right to talk about them!'

He shook his head, suddenly looking drained. He let go of her arms. 'Why do you keep doing this? Why do you keep –?'

He bit off the rest of his words, but she could guess what he'd been about to say. The last time the two of them had fought it had been over Sathi's father and his total lack of concern for his teenage daughter. Especially as said teenage daughter had set out to a foreign country without any means of support. She hadn't been able to bear any criticism against her father, and she'd blown up pretty spectacularly at Zakiy in what had been a completely unreasonable way.

She had more or less accepted the unsavoury truths about her father now, but here she was reacting in that same unreasonable way about her great-aunt and great-uncle. She didn't want to keep making the same mistakes again, she didn't want to fight with Zakiy, but her emotions were yet again all over the place, scattered so much she couldn't control them. Half the time she didn't recognise the words coming out of her own mouth. Even now there were two parts of her warring for control; one wanted to agree with Zakiy, tell him he was right, she was obsessing over something pointless; the other wanted to scream at the arsehole to mind his own business.

Slowly she realised that Zakiy had been talking while she tried to figure out what was going on inside her own head, and she tuned back in just as he said, '… told you before, family isn't about blood or relations. It's about being there for someone no matter what; it's taking comfort in the presence of another person, about *real* love and affection. It doesn't matter that they're your blood relatives - they're not your family.'

'Easy for you to say,' Sathi muttered under her breath. Fully aware that she sounded like a petulant brat.

'What?'

'I said, that's easy for you to say,' she repeated loudly. Somehow that part about sounding like a brat didn't bother her too much anymore. Envy and spite lent force to her accusations. 'You have parents who love you and siblings who adore you,' she spat. 'What the hell do you know about not having a family?'

Zakiy looked at her as though she'd slapped him. The hurt on his face should have been enough to make her stop, make her take back those horrible words.

Should have.

She stayed silent.

Finally he said, 'You're not without a family. That's what I've been trying to tell you. My family is yours, Sathi. I thought you'd know that by now. Do you know how happy, how content I felt every time Zoya insisted you put her to bed? When Amma decked you out in that half-sari. Why do you think I was so angry with Dad for treating you like an outsider those first few weeks? *We're* your family, Sathi.'

She felt like she had been caught in the middle of a tornado. Her turbulent and chaotic her feelings churned within her, twisting and pulling at her mangled heart. Overwhelming gratitude for his thoughtfulness. Grief at the truth of his words about Great-uncle and Great-uncle and the heart-breaking knowledge that they didn't love her. Cautious joy at this possibility of an alternate family, one that would love and accept her for who she was. Annoyance that he was right, at how logical and reasonable he was, and how illogical and unreasonable *she* was in comparison.

Sathi searched for words to convey all of this, to explain how conflicted she was, how she was feeling opposing emotions in a way that made no sense to her, in a way that scared her and made her fear for her sanity. Instead what came bursting out from her mouth was:

'I don't want to be anybody's charity case!'

Reeling inside, she watched with a sort of clinical interest as shutters slammed down on Zakiy's face, a face that had been open and earnest and filled with hope just moments ago. Truly amazing, she thought to herself, how human beings could express strong emotions with such subtle movements of the eyes, lips, eyebrows...

His face, just for a moment, became filled with inner agony and she was reminded instantly of how he'd looked when he'd been helpless to do anything while Aman was having a violent episode. The comparison punched a hole in her chest, but her new capacity for distancing helped to numb that impact, putting a temporary bandage over the wound and prolonging the moment when it would break through, raw and bleeding.

Zakiy looked away and took a deep breath before he spoke again. 'I'm... very sorry that you feel that way,' he said, his voice almost breaking. Then it hardened as he threw the articles back on the bed. 'I won't keep you any longer. My parents and Zoya are staying for a couple of days, but I'll make sure they keep out of your way.' He glanced back at the papers flung haphazardly on the bed, and his lips twisted. 'I wouldn't want to take you away from your precious *family*.'

'Please don't do this,' he begged, his heart breaking as he looked at the man he had respected, even worshipped. Now he wore the face of a stranger. 'Don't do this to me.'

'Get out. You don't belong here. And you never will.'

Howling, he turned and ran.

Chapter Seventeen

The Battle

For a long time, Sathi just sat there, staring blankly at the door Zakiy had banged shut on his way out. Dread suffocated her, bearing down on her chest. What had she done? She couldn't make sense of her emotions and her behaviour. What had happened to her? Why was she so out of control? Why did she often feel simply like a vessel for her emotions – something that had no control, but just had to ride out whatever hit her at the time?

Even as she insulted Zakiy there had been a part of her that looked on in horror, unable to believe the spite with which she responded to his kindness.

What he'd said about her great-aunt and great-uncle still stung. She couldn't bring herself to accept the truth of his words, because if she did it would be like losing her Amma all over again. She would have no more claim to her mother, to the dream of belonging to a family.

But did she want to belong to what was, essentially, a family of villains?

The great-villains, a voice whispered, and she chuckled and then winced at the pain in her chest.

Zakiy had been her best friend for only a short time, but she couldn't imagine life without him. She also couldn't imagine carrying on like this, fighting with him every moment. Until this morning they hadn't even spoken to each other since... She thought back, a troubled frown taking root on the folds of her forehead. They hadn't spoken to each other since their last fight, the one that had ended in her slamming the door in his face.

Her head fell forward in shame and disbelief. She couldn't believe she'd behaved like that. What a horrible way to treat her friend. Sathi felt like such a failure in so many ways already that it was depressing to think she'd also failed as a friend.

Closing her eyes she shuddered out a breath and rested her head on her knees. She didn't know how to fix this – any of it.

She should apologise to him...

No! What if you apologise and he doesn't accept? What if he sneers at you again?

He didn't sneer! she told herself quickly.

That other part of her ignored the denial. *Let him apologise. He started it!*

No, she thought sternly, he hadn't. *She* had. She'd been taking out all of her anger and frustration on him, and then she had let her hurt and jealousy his closeness to Ruhaan get the better of her. It wasn't fair to blame him.

Who cares about being fair? Didn't you get the memo – life isn't fair. Was it fair your mum died before you could know her? Was it fair your dad let you believe you killed your mum? Was it fair when, after all that, your only chance at belonging to a family turned into yet another failure?

Sathi put her hands on either side of her face in a pathetic attempt to contain her chaotic thoughts. Being reminded, even if it was by herself, of all the things that were weighing on her wasn't helping matters.

Failure. It was an awful word. The thought of being a failure was like a knife twist in her gut. Even worse than failing at being a good friend, she had failed at being a good daughter. She felt physically sick as she tried to analyse her avoidance of Vidhya and the crime she'd committed against her mother. Sathi couldn't understand her reticence. It filled her with shame, and even when she wasn't actively thinking about it she could feel it lurking under the surface of her every thought and mocking her until she thought she would go mad.

Maybe you are going mad...
What? No!
But how do you know?
Sathi kneaded her knuckles into her temples, hard. You're not going mad, she intoned, trying to convince herself.

Her argument with Zakiy ran through her mind yet again, both his hurtful but true words and her own disgraceful response to them. Remembering that he hadn't bothered to tell her about Aman going off his medication made her feel even worse.

Why hadn't he told her? She had done so much for Aman, and while she hadn't done it expecting anything in return, she had thought she at least deserved to know something so wonderful. Maira and Narayan's gratitude meant little in the face of Zakiy's betrayal. How could he have dismissed her so easily?

The more she thought about it, the more her sadness changed into anger. Hot lava began to boil in her as she stewed over the injustice of it all. *She* had been the one to spend hours looking up imaginative venues for Aman's treatment. *She* had been the one to find Bushy, through Anna. Zakiy had no right to exclude her like this!

Then, unwillingly, the memory of how she had treated him interrupted her rage. Zakiy had done much more for her when she had been trying to gather information about her mother back in Nelliampathi. And she had rubbished all of that, rubbished *him* when he had – not unreasonably – wondered aloud why her father hadn't come with her when she set out to Kerala instead of letting her undertake the journey alone.

I'm a hypocrite, she thought miserably, the guilt heavy in her stomach. *I have no right to blame him.*

With that realisation she sank into despair again and buried her head in her arms. She breathed in and out slowly as she tried to calm down, but she couldn't stop the memories of the argument from tormenting her:

His hurt expression when she'd yelled at him.

His parting words – made worse because they'd been a reflection of the pain she'd caused.

How she'd argued with him about Beth and Luke, and hadn't seen through those two from the start. She'd been blind to their condescension and air of superiority.

Aman smiling affectionately at Ruhaan and calling her "choti".

Great-uncle's cruel smile and cold, dead eyes.

How Ruhaan and Zakiy seemed to be so perfectly in sync, and the way he seemed to seek out her company over Sathi's.

That kid's mother who'd snubbed her for no reason.

The stuff Bushy had told her about kaivisham, and the fact that people could do such terrible, unspeakable things to each other for petty reasons.

Great-aunt giving kaivisham to Maya, her daughter-in-law.

Her dad's agonised expression when she told him she was setting out to Kerala - the place where her mother had been murdered.

Murdered by her supposed best friend – whom Sathi didn't even have the guts to try and track down, like she'd promised herself she would.

She gripped her head with her hands and her nails began to dig into the soft flesh at her temples. It hurt, but it was nothing compared to the raw throb in her chest. She deepened the pressure, branding the skin with her sharp nails until she got what she wanted: the physical pain grew too intense to ignore. She started breathing more easily as the weight of her guilt and sorrow lifted. Her hands relaxed in response.

As soon as the pain abated, though, waves of torturous shame began to wash over her, unrelenting. What kind of a person was she? Why was she doing things like this? Was she finally going crazy? Had her mind completely given up on her?

Sathi started shaking. She was afraid, she was so terrified of herself; her mind was a stranger, and she didn't know what she would do if she couldn't trust her own mind.

She clamped her lips against the whimpers that were struggling to break out, trying to hold in her fear. She felt sobs starting to make their way up her throat, squeezing everything together until she couldn't breathe properly. Her head was pounding, all he nerve endings at breaking point with the pressure she was putting on them.

She was a horrible human being, a horrible, useless human being, a failure. She was good for nothing – a dead space. She didn't want to carry on like this, carry on feeling like a waste of space. She felt like she was about to explode with all these... these volatile emotions she was bottling up and suppressing, like she was drowning in her own mind. She wished there was someone she could reach out to, someone who wouldn't judge her. She thought of her dad with longing. She needed someone who would listen to all of her awful thoughts and not think any less of her for it.

Obviously, Zakiy was out of the question at the moment – or maybe forever. And she really didn't feel like she could talk to anyone else.

You can speak to Devi, a small voice whispered within her.

For a moment Sathi felt an overwhelming urge to open her heart to her goddess and beseech her for help. Then she hung her head. She didn't deserve Devi's love. She wasn't worthy of it. She'd thought and said and done terrible things, things that made her shudder to think of even now. She didn't deserve Devi's help or forgiveness. *I am a horrible person*, Sathi repeated to herself, the single tear that had been left behind rolling down her cheek.

Her heart now felt as though it was trying to claw its way out of her chest cavity. Sathi thought back over her every action and word that had hurt someone, coming to the end of the cycle only to begin the painful loop again. Her every mistake, her every hurtful deed... all of these ganged up on her and battered her brain until she felt ready to scream.

I'm a horrible person. I'm a failure. I hate myself. I'm a horrible person. I'm a failure. I hate myself. I'm a horrible person. I'm a failure. I hate my–

'Enough!' Sathi half-yelled and shot to her feet. She shoved her hair out of her face where strands had become stuck to her wet cheeks.

'Fuck this!'

Her hands shook, and her breathing was ragged and painful. She couldn't deal with this anymore. She couldn't feel this intense guilt day after day and keep holding on to her sanity.

She didn't know what she was supposed to do. She couldn't think straight; she couldn't understand how she was meant to carry on like this. Even when she'd believed that her mother had died in childbirth, when she'd essentially believed that she'd caused her mother's death, she hadn't been like this. She hadn't felt like she was losing control of her mind. She hadn't felt like death was truly better than this miserable existence.

Is this what Aman used to go through? Sathi wondered suddenly, and then shuddered at the thought. If it was, she didn't understand how he'd put up with it for fifteen long years. At least this hadn't started happening to her until a few months ago, ever since...

Sathi felt the air being punched out of her lungs, and she actually choked on the breath that had gotten caught in the vacuum left behind. She dropped involuntarily down onto the bed as her knees gave out beneath her. She actually couldn't breathe for a few panic-stricken moments, and that was what finally forced her to calm down and take stock of the situation.

She had been having wild mood swings, including dark, low moods where she couldn't find even a ray of hope in the utter bleakness the world seemed like in those moments; she'd been increasingly short tempered, in a way that was extreme even for her; she'd even – how she hated admitting this – she'd even contemplated killing herself.

And all this had started after the three months she'd spent at her great-aunt and great-uncle's house.

Sathi felt herself become very still as she considered the possibilities.

Both the guy from the temple in Mysore and Whitebeard had told her there was "something" inside her. Something she needed to get rid of, according to them.

The night she'd left that the house, the night Great-uncle nearly raped Maya, she had had a dream where she had felt Devi's divine eye destroying pools of darkness in her body. At first she'd assumed that the black sludge was symbolic of the evil inside her, which she had cultivated by ignoring the evil that was taking place around her. But now... what if it had been the effects of black magic? What if that dark sludge had been indicative of dark energy that had been forced into her body, violating it?

She thought back over how eager her great-aunt and great-uncle had been to feed her and stuff food down her throat. She thought of Great-aunt handing Maya a glass of milk and using a finger to tip it up so that her daughter-in-law had to drain the last drop. She thought of the blank, zombie-like expression of Maya's face as she walked into Great-uncle's room.

Was it possible that she, Sathi, had been given kaivisham?

Not just possible, she realised. It was highly probable. The more she thought about it, the more she realised that her behaviour while at that house should have tipped her off to something else going on. She had started acting oddly a few weeks into her life there, being entirely too understanding and sympathetic towards them, easily accepting and forgiving the atrocities they had committed. They'd been using their gross expertise in black magic to enslave her will, making her more docile, more willing to bow to *their* will.

She couldn't believe she'd been so blind! How had it taken her so long to figure this out? She'd been acting like a crazy person, she'd been acting unlike herself, because *she hadn't been herself!*

The leaden weight in her chest lifted as she realised that her volatile behaviour for the last few months may not have been entirely her fault. Her great-aunt and great-uncle had done all they could to try and mould her into their little puppet, and they'd nearly succeeded. She would still be under their control if it hadn't been for Devi.

As her mind whirred she could feel the rightness of her thoughts, and knew that she had no one but her goddess to thank for this insight – otherwise she would have truly driven herself mad.

Or killed herself.

Gratitude flowed through her, pure and sweet, and she slipped off her shoes and shifted on the bed so that she was sitting cross-legged. Then she reached for her phone and scrolled through it until she had found the song she's copied across from the CD Narayan had given her, the Gayathri Manthram. Closing her eyes, she listened to the opening music and focused on Devi, drawing strength from the sweet knowledge that she wasn't alone. She allowed the lyrics of the manthram to wash over her, and began to recite the words:

Om bhur bhuvah svah
Tat savitur vareniyam
Bhargo devasya dhimahi
Dhiyo yo nah prachodayat
Om bhur bhuvah svah...

Sathi lost count of how many times loops she went through, but listening to the music and following along was having a calming effort, allowing her to think more clearly than she had been able to for months. As she did, the image from her dream came to the forefront of her mind: her body, with black sludge everywhere, polluting it. Seeing it, Sathi got an idea: she began to visualise a light that Dream-Sathi could apparently draw out from the luminous earth, using it to flush out the darkness. Unlike the golden light that had been Devi's weapon, Sathi imagined this one as being green-tinged, drawing inspiration from the lush grass in the meadow where the dream had taken place.

Over and over she repeated the words, all the while visualising that green light dislodging the kaivisham in her body. She wasn't sure how much time had passed; she also wasn't sure when she fell asleep and began to dream.

The temple was filled with soft evening light as the sun bid goodbye; hundreds of oil lamps with flickering wicks of flame waited for their light to be needed, playing tag with the breeze as they illuminated the indulgent faces of the idols of the gods. Garlands of flowers wreathed their necks in bright colours and bells rang out as the puja began—

A young boy, no more than ten years old, stood in the middle of a sitting room with a man and a teenager. They stood and talked and laughed with each other, and it was obvious that the boy adored the other two. Then a woman came into the room carrying a glass of something. Smiling, she handed it to the boy, who accepted it eagerly and drained it in one go.

Wiping his mouth, he thanked the woman and then went back to the conversation. That's when things went wrong; the boy's face twisted, he started shaking violently and he began to shriek wordlessly. The glass slipped between his fingers and splintered into a thousand shards as it smashed against the hard floor. The boy fell like a puppet whose strings had been cut.

Sathi woke up with a gasp. It took her a moment to shift herself out of the dream, separating it from reality. She thought about the dream for a moment, but like the dreams that had grown in frequency over the last few days, she couldn't make any sense of it. She felt weirdly edgy and off balance, and she had to blink around the dark spots dancing across her vision. Slowly, stiffly, she stretched out her legs from under her and sucked in a breath as the blood circulation returned to them. Somehow she'd managed to fall asleep without moving from her cross-legged position.

She felt oddly drained and achy - almost as though she was recovering from a fever. On the plus side, her mind felt surprisingly clear despite the weird dream, and she felt like herself again.

She had a fierce urge to get out of the room, though. The walls seemed to close in on her and she was starting to feel claustrophobic. She wanted to be outside, to breathe in fresh air and be surrounded by nature. Most of all, she wanted to think about the revelations she'd had and figure out the implications of it all, and she couldn't do that in this tiny room that had become a prison to her over the last months.

An idea of where she could go occurred to her. Smiling, Sathi rose on wobbly legs and, one step at a time, made her way back outside.

Chapter Eighteen

A Drop of Mother's Love

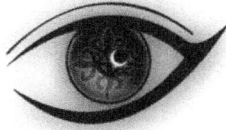

Breathing in the heavenly fragrance of freely growing jasmine bushes, Sathi knew instinctively that she'd made the right decision in coming here. She looked around in pleasure at the gorgeous public gardens that formed a part of the park near the hotel. As well as the jasmines, hibiscus, lilies, geraniums, dahlias and bougainvillea had burst into brilliant blossom and were showing themselves off to the sun. Sathi set off at a languid pace around the various sections of the garden, trailing her fingers over the brightly coloured petals as she walked.

Her mind was racing with what she'd just found out about herself. Now that she was thinking clearly enough for it to have occurred to her, she knew she was right. Her moods swings, the things Bushy had told her about kaivisham affecting the mind... it all fit!

That wasn't to say she hadn't had low moods or a short temper before met her great-aunt and great-uncle. Cringing, she remembered her spectacular show of temper at Zakiy when he criticised her father. No, she definitely didn't claim she was a saint beforehand.

But it also couldn't be disputed that things had gotten so much worse in a short amount of time. If she'd been a 4 on scale of 1 to 10 of short-temperedness before, now she was a 90. No matter how upset or angry she became she'd never reached a point where she felt physical symptoms or considered killing herself.

Sathi reconsidered. Well, no. The first time she really considered that wasn't after she had left that house. It had been the day Great-aunt faked a heart attack in order to prevent her from going out to meet Ravi, her colleague at the resort where she used to work. In the hospital she had gazed at her great-aunt's sleeping form with fear in her heart – fear that she would lose her, lose her only family. That day she had vowed that she wouldn't continue to live in a world without her great-aunt and great-uncle. That she wouldn't go back to living her lonely life before she met them.

She closed her eyes briefly and concentrated on Devi for a few minutes to get her emotions back under control. Then she began walking again, her stride lengthening in response to the anger that was growing within her.

In all this time since she had learnt Great-aunt and Great-uncle's true nature, she had been repulsed by them, frightened by them, despaired over them, wept for them... As she considered how the two of them had tortured her mind to the point of her wanting to end her own life, she realised that anger was too mild an expression to describe how she now felt. Rage. Fury. It wasn't like her earlier fury, though. That had been an out of control, confused, choking anger, one accompanied by guilt and shame.

This was different. It was a righteous anger, an anger that fortified instead of depleting strength. In fact, she was surprised by how invigorated she felt as outrage coursed through her veins. She knew one thing then with absolute certainty: there was no forgiveness for her great-aunt and great-uncle.

A hand softly touched her shoulder, and Sathi spun around to find Maira smiling serenely at her. 'I see you're out to enjoy these gorgeous blooms, just like me,' she said, gesturing to the flowers around them.

Sathi nodded, not quite able to smile back. The sight of Maira had reminded her of her behaviour, and she felt ashamed of herself.

Maira fell into step next to her, and they strolled along silently for a while. Then, like she'd just remembered, Maira said, 'Zoya was asking for you. Well, I think throwing a tantrum demanding to see you would be a more fitting description.' She laughed, her normal warm laugh, and Sathi felt her insides become less tight.

'I'll need to appease her, then,' she mused, managing to locate and utilise her cheek muscles more effectively this time.

'Unless you want to deal with Zoya at her very worst, then yes, you do,' Maira concurred, chuckling again.

They fell into silence again, but it was less awkward this time. They rounded a corner, and Maira gasped in delight, running over to the large clusters of rose bushes that dominated this section of the gardens. 'Sathi, look,' she called, beckoning to her. Maira bent down over the deep blush-coloured blossoms and inhaled deeply, a blissful smile tilting up her full lips. 'They're native roses,' she told Sathi over her shoulder. 'Their scent has no comparison.'

She breathed deeply once again, and then turned to gesture encouragingly to Sathi. She smiled back tentatively and mimicked Maira's movements as she bent her face towards the nearest cluster of roses. Her eyes closed at the unexpectedly potent, sweet fragrance wafting out from the delicate petals. Yet it was not overly sweet; it had a definite bite of spice to it.

Sathi looked up at Maira, straightening. 'It's amazing! You're right, the smell is completely different to the ones you get in the UK.' Unable to help herself, she leaned down to get another whiff.

Maira laughed at her enthusiasm and deftly plucked a deep pink petal. She held it out to her and said, 'Open up.' She popped it into Sathi's mouth when she opened it in surprised protest.

'Chew,' Maira urged when Sathi just looked confused and pushed the velvety petal around her mouth with her tongue.

Unsure, she obeyed and then grinned as her taste buds got to experience that same intoxicating mix of sweet and spice, combined with the soft crunchiness of the fresh, water-swollen petal.

'Wow,' she whispered when she'd swallowed, her eyes wide.

Maira's eyes danced with amusement. She looked around surreptitiously at the deserted garden, then reached down and broke off the stalk of one of the half-open blossoms. She then motioned for Sathi to turn around and tucked the rose within the thick folds of her hair before gently turning her so that they faced each other again. 'There,' Maira said, smiling softly.

Gazing at her, Sathi's eyes prickled. Maira's expression softened and leaning down, she pressed a kiss to Sathi's forehead

Maira pretended interest in the small board detailing the species and origin of these particular roses as Sathi hastily wiped at the moisture in her eyes. Maira then linked her arm with Sathi's and suggested, 'Let's keep walking.'

They slowly ambled over to the next section of the gardens. 'Did Zakiy ever tell you that Zoya was adopted?' Maira asked, pausing to finger a beautiful ivory coloured blossom Sathi couldn't put a name to.

'Yes,' she replied. 'He said you found her in the middle of a storm...?

Maira nodded. 'That's right. We asked around everywhere, you know, to try and find her birth parents; but no one came forward to claim the tiny thing.' She smiled, but the expression was marred by sadness and anger. 'Narayan and I thought long and hard before we actually decided to take her in. Not that we didn't love her,' she hurried to add. Her voice became rueful. 'I think we all fell in love with her the instant we saw her. But I used to work as a sort of liaison in an adoption agency, and I know first hand just how complicated adoption can be.'

'What do you mean?' Sathi asked.

'Even when the adoptive parents and the child are a good match and the parents want the child for all the right reasons, it's still very difficult to make it work. The kids, once they reach a certain age, almost always come in asking about their biological parents, even when they're happy with their adoptive parents.' Maira sighed. 'I don't know what it is that makes them crave knowledge about their "real" family,' she said, making air quotes, and Sathi dropped her gaze to the floor, beginning to see where this conversation was going.

'No matter how happy they are with their adoptive family, no matter how well looked after they are, in the end that curiosity overwhelms them. And of course that breaks the hearts of their adoptive parents.'

Maira stared at nothing for a moment, looking as though her thoughts were far away. Then her gaze flicked to Sathi's face, those dark eyes measuring her expression. Maira seemed troubled by what she found there. 'In all these years, Zakiy's never formed a close relationship with anyone – not his school friends, not even with Ruhaan and Dhameer. Of course those two knew about Aman, but Zakiy never talked about his worries and fears about his brother – he preferred to act like everything was fine. That was his coping mechanism, I suppose... because the reality was too painful for him.'

Maira's forehead creased, reflecting her sorrow over her son's pain. 'I don't know if I can describe just how horrific it was, to live with a child who looked at you with the eyes of a monster; who might very easily kill you in one of his blind, paranoid rages.' She paused, and a teardrop escaped from under her closed eyelids. She did not bother to brush it away, her gaze still under the shackles of memory.

Maira sighed heavily. 'It was much worse for Zakiy – he was just a child himself back then. We all just... we learned to live with it. To be careful, to not let anyone in, to make excuses whenever our friends wanted to visit us. We avoided the rest of the world, and eventually everyone got the message and began to avoid us in turn.' She paused and seemed to be gathering her thoughts. She looked at Sathi. 'Until now. Sathi, you're the first person to come into our family in such an intimate way. Zakiy's never before formed a friendship strong enough that he's opened up about Aman. I don't know if you realise just how significant that is to Narayan and I, when we had all but despaired of Zakiy ever having a normal life. And that's not even taking into account how pivotal you were in Aman's recovery. Our whole family will owe for eternity for that.'

Sathi finally found her voice within the clogged mess that was her throat. 'Don't be silly,' she muttered.

'I'm just acknowledging how grateful we are to you.'

She had to look away from those kind black eyes. 'There's no need to. Besides,' she said in a low voice, 'Zakiy... he helped me out a lot back when... when I was trying to find out about my mum. I'm just returning the favour, really.'

They walked on for a few minutes in silence after that, and Sathi received the distinct impression that Maira was building up to saying something. Sathi waited, her stomach twisting itself into knots.

'Sometimes it's hard to know who your family is, don't you think?' Maira asked.

Sathi didn't say anything.

'That's one thing I learned in life,' Maira continued. Her voice had a brittle quality that it didn't have before. 'Blood doesn't mean anything if there's no love behind it.'

Sathi suddenly felt stupid. She remembered how Maira's family had all but banished her because she married outside her religion. Compared to that she, Sathi, was lucky. 'I'm sorry,' she mumbled awkwardly. 'I wasn't thinking... What your family did... that's awful.'

Surprisingly, Maira laughed. 'Oh them,' she said dismissively. 'No, I rarely waste my time thinking about them anymore.' Her face clouded over once more. 'I was thinking about something else.'

When Sathi didn't respond, Maira glanced over at her teasingly. 'You're not really one for prying, are you?'

Sathi felt a reluctant smile tugging at her lips in response. 'It's not really any of my business.'

'I disagree,' Maira said firmly. 'You're like a daughter to me, and in my book a daughter has the right to ask as many questions as she likes.'

A pleasant heat warmed her veins at Maira's words. 'All right,' Sathi said in defeat, 'I admit I'm curious. What were you thinking of earlier when you said blood didn't matter?'

'Back when we were all living in Nelliampathi, when Aman and Zakiy were small, Narayan used to run a temple.' A wry smile crossed Maira's lips. 'You know how he is with his Hindu gods. He loved it, loved being immersed in that world of the gods. Anyway, he built this temple with another man, his... well, I'm not exactly sure how they're related, just that he's a distant relation from Narayan's father's side. Our families were very close, and like I said, Narayan and Kaka – that's what I used to call him – ran this temple together for years. I'm not sure exactly what happened, but something went wrong between them and the relationship began to sour. And suddenly one day we found out that Kaka had written the deed for the temple over to one of his sons and made Narayan an outsider in the very temple he helped to build. Kaka took away all his rights and told Narayan to get out.'

Maira closed her eyes and pinched the bridge of her nose with her thumb and forefinger. 'Narayan was utterly broken. He'd respected Kaka like a father, you see.'

'What did you do?'

Maira shrugged. 'What was there to do? The paperwork was airtight and besides, Narayan refused to fight Kaka over property. I still don't know what went wrong. Narayan wouldn't talk about it, and Kaka... well, let's just say I saw a whole different side to him when I confronted him about it.

'The hardest thing to bear about his betrayal was the way it ripped apart our families – especially the kids. Aman and Zakiy were always playing together with Kaka's kids. They loved spending time with each other, even though Kaka's kids were much older, almost grown men really. After Kaka and Narayan parted ways, though, he started being very unpleasant if any of us went there. Aman, in particular, would go there even after we told him not to – Kaka wasn't above taking a cane to the kids if they annoyed him, and we couldn't bear the thought of that happening to Aman or Zakiy. But Aman wouldn't listen to us. He snuck out all the time to go there. Narayan and I didn't have any peace of mind until he got back home.'

'Did something happen to Aman?' Sathi asked, uneasy for reasons she couldn't explain.

'No. I guess it sounds silly now but at the time it was nerve-racking, that's all.' Maira shook her head as though to shake off her fears, and then froze mid-motion. 'Well, there was that one time... but that wasn't anyone's fault.'

Sathi's feeling of foreboding increased, anxiety curling fists around her stomach. 'What happened?

Maira made a face, like she didn't want to talk about it. 'The last time he was there Aman fainted.'

Sathi stopped in her tracks, the breath rushing out of her. A strange heaviness pressed down on her, and for a moment the rich greenery around her dimmed in her vision. Her heart thudding in a place in her chest that seemed too high up to be normal, she asked, 'What was his name?'

'Hmm?'

'Kaka's name. What was it?'

Maira turned her quizzical gaze to Sathi. 'Bhaskar. But why– Sathi? Sathi, what's wrong?'

Her voice rose with worry – or maybe it just sounded that way because of the odd ringing in Sathi's ears.

Maira reached out and shook her shoulder. 'What's wrong?' she asked again.

Images from the dream she'd had flashed before Sathi's eye; the temple, the idols wreathed in garlands, the boy who collapsed among chairs, his body limp with unconsciousness, and lastly those terrible eyes, the familiar eyes that had haunted her nightmares for such a long time...

Her vision cleared enough to allow her to focus on Maira's worried face. The face of a mother who had, just minutes ago, been relating her sorrow over her son's debilitating illness. A mother who had suffered for years, all because of–

Working around the bile that filled her mouth, Sathi choked out, 'We need to find Narayan. I need to speak to you both.'

Chapter Nineteen

Moment of Truth

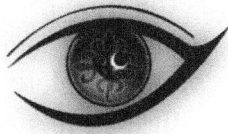

Sathi steepled her fingers together as she waited, forcing calm.

Back in the garden, Maira had searched her face for a moment before giving her a nod of acquiescence and dispatching herself to find Narayan. Sathi had followed slowly and made her way back to her room, trying hard to think clearly instead of freaking out. She needed to do this. She owed it to them.

A sob began to claw its way up through her throat, and she quickly shoved it back down. She couldn't go to pieces. Not yet. Too soon, a knock sounded at the door, and she straightened and psyched herself up briefly before calling out to them to come in.

Sathi stood as Narayan and Maira entered the room, then blinked in shock when Zakiy and Aman piled in after them, looking confused. The room suddenly felt very crowded with all those stared directed at her.

'Sathi?' Maira gazed at her in concern. 'You said you wanted to talk to us about something?'

She took a deep breath. *Keep it together*, she ordered herself. 'Yes. I need to tell you something... something about Aman's illness.' Her eyes flickered automatically to Aman, who looked confused. She could feel Zakiy's eyes on her, but she couldn't bear to look at him. Not now. She looked back at Maira and Narayan instead. 'I don't think Aman's schizophrenia was normal,' she began, directing her gaze to a spot somewhere between the two of them.

'What do you mean?' Narayan asked, puzzled.

Sathi glared down at her trembling hands. 'Vinod Kani was telling me the other day that his medication – the one he gave us for Aman the very first time we came here – shouldn't have worked so quickly. He was saying that the reason it worked so quickly must have been because Aman's body was already fighting against the disease. The... the manthram in the medicine was the final push his body needed to finally throw it off.'

For a few moments there was complete silence in response to her words. Then, speaking for the first time since he came into the room, Zakiy asked, 'What does that mean?'

She dared a peek at him and instantly wished she hadn't. His expression was hard, and the muscles in his jaw jutted out in stark contrast to his normally relaxed features. Looking at him, Sathi felt all the emotions she'd been tamping down rise to the surface.

Why? she shrieked at the unfairness of it all. *Why did this have to happen?*

Sathi gritted her teeth momentarily, trying to regain control. Just because she knew the reason for her mood swings, that didn't diminish their severity. 'The schizophrenia wasn't natural,' she repeated, her throat dry. 'Someone– something instigated it.'

'Spit it out, would you,' Zakiy snapped, his expression rigid with tension.

'Zakiy!' Maira reprimanded sharply, but Sathi knew this was only a fraction of the anger she deserved. Bleakly, she realised that none of them would forgive her once they knew the truth. For some reason, the realisation somehow made it easier to forge ahead. After all, what good would it do to hold back? 'I think Aman was given kaivisham. I think that's why he got ill.'

The pin drop silence lasted for about five breaths.

'That's impossible,' Zakiy said finally, exchanging glances with his mother.

Narayan, she noticed, hadn't said a word.

Sathi swallowed nervously. 'Vinod Kani says kaivisham can affect the mind in the worst way – it disrupts neuron activity and causes mental imbalance.'

'So?' Zakiy challenged. 'There are hundreds of people who suffer from mental illness. Are you saying they're all like that because they've been given kaivisham?'

Sathi hated the sarcastic edge to his voice. She knew it was simply a reflection of his pain, but that didn't halt the moisture stinging her eyes.

'No,' she said quietly. 'But Aman *has* been given kaivisham.'

'By whom?' he demanded in exasperation.

Sathi stared at him for a moment, committing his expression to memory; it showed anger, hurt, agony... but not hate. Not yet, at least.

She had asked herself earlier what she had to lose. Now, staring at Zakiy, at all of them, she was beginning to understand just exactly what she was going to lose. How ironic, how unfair that the answer to his question was going to cost her everything she had only just begun to value.

'The great-villains,' she told him.

His expression turned blank with shock. 'What?' he whispered, his horror-struck eyes never wavering from hers.

'What are you talking about?' Maira asked, tearing Sathi's gaze away from his tortured face.

Sathi flexed and unflexed her fingers. 'My mother's aunt and uncle. They're the ones behind this, I'm sure of it.' She described the dream she'd had, particularly focusing on the young boy in the room who had twitched, shuddered and finally collapsed in the middle of the room.

Maira gasped when she finished. 'That's exactly what happened to Aman, just like I was telling you earlier.'

'What happened to me?' Aman asked his mother.

Maira, still looking shaken, regarded Aman with worried eyes. 'I don't know if you remember... you used to be good friends with Kaka's sons, Karan and Girish. Once when you were at Kaka's house you fainted. It was after that you... you fell ill.'

'Oh.' That was all Aman said, lapsing back into perturbed silence.

'What does that have to do with anything?' Zakiy asked through gritted teeth. 'Kaka was like a family friend or something, wasn't he?'

Maira didn't reply, her gaze fixed on her husband's ashen face suspiciously.

Sathi was the one who answered. 'I don't know who he is to you, but I know one thing: Bhaskar is my mother's uncle. Karan and Girish are her cousins.'

Zakiy gaped at her for a few moments; she could only imagine what he was thinking. He held up his hands as though warding off her words. Then he shoved them through his hair, huffing out a frustrated breath. 'Okay, say you're right about the kaivisham part. And say this Kaka is the same person as the great-villain. But why should he want to hurt Aman?'

Sathi hesitated. This was the part she didn't understand, either.

How would her great-uncle profit from inflicting such a horrific illness on a ten-year-old?

'Narayan,' Maira said suddenly. She walked over to stand directly in front of her husband, her gaze boring into him. 'You know!' she accused, her eyes narrowing. 'Only you can answer your son's question. What happened fifteen years ago? Why did Bhaskar throw you out of that temple? Why did you insist that we run away from our home like fugitives? It's time you told us the truth, Narayan.'

Sweat beaded on Narayan's forehead, and his eyes roved pleadingly around the room as though searching for an escape route. Then his eyes focused on his sons, who were staring at him, stone-faced.

'Zakiy, take Aman outside, please.'

Zakiy began to protest, but Aman beat him to it. 'No, Dad,' he asserted in a calm, self-assured tone of voice that Sathi had never heard him use before. He put a hand on his brother's shoulder. 'We're not going anywhere. We have a right to know. *I* have a right to know,' he added more quietly.

Narayan's eyes were wide as he gazed at his elder son, speechless.

'They're not kids anymore,' Maira reminded him softly.

182

Narayan nodded almost vacantly in response to his wife's words, and squared his shoulders. 'You're right. It's time you knew the truth. All of you,' he added, looking up fiercely at Sathi, and she felt a shock thrill through her at the sweet realisation that, despite everything, Narayan viewed her as part of his family.

Then his shoulders slumped as he resigned himself to relating his story. 'Bhaskar Kaka and I have known each other for a long time – he was a distant cousin of my father's and the two of them were close friends, too. They were devout Hindus, and as Bhaskar and I were both drawn towards the divine, my father encouraged me to start a temple with him.' His expression clouded over. 'However, as I found out later, he and I had very different ideas on the divine. We were both blessed, you see, we had certain talents that showed that the gods had marked us with their favour.'

'Like what?' Zakiy asked, his intent gaze never straying an inch from his father's face.

'Our temple was one devoted to Devi, the mother goddess.' Zakiy's eyes flashed to Sathi, and she nodded slightly. The temple in Nelliampathi, the one near her great-aunt and great-uncle's house... Sathi was pretty sure it was the same as the one Narayan had built. Narayan hadn't noticed the exchange and continued, 'Every year, at the harvest festival, we would boil a small handful of rice to make *pongal* to offer to the goddess in her Bhadrakali form – as you know, Bhadra is Devi in her angry, blood-thirsty incarnation, when she drinks enemies' blood and wears their detached heads as garlands. But she is a righteous goddess; she will only take this form when roused by extreme injustice. It is a form she has to take in order to destroy enemies, because as Devi she is too much like a mother. Anyway, every festival day we would boil the pongal; when the water boiled over Bhaskar would scoop out a fistful of it to present to the goddess – with his bare hands.'

Sathi and Zakiy exchanged startled glances and Aman asked, 'How could he do that without scalding himself?'

'Because he was channelling the goddess,' Narayan replied simply.

Sathi made an embarrassing squeaking noise.

183

Narayan half-smiled. 'Devotees from all around us gathered on the day of the festival to witness this miracle for themselves.'

'But isn't it possible to get your skin used to very hot temperatures?' Sathi asked, recovering herself. She remembered a friend of her father's who'd taught her the basics of Indian cooking. 'I've seen someone pick up pots and pans that have been sitting on the stove on full heat for hours without injury. She's been doing it so long that her skin doesn't feel the heat or get burned by it.'

Narayan, instead of getting angry as she'd expected, nodded as though she'd made a good point. 'Yes, you're right. And I'm sure that less... scrupulous individuals have taken advantage of that fact to fool devotees. But Bhaskar was different. He could only touch the pongal when he was channelling the goddess. You could see physical changes when that happened; the posture, the stride, the facial expressions... they all change, they become foreign when another spirit enters you.'

You could hear the fervour, the wistful awe in his voice as he spoke – it was obvious he'd had personal experience of channelling gods, too.

'What could *you* do, Dad?' Aman asked in a hushed voice, his eyes wide with awe.

Narayan smiled at him, though the expression was bittersweet. 'I was blessed with healing powers. People would come to me seeking relief, and the goddess would reach through me and put *bhasma* on their foreheads, and they would find that they felt better almost immediately. There was no one I couldn't heal with her help... except for my own son.'

Aman crossed the room to comfort him when his father's voice broke, but Zakiy stayed where he was. He hadn't relaxed a muscle, and looked like he would snap at any moment. Narayan regained his composure. 'Anyway as time went on the two of us became more and more renowned for our abilities. People visited the temple in droves, and it flourished. After all, the gods gain their power from the unwavering faith of those who worship them.

'But as our popularity grew, Bhaskar changed. He revelled in his power, and he began to feel and act like *he* was a god himself. He began to view himself as someone to be worshipped. I didn't feel that way. Even when the people I healed said they would be grateful to me all their life, I told them that their gratitude was misplaced. I always reminded them that it was the goddess who healed them, and that it was her they owe their gratitude to. Bhaskar and I were simply human beings who'd been fortunate enough to be chosen by the goddess to carry out her will and help her devotees. We deserved no worship.' Narayan paused, troubled. 'But Bhaskar's power went to his head, and he began to make demands on the people to worship him.'

'Worse still, he began to order the gods to serve his own purposes. If someone stole a coconut from the temple grounds he would demand to the gods, 'Go, go and get revenge!' He would pray for all the wrong reasons, demanding money and wealth, and forcing the gods into doing dark deeds. I tried to point out the wrongness of what he was doing. I warned him that he would lose favour with the goddess if he carried on the way he was. But he was too drunk on power to listen to me. Then my fears came true. He began to gradually lose his goddess-given powers.' Narayan heaved a sigh. 'Come the festival one year, the goddess refused to enter his body, and he couldn't offer the pongal. In the end I put bhasma on his forehead, and the goddess finally graced us with her presence again. From them on I had to apply bhasma on Bhaskar before the goddess would allow him to channel her.

'Bhaskar was angry and humiliated, and he began to resent me for being more powerful than him. I tried to tell him that he only lost his power because of what he had been making the gods do, and that if he asked forgiveness and changed his ways the goddess would bless him again. I was the last person he would listen to, though, and he brushed me off and claimed he didn't need the gods anymore. His goals had shifted from the spiritual to the material, and he became consumed with accumulating wealth.

'Then one day an astrologer came and told us there was great treasure within the temple. Of course, as soon as Bhaskar heard this his eyes glazed over and he became obsessed with finding this so called treasure. He even managed to find some gold from somewhere, and claimed he'd had a divine vision showing that the rest of it was under the main pedestal of the goddess. He said our ancestors had buried it in the land the temple was built on. He wanted to break apart the pedestal and dig under the seat of the goddess for the rest of the gold.' Narayan's expression reflected the horror that spiked in his voice. 'I couldn't believe he would even consider doing such a thing, and I told him there was absolutely no way the goddess would want her temple uprooted in such a blasphemous way, treasure or no treasure.

'Bhaskar turned very nasty when I said that, and he said, 'You want it all to yourself, don't you, that's why you're acting so indignant. You bloody hypocrite!'

'I was shocked. I told him again, 'I don't want any treasure. If there had been a way to get it without breaking down the temple, I would happily let you have all the treasure down there. But I won't allow the temple to be ruined for the sake of gold.'

'Bhaskar didn't like that, and he yelled abuse at me before storming off. I didn't see him for more than a month after that. I was worried and upset; I had respected and loved him like a father, and it pained me to deny him anything. When he finally returned, I was so relieved that I didn't care about his cold expression when I ran out to greet him. Then he handed me some documents.

"What's all this?' I asked, surprised.

'He said, 'They are legal documents proving that my son Girish is the sole owner of this property and the temple built on it.'

'Shocked, I stared at the papers speechlessly. 'Bhaskar, what have you done?' I whispered, disbelieving.

'His expression was the cruellest I'd ever seen it. 'You are trespassing on private property. Please remove yourself immediately from these premises, or I will be forced to do it for you.' As he spoke, his two elder sons suddenly flanked him on both sides, no sign of friendliness on either of their faces even though we'd been close for years.'

Narayan paused to take a deep breath and then let it out again slowly. 'Since then I tried many times to talk sense into Bhaskar, but he refused to even meet me. In a single day, he made me an outsider in the temple the two of us built together. I couldn't bear it, especially when I heard that Bhaskar was going to demolish the temple in search of the gold. He'd convinced everyone about the treasure in the temple, and they all joined together to dig up the gold.'

Narayan's pained expression then changed, becoming filled with awe. 'But when the door to the pedestal was opened, they saw a miraculous sight; the mandapam was crawling with snakes, swarming around the idol of the goddess and hissing at anyone who tried to get closer to the statue.

'From then on it was impossible for anyone to conduct prayers or pujas there, and anyone who came close to the temple was scared off by snakes. The temple slowly crumbled to ruins.

Chapter Twenty

Serpent's Dance

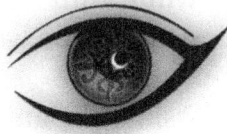

'Bhaskar's anger at me grew and grew,' Dad continued, 'because not only did he fail to get his gold, he also lost all the prosperity from the temple. And he held me responsible for all of it.' Dad sighed, and Zakiy thought he looked like he'd aged ten years with just one conversation. 'He never considered the possibility that all this happened because of his own greed. He did everything he could to make our lives miserable in Nelliampathi. I respected him as a father, and couldn't bear the thought of hurting him but-'

He faltered, glancing at Aman with pain in his eyes. 'If it's true that he did this to Aman...'

Zakiy unfroze, whipping his head around to stare at his father. 'Why would he do that? Aman was just a kid, he had nothing to do with all that temple business.'

Dad sighed. 'Bhaskar had so much anger and resentment towards me – I wouldn't be surprised if he targeted Aman out of spite. He knew nothing would hurt me more than if he harmed either of you.'

Zakiy's mind was racing ahead, trying to see the whole picture. 'But you don't know for sure he did this – that he gave Aman kaivisham?'

His father opened his mouth to reply, but Sathi's quiet voice got there first: 'I'm sure.'

He forced himself to turn in her direction. The sight of her vulnerable expression warred with the memory of the accusations she'd hurled at him the other day, and he fought back a grimace. 'How can you be sure?'

Sathi seemed to steel herself. 'Because when I was in their house they gave me stuff as well. At first to keep me quiet and docile, to stop me from reacting to all the disgusting stuff they did, and then after I'd left to discredit me if I talked about it to someone.'

'What do you mean, *discredit* you?'

She bit her lip. 'You've noticed how... how crazy I've been acting recently. My mood has been out of control, and my emotions have been all over the place. I haven't even felt like myself in months.'

Zakiy frowned. 'So they gave you kaivisham?' he asked. 'That's why you've been acting... oddly?'

She nodded mutely.

Some part of him felt relieved to have a reason for her erratic, unreasonable behaviour. But that didn't erase the hurt of the things she'd said and done. He glanced away, and his gaze fell on his brother. Aman was still absentmindedly patting Dad on the arm to comfort him, his expression confused and puzzled. Seeing that confusion was like a shot of ice to Zakiy's veins. Aman was one of the most brilliant people he knew; that confusion did not belong on his face. Staring at the shadow of what his brother used to be, Zakiy's vision became tinged with red. He was immobilised by the force of his fury, and through his outrage he reached a decision. All those years he'd spent discouraged that he couldn't do more to help his brother. A big part of that had been frustration that there was no tangible enemy he could fight and defeat. With his schizophrenia, Aman himself had been the enemy – how could you fight someone you loved, someone who wasn't responsible for his own actions?

But now, hearing that his illness may have been brought about by more than just cruel fate, hearing that another human being may have been responsible for his brother's suffering... Well, that shifted his whole perspective. Now he had only two goals. One, he would find out the truth for himself. And two, if it turned out that this Bhaskar was responsible, then...

Zakiy would make him pay.

His mind made up, he pulled himself back into the here and now and noticed Sathi watching him anxiously. His lips flattened into a flat line as he considered for the first time what his decision meant for her. He couldn't let himself think of that now. Zakiy turned to face his parents. Clearing his throat to get their attention, he told them flatly, 'I'm going back to Nelliampathi. I want to find out the truth for myself.'

Silent tears started coursing down Sathi's cheeks. Zakiy clenched his jaw and crossed his arms stiffly, stifling the impulse to go over to her.

'Absolutely not—' Dad began to thunder predictably, but Amma silenced him with a touch and glanced between Zakiy and Sathi with troubled eyes. 'What is going on with the two of you?'

Sathi just shook her head, and he said nothing.

'Zakiy,' Amma said, her sharp tone a demand.

He looked only at his mother as he resigned himself to the inevitable. 'Conflict of interest, I suppose you'd call it,' he said as glibly as he could. 'Sathi considers Bhaskar and that lot her family, and I... well, let's just say I disagree with that sentiment.'

Amma's face filled with compassion. She walked over to Sathi and put her arm around her. The affectionate gesture crumpled Sathi's tenuous control; she turned her face into Amma's shoulder and began to sob in earnest. 'Shh it's okay, let it all out,' Amma crooned, as though to a young child. She then threw Zakiy a look that plainly said, *Sort this out!*

Zakiy felt himself soften as he looked at his best friend tucked under his mother's arm, her face sodden with tears. He thought about everything she'd done for him, how much time and energy she'd sunk into making Aman better. He thought of how, even after finding out that her great-uncle may be responsible for Aman's illness, she'd had the decency to tell them everything. And if she was right about them giving her kaivisham, then wasn't she just as much a victim as Aman?

Zakiy strode over so he stood next to his mother and Sathi, and gently bumped his shoulder into Sathi's. 'Cheer up. Otherwise we'll have to turn a hose on you,' he threatened.

She gave a half-hearted chuckle that soon gave away to another sob. Zakiy sighed. 'Look, it's okay. I don't claim to understand what you're

going through – what with them being your only link to your mum...
well, I can't empathise, but I *can* sympathise.' Then his voice hardened.
'But if they're the ones who did this to Aman, I'm not going to let them
get away with it. I don't expect you to forgive me for that, seeing as
they're your family and everything, but–'

'No,' she interrupted him abruptly.

Zakiy stared at her. 'What?'

Sathi lifted her chin and rubbed at her face haphazardly, her
expression fierce. 'No,' she repeated, her voice strong and sure. 'You
were right all along, Zakiy. My mother's aunt and uncle may be my only
blood relatives, but they're not my family.' Fresh moisture dewed in her
eyes as she glanced at each of them. 'You guys are. You've treated me
like a member of your family, and it's about time I stepped up and
earned that honour.'

'Sathi, you don't need to earn anything,' Zakiy assured her, his own
voice tight with emotion. Joy was flooding through him as he gazed at
her determined expression. He had his best friend back...

Sathi shook her head emphatically. 'It's past time those vile monsters
were stopped. I'm coming with you to Nelliampathi. And together we're
going to make them regret the day they decided to mess with our family.'

Dark clouds had just begun to encroach on the drowsy horizon when
they pulled into the small hive of activity that was Nelliampathi town.
Sathi looked around in pleasure at her hometown as they left Toothless
parked at the side of the road and set out on foot to make the familiar
ascent up through the tea estate at the edge of town. They didn't speak
much as they walked, each consumed by their own thoughts. The
intoxicating scent of fresh tea washed over them, and Sathi sighed in
contentment at the familiarity of it.

When they reached the top of the small hill, Zakiy glanced at another
pedestrian walking towards them, and gave Sathi a sidelong glance. She
nodded minutely.

Zakiy stepped forward right the man's path, forcing him to stop. 'Excuse me,' Zakiy said, putting on a charming smile. 'Could you tell us the way to the Durga Devi Temple around here?'

The man stumbled back a step, all the colour leaching out of his face. 'You can't mean the one in Nelliampathi,' he said.

Zakiy nodded, making sure his expression reflected mild puzzlement.

The man shook his head emphatically. 'No, sir, don't go there. It is not fit for human beings, only demons and devils.'

'But it's a Devi temple, isn't it?' Sathi asked, her voice the perfect mix of confusion and apprehension.

'Yes, madam, it was but the great goddess Durga has left the temple – it was unfit for her. Now demons have the run of the place. No one can go inside the temple because of the vicious snakes.'

'Snakes?' Zakiy repeated, widening his eyes.

The man nodded. 'Yes, the temple is teeming with snakes. No one has the courage to go inside. Please, sir, do not go there,' he urged, concern for them leaking into his words.

They nodded and thanked him, then waited until he was out of sight before continuing along their original path. After a moment Zakiy asked quietly, 'What do you think?'

Sathi shook her head. 'I've been in there twice so far, once at night, and I've never seen anything.'

'Just rumours?' he suggested.

'Maybe. Though from what your father said...'

He made a vague grunting sound in response. They didn't speak again until they turned into the tiny pathway that led to Sathi's great-uncle's house and near it, the Devi temple. As they approached the temple, Sathi's eyes flicked to the house looming in the distance, away to the temple and then back to the house half a dozen times. Her movements became more and more jerky like she had to force herself to keep moving forward. Zakiy moved closer to her and casually linked his arm through hers. Sathi shot him a grateful smile.

The archway to the temple had cobwebs stretching across it from one wall to the other; the fine silky threads the brightest thing among the pitch black that was the inside of the temple. Squinting, they could just barely make out the different pedestals, each devoted to a different god or goddess. Both of their eyes searched anxiously for anything that might be slithering around on the ground. Sathi and Zakiy exchanged a look filled with trepidation and stepped inside the archway.

For a few moments they stood still, blinking as their pupils slowly adjusted to the lack of light. Darkness hung over the various pedestals like a living thing, and the unlit oil lamps spread around haphazardly everywhere seemed to emphasise it. Sathi shivered as she took in the deserted temple and remembered how it had looked in her dream, when the lamps had been lovingly lit and the gods had been offered prayers with garlands of flowers and incense sticks. The reason for the temple's current state made bile rise to her throat.

Zakiy tugged on her arm and she followed his gaze to the main pedestal. It was shut, immersed in shadows within shadows. Sathi gulped and said a quick prayer to Devi. Then, as one, they moved towards it.

The dust was a thick sheet coating the wooden double door and the three steps that led up to it were covered in the same way. A dead spider had its legs tangled up in the cobwebs that hung from the ceiling.

Zakiy reached over, his hands shaking, and flung the doors open. Taking a deep breath, the two of them leaned inside to peer into the tiny room that held the main figurine of the goddess. Sathi stared in wonder at the statue; even with the opaque layer of grime obscuring the face, the power that exuded from it was unmistakeable. It showed the goddess seated atop a magnificent bronze lion, a sword in her hand and her expression strong and serene. Entranced, Sathi walked forward to get a closer look but Zakiy's words stopped her.

'Did you hear that?' he said in a hushed voice as his eyes roved around the floor of the pedestal.

Now that he'd pointed it out she could hear it too. A vague rusting noise was coming from a spot just behind the goddess statue, getting louder as though–

'Argh!' Zakiy yelled, yanking her with him as he jumped back.

Sathi felt her expression freeze in a mask of shock as the cobra uncoiled itself from the corner where it had been waiting, and slowly advanced towards them. Heart thundering in her chest, she suddenly understood what the phrase "rabbit caught in the headlights" truly meant. Her muscles frozen in place, she could only watch in terror as death approached.

Once the snake reached the statue, though, it paused and lifted itself up, the fine membrane of its hood spreading out as it gazed up at the goddess. Then it abruptly turned and slithered towards the open doorway in a movement so rapid and graceful that they had barely enough time to flinch back another step. Even in the dim lighting, the serpent's sleek scales shone a brilliant bronze as it slithered out and down the steps.

For a few minutes the only sound was that of their beating hearts, unnaturally loud in their ears. Sathi could feel Zakiy trembling next to her, or maybe it just was her trembling. She really couldn't tell at the moment.

'Guess they weren't just rumours, huh?' Sathi finally managed to huff out.

Zakiy made a strangled noise. 'Yeah. Though it wasn't exactly the nest of snakes everyone claimed.'

Despite his nonchalant words, he peered apprehensively into the dark corners of the room. She was too worried herself about any more surprise visitors to tease him for it.

Sathi turned her attention back to the figurine of Devi, reaching out tentatively to rub off some of the grime from the goddess's face. Her goddess...

'The warrior goddess,' Zakiy said suddenly from behind her, his voice thoughtful.

Sathi glanced back at him. 'Huh?'

'Durga devi,' he said, nodding to the statue. 'She's the warrior goddess, riding into battle riding a lion and wielding her sword to defeat evil.'

He smiled at her, though she thought there was a hint of nervousness hiding under the surface. Sathi turned back to face the statue. It was so wrong, she thought, that a temple could be in such ruin, and that a beautiful statue like this could be so badly neglected. Even after clearing away some of the dirt, the goddess's face was still deep in shadow.

On impulse she scanned the floor near the statue and found an abandoned matchbox. She stooped to pick it up, and her eyes fell on an oil lamp placed at the goddess's feet. Sathi managed to locate a small stub of a wick among the grime, and held a lit match to it, watching with satisfaction as the flame grew in strength. It wouldn't last long without any oil, but for now it was good enough. That small orb of light transformed the whole room, and best of all, lit up the statue so that the warrior goddess's face was awash with a soft, flickering light.

As though in response to the warmth of the flame that was causing shapes to dance across the room, corresponding warmth was spreading in her chest, finally dislodging that hard ball of grief and anger she had been carrying around for so long. The relief was so great that it brought a smile to her face.

Without turning, she said quietly, 'I meant what I said, you know.'

Zakiy waited, not even sounding like he was breathing.

Sathi felt a wave of remorse for the hurt she had caused him and turned so that he would be able to read the truth in her eyes. 'I'm not going to make excuses for them anymore,' she told him steadily, her eyes completely dry. 'Everything they've done – the manipulation, what they did to Maya – it all pales in comparison to what they did to Aman. I... I can't even imagine being so twisted that you'd something so vile to a child, out of spite. That's something inexcusable. Unforgivable.'

Sathi had watched him as she spoke, and with every word a strange kind of happiness had begun to grow in his expression; no, happiness was the wrong word. It was a deep, fierce sort of joy, one that erased all the pain and anguish that had been darkening his face. With a jolt she realised that she was looking at her old Zakiy again – her cheeky, exasperating, indomitable best friend.

Zakiy stepped closer to her. 'Promise?' he whispered, holding out his hand.

Sathi smiled at him and put her palm on his. 'I promise. I will be with you every step of the way to avenge what they did to Aman – my brother.'

'Hey, he was my brother first,' he teased weakly despite the fact that his voice broke.

Sathi cut him a look. 'Then you'd better learn to share.'

He chuckled, and for a while they just basked in the sweet knowledge that their friendship was intact.

'So the battle is on, then?' Zakiy asked after a few minutes.

Together they turned to face the warrior goddess again, their shoulders brushing.

'You bet,' Sathi told him.

PART TWO

Chapter Twenty-One

Lion's Den

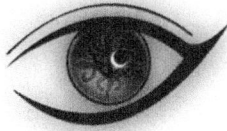

Zakiy looked over his shoulder, through the thick trees to the other side of the driveway where Sathi had insisted on waiting for him. Even though he couldn't actually see her he couldn't deny the comfort the knowledge she was nearby brought him.

Taking a deep breath, he turned to face the door. He lifted his fist and rapped once with his knuckles.

After a moment's delay the door was flung open by a man whose closely cropped hair had completely greyed over. 'Yes? Can I help you?'

Hate was a gushing river of fire through his veins as he stared at this man who could be none other than Bhaskar. Even if he wasn't responsible for ruining Aman's life, it was indisputably true that he'd deceived and betrayed Zakiy's father, driving him out of the temple and home he loved.

Zakiy forced his resisting lips to smile. 'Hello, sir. You may not know me, but I know you. May I come in?'

Confused, the great-villain let him in and led him to a rather generic living room, where he was joined by an old woman with a sour expression on her face. 'Who's this, Bhaskar?'

'My name is Zakiy,' he answered. 'I'm your friend Narayan's son.

He watched closely as the great-villains exchanged a startled look. Bhaskar recovered first, adopting an unctuous smile that made Zakiy want to cringe away from him.

Instead, he allowed Bhaskar to fling an arm around his shoulder and steer him to the sofa. 'How are you, moné? How many years it has been since we last saw you! How is dear Narayan? And Aman?'

It galled that he acted as though Zakiy's mother didn't exist – she was only a lowly Muslim after all. But worse than that his blood boiled at the casual way he asked after Aman, as though he had the right to even utter Aman's name. Saliva gathered in Zakiy's mouth, and he had to force himself to swallow instead of spitting in the miserable wretch's face.

'They're well,' Zakiy said slowly, keeping his eyes trained on the great-villain. He did not want to miss even a minuscule change in his carefully nonchalant expression. 'Considering.'

Bhaskar's eyebrows rose in polite puzzlement. 'Hmm?'

Zakiy leaned back lazily, propping one elbow up on the back of the sofa. 'Well, yeah. Considering what you did to Aman.'

The crone let out a low oath and her gaze jumped to her husband, whose expression had frozen as though determined to give nothing away.

Zakiy's hands curled into fists as the great-villains' reaction confirmed his fears. So Sathi's suspicions had been right. He couldn't believe it. How could they even live with themselves? Bile rose in his mouth again, and he resisted the urge to leap over and strangle the two of them with his bare hands. Zakiy fought to keep his temper under control, and finally he could speak again.

'Are you wondering how I found out?' he enquired in a conversational tone.

The great-villains exchanged the tiniest of glances, as though they were calculating how to proceed. Then Bhaskar gazed back at him in concern, or something designed to look very much like it.

'Zakiy, moné, I think you must be tired from the long journey.' He nodded to a tired-looking woman who had appeared in the doorway off the living room, and she disappeared inside again. 'Let us get you something to drink first.'

'Yes, moné. Here, have this,' the crone simpered, taking the glass the servant had brought and holding it out to him.

Oh, they're good, Zakiy thought. He smiled, making no move to accept the drink. There was no warmth in his expression. 'What, no watermelon juice?' he mocked, raising his eyebrows.

Shock flitted across their faces; they were panicking a little now, trying to work out how he knew so much.

'We don't have any in the house at the moment,' Bhaskar said cautiously, 'but we can send out for some if that's what you prefer.'

'The watermelon or the kaivisham?' Zakiy queried.

He took a grim satisfaction from their *Oh crap how does he know?* faces.

Then: 'Kaivisham? What are you talking about, moné?'

Finally tiring of the pretence, Zakiy leaned forward. 'I know you gave Aman kaivisham all those years ago. I know you're the ones responsible for making him a schizophrenic.'

They didn't even flinch this time – just exchanged looks of pity. Bhaskar reached across and patted his knee. 'Moné, you're obviously very upset. Aman's illness was very unfortunate, and you were both very young when it started, of course. I can see how upsetting that must be for you still. And of course,' he added, a sly note entering his tone, 'dear Narayan had to regrettably leave Nelliampathi, his home for so long...'

Disgust rolled over Zakiy in a suffocating wave and he jerked to his feet, throwing off the placatory hand. 'Do NOT insult my intelligence. You drove my dad out of the temple he loved, you poisoned my brother and now you're acting the innocent? Well guess what?' He lowered his voice to menacing whisper. 'I. Don't. Buy. It. I know what you've done, and you mark my words because I'm going to make you pay for it!'

The crone hissed, 'How dare you speak to–?'

'Shut up, Goudhamy!' Bhaskar barked, his composure breaking momentarily as he glared his wife into submission. She looked shocked, taken aback, and then scowled balefully at Zakiy.

Bhaskar's turned his attention back to Zakiy, and his expression was guarded, thoughtful. 'Moné,' he began carefully, 'I can see that you're very upset, but I cannot let you disturb my family like this with wild accusations. Please leave now, or I will ask my son to call the police.'

As he spoke a man had slunk into the room; he was solidly built, and his arms were positioned oddly, almost like he was a... bodyguard.

Zakiy looked from the menacing expression on the son's face, to Goudhamy's resentful glare and finally the great-villain's calculating stare.

A tidal wave of unease and revulsion swooped low in his stomach, and he turned and left without another word.

Sathi paused for the hundredth time to anxiously scan the empty pathway and then went back to her nervous pacing. Her ears were strained so hard to hear the slightest noise over the chirping birdsong that she nearly jumped a foot in the air when she at last caught the sounds of footsteps stomping in her direction. She shrank back under the cover of a large jackfruit tree, peering through the fronds with her heart in her throat. The footsteps became louder.

She nearly cried out in relief when she glimpsed Zakiy emerge through the thick bushes and look around. 'I'm here!' she hissed from her hiding spot.

He spotted her and walked over, whispering, 'You could have stayed at the resort. You didn't need to hide out here.'

Sathi shook her head adamantly. 'I wasn't going to let you go alone – I should have come in with you,' she muttered, ashamed.

He brushed off some dry leaves from the top of her head, looking unusually grim. 'Stop it. We agreed this was better, remember?'

'What happened?' she asked, scanning his strained expression.

'Not here.' He glanced back at the pathway and shuddered slightly. 'Let's go back to the resort.'

After hours of discussing strategy they had come to the decision that a direct attack was best in terms of finding out whether the great-villains were responsible for Aman's illness. Zakiy had told her it would be better for him to go alone that first time – her presence would complicate matters and Sathi, thinking of her great-uncle's cold, calculating gaze, had been far too revolted at the idea of facing him to argue with Zakiy. Much.

They soon reached the resort where she had resumed work as cook-cum-waitress. She closed the door of her cottage room and turned to face him. 'Talk.'

Zakiy slowly shook his head. 'It was them, Sathi. They all but admitted it.' He told her everything that had happened, from Bhaskar's fake concern to Goudhamy's open animosity and Girish's blank expression.

It felt as though her spinal cord had been injected with ice. She realised then that she'd been holding out a tiny shred of hope that her mother's aunt and uncle hadn't done such a heinous thing.

Zakiy was watching her sympathetically. 'I'm sorry.'

That shook her out of her stupor. 'What? My disgusting excuses for a great-uncle and great-aunt make your brother into a psychiatric patient and *you're* apologising?'

He flushed and mumbled, 'I don't like upsetting you.'

A rush of warmth flooded her, and for what was probably the first time she realised what the true meaning of family was. The news that had seemed so heart-breaking when she first heard it, the news that the great-villains had indeed been responsible for bringing about such a cruel fate on a ten year old child, no longer filled her with such pain.

On the contrary a fierce thirst took root in her – a thirst to make them pay for what they'd done.

'I won't let anything about them upset me anymore,' she promised him, and herself.

Zakiy searched her expression for a few moments, and seemed satisfied by what he found there. 'Okay.'

'So what are we going to do?'

'I want to know how they're doing it,' he said immediately, like he had spent a long time thinking about it. 'If you're right, and they *did* give kaivisham to you and to their daughter-in-law, then I want to know exactly how they're going about it.'

She looked at him expectantly. 'How?'

His face fell and he shrugged at her in a comically helpless way. 'I haven't worked out that part yet.'

Sathi chewed her lip, thinking back over the time she'd spent at their house. There had to be something there that could help them. Slowly, a memory surfaced. 'They used to go out together,' she remembered, looking up at Zakiy. 'Alone. They didn't want anyone with them then. I know because I offered to go with them once and they fobbed me off and manipulated me into staying behind.'

'Hmm... you reckon they might have gone to practice black magic then?'

She nodded slowly, still casting her mind back. 'I'm sure of it. The first time they went out alone while I was there was the day Girish and Maya were scheduled to go to dinner with Maya's friends. And you know she fainted so they couldn't go after all.'

'Did they go out like that again?'

'Yeah...' she scrunched up her nose, trying to remember. Then she gulped. 'The night they... uh, the night I left the house.'

Zakiy's eyes widened first in understanding, and then in horror. 'In other words the night Bhaskar almost raped Maya.'

She nodded weakly.

'So the two of them went out and got something to give Maya to make her go into that zombie state and go to Bhaskar's bedroom.'

'Twisted doesn't even begin to cover it, does it?' she said shakily.

'Nope.' His focus was far away though.

'What? What are you thinking?'

'I think I've got an idea to find out how they do it.' The ghost of a smile flickered across his features. 'But you're not going to like it.'

Apprehension fluttered in her stomach. 'What is it?'

Before he could answer a sharp, impatient knock came at the door. Sathi nearly growled at whoever it was to go away – then her boss appeared around the door. 'Sathi. Can I borrow you a minute?'

Tall with shoulder-length hair arranged into a careful bun, Nidhi was a fair and reasonable boss. She had been understanding when Sathi had to leave to go to Zakiy's house in Mysore, and had been pleased to reappoint her when she came back. Having said all of that though, she was a tough businesswoman and Sathi wasn't quite brave enough to follow her earlier impulse and yell at her to go away.

'No problem,' Zakiy said, jumping up and grinning at Sathi. 'I'll meet you at the campsite tonight.'

She almost threw something at his retreating back as he ambled out, whistling. The cheater! He knew how much she hated being kept in suspense like that.

'Sathi?' Nidhi raised her eyebrows enquiringly.

'Uh... right, sorry, what can I do for you?'

'Well, I wanted to introduce you to the new head cook since you'll be working together a lot from now on.' Nidhi gestured to someone standing just outside the doorway. 'This is Veena.'

The woman who came shyly into the room had a sweet-looking face was creased with worry-lines, and her eyes had dark shadows under them.

'Veena, this is Sathi,' Nidhi said briskly. 'Now Sathi, I know you worked this morning but can you help out with waiting tonight? Ravi's gone home because his baby's sick and we're a bit shorthanded.'

'Yeah, Ravi already asked me. No problem, I can cover.'

Nidhi nodded, looking relieved. 'Great. Right, I'll leave the two of you to get acquainted, shall I?'

She hurried out without waiting for an answer, and Sathi smiled at the quiet woman. 'Quick, isn't she?'

Veena's gaze rose to meet hers and she smiled back tentatively. 'Yes, but I like her.'

'So do I.' Sathi glanced at the clock and groaned. 'Nearly time for us slaves to get to work. Come on.'

They cut through the small resort, Sathi pointing out the gorgeous, unique cottages that formed the guest rooms along the way. The cottages were enveloped within the thick woods of Nelliampathi, teeming with both plant and animal life. Sathi waved at some of the regulars who knew her from before, stopping for a few moments to say a few words to some of them and introduce Veena. Then they headed over to the slightly larger structure that was the restaurant, through the dwindling lunch crowd and into the kitchen behind. It was mercifully quiet compared to the hullabaloo that was the restaurant. Sathi went over to a cupboard and rooted around for the last of the white chocolate and macadamia nut cookies she'd baked the day before.

She frowned down at the broken remains of it before offering the tin to Veena. 'Zakiy's obviously found my secret stash – this tin was full this morning. Or it could've been Ravi, actually. The pair of them clean out the kitchen before I can finish stocking it.' She shook her head as she took a piece herself.

Veena giggled, a sound that made her seem years younger than her appearance. 'Boys are like that. You'd think they have bottomless stomachs, to see the way they eat.'

'You sound like you have too much personal experience,' Sathi commented, starting to get plates out of a cupboard and stacking them on the counter nearest to the door.

'I have two younger brothers and trust me – growing up doesn't mean anything when it comes to men and their appetites.' Veena laughed and opened a nearby drawer, pulling out handfuls of cutlery.

'So are you new to Nelliampathi?'

The older woman paused and a strange, wistful expression crossed her face. 'I guess you could say that – though Nelliampathi isn't new to me.' Seeing Sathi's confused expression, she smiled. 'I used to live here when I was a young girl like you.'

Sathi was about to ask why she'd left when Jagdish, a very newly appointed member of their wait staff, came rushing in. 'Sathi! A huge crowd of tourists just came in and they're demanding all sorts of specialties. I can't deal with them on my own!'

Sathi nodded swiftly, setting down the last of the plates. She caught up a notepad and pen and stuck them into his hands. 'Alright, you think you can handle taking the drink orders?'

He nodded, but looked scared to death at the prospect. Sathi swallowed a grin and glanced at Veena. 'You okay for us to leave you for a bit?'

'Don't worry about me,' she said, already filling a massive wok with oil and expertly balancing it on top of the lit stove.

Sathi turned back to Jagdish. 'Right. Take a deep breath and plunge straight in,' she advised him, grabbing another pad for herself. Face pale but set with determination, Jagdish marched through the door, the notepad sticking out in front of him like some sort of shield.

'That's the spirit,' she murmured, smiling faintly as she followed him out.

The three of them regrouped in the kitchen nearly five hours later, tired out but panting with a sense of accomplishment. The last of the satisfied customers had left, and they were finally enjoying a brief moment of peace. Sathi looked at Jagdish. 'Well done. You were great out there.'

He beamed and flushed dark with pleasure. 'Thanks. I don't think it will be so bad again.'

Veena nodded. 'You're right. That first time is always the worst, and now it'll only get easier.'

Sathi smiled teasingly at her. 'You weren't so bad yourself. Who are you, superwoman?'

Veena had been truly amazing, the way she singlehandedly managed the orders Sathi and Jagdish kept bringing through to her in a continuous stream. Sathi had returned several times to the kitchen to try and help her out, but Veena had kept shooing her back out, assuring her she could handle it.

'I'm used to cooking for hungry boys,' Veena replied, her eyes twinkling.

'Of course, we've only won a battle – the war is still on!' Sathi said, glancing around at the kitchen that had been spotless just that afternoon and was now teeming with dirty dishes. Every surface was covered with half-full pans or vegetable waste or open spice bottles.

The three of them sighed, glanced at each other, and wordlessly began to clear up the room.

When the kitchen was gleaming again they locked up and exchanged tired goodnights before dispersing. Sathi headed towards the familiar woods that were deliciously cool at this time of night. She followed the well-trodden path to where Zakiy had set up his tent. Even though there was a huge house belonging to his parents in Nelliampathi, he hated staying there because of the bad memories with Aman. So he camped out in the woods whenever possible, and Sathi had set up her own tent next to his. When she entered the campsite a small fire was already crackling cheerfully. Zakiy had balanced a small saucepan of milky cocoa on top of it, and she had to smile at the sight. It was a tradition of theirs now.

He glanced up as she went to the hamper hanging on a nearby tree and began rummaging around. 'What are you looking for?'

'Marshmallows,' she replied without turning around.

There was the sharp ripping sound of a plastic packet being pulled open. 'Way ahead of you,' Zakiy said smugly as he held it out to her.

She made a face at him but accepted the packet of mushy goodness and sat down. She watched silently as he poured out the steaming cocoa into two mugs and handed her one. She tipped in a generous amount of tiny marshmallows into both cups.

'So,' she said eventually, 'what's this idea you've got that I'm not going to like?'

He peered at her over the rim of his cup. 'You know I want to know how the great-villains get their hands on kaivisham?'

She nodded.

'And you said they probably do it when they go out alone together?'

'Yeah.'

Zakiy said in a rush, 'I want to follow them when they go out again.'

She choked on her mouthful of cocoa and started coughing. Zakiy thumped her back, but she brushed him off and stared incredulously at him. 'Let me get this straight,' she said once she could breathe properly, 'you want to play spies?'

He gave her a reproachful look. 'Not *play*.' Then he grinned. 'We'll actually *be* honest-to-God spies.'

Sathi buried her head in her hands, beyond words.

'All right, all right, kidding aside... Think about it! If we follow them we can find out exactly how they do it.'

She lifted her head to look at him. He was almost feverish with excitement. 'Okay, say for one moment that your idea makes any kind of sense. Are we supposed to tail them day and night? Set up twenty four hour surveillance outside their house until they decide to go out and do some black magic?'

A chagrined expression crossed his face. 'Well, I've been thinking about that as well...'

Sathi groaned.

'No, hear me out! We won't have to wait long for them to go out again. In fact, I wouldn't be surprised if they go out as early as tomorrow morning.'

'What are you talking about?'

'Well, there's someone they're very angry with at the moment. They probably won't wait long before they try and give kaivisham to him.'

She frowned at him for a few moments before the lines on her forehead slowly straightened out. She regarded him thoughtfully. 'You.'

'Me,' he agreed. 'I saw their faces. They were so shocked, shocked and angry that I knew their most vile secrets and laid them out like that. They're probably thinking up all sorts of horrible things to do to me,' he added cheerfully.

For a moment fear and rage clutched her throat and cut off her ability to breathe. The thought of them harming her had been painful, heart breaking... the thought of them harming Zakiy made her see red and want to destroy everything in sight. Starting with the great-villains' necks.

Zakiy nudged her with his shoulder. 'Don't worry. Knowledge is power – and now we both know everything they can't affect us so much. Especially now that they can't keep us divided anymore.'

'Huh?'

'Well, think about it. We haven't exactly been acting like friends these last few months. We've been at each other's throats all the time. I think they drove a wedge between us to keep our attention away from what they did to Aman.'

Thinking over his words, Sathi realised the truth in them. Her weird mood swings and touchiness had turned what was a close friendship on its head, making them both miserable and unable to confide in or gain support from each other. But now that they knew kaivisham was the cause of it at least they knew what they were fighting against.

It was the difference, Sathi speculated, between wrestling with empty air and grappling with something invisible but with substance. Elusive as it was, you could grasp it and control it, fight against it.

It made a world of difference.

She exhaled and nodded. 'All right,' she said. 'What's the plan?'

Chapter Twenty-Two

I Spy

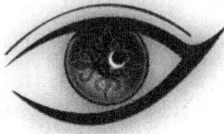

'Zakiy,' she growled, 'I *cannot* believe you bought us kids' walkie-talkies!'

She could almost picture his injured expression. 'What exactly are you annoyed about? The fact that I got us walkie-talkies, or that I got us kids' ones?' he demanded, his voice weirdly muffled through the toy's tinny speakers.

Sathi frowned down in his general direction since she couldn't actually see him. 'Both.'

It was the next morning, and they had been "staking out" the great-villains' house since dawn. As usual, Zakiy had been diligent to a fault in organising the whole venture. He had dragged her out of bed kicking and screaming before the sun had even risen and alternately encouraged and taunted her all the way to the house. Then he had somehow persuaded her to climb up into a tree, blathering something about "vantage point" and "bird's eye view", and hid himself down in the bushes below her. Now tired and hungry with fire ants crawling all over her, she really wasn't in the mood to play with walkie-talkies.

Zakiy ignored her grumpiness. 'Still nothing to report, m'lady. Will keep you updated on the G-V's whereabouts. Over.'

Despite herself, she smiled. She had to admit it was good to see him back to his normal, mad self. G-V. Sathi shook her head. Honestly.

For another half an hour or so they waited in silence. Then a very subdued voice came through her walkie-talkie. 'Sathi?'

'Yup?'

'Do you have anything to eat?'

Sathi rolled her eyes. 'No I must have forgotten to pack a picnic lunch while you were waking me up at an unholy hour.'

'Fine, be that way.' He sulked for a few moments before asking hopefully, 'You don't have any ripe mangoes hanging on that tree, do you?'

Her lips twitched. 'No, mangoes usually don't grow on jackfruit trees. I have a jackfruit hanging here, though, about two, three times the size of your head. Shall I toss it down to you?' she asked sweetly.

'Er, no, that won't be necessary,' he said hurriedly.

Another five minutes passed in silence. Sathi was just about to relent and suggest that they take a break from their stakeout when Zakiy gave a sudden shout.

'They're here!' he said, his voice rich with excitement.

Sathi took a deep breath and leaned over carefully. Sure enough, her great-aunt and great-uncle had come out of the house and were slowly making their way towards the waiting auto-rickshaw at the end of the driveway. Emotions threatened to overwhelm her, but she pushed them down. She couldn't afford to let them control her now.

'Okay, I'm going after them,' Zakiy whispered urgently. 'Follow the plan, wait a minute then meet me at the rendezvous spot. Over and out.'

'Wait. Zakiy!' she hissed, but there was nothing but a weird crackling noise from the walkie-talkie. Sathi cursed. She squinted down anxiously and spotted a bushy brown head bobbing between the greenery as he followed the great-villains. As soon as they got into the auto Sathi slipped down from the tree and looped her way around the clump of trees, trying to be stealthy as well as fast. She reached the end of the great-villains' driveway and cautiously looked around. The welcome sight of the auto-rickshaw turning the corner met her, and she started sprinting. A second rickshaw was idling at the top of the hill and Zakiy leaned out of it to gesture urgently at her, tapping an imaginary watch on his wrist.

Sathi rolled her eyes again even as she ran. Always the drama queen. She reached the rickshaw and pulled herself into it. Zakiy immediately turned to the driver of the rickshaw. 'Right, Raju! The chase is on.'

Raju lost no time in obliging, and the rickshaw began to bump its way down the hill.

'They didn't spot you, did they?' Sathi asked, her heart still racing.

He shook his head. 'Please. Don't insult my ninja skills.'

She glanced at the driver and lowered her voice. 'Won't he think it's odd that we're following them?'

'Nah. He thinks we're child genii who graduated early and became police detectives.'

Sathi eyeballed him.

'Oh all right! I told him they're our grandparents and that we want to surprise them for their wedding anniversary.'

She nodded and sat back against the seat of the rickshaw. Raju made sure to keep the other rickshaw in sight but otherwise left a good gap between them. Despite that her pulse was jumping madly in her wrists and she had to literally sit on her hands to stop them shaking. It was all right when it was more of a joke, with toy walkie-talkies and tree climbing. But now that it was real... she was beginning to lose her nerve.

Sathi closed her eyes and forced her breathing to calm. She made herself think of all the horrible things the great-villains had done, one by one. Maya. Narayan. Aman.

Out of all those what the two of them had done to Aman kept circling through her mind. A ten-year-old boy. That's whose life they had played with, using dark magic and spite to create a toxic stew that had culminated in the mental illness of a child. There was no forgiveness for that. No mercy.

Sathi opened her eyes.

Their auto rickshaw had come to a stop. She stuck her head out, and then withdrew it just as quickly. 'Quick! Go behind that wall,' she urged Raju, pointing.

Zakiy pulled on her arm. 'What? What's going on?'

'Ajay. He's standing next to their rickshaw. He must have been driving it,' she realised, twisting around in the seat to check that they were out of his eyesight.

'Who is he? Does he know what they do?'

'I don't know. He's like the great-villains' own personal rickshaw driver or something. He knows me, so we can't let him see us.' She started chewing her lips – this idea was looking more ridiculous by the minute.

'Chill,' Zakiy told her, peering out at Ajay with narrowed eyes. Then he met her anxious gaze. 'Plan B?'

Sathi glanced at the bulging backpack strapped to his back and sighed. She gave him a resigned grin. 'Let's do it.'

Ajay was slouched against his rickshaw and staring moodily at the ground like it had offended him. He hardly noticed an elderly couple clad in the dark orange clothes of devout temple-goers as they plodded their way past him and inside the temple grounds. Once they were behind the gate and out of sight they exchanged relieved glances and the old man reached up to scratch the edges of his grey beard like it was irritating his skin. If you looked closely you could see hints of brown underneath his silvery hair. As they followed the stream of devotees heading towards the pedestals of the gods, he leaned close to the woman and said in a voice that didn't reflect his age, 'That wig suits you – you should keep it.'

'Shut up!' Sathi whispered out of the corner of her mouth. Her legs were too trapped in this contraption he'd made her wear to kick him. Plus that would kind of ruin their cover.

For once he actually listened to her, and they allowed themselves to be carried along on the tide of the crowd while they kept their eyes peeled for the great-villains. Finally Sathi clutched his arm and nodded towards an out-of-the-way pedestal. Her great-aunt and great-uncle were standing outside, their eyes shut and palms pressed together in prayer. Watching their lips move silently, a surge of revulsion and hatred rose in Sathi's chest, surging upwards to form bile in her mouth.

She felt a mad urge to tear off her wig and stalk up to them. To announce to everyone what they'd done – the evil they were capable of.

Zakiy's hand closed over her wrist and gripped tight as though he knew exactly what she was thinking. He gave her a look that somehow managed to convey both understanding and a warning, and tugged her behind a nearby shed that was deserted and more importantly out of sight of the great-villains.

'How can they do horrible things and then pray?' Sathi exploded. 'Don't they have any shame?'

Zakiy's expression was tight with the same disgust she felt. 'I think it's the other way around. They pray to make those horrible things happen, things that will turn their selfish wants into reality.'

She went still as the impact of his words sank in. 'Oh God, you're right.' She slumped against the wall, tasting bile. 'It's horrible. It's so twisted to pray to gods to help you do evil.'

'That's the basis of black magic though, isn't it?' Zakiy peered out from behind the shed to check on the G-Vs. Then he glanced back at her. 'You force the gods to do your bidding, to turn into an evil aspect that harm people instead of protecting them.'

'Like White Beard told me once,' Sathi recalled. 'Your dad's temple in Nelliampathi – he said it fell to ruin because the people running it – as in, Bhaskar – started abusing the gods, using them for the wrong reasons... White Beard said the gods abandoned the temple after a while.'

'I don't blame them,' Zakiy retorted grimly. Then he stiffened. 'Something's happening.'

She leaned her head around his so they could both watch as the great-villains moved around to the doorway of the pedestal and stood to one side of it, heads bowed, hands clasped, the picture of devotion. As they watched the priest came up to the doorway with *prasadam* in his hands – a small amount of some of the flowers, *chandanam* and saffron powder and a banana – which had been offered to the gods with prayers. Sathi waited for them to accept it and then leave like the rest.

216

Then something interesting happened: instead of taking the offerings from the priest, Bhaskar gave an almost imperceptible shake of the head and laid a hand on his wife's arm and steered her away. Sathi exchanged puzzled glances with Zakiy, and they followed the great-villains back to where Ajay was waiting with the rickshaw. As soon as they got in, Sathi and Zakiy marched to Raju, who had parked his rickshaw out of sight and was waiting for them.

'We need you to follow them again, mate,' Zakiy said, quickly following her in.

Raju glanced back, puzzled, as he cranked up the starter lever. 'You did not surprise your grandparents?'

'Oh trust me, they'll be getting the surprise of their lives,' Zakiy said tersely, leaning forward to keep an eye on Ajay's rickshaw.

Sathi shivered at his expression. His face was cold and harsh, emotionless. Nothing like that carefree boy she'd met less than a year ago.

She turned her face to watch the sleepy town rush past. Had that boy ever existed though? she asked herself. Hadn't the cheery smile just been a cover to hide his pain, to get away from the constant misery his life would have been if not for that small escape?

The great-villains just went straight back home.

Sathi couldn't understand it. She'd been so sure their outings had been to procure whatever disgusting items they needed for more black magic. But all they'd done was go to a temple!

'What now?' Zakiy asked in a low voice.

'I don't know... maybe they'll go out again?'

Even as she said it though she knew it was unlikely. Had she been wrong then, about those two times when they'd left the house on their own?

Zakiy shook his head. 'I don't think so. No, I think whatever they wanted to do they've accomplished today.'

'We must have missed something then.'

'But we were with them the whole time.'

'I know but what else?' Sathi asked, starting to feel frustrated.

He didn't reply, just tapped his fingers against his knee as he thought. Then they abruptly stilled. 'That exchange between the great-villain and the priest - what was that about?'

'I wondered the same thing. Also, why didn't they take the prasadam?'

Zakiy shrugged, no closer to answering that than she was, but Raju spoke up unexpectedly. 'Are you talking about the priests at the temple I just took you to?'

The two of them turned to stare silently at him, and his skin slowly darkened. 'I could not help overhearing,' he appealed.

Sathi batted his apology away. 'Never mind that, what do you know about the priests there?'

He wouldn't meet their gaze. 'I have heard other passengers speak about that temple when I take them there. They say it is somewhere you can pray to get relief from illness or maladies that were not naturally caused.'

Sathi glanced at Zakiy excitedly; "not naturally caused" – could he be talking about kaivisham?

Raju continued, 'Some of the priests there tell those people not to take the prasadam.'

'Why?'

'I am not sure. I think it is because leaving it at the temple will make sure the black magic does not go back to those people.'

'Huh,' Sathi said, chewing her lip. 'So the temple helps people who are victims of black magic?'

'Yes,' Raju said, looking relieved that she understood.

She looked across at Zakiy. He clearly didn't know what to make of this new information either.

'You will go in to surprise your grandparents now?' Raju enquired.

Zakiy huffed out a mirthless laugh. 'I think we're going to have to postpone that, Raju.'

And he gave the confused rickshaw driver directions back to the resort.

Chapter Twenty-Three

The Root

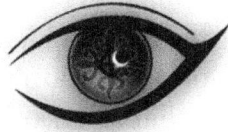

Veena was wiping down the counters when they went into the kitchen of the resort to try and scrounge some lunch.

'Oh hey,' Sathi greeted her. 'Veena, you haven't met Zakiy, have you?'

'Ah, so this is the cookie-stealer,' Veena said, smiling at him.

Zakiy grinned. 'That's me. And it doesn't have to be cookies – no food is safe from me!'

'Then it's a good thing I hid that chicken curry I made earlier,' Veena said. 'I was saving it because I had a feeling two little scavengers would come wandering in at some point,' she added, her eyes twinkling as she lifted a big saucepan from a bottom cupboard.

Sathi threw her arms around Veena and squeezed the breath out of her. 'You're the best!'

Zakiy sniffed eagerly at the curry, and Veena tried to fend them both off, laughing. 'I agree! How did you know I was craving this?'

'We'll just call it intuition.' Veena brought the curry to the table and Sathi snagged a half-full packet of the slightly sweet white bread that was available in India. On second thought, she went back and grabbed a second packet – Zakiy would inhale the first one in seconds.

Then the two of them fell on the food like they hadn't eaten for days, while Veena watched on indulgently.

Jagdish came in and said someone was outside who wanted to speak to Veena. She frowned. 'Who is it?' she asked.

Jagdish shrugged. 'He wouldn't say. He just said he had to speak to you urgently.'

Veena bit her lip, her expression clouding over, but she followed Jagdish out of the room.

While Sathi was worried about whatever was making Veena so anxious, she was glad of the opportunity to speak to Zakiy alone.

'I've been thinking about what Raju said, and it doesn't make sense.'

Zakiy gave her a sidelong look, but didn't say anything, just kept on munching. She decided to take that as encouragement.

'I mean, why would they care about taking the prasadam? They're the ones giving the kaivisham, not the victims of it.'

'It's hard to picture those two being the victims in any scenario,' he said.

'Exactly. So it doesn't make sense that they'd worry about it.'

'No,' Zakiy said slowly, shaking his head, 'actually that's what they would worry about the most. Think about it. A liar always suspects others of lying because that's what they themselves do. So if the great-villains are always using kaivisham to do horrible things to other people –'

'Then they always suspect that other people are doing horrible things to them,' Sathi finished, stunned by the logic. 'You're right.'

'Course I am,' he retorted, smug now.

'Oh shut up.' Sathi thought for a moment. 'But if that's what they're doing on the outings then how – and when – are they preparing kaivisham for other people?'

'That I don't know,' Zakiy admitted.

She pretended to scowl at him. 'What good are you anyway?'

He made a face at her. 'But seriously, how are we going to find out? Maybe they don't leave the house to do it?'

Sathi thought back over the time she'd spent at their house. 'Maybe. I've never noticed them go off alone inside the house though. Mostly they just sit there like... like King and Queen Slug.'

'Seriously? Slug royalty?'

220

She shrugged. 'That's the mental image I get, a pair of oozing sickening slugs.'

Zakiy snorted. 'I sometimes forget how nuts you are.'

She sniffed indignantly. 'I find that highly offensive.'

'Sorry.'

'Anyway, I don't know how they do it. Unless they get up in the middle of the night or something.'

'Like bubble, bubble, toil and trouble?'

Sathi shook her head at him, then sobered as she thought of the situation at hand. 'How do we find out?'

He chewed thoughtfully on a piece of bread for a few minutes. 'I don't think our spying skills will get us much further.'

'No,' she agreed, rolling her eyes.

Zakiy suddenly brought his fist down on the table, hard. 'Damn it, I really thought we were onto something today!'

Sathi froze for a moment, taken aback at the abrupt leaking through of his very real frustration. Then she reached out and covered his fist with her own hand. 'Hey, it's okay. We'll figure this out, I promise.'

He slowly exhaled, air hissing out through gritted teeth. Then he opened his eyes and flashed her an apologetic look. 'Sorry. This is getting harder.'

'What is?'

Zakiy kneaded his eyes with his fists. 'This. Keeping it all under control. Usually making jokes makes me feel like I'm in control but lately it's been more difficult to keep up that mask. I can't control it anymore.'

She took a moment to reply, wanting to be sure of what she was saying. 'I think that's a good sign, Zakiy. Back then you needed that mask, that flippant humour, because otherwise the dark stuff in your life would have been too much to bear, it would have destroyed you. But now it's different, because you've become stronger – you've faced it, and you're fighting it. You don't need that mask anymore, because you've outgrown it.'

His gaze bore into her; he looked like he wanted to believe her but was also scared to. 'Do you really think so?'

'*Yes*. I remember the guy you were more than a year ago, when we were sitting across a table just like we are now, and you told me about Aman for the first time. I can see how much stronger this man who is sitting in front of me is compared to that broken guy. Trust me, I can see the changes.' Sathi smiled encouragingly and squeezed his hand, still under hers.

The grateful smile that flashed across Zakiy's face was all the reward she could ever ask for. But his reply contained all his trademark flippancy:

'What does it say about us that we have all our most profound conversations while we're stuffing our faces, eh?'

Sathi left Zakiy to polish off the last of the chicken curry and bread, and went in search of some coffee: India had made her into a severe caffeine addict.

As she emerged from the back door raised voices caught her attention. Frowning, she walked along the veranda to the section that looked out onto the encroaching forest. She stopped when she spotted Veena and a man standing a little way into the forest, under the cover of the trees. Though she couldn't make out what they were saying – or rather shouting – at each other, Veena was visibly upset and had tears streaming from her eyes.

With a jolt, Sathi realised that she recognised the strange man. It was Jayaram, the half-crazed guy who had once shouted at her for no reason, ranting on about kaivisham.

Anger flooded her at the sight of this guy picking on Veena. Sathi stalked forward and thrust herself between Veena and Jayaram. 'What the hell do you think you're doing?' she demanded, scowling fiercely at him.

He looked taken aback at her sudden appearance, and then he seemed to recognise her as well. To her surprise, unease skittered across his expression and his eyes flickered to Veena.

Sathi moved to put herself in his line of sight, and leaned up on her tiptoes so he had no choice but to meet her furious gaze. 'I don't care what your problem is, but I don't want you coming near my friend ever again, understand?'

The guy's expression hardened. 'Don't tell me what to do, you silly girl.'

Her face was heating up with the force of her anger. 'Either you go away right now or I will call the police,' she said clearly and distinctly, barely keeping her voice steady.

'Sathi...' Veena began, reaching out to touch her arm but Sathi shook her off.

'Let me handle this guy, Veena. I know him from before, he's crazy.'

Jayaram took a step forward, his face contorted with rage. 'Crazy? Crazy? Do you have any idea what you're talking about, you silly little girl? Do you know –'

'Enough!' Veena said, cutting him off. She levelled a steady glare at him. 'Leave now. Otherwise it will be me calling the police.'

As he stared back at Veena, all the anger drained out of his expression, leaving him with an oddly blank look. His shoulders slumped, and he turned and walked off without another word.

Feeling unsettled, Sathi glanced at Veena. Her eyes were squeezed shut, as though in pain. Sathi hesitantly reached out and touched her shoulder, and she slowly opened her eyes. They were red.

'Veena?' Sathi's voice was hesitant, unsure, confused.

Veena forced a tight smile onto her face in response and shook her head twice. Then she walked away, back into the resort, leaving Sathi to wonder what the hell had just happened.

Later that night Sathi finally climbed gratefully into bed – or well, her sleeping bag, since she'd opted to sleep at the campsite again – and sighed in relief as her body sank into the soft padding. What with waking early and climbing trees her tired muscles definitely appreciated the cushioning.

She sighed again, and rolled over onto her back. It had been a long day, emotionally as well as physically. She and Zakiy had stayed up for ages discussing the issue of the great-villains and kaivisham, talking in circles and coming up with no fresh insight. Discouraged, Zakiy had finally slouched off to his own tent and she had followed suit, trying to keep the same despondency at bay.

As she had done every night since they returned to Nelliampathi, Sathi closed her eyes and pictured golden light infusing her body, flowing through her limbs and driving out the black sludge that she associated with the kaivisham that had poisoned her body and mind. She had no idea if doing this helped because she was actually somehow purging that poison, or because the process involved deep breathing that sent her into a meditative state where her mind was both clear and focused. Either way, the important thing was that since she'd begun this routine she'd noticed she was feeling more settled than before, and she felt more in control of herself and her chaotic emotions. Her explosive, irrational rage in particular had calmed somewhat.

Even better, her sleep had improved seeing as she usually fell asleep a few minutes into her visualisations. Sure enough, Sathi felt herself begin to drift off and said a sleepy 'Goodnight!' to the pictures of Devi and Amma taped to the inside of tent before she fell into a deep sleep.

The crowd of people spilled outside the gate, bodies pressing together as their owners strained for a good view into the temple. Two men stood in a circle of cleared space in the middle, both wearing only a kavi mundu that marked them as priests. Their bare chest and upper arms had streaks of bhasma *dusted across them, and more marked their foreheads. One of the men, much older than the other, had his eyes shut in intense concentration, his lips moving in barely audible prayer. He stood in front of a pedestal with the figurine of a goddess with her tongue hanging out between blood-red fangs and the severed heads of asuras strung around her waist, their dead eyes staring blankly.*

The younger man was making a small fire on the floor and had balanced a rounded clay pot filled with some milky liquid on top of the flames. Brilliantly lit oil lamps were everywhere, the hundreds of wicks dancing in the breeze. As the liquid in the pot began to bubble and froth, the older man's chants grew in volume, until his voice filled every corner of the temple and sent shivers down the spines of the watching devotees with its power.

The boiling liquid rose higher and higher in the pot and then spilled over the edges, froth streaming down the sides and onto the floor. The chanting man's body began to tremble, and his chants came to a stop as his tongue came outside his mouth and was clamped between his teeth in a terrible grimace. Trembling became violent shaking, and yet he seemed to be in no danger of losing control or falling.

The gathered devotees gasped in awe as he reached down and lowered his arm into the pot, cupped some of the boiling liquid in his hand and smoothly poured it down his throat—

The temple abruptly went dark, all light leached from it. It was still the same place, but there were no people, no lamps, and the floor and walls were covered in a thick layer of grime and dead leaves. The whole place had the feel of a ruin, and the pedestals were covered in cobwebs. Neglect and abandonment had stamped its mark on it. The main mandapam devoted to Devi was likewise in ruin, cracks running like veins along the walls. Inside, the timeless face of the goddess statue showed an endlessly patient and yet immeasurably sad expression that—

Fire blazed again, but it had no clay pot balanced on it this time. Instead an old woman clad in black huddled around the crude brick structure that housed the fire; muttering with excitement, she drew out a wooden box that opened to reveal a lock of curly black hair. She shook it out into her hand and then dropped it into the fire, where seven pairs of eyes gleamed among the fiery tendrils of flame...

Sathi gasped and bolted upright, her heart thundering in her chest. She tried to take deep breaths to calm herself but it was difficult when it felt like her rib cage was crushing her lungs. Her clothes were drenched with sweat where they clung to her skin.

'Sathi! You okay in there?'

Before she could reply there was a ripping sound as the Velcro of her tent was yanked apart. Zakiy stumbled in, his eyes screwed shut and his arms out in front of him.

The sight – combined with anxiety that he would fall and break his neck – momentarily distracted from the awfulness of her nightmare. 'What are you doing, you idiot?' she demanded, jumping up and grabbing hold of his arm before he tripped over his own feet.

'You don't know what a minefield girls' bedroom are! Or tents, whatever. I didn't know if you were dressed!'

Sathi half-sighed, half-laughed. 'Well rest assured, I'm completely decent and fit for company.'

Zakiy opened his eyes, and they immediately focused on her, warm with concern. 'What happened? I heard you shout out.'

The dream – or was it dreams? – raced through her mind, and she related them to Zakiy. His face was thoughtful when she finished. 'That bit at the beginning, with the guy who put his hand into the boiling pot – that sounds like what my dad was telling us about Bhaskar and how he could do that without scalding his hands when he was channelling the goddess.'

She nodded. 'Yeah, and I'm pretty sure that other guy with him was a younger version of your dad.'

'But then it showed the temple dark and neglected again?'

'Like it is now,' Sathi agreed.

'Hmm.' Zakiy stared off into the distance, thoughtful again.

Hesitantly, she brought up the last and most horrifying part of her dream. 'Then it showed that old dream, with Goudhamy aka my darling great-aunt doing black magic.'

Zakiy's gaze returned to her. 'What about that thing you see in the fire, with seven pairs of eyes? You've seen that before, right?'

'I don't know what it is. It's always there in that fire, and sometimes she talks to it, like it's a pet or something. It has scales,' she remembered.

'So it could be something reptilian. But what?'

She shrugged, out of answers. They were silent for a while, and Sathi thought back over the dreams, wondering again at how they'd jerked from the temple as it was when Narayan and Bhaskar were in charge of it, to how it was now, and finally to her great-aunt's misdeeds.

'The temple,' she realised suddenly. That was the key they were looking for, the puzzle piece without which the mystery of kaivisham could not be solved.

'What about it?' Zakiy asked, looking confused.

Sathi looked at him, and saw not him but Whitebeard standing in front of her, repeating the same words he'd told her the first time she'd met him, standing in that temple.

'Of course, it's a paradox. You do something the gods don't like and they leave and go about their business elsewhere. Without them, what's the point in having a fancy house? So the temple falls to pieces.'

Sathi thought of what Narayan had told them, how her great-uncle had started to use his powers in the wrong way, ordering the gods to do his bidding. She thought of her great-aunt and the grotesque creature in the fire. She thought of her aunt, and the zombie-like expression as she glided into her great-uncle's bedroom.

'Sathi.' Something made her think this wasn't the first time Zakiy had said her name. He gripped her arms, looking worried. 'What's going on?'

She blinked, focusing on his face and remembering the pain there when he thought of his brother's illness.

Sathi swallowed. 'I think I know where the great-villains make kaivisham.'

Chapter Twenty-Four

Surprise Visitor

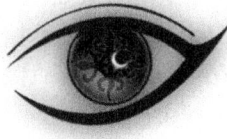

W hen she explained that the room in her dream could actually
be in that temple, Zakiy was all for setting out then and there
to find out. Then Sathi pointed out that they would have better
luck finding the room in daylight. Besides, the thought of encountering
the snake again at night terrified her.

Instead, they made plans for the morning and retired to their separate
tents. When morning came, though, it was obvious those plans would
have to be put on hold. Jagdish from the resort rushed up to her in the
campsite and blurted, 'Sathi, come quickly! That crazy man is back and
Veena... Veena is crying!'

Sathi didn't know whether to laugh at Jagdish's horrified expression
at a crying woman or feel angry with Jayaram – because she had no
doubt he was the "crazy man" – for upsetting Veena again. The latter
emotion won out as she hastily scraped her hair into a sloppy ponytail
and marched down to the resort with Jagdish at her heels.

They found Veena in her cottage room, alone. 'Where is he?' Sathi
demanded, looking around like Jayaram might be hiding under the bed
or something. 'I swear when I get my hands on him, he'll wish–'

'He's gone,' Veena broke in, her voice subdued. Her eyes shone with
unshed tears.

The sight only fed Sathi's outrage. In the short time since she'd known
her, she had come to care about Veena and the thought of anyone
upsetting her friend was unbearable. 'Which way did he go?' she asked,

fully intending to drag his sorry butt back and make him apologise to Veena.

Veena just shook her head. 'It doesn't matter. He's gone now.' Sathi opened her mouth to protest but stopped herself when she saw Veena's lips trembling. 'He's gone, and he's not coming back.'

The heartbreak in her voice brought Sathi up short. This was more than just distress over some random guy's ravings. This was pain, pain and agony that came from genuine emotion.

Sathi studied Veena's face again and made a quick decision. Glancing back, she gave Jagdish a meaningful look, one that he was all too eager to obey as he scurried out of the room, closing the door behind him.

She went to sit on the bed next to Veena, and took her hand in her own. 'Who is he?' she asked softly.

Veena shook her head, tears spilling over onto her cheeks. Sathi squeezed her hand, but waited silently. Finally, after several minutes, Veena choked out, 'Jayaram... he was my brother's best friend from childhood. We...' Her eyes flashed up to Sathi's face, and her voice was more composed when she continued. 'The three of us were always together when we were kids. Then we lost touch and never saw each other again.'

'Jayaram...he wasn't just your brother's best friend was he?'

Shutters instantly began to fall over Veena's face – then she looked at Sathi and her expression softened. Dropping her eyes to the bed, she shook her head. 'No. Jay and I... we loved each other.'

Sathi couldn't imagine anyone loving Jayaram, but maybe he'd been less antagonistic when he was younger. Veena glanced up and seemed to get what she was thinking. A wry smile lifted her lips. 'He's more sensitive than you think. He's a very kind man, a loyal man.' Then her wistful expression clouded over.

She was probably thinking of what had caused the change in him – Sathi tried to remember what Jayaram's friend had told her. 'Oh! He's grieving because his best friend died...'

Sathi trailed off as a flash of pain passed through Veena's eyes, and she reconsidered her words. Jayaram's best friend had also been Veena's brother. 'I'm so sorry,' she whispered.

Veena gave her a bittersweet smile. 'It's fine. It all happened a long time ago.'

Sathi's thoughts went to her mother. 'Yeah, but the pain never really goes away.'

The older woman studied her face for a long moment. 'You're right.'

Sathi changed the subject: 'So why did you and Jayaram lose touch?'

Veena sighed. 'When Vijay died I had to end my studies and find a job to support my family. It just wasn't possible for us to be together.'

'Why, couldn't he handle a long distance relationship?'

'No, no, of course that's not the reason,' Veena said defensively. Then she averted her eyes. 'I didn't tell him I was leaving. Vijay never knew about our relationship, and after his death... well, it seemed like we would be dishonouring his memory to let it go on. It just wasn't appropriate.'

Sathi hesitated. 'Do you still love him?'

Veena didn't look up as she answered. 'No. That was all a long time ago. It's just, seeing him again after all those years... It brought back a lot of memories.'

Sathi thought back to the time when she had seen them arguing. 'What does he want now, then? Why does he keep coming and arguing with you?'

Just like that the old shutters fell over Veena's expression, except this time there was no going back. Sathi was sure though that in the last glimpse of emotion a glimmer of fear had passed through Veena's eyes.

'I think you've wasted enough time over me today,' Veena said. 'Now I must go, I'm needed in the kitchen.'

And without another word or a backward glance she rose and left the room.

'And she didn't say anything else?' Zakiy asked as they made their way towards the temple, weaving through the tea estate.

'Nope. She wouldn't say another word on the subject.' Sathi frowned, worried. 'I wonder what's going on with her.'

'I'm sure she's fine. It's probably just seeing Jayaram again. It can't be easy to come to terms with, after all those years.'

'Yeah...'

Sathi couldn't help but think there was something more to it, though. However, the mystery of Veena took a back seat as the temple came in to view. Apprehension raised its head within her but Sathi forced herself to push it down staunchly. She could tell from the way Zakiy was walking that he was feeling the same tension. Just like the last time they'd entered the temple, they exchanged fortifying glances before they stepped inside the temple.

The neglected, dark state of the temple was a gruesome contrast to the light-filled, peaceful scenes in her dream. A temple should not have suffered so much neglect. It should never have been allowed to fall to this level of degradation.

Then she thought of the reason for that degradation and shuddered. *Focus.* 'I'm pretty sure that room in my dreams is in here. There's some kind of trapdoor the crone uses to get into it.'

'How do you know?' Zakiy asked in surprise. 'You didn't mention a trapdoor in your dream.'

'It wasn't in the dream I had last night, but I've had that dream loads of times before,' she explained. She'd actually had the same dream every single night for a while when she'd first arrived in India. 'Right at the beginning the crone pulls herself into the room through a trapdoor.'

Sathi glanced around the temple, making herself focus on the structures and possible places for a hidden door. Wordlessly they split up and scoured the building, poking and prodding into dark corners.

'Nothing,' Zakiy said after more than half an hour of fruitless searching, yanking a cobweb from his hair in disgust. It was only one of a few dozen still trapped in his brown curls.

Sathi suspected that she didn't look much better as they stood and gazed around once more, this time in resignation. She was sure that the dream last night had been a sign from Devi, giving them a push when they were at a standstill with this kaivisham mystery. And yet now that they were here in the temple it was hard to believe anyone had been using it as headquarters for carrying out black magic.

She glanced at Zakiy. The worst thing in all this was the fact that he was looking at her for guidance, he was depending on her because it had been *her* dream and *her* bloody grandparents and *her* idea to search for a trapdoor. She didn't know how she could offer up any kind of encouragement when it already felt like she was floundering aimlessly. She'd felt so certain that they'd find the answers they needed here.

Sathi felt a tension headache begin to pulse above her eyes, and walked away a few paces as she tried to think. She stopped in front of the biggest pedestal, the one belonging to Devi.

Come on. You got me this far – what am I missing?

She didn't really expect an answer, and she didn't get one. Sathi sighed and closed her eyes, trying to remember every second of the dream. Thinking of Bhaskar and the pongal, she retraced her steps to the pedestal for Bhadra, the violent incarnation of Devi who drank the blood of her enemies and whose rage was all-consuming. The figurine was just as Sathi'd seen in the dream, except covered in layers of grime like everything else in here.

A shudder went through her as she remembered the horrific grimace Bhaskar had made when he was channelling the goddess. Bhadra was supposed to be an extreme form of Devi, ruled by blind rage and bloodlust – but Sathi couldn't understand how that worked. How could a goddess as serene and forgiving as Devi ever take such a monstrous form? She'd once heard a myth in which Bhadra had been in such a rage that she only calmed down when Lord Shiva laid down in her path and she stepped on him. Only the horror of what she'd done had brought Devi back from that murderous state.

Sathi could only imagine that Devi couldn't destroy enemies when she was in the form of a mother, and since all human beings were technically her children...

She looked back at the pedestal for Bhadra. She supposed that if it was the only way people like the great-villains got their comeuppance then it was worth it.

'Sathi?' Zakiy said quietly, looking at her in concern.

She shook her head and forced herself to refocus. The dream. That was the key. Letting her eyes roam around the temple as she followed the dream from Bhaskar scooping up the boiling pongal to the moment when her great-aunt opened the trapdoor–

Her eyes snagged on the main pedestal for Devi as she remembered how the dream had focused there before switching to show the crone in that God-awful room. Not entirely sure of what she was doing, but trying to follow her instincts, Sathi walked over and fingered the door. Her hand came away smudged with dirt – it certainly didn't look like anyone came here on a regular basis. Sathi started to push open the door.

Zakiy was by her side in an instant. 'Wait. I'll go in first.'

She turned to him, one eyebrow raised. 'I can take care of myself. I'm not scared.'

'Yeah, but I don't want to stay out here by myself!' And he shrugged his way past her.

Despite herself, Sathi snorted and followed him in. Inside, they stood still for a minute – she knew they were both waiting for the snake. When there was nothing but silence she exhaled and started poking around in corners again, trying to find anything that might resemble a trapdoor.

'Sathi?'

The urgency in Zakiy's voice had her off the filthy floor where she had been crawling around and standing next to him where he was peering at the wall behind the statue of Devi.

'Look,' Zakiy said, pointing at a section of the wall. 'There's something here. Look at this crack.' He inserted his nails into the crack and heaved, and there was a strange grinding noise that made her hair stand on edge. A section of the wall slid away, leaving a large rectangular crevice that a person could easily slip through.

Sathi thumped Zakiy's arm in excitement. 'You genius! I can't believe you found it.'

Zakiy was trying hard not to look too pleased with himself – and failing miserably. But she figured he deserved it. 'After you, m'lady,' he said, gesturing with a flourish.

She took a deep breath, held it, and ducked through the makeshift doorway.

'It's like Dracula's crypt in here,' Zakiy observed, looking around with interest.

Sathi silently concurred as they navigated the narrow stairway. Although calling it a stairway was being over-generous – it was no more than a rickety old ladder, and she was relieved when they finally reached stable ground again. She stepped off the last rung and then stood still in shock. It was the room from her dream!

It was surreal. Sathi took in the shelves against one wall, the low ceiling that could make a tortoise feel claustrophobic and more disturbingly, the brick square she had seen the crone hunching over countless times as she crooned to that horrific creature in the flames.

Goosebumps broke out over the surface of Sathi's skin. She couldn't believe she was actually in the place where her disgusting grandparents carried out kaivisham, the centre of their evil. This. This was where they had concocted whatever horrible mixture they'd given to Maya so she would walk, zombie-like, to her father-in-law's bedroom. It was where they'd found a way to destroy Aman's brain and make him a prisoner in his own mind.

A wave of revulsion rose in her until the bile made her feel physically sick. How could she be related to people like them?

Zakiy's hand dropped onto her shoulder, warm and familiar, and she took a ragged breath in. 'Come on,' he said quietly, gently tugging her forward into the room. Woodenly she walked towards the bricks. They had scattered out of formation, the edges crumbled and rounded, covered in orange-brown gunk. The sand on the floor in the middle of the brick square was black.

Looking away from the gruesome sight, her attention was caught by the shelves. Remembering the dream, Sathi shuffled closer and

234

examined the many glass bottles that filled them. She was half-expecting to see the grotesque components of the black magic the great-villains used, and was relieved when she saw that the dusty, dirty bottles were mostly empty – at least of anything distinguishable.

'This is weird.'

She turned to see Zakiy still standing by the brick square, peering at something on the ground. She returned to his side. 'What?'

'Those,' he said, waving a hand towards what looked like crusty, orange-brown boulders on the floor next to the brick square. 'They're termite mounds. There's no way they've grown that big *that* quickly.' Zakiy leaned down over the bricks. 'Look, there's more in here as well. This place hasn't been used in a while.'

Sathi pursed her lips as she considered the mounds. 'Well, the great-villains probably haven't used it in the last few weeks...'

She trailed off as he looked up at her with eyes that were slightly too wide. 'Sathi, this didn't happen in the last few weeks,' Zakiy said slowly. 'Last few months maybe – or years.'

They were both lost in their own thoughts when they left the temple.

They only resurfaced when Zakiy's phone rang. He glanced at the display and then pressed the phone to his ear, mouthing 'Amma' at Sathi.

She nodded to let him know she didn't mind, and they continued walking as he talked to Maira. 'Yeah, we're both fine. Yes, Sathi's fine too. What – okay, I'll tell her' – Zakiy rolled his eyes and said, 'Apparently Zoya is turning the house upside down with her tantrums because she misses you so much.'

Sathi grinned. 'Ask Maira to tell her I love her. And not to destroy any property.'

He relayed the message and then was silent for a long time as he listened to whatever his mother was saying. The smile faded off his face as he listened, and his one-word responses became more and more glum. Finally he sighed, 'I will, Amma. Love you too' and shoved the phone back into his pocket.

'What happened?' Sathi asked.

Zakiy glanced at her wearily. 'She wants me to go and check on the house. Well, she said house but she meant Abdullah.' He shook his head. 'There's no telling what he and Dattu will get up to if left unsupervised for too long.'

Abdullah was Zakiy's parents' housekeeper and was a pompous, overbearing man who was at always at odds with the younger, more mischievous Andhra worker, Dattu. Sathi knew Zakiy hated visiting their old house because of all the bad memories it held.

'It's probably a good thing,' she teased, trying to lighten the mood as they walked, 'you don't want to deprive Dattu the pleasure of seeing you.'

Zakiy flashed her an exasperated look. 'For the last time, Dattu isn't gay and he *does not* have a crush on me!'

'He has a big brother crush on you then,' Sathi countered.

'Okay, that could be true. I think he misses his family.'

'Can you blame him, being stuck with Abdullah all day every day?' She shuddered.

'Don't remind me.'

For a while they walked on in silence. She could tell her attempts to cheer him up hadn't really worked. She also knew it wasn't just the prospect of going to his house that had brought him down.

'It doesn't make sense does it?' she sighed.

Zakiy was instantly on the same page. 'Nope. I mean, you *know* for a fact that they made kaivisham to give Maya and, well, you, and you even dreamt about it – but that room hasn't been used for ages!' He ran his hand through his hair in frustration. 'I just don't get it.'

'They must be doing it somewhere else.'

'But where? The only place they went to was that other temple. And they didn't do anything!'

Sathi shook her head. 'I don't know. All I know is they're guilty.'

That was about the only thing she was sure of at the moment.

'Aargh! HELP! Someone help me!'

The cries greeted them as they drew closer to Zakiy's house, and startled, they ran the last few yards and saw that it was Dattu yelling – because a man was gripping his collar and shaking him.

'Where is she?' the man was demanding, sounding half crazed. 'If you don't tell me where she is right now I will make you regret the day you were born!'

'Hey, what do you think you're doing?' Zakiy rushed forward, outraged, and wrenched the man away from Dattu.

Sathi came to a stop, feeling as though all the breath had deserted her just when she needed it most.

The man's eyes widened in recognition and he shook his fist in Zakiy's face. 'So you're the boy! What have you done with her? Tell me what you've done to my daughter or else I swear I'll –'

He broke off suddenly as he saw Sathi standing there, speechless. His fingers collapsed from the tight fist they'd been making.

Sathi's feet took her closer to this miracle and she wondered if she was hallucinating. She stared at the apparition before her.

'Dad?'

Chapter Twenty-Five

A Reunion

Dad?' Sathi repeated, not quite trusting what her eyes were telling her. 'What's going on?' *Am I hallucinating?* she wondered again.

Her dad didn't reply. He looked like he was drinking in the sight of her, just like she was doing with him. He was wearing jeans and a ratty old shirt instead of the smart suits she was used to seeing him in, and his hair was longer too and rumpled like he hadn't bothered to brush it. And was she imagining it or was his dark hair peppered with a lot more grey than when she'd last seen him?

'Nakul!'

Manish the tea maker ran up to them, calling *her father's name* – could the situation become any more bizarre?

Her dad unfroze. 'Sathi, thank God you're safe,' he said, like a prayer. Then something even more bizarre happened.

He rushed forward and hugged her.

Sathi stood there like a rigid plank as she felt a thousand emotions course through her at the feel of her father's arms around her, encompassing her in warmth, making her feel safe and loved and cherished in a way she hadn't felt since she was a small child. Dad held her close for what seemed like both an impossibly short and impossibly long amount of time. Then he pulled back to look at her, and Sathi was shocked to see that there were tears pooling in his eyes.

'Don't ever do that to me again,' he told her sternly. But there was none of the usual annoyance or brusqueness in his voice, just genuine worry and overwhelming relief. He leaned forward and pressed a kiss to her forehead.

At that moment Sathi realised that intense happiness could hurt your heart in much the same way as intense pain could. And for once she was experiencing the former instead of the latter.

Zakiy stepped forward. 'Look, Mr Varma' – her father wrenched his gaze from Sathi to glare suspiciously at him – 'I don't claim to understand what's going on but may I suggest that we move this conversation to somewhere more private?' Zakiy gestured towards his house.

Her father seemed to be on the verge on declining – rudely – Zakiy's generous offer, but seemed to reconsider as he looked around and realised that they were providing free entertainment for a gaggle of tea estate workers who were watching the drama with rapt attention. So her father squared his shoulders and curtly nodded before putting an arm around Sathi's shoulders and following Zakiy into the house, with Manish, Abdullah and Dattu trailing after them.

Zakiy's house was truly palatial in structure, with rooms that were large and airy with high ceilings and arching beams. Zakiy led them into the spacious living room and then, after a glance at the mute father and daughter, cheerfully offered to give Manish a guided tour while steering Abdullah and Dattu out of the room with instructions to prepare snacks for the visitors.

Silence descended as Sathi stared at her father, still not able to quite believe that he was actually here in front of her, sitting next to her on the sofa and looking at her with a strange tenderness in his eyes. A thousand questions teemed in her mind, but she was afraid to speak in case it broke this spell, in case she woke up and realised that this was a dream.

Dad didn't seem to be in any hurry to speak either and she opened her mouth at last meaning to give voice to her questions, but what came out were sobs. Reaching out and flinging her arms around Dad's neck, inhaling his crisp, familiar scent, all the grief and love and sorrow and hope she was feeling broke down into an unspoken language that her father seemed to understand as he wound his arms around her and murmured comforting sounds into her ear.

When the floodgates of her emotions slowly emptied she became aware that her eyes and nose were leaking disgustingly onto the soft fabric of Dad's shirt, but he didn't seem to notice – or care – as he held her close and rubbed warm circles on her back. Tucked under her father's arm, her sobs quieted into sniffs and then faded to silence. Sathi maintained that silence for a while; processing her grief as well as trying to form the question she wanted to ask her father. Despite the preparation, the question still came out slightly incoherently: 'How...? How are you here?'

Dad didn't reply immediately, and instead hugged her tightly for a moment before taking his arms away. Terrified of the rejection, Sathi twisted to scan his expression and was shocked – not to mention relieved – to see that he looked sheepish. An expression she had never seen on her father's face before.

Emboldened, she reached on a hand and hesitantly touched his arm. 'Dad?'

How sweet that word was on her lips!

Dad sighed and then took what could only be described as a gulp of air before speaking. 'Sweetheart, I was keeping tabs on you.'

Only the significance of what he'd just said could trump the shock of hearing the endearment, the endearment for *her*. She opened her mouth to say something, but could only gape wordlessly.

He seemed determined to go on now that he had begun. 'Manish was keeping an eye on you for me.'

'*Manish?*'

'Yes. I've known him since I was a boy, and I knew he would never leave Nelliampathi. So when you left London I called him and asked him to look after you.'

Sathi thought of all those phone calls between herself and Manish in the past months, the way he got panicky if he couldn't get hold of her on the first try. He would keep calling until she picked up, and he would admonish her for worrying him. She had always loved the way he looked after her, thinking that she had been lucky enough to stumble across someone who seemed to care for her like a father, a sort of divine compensation for having an actual father who *didn't* care. Now the revelation that the worry and concern behind Manish's actions had actually been her father's was too monumental for her to take in.

Dad continued, 'Then he called me yesterday in a panic saying that he couldn't get hold of you or find you anywhere. So I jumped to conclusions and well... here I am.'

Right. She'd left her phone on silent while they tracked the great-villains and had been too busy with Veena and the temple to go and see Manish.

Dad's slightly nervous expression shifted to worry when she didn't say anything. 'Sathi?'

She looked up at him and remembered something else: 'I caught Manish making furtive phone calls a couple of times and he always put the phone down as soon as he saw me. I accused him of having a secret girlfriend.'

Her father laughed, a rich, wonderful laugh that took her by surprise. Warm honey poured into her chest at the thought that she had made him laugh, and her own lips curved upwards in response.

'Darling, that man is married to his tea shop,' Dad said, his eyes crinkled from laughter.

She snuggled back into his arm. 'Yeah, but it's not unheard of for married men to have mistresses.'

Dad chuckled again and mussed her hair with his hand. Sathi closed her eyes and sighed in complete, blissful happiness. Her father. She had her father back.

For a few minutes neither of them spoke, then Dad broke the silence. 'Sathi, can I ask you something?'

'Of course.'

'When you saw me today... you looked completely shocked. You looked like you couldn't believe your eyes, like you couldn't believe I would come after you. Did you...?' He trailed off and then rushed on, 'Did you really think I would abandon you like that?'

Sathi stiffened and then leaned back to see his face. It was tortured and haggard, with lines that hadn't been there before, lines that she now knew were a result of worrying about her. She hated to see his pain, would do anything to erase it, but she was unable to prevent her own pain from showing in her eyes as she silently answered her father's question.

Dad's head fell into his hands. 'I've failed as a father.'

Her heart broke, and now she was the one comforting him. 'No, don't say that.' She laid her head against his cheek and hugged him to her.

'When... when you mother died I couldn't bear it. I loved her so much and her loss was the worst thing I could imagine. I was angry at the world, angry with God for taking her away, and I rejected everything else I had as a stupid kind of defiance. I was too wrapped up in my own pain and rage to realise that there was someone else who needed me, someone small and precious who had lost infinitely more than I had.' Dad cupped her cheek in his hand, and she felt her eyes filling again. 'I ignored the needs of that tiny little girl while I churned over my own feelings. I was selfish, and what I did was inexcusable.

'When that initial, overwhelming pain had faded I was left feeling empty, hollow, just a body with no emotions. And by then you'd grown, and every time I looked at you all I could see was my Madhu – and you do look so much like her, darling. By the time I realised that God had given you to me to soothe the pain of losing her, I had grown so far away from you that I didn't know how to set about repairing the damage. You loved me, I knew that, but I knew you also felt betrayed by me, by my neglect, and the thought of you hating me – no matter how well justified – terrified me.

'So I did what I do best and ran away from it. I made every excuse to be away from the house, away from your pain and unhappiness, away from a young girl who'd lost her mother and – in effect – her father. I made what was a bad situation much worse because of my own selfishness. I forced us to live like strangers in the same house.'

The tears had overflowed onto her cheeks now, but Sathi couldn't speak, not with her throat so swollen with emotion.

'Then, when you suddenly said you were going to come out here, here where–' Dad abruptly cut himself off and then continued, 'When you suddenly left I was jolted out of my self pity and I realised just how much you meant to me. I panicked, knowing that you would be out here, alone, and you don't know how close I was to jumping on a plane then and there to come after you. Then, I realised that if I came after you like that and tried to drag you back to London I would end up just alienating you further. That's why I called Manish. Until he told me that you were safe and well, that he'd seen you, I don't think I breathed properly.'

He looked into her eyes with a sudden fierceness. 'But there's one thing you should never ever doubt, and that's how much I love you. That has never changed since the moment I first laid eyes on you when you were a tiny little thing, and it will never change. You are my daughter, my precious daughter, and I love you very much.'

Sathi couldn't look away from the intensity of the gaze. Leaning into his embrace, she said the words she had wanted to say for a very long time, words that had festered within her for years because she couldn't express them. 'I love you, Dad.'

With excellent timing, Zakiy walked in with a tray of snack and drinks, beaming at them like it was perfectly normal to have guests in his house, a house that had stood empty and desolate for years. Sathi's heart suddenly overflowed with affection for him and his thoughtfulness, and she motioned for him to stay with them when he tried to leave discreetly. Turning to her father she said, 'Dad, let me introduce you to my best friend. This is Zakiy.'

They shook hands, and she was relieved to note that Dad's expression had lost some of its earlier hostility – though not the sternness. 'Pleasure to meet you, young man.'

An awkward note returned as they munched on hot samosas, largely because her father looked like he was sizing up Zakiy. 'So,' he suddenly boomed, 'what do you do, Zakiy?'

Zakiy gulped down the big bite of samosa he'd just taken. 'I just finished my engineering degree, sir.'

'I see. Do you have a job?'

'No, not yet. My...' – he quickly glanced at Sathi – 'my family is in Mysore, and I'm hoping to find a job close to them.'

Dad frowned. 'Don't engineering students have job interviews at the end of their final year?'

'Um, yeah. But I, er, opted out of them.'

Dad's tone became coloured with disapproval. 'Why would you do that?'

Zakiy sent Sathi a pleading look, and she put her hand on her father's arm. 'Dad...'

'I'm just curious, sweetheart.' He gave her an indulgent look that vanished when he turned back to Zakiy. 'I just wanted to know what your young friend here does with his time.'

Crap. Why was her father on the warpath? She'd seen him like this before, and things never ended well for his victims. Sathi had to intervene: she would have to take desperate measures. She glanced at Zakiy, both apologising and asking permission, and he gave an imperceptible nod.

'Dad, Zakiy's brother suffers from schizophrenia,' she said quietly.

Her father's expression turned blank, giving nothing away. He stared intently at Zakiy for a few moments before nodding. 'I'm sorry.'

'That's okay, sir. Because of your daughter's help I've been able to find an Ayurvedic doctor who was able to help Aman get better.'

'Good.' He regarded Sathi with pride and affection. 'Well, now that's all sorted there's no sense in delaying.'

Sathi blinked at him. 'Huh? Delaying what?'

'Our return to London, of course.'

Sathi dreamt of Vidhya Raman that night.

It wasn't like her other dreams – those had something special about them, definitely, because they showed things, true things, that she couldn't possibly have known about like the temple.

In this dream, she saw Vidhya and her father together, talking, but because she didn't know what Vidhya looked like as an adult, she was in

244

her thirteen-year-old body. But worst of all she was flirting with Dad. The sight of an adolescent flirting with her father was already sickening enough, but when it was Vidhya? Nauseating.

Then it showed her mother and mini-Vidhya arguing on the edge of a cliff, their hair lashing their faces as a strong wind swirled around them. Mini-Vidhya was doing most the shouting (though the dream didn't have audio) and her face was pinched and ugly as she yelled at Amma.

Then she reached out and shoved Amma over the cliff.

Sathi woke up with a yell, her hands stretched out above her as though to catch her mother before she plunged to her death.

Tears prickling her eyes, Sathi put her palms over face and tried to force the horrific image of Amma falling into empty air out of her head. A flood of hatred washed through her, hatred at Vidhya, at the woman who'd betrayed her mother, her best friend. Sathi's murderous thoughts gave away to despair at her father's assumption that they would leave India imminently.

She got up and left her room at the cottage, going out into the veranda and sitting on the parapet there. Looking out at the beautiful hills and forest of Nelliampathi, she felt a pang within her at the thought of leaving it. And that wasn't all that she would miss.

She couldn't bear the thought of leaving Zakiy, her best friend who'd stuck with her through thick and thin, who'd been her partner in crime in finding out about her mother as well as finding ways to treat Aman's illness. How could she leave him? Not just Zakiy, but Maira, Narayan, Zoya, Aman, Manish, Anna, Ravi, Veena... even Nidhi. In just a few months she'd formed so many more meaningful attachments with others than she had in years in London. How could she leave all that behind?

And then there was the most important reason why she couldn't leave: the tool with which her subconscious had chosen to torment her today. She hadn't achieved what she'd come to India to do, to avenge Amma. She even knew the identity of her mother's killer.

The problem was, so did her father.

Sathi had known before she set out to India that there was a far simpler way of finding out the identity of Amma's murderer than trekking out to an unknown country. Her father knew. He knew it was Vidhya because of the letter written from her mother to her father, in which Amma had confided in her husband about the people who visited her at the hospital, who had unnerved her, who they both knew the identity of, even though Amma simply referred to them as "they".

Of course he knew – how could he not? He knew Vidhya had killed his wife, but he hadn't done anything about it. Sathi didn't know why, but she knew that it was a forbidden subject with him still. All the joy she had experienced yesterday, the joy of realising that her father did really love her, had been marred by that one wall that was still erect between them. Her father had begun to say something about her coming to Nelliampathi and had then cut himself off and changed the subject.

She hadn't challenged him on it yesterday, and she wasn't sure she would ever have the courage to. She was terrified that doing so would force the return of the cold, angry father she was used to living with – and erase this loving father whom she couldn't quite believe was real.

She was terrified of losing him again.

She was locked in the iron grip of an impossible decision; would she go along with her father, cut her losses and return to London with him? Or would she risk his alienation to finish what she had started and avenge her mother's death?

'Hey Sathi!'

While she had been zoned out Zakiy had walked up to her and now wore a cheerful grin. Seeing him, her heart lurched but she somehow managed to smile back. 'Hey.'

She scooted over to make space for him and Zakiy sat down next to her. For a few moments they sat silently, enjoying the crisp breeze rusting their clothes and each other's company.

'I'm going to Mysore,' Zakiy said eventually.

Sathi turned her head so sharply pain that shot through her neck. Seeing her panicked expression Zakiy hastened to add, 'Just for a few days! I want to see how Aman's doing. And I didn't want to, well...'

He trailed off and she understood the message perfectly. He was giving her space, space to make this impossible decision without having to contend with him as well. Tears filled her eyes again and she thanked Devi – for the millionth time – for giving her such an amazing friend.

How was she supposed to give him up?

'I'll come with you,' she said automatically.

He was shaking his head even before she'd finished speaking. 'Don't be idiotic. You need to stay with your dad.'

'Zakiy...'

'Shh,' he told her, putting his arm around her. 'Look, don't give yourself an aneurism over this. If you stay, you stay. If you go, you go. That's all there is to it, and whatever you do we'll still be best friends, okay? You're not getting rid of me that easily!'

She shook her head, rebelling against his words. It wasn't that simple. 'I made you a promise.' *Just like I made myself a promise,* she thought. 'I promised I would help you make the great-villains pay for what they did.'

Zakiy didn't reply for a few moments, but the arm around her tightened. 'Well, I hereby absolve you from your promise.'

'Stop that.'

He looked at her, startled. 'Stop what?'

Sathi sniffed, feeling thoroughly miserable. 'Stop being so nice.'

Zakiy chuckled and stood up, saluting her. 'Yes ma'am.' Then his grin faded. 'I'll have to get going now.'

'Wait!' She leaped up and clutched his arm. 'How long are you going for?'

He looked into her eyes intently. 'That depends.' He gave her one last hug and walked away.

Aghast, she stared after him. Then she blurted, 'I'm not going anywhere until you get back!'

Zakiy's only answer was to give her a sad smile over his shoulder while she stood and watched him walk away, wondering why she couldn't have promised him that she wasn't going anywhere, period.

Chapter Twenty-Six

Decisions & Revelations

Her life was a complete shambles, so Sathi went shopping.

In fairness to herself, it wasn't just a shopping trip; after Zakiy left, Jagdish from the resort had rushed up to her and – in a weird mimicry of déjà vu – informed her that Veena was upset because Jayaram had come again and apparently they'd had a very public, very loud fight right in the middle of the restaurant. Nidhi might be fair, but a spectacle like that with her staff wasn't good for business, and she'd given Veena an official warning and told her she would be fired if a repeat incident occurred.

So, in a desperate effort to cheer both of them up Sathi had dragged Veena to a huge market nearby and convinced her that a break from their respective troubles for a day was exactly what they needed. Or maybe calling it "running away" might be more accurate – perhaps she had more in common with her father than she thought, Sathi realised uneasily.

Dad hadn't been keen on spending the day away from her, but when she explained what had happened with Veena he gave in, and they made plans to meet up later in the day. He'd told her that he had a surprise for her.

For a minute her father's excitement when he told her that cheered her up; then the thought that he might be looking up flights back to London right now made her smile turn into a grimace.

Later, she told herself, *I'll think about it later.*

Veena was looking half-heartedly through a pile of tops and Sathi stood watching her, shifted out of feeling sorry for herself by the dark circles under her friend's expressive eyes. The usual immaculate braid that slivered down her back was scruffy with strands sticking up, and her shoulders were slightly hunched in as she stood. Now that she was paying attention Sathi could see just how tired and weary Veena looked; she kind of hated Jayaram for hurting her again and again, no matter his good intentions.

Veena turned and caught Sathi staring. She lifted her eyebrows. 'What? Why are you looking at me like that?'

'Nothing.' Sathi went over to her and impulsively gave her a hug. Veena stiffened in surprise before relaxing and hugging her back.

'So,' Sathi said, pulling back, 'do you want to talk about it?'

'There's not really anything to talk about. He came, we argued, he walked off in a huff. It's the same old story.' Veena shrugged, feigning nonchalance.

'I'm sorry.'

Veena squeezed her hand in response, and then sighed. 'I just wish he would let go. I wish he would forget about me and move on with his life.'

'If he hasn't forgotten you in all these years he's hardly likely to forget you now,' Sathi pointed out.

'He must. He will, I'll make sure of it. He's living in a dream world right now. Do you know what he suggested? He asked me to go with him; he said we would get married! Ridiculous.'

'What's so ridiculous about that?'

'We haven't seen each other in twenty odd years!' Veena shook her head. 'I told you, Jay is living in a fantasy of his own making. It would never work with the two of us. It's too late.'

'Why is it too late?' Sathi argued. 'Is it because of your brother? Because surely he would rather you be happy than make yourself miserable for the rest of your life for the sake of not disrespecting his memory?'

She wasn't entirely sure why she was pushing Veena with this – she didn't even like Jayaram. But she had to admit that there was something noble, something admirable about his refusal to give up on Veena and their love, and she couldn't understand why Veena seemed immune to that.

Anger flashed through Veena's eyes, but she visibly controlled it. She said firmly, 'Look, let's just agree to disagree on this.' Shrewdness took over her expression as she stared at Sathi. 'Now it's your turn.'

'Huh?' Sathi said, startled and playing for time. She had the distinct sense of being wrong footed.

'Don't act smart with me, young lady!' An ironic smile played around Veena's lips. 'You've made me spill my deep dark secrets, now it's your turn. Why are you so down?'

A ready denial rose to her lips, but Sathi realised that the thought of voicing her dilemma was very appealing – and Veena was the closest friend she had access to at the moment, one without much vested interest. A non-partisan, if you will.

'My dad's here,' she said.

Veena's playful expression turned to shock. 'Nakul? Here, in Nelliampathi?'

'Yeah, and–' Sathi cut herself off and frowned. 'Wait, how do you know his name?'

'Oh, you told me once. Anyway, why has that made you sad?' Veena asked quickly.

'He wants me to go back to London with him.'

Veena looked puzzled. 'Wouldn't you have done that eventually anyway? You're here on a gap year, aren't you?'

'Yeah, but Dad wants me to go right now, in the next couple of days.'

'And you don't want to leave.'

Sathi didn't reply. The problem was, she didn't know *what* she wanted. Or maybe it was that she wanted too many things.

'I guess it's only the matter of a few months, isn't it?' Veena offered. 'Then you'd have to leave anyway.'

'It's not that simple,' Sathi said. Damn. The problem with opting to unload your problems was that the person you were unloading to had to know the full story. Which Veena definitely didn't.

'Why not?'

Sathi squirmed internally. Why had she opened her big mouth? She wasn't sure she was in the mood to go through this again with someone.

Then it occurred to her that she was being a hypocrite. She had forced Veena into confessing what was obviously a painful past and here she was shying from doing the same. She couldn't treat Veena like that.

'Let's go and have a coffee. This is going to be a long conversation.'

Zakiy had put on a good face for Sathi, but the truth was he was terrified. He'd assured her that they would remain friends even if she chose to go back with her father, but he knew that the logistics of that were never going to work. *He* hadn't believed a word he said and he knew Sathi hadn't either.

But she'd wanted to believe him. He'd seen that in her eyes, that longing to make everyone – both her father and Zakiy – happy, all at once. Of course she put herself and her own needs last on her list of priorities.

That's when he realised he needed to leave, give her some space to figure out what she wanted without the guilt and anguish his presence undoubtedly ignited in her.

The knowledge that he had acted for the greater good did nothing to lessen the pain of parting on such uncertain terms, though – he missed his best friend.

And apparently he wasn't the only one.

His father opened the door back in Mysore and, upon seeing his son, immediately looked around. 'Where's Sathi?' he asked.

Zakiy pushed past his father, seeing as he wasn't giving any indication of stepping aside to let him in. 'It's just me this time. Sathi had to stay behind in Nelliampathi.'

Dad looked crestfallen. 'Oh no, I really wanted to tell her about the new CD I bought for the puja room. I know she would have liked it...'

Zakiy left his father staring dejectedly at the floor and walked into the kitchen, where Zoya immediately pounced on him. Then she realised that her Sathi chechi hadn't come to see her, and she started wailing with a volume that would put an ambulance to shame. Nothing would console her or Ricku the dog who, after sniffing hopefully around Zakiy, flopped down and started up a low whine to complement Zoya's wails.

'What on earth is going on here?' Amma asked, walking in and staring at the kid and dog duo in surprise. Then she caught sight of Zakiy, and a joyful smile spread across her face as she rushed over to kiss his cheek.

Then she looked around. 'Where's Sathi?'

'Oh for God's sake, I thought *I* was your long-lost child,' Zakiy said in mock rage. In truth he was overjoyed at his family's reaction to Sathi. Although given recent events the joy was bittersweet.

Amma gave him an affectionate smile and tucked in the tag at his shirt collar. 'Sathi's like a daughter to me, too.' She looked down at Zoya, who was beating her big brother with her small fists, and her eyes sparkled. 'A more respectful, better behaved one.'

Zakiy rolled his eyes. 'Well, can you please remove your *other* daughter from my leg? I can't walk.' To demonstrate his point, he shook the leg that Zoya was clinging to with both hands. Another minute, and his belt would probably give away.

Amma laughed and leaned down to peel Zoya off him. Bouncing her in her arms, Amma told her, 'You'll see Sathi chechi soon, *vavé*, don't cry. She'll come to see you soon.'

She glanced up at Zakiy and caught sight of his grimace. Frowning, she put Zoya down and told her to go to her father before turning to cast a concerned look at Zakiy. 'What's wrong?'

'I'm not sure Sathi will be able to come anytime soon,' he said carefully.

Amma looked surprised. 'Oh. Well, in that case we'll try to come to see you two in Nelliampathi.'

Zakiy shook his head mutely.

'What? What is it?'

'Her father came from London, and he's planning to take her back with him.'

'I see.'

Amma looked at him, and something about that steady, unflinching gaze made him want to run away. Zakiy turned and opened the fridge for the sake of looking away from his mother. 'Yeah. She's wanted her dad to come after her for so long, you know? Now that he has she can't believe it. I'm glad she's happy.'

A hand softly touched his shoulder. 'Zakiy, I know this is hard. But sometimes caring about someone is about being able to let them go.'

His face still turned away from the understanding in her voice, he nodded.

The doorbell rang at that moment, and Zakiy jumped at the chance to escape. 'I'll get it,' he said, straightening and rushing from the room.

When he opened the door he was surprised to see D. 'Hey! What are you doing here?' he asked, hugging him.

'Hey, hey, careful with the hair,' D protested, pulling away and touching his precariously arranged hair.

Zakiy raised an eyebrow at him. 'As vain as ever, huh? Glad to see there's no change.'

'At least I brush it, unlike *some* people,' D shot back.

For a moment they regarded each other silently before bursting into laughter. 'Ah, I've missed you,' Zakiy said.

'Funnily enough, so have I. So why are we standing around? Let's go somewhere!'

Zakiy agreed good-naturedly and the two of them wandered through Mysore town, catching up. 'How's Ruhaan?' Zakiy asked.

D made a face. 'As sweet-natured as ever.'

'That bad, huh?'

'Worse.' D's voice became closed off suddenly. 'Ever since we left she's been a nightmare.'

Zakiy shook his head ruefully. 'I don't know why she acts like that. She's always fine with me.'

'Seriously?' D burst out. 'Do you actually not know why she acts like a diva?'

Shocked, Zakiy shook his head.

'She thinks she's effing in love with you, that's why!'

'What?' Zakiy squawked. 'She does not! She's like a sister to me.'

'Well, she doesn't quite see it that way. She's been obsessed with you since she could talk, and that mother of hers doesn't help. She's over the moon about getting you as her son-in-law someday.'

'Over my dead body!' Zakiy shuddered at the thought of having Fadilah as his mother-in-law.

'Yeah, well, unless you do something about it that's how things are going to end up,' D said bitterly. 'Ruhaan's not going to let her dream guy slip through her fingers.'

'Look, why are you acting like this is my fault?' Zakiy demanded, getting angry now.

'I didn't say that.'

'No, but you're acting like it.'

They glared at each other. Then D's eyes inexplicably filled with pain and he glanced away.

Zakiy felt as though an anvil had hit his chest. 'You love her,' he realised, dumbstruck. 'You love Ruhaan.'

D choked out a strangled laugh that somehow made him sound as miserable as he looked. 'Masochistic, or what, eh?'

'No, of course it's not,' Zakiy assured, still reeling. 'How long's that been going on?'

D shrugged. 'Pretty much forever. But she's never even thought of me that way. She only ever has eyes for you.'

'Couldn't that be because you're always mean to her?' Zakiy pointed out.

D laughed, though this time it was genuine. 'No, you don't understand. I'm mean to her because that's the only way she'd notice me, or interact with me as a human being. I'm the only one who challenges her and her, well, let's say *difficult* personality. I just keep waiting and hoping that one day she'll realise that and wonder what the hell she ever saw in you,' he teased.

Zakiy shook his head, awed at the depth of character his friend had suddenly revealed. D had always been a player where girls were concerned, constantly setting his sights on and hitting on anything female. That had been why Zakiy had been uneasy about the closeness that had sprung up between D and Sathi – no matter how long he and D had known each other, if he messed with Sathi Zakiy would have punched him for sure. Now he realised that D's flirty persona had all been an act, one probably cultivated to hide his feelings about Ruhaan. 'I can't believe I never realised.'

'Well, you've always needed a nudge to see what's right in front of you.'

'Hey, what's that supposed to mean?'

D blinked, his grin fading into incredulity. 'You mean you haven't figured it out yet?'

'Figured *what* out?' Zakiy asked.

'Maybe it's not a nudge you need; you need a proper *shove* in the right direction.'

'D!' Zakiy growled. 'What are you talking about?'

'I'm talking, my dear, stupid friend,' D said, 'about the fact that you're obviously in love with Sathi.'

'So let me get this straight,' Veena said, pushing her coffee cup away. 'You think your Amma was murdered and you came to India to try to find the responsible party?'

'I *know* Amma was murdered,' Sathi insisted.

Veena raised her arms, palms out in surrender. 'Okay, fine, say you're right. What chance have you got of tracking down her killer? Wouldn't it be better to abandon this fruitless venture and go back home with your father?

Sathi didn't reply, frustrated that Veena didn't understand. She'd never thought that she could be so unhappy after having her father come after her like she'd always hoped he would, come after her and tell her that he loved her despite everything that had gone wrong between them. It was so unfair! She'd got what she asked for, but at what a price!

And worst of all was the knowledge that a fair share of the blame for the cause of her unhappiness rested with herself. If only she had the guts to confront her father, to tell him honestly that she didn't want to leave before she avenged her mother. If only she could look him in the eye and tell him she was staying, that she wouldn't go back with him yet.

If only she weren't so tempted to go with him, to forget this whole mess and return to London where they could start anew, safe and happy in the knowledge that her father loved her.

The thing was, she wasn't sure she would be able to live with herself if she took such a cowardly course of action.

And like that, the load on her chest lifted. Sathi felt like she was breathing properly again for the first time in two days. Realisation had illuminated the way to her decision, as effortlessly as water gushes through an aperture.

'Sathi?' Veena touched her shoulder in concern.

She beamed at her friend, knowing that she wouldn't have been able to make this decision without her. 'Excuse me a minute,' she said, walking away a few paces and pulling her phone out.

For a moment Zakiy couldn't do much more than gape at his friend. '*What?*' he spluttered out eventually. If he'd felt like an anvil had hit him earlier, now it felt like a grand piano had ploughed into him, Tom and Jerry style. Except he didn't have an umbrella ready to deflect the blow.

'D, that's not even remotely funny,' he warned through gritted teeth.

'I'm not trying to be funny – it's just one of those facts of life. The earth is round. The sun rises in the – wait, I always have to think about this - in the East. You love Sathi.' D shrugged, and the bizarre thing was, he looked deadly serious.

'We're just friends. *Best* friends,' Zakiy repeated, his skin starting to burn with embarrassment. Why did everyone seem to be making the same mistake?

D gave him a pitying look. 'You really don't have a clue, do you? And I thought Sathi was bad.' He shook his head, half-sighing, half-chuckling.

'What are you going on about?' Zakiy demanded, his heart fluttering like the wings of a trapped bird inside his throat.

'Well, she's obviously in love with you, too.'

When he received no response but dumbfounded silence, D gave his friend a look that was a blend of exasperation and curiosity. 'Could you be any more blind? Are you two really that oblivious?'

Zakiy transformed his confusion into annoyance. 'You're talking nonsense. There's nothing like that between us.'

'Are you kidding me? Most of the time you two act like an old married couple. And when Ruhaan was drooling over you Sathi was so jealous she couldn't see straight!'

'Well, if that's true why did she hang out with you all the time?'

Uneasily, Zakiy wondered where that petulant outburst had come from. Hadn't he just told himself that the only reason he didn't like Sathi and D hanging out was because he thought D was a player and would end up hurting her? Was D right – had he really been lying to himself?

'Oh, that was one of my ingenious plans to win Ruhaan over and make her realise she was wasting her time with you; then I saw hopeless you and Sathi were, and I realised it was the perfect way to kill two birds with one stone. You see, I was hoping that seeing me and Sathi spend time together would make you jealous – which it did – and force you to realise how you felt about her; that was obviously a severe overestimation of your intelligence on my part. At the same time I hoped that it would make Ruhaan jealous over me.' D frowned. 'I think I need to work on that one.'

Despite his overwhelming confusion Zakiy felt the need to make D feel better, especially after hearing how much he had been trying to do for Zakiy's sake. 'No, she was definitely jealous,' he said. 'She mentioned to me later that she missed having you around.' Zakiy grimaced. 'Well, being Ruhaan, she didn't put it quite that way but that was the sentiment. She takes you for granted so much that I think it startled her that you weren't always around.'

D looked hopeful. 'Really?'

'Positive. You know, that could explain some of her resentment towards Sathi, too.'

'Maybe.' D sighed. 'I guess I just need to keep at her and wear her down slowly.' Then he grinned. 'In the meantime, I can take credit for uniting one couple at least – I can take it as an omen for my own love life.'

Zakiy shook his head dubiously. 'I wouldn't be too sure of that.'

When D opened his mouth to protest, he rushed to forestall him. 'No, listen. I love Sathi – she's my friend. But I'm not *in love* with her...'

D rolled his eyes heavenward. 'Oh my God. This is like trying to explain elementary definitions of like and *like*. How can you be so much in denial?'

Zakiy was just about to protest that he wasn't in denial when his phone rang. Troubled by the conversation, he lifted it to his ear without checking the caller ID. 'Hello?'

A very familiar voice sounded in his ear. 'Zakiy, come back. I'm not going anywhere.'

Two sentences. That's all it was. But hearing them was like taking that first breath after a deep dive. It was like seeing those first pricks of light when you're walking down a dark street. It was like the sun breaking through after a storm, drenching you in liquid warmth that seemed to reach all the way into your soul.

Hearing her voice then, Zakiy realised that D was right. He really had been lying to himself all along.

When he finally found his voice, it was thick with tears. 'You're the best,' he told her. *I love you*, he added silently, reverently.

He could hear the smile in her voice when she answered: 'Nope. That's still you.'

Sathi wasn't going. She was staying with him.

Zakiy was in love with his best friend.

He was in big trouble.

Chapter Twenty-Seven

Double Role

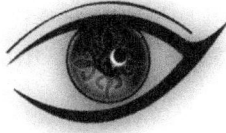

Disconnecting the call, Sathi went back to Veena. 'I'm not going,' she informed her, feeling as though she were floating on air. The relief she felt was overwhelming.

She would tell her father her decision in the evening. The idea of saying no to her father still filled her with apprehension, but the knowledge that she was doing the right thing would help bolster her courage.

Veena looked even more worried than before. 'Sathi, are you sure–'

She was interrupted by the waiter, who came by to give them the bill for their coffees. 'Oh, Veena, can you take the money from my purse? It's there on the seat next to you.'

'I can pay,' Veena argued.

'No way, it's my turn,' Sathi insisted.

Veena shook her head but took some money from Sathi's purse and handed it to the waiter. As she did, a piece of paper fluttered out of the purse and down to the table.

'What's this?' Veena asked, picking it up. Her expression froze.

Sathi glanced at the paper and smiled. 'It's a picture of my mum. She won this art competition when she was thirteen, and I found this photo of her in a newspaper. It's one of the only pictures I have of Amma, so...' She shrugged.

Of course, the picture didn't *just* show her mother. As though reading her mind, Veena fingered the crease where the photo had been folded over, and seemingly almost against her will, lifted the flap so that the whole picture was visible.

'That's Vidhya Raman,' Sathi told Veena, who didn't look up. 'She's Amma's supposed best friend.'

'Supposed?'

'Well, yeah.' Sathi hesitated. 'She's the one. She's the one who killed her.'

Veena's head whipped up, and her eyes bore into Sathi's. 'What?'

Sathi nodded. 'Vidhya was jealous of Amma. And she... she liked my dad, wanted him for herself.'

'Who told you this?'

'Amma's uncle. He and her aunt adopted her when her parents died.'

Veena looked stricken, and if Sathi wasn't mistaken, her hands were trembling. Concerned, Sathi touched her arm. 'What's wrong? Are you okay?'

'I...' Veena looked up at her for the first time, true panic in her eyes. 'I've got to go. There's something... there's something I've got to do, I just remembered. I've got to go,' she repeated, standing up and making for the door without another word.

'Wait!' Sathi rushed after her, following her outside, but she had disappeared into the crowd. Her phone rang; it was her dad, asking her to meet her at a certain address. Still scanning the landscape for Veena's slight figure, Sathi agreed distractedly. She eventually gave up and set out to meet Dad, her mind churning over what had happened. What was up with Veena?

When Dad saw her coming he rushed to close the last few steps between them and gathered her into a big hug. He pressed a kiss to her forehead before he drew away. 'I missed you.'

Sathi felt her anxiety over Veena fade as blissful love washed over her. She clung to her father's arm, feeling like a little kid again. 'I missed you too, Dad.'

Tucking her hand securely into the crook of his arm, Dad started walking.

'So what's the surprise?' Sathi asked as they headed further away from the Nelliampathi town centre.

'You'll love it,' Dad replied mysteriously, refusing to say any more on the subject despite Sathi needling him for details.

Around ten minutes later, they came up to a house built into the edge of the forest. Sathi gasped when she saw it; constructed in a way reminiscent of a tree house, the single-story building was at the top of a flight of stairs, supported by sturdy, exquisitely placed pillars that made it seem as though the house was resting on air alone. The house itself was built very simply, with a thatched roof and a charming removable door. All in all, surrounded by the woods, the little cottage looked like a scene straight out of a fairy tale.

As soon as she saw the house, Sathi knew her mother had to have designed it. It was perfect. Her hunch was confirmed when Dad put his arm around her shoulders and said, 'This is where your mother and I used to live. This little piece of heaven was her pride and joy.' When she didn't move, he gave her a gentle push forward. 'Go on. I know you're dying to explore it.'

That was all the encouragement she needed, and she walked up the steps as though in a dream and paused on the tiny porch in front of the door, admiring the view of the mountains afforded to her while Dad unlocked the door. He stepped back to let her go in first. The little sitting room inside made her eyes fill as took in the little touches that her mother must have made in the process of making this house into a loving home; the soft rug on the floor that matched the maroon of the sofa; the lace curtains with rose patterns that covered the floor-to-ceiling glass of the north wall; the walnut coffee table with the antique-looking candle holder at its centre.

It was the opposite of their large, impersonal house in London. It was perfect.

Sathi wandered around the small rooms of the cottage, taking in every detail and revelling in the knowledge that it was her mother's mind that thought it all up. She trailed her hands along everything, touching everything her mother's hands had once touched, her eyes drinking in everything her mother's eyes had once seen.

Her dad seemed content to let her walk about, watching her affectionately. Finally she joined him on the sofa and leaned her head on his shoulder. 'I thought you'd sold this house years ago.'

Dad's hand tightened around her. 'I could never sell this house. Madhu designed every stone of it herself; it was her dream house. You know, everyone thought she was mad for building such a small house, but she was deliriously happy with it. It was our sanctuary, where we were truly cut off from the rest of the world.'

'Thank you for bringing me to your house, Dad.'

'It's yours, too, sweetheart.'

Sathi sighed, contentment permeating her every cell of her being like a drug, intoxicating her. Could there be a greater happiness?

'I've heard wonderful things about your cooking, you know,' Dad said, sitting up. 'Why don't we make a day of it, spend the night here and we'll cook up a meal together?'

'Okay,' she agreed, excited about the prospect of cooking for her father. She followed him into the kitchen and began to pull open cupboards. It was no good, however; there was nothing edible in there, just various pots and pans.

'We'll have to go shopping,' Dad sighed. 'Otherwise I'll have to wait until we go back to London for me to taste your cooking!'

Sathi had just pulled out a photo frame from an otherwise empty cupboard, and pulled a face at her father's words. Right. She still needed to tell him that she wouldn't be going back yet. Trying to buy time, she looked down at the photo in her hands, which showed Amma with her arms around–

'What the hell?' she exclaimed.

Dad hurried to her side. 'What is it?' He saw the photo and brushed off some dust from it. He smiled. 'Oh yes, you wouldn't know who this is with your mother, of course. She was Madhu's best friend, Vidhya. Vidhya Raman.'

Sathi stared uncomprehendingly at the photo, unable to believe what her eyes were telling her. She thought about the last few weeks, a million connections forming in her mind, connections that she'd been too blind, too stupid to see.

Her father said the woman in the picture was Vidhya Raman.

But Sathi recognised the woman as someone else, a younger version of someone she knew very well.

The woman in the picture was Veena.

Sathi sprinted all the way back to the resort.

Her father followed her, frantically calling out questions she didn't have the answers to. Not yet. When the two reached the resort Sathi immediately ran into the kitchen. Finding it empty, she rushed to the staff cottage and threw open the door of the room next to hers. It, too, was empty, but that wasn't the worst thing: the room had been stripped of Veena's belongings, save for a half empty tube of toothpaste at the sink and a bottle of eyeliner in front of the mirror. Just like someone had left in a hurry, forgetting those small, insignificant things in the rush to get away.

'Oh, didn't you know?'

Sathi turned to see Jagdish standing in the doorway. 'Veena left,' he continued, looking a bit shell shocked. 'That guy Jayaram came again, and she went with him.'

Of course. She should have known. All his deranged rants and Veena's – *Vidhya's* – heartbroken act had been just that. An act. A way to gain Sathi's confidence and find out how much she knew about Amma's murder. And just a few hours ago Sathi had given her the answers she was seeking, and Vidhya had melted again into the shadows like a sly fox.

'She told me to give you this.'

The words snapped her mind to attention, and she reached out with shaking hands – shaking from rage – to take the sealed white envelope Jagdish was holding out. She ripped it open and lifted out the single sheet of paper.

Sathi–

I'm sorry. I'm so sorry for doing this to you. I can't stay, not now that you know who I am. I've never been brave like your mother; I'm a coward. I've run before and now I'm running again.

But there is one thing you need to know. I did not kill your mother. Sathi, you have to believe me. I don't know for sure who did, but there is a way for you to find out. Your mother left me her diary before she died, and she made me swear not to read it. But if anyone has a right to see it, you do. The diary is safe at the address at the bottom of this page.

I've never had the guts to try and find your mother's murderer; but you, wonderful as you are, have obviously inherited her courage. You must find out the truth, Sathi. No one loved your mother like I did, and her murder is a heinous crime that they've tried to cover up. You can't let them win. You need to find out the truth.

And if I were you, I would look first at those who fed you those lies about me – yes, I'm talking about your mother's family. They are responsible for your mother's death, I'm sure of it!

Find the truth, Sathi.

- Vidhya

To be continued - and concluded! - in the
third and final novel in the trilogy, Serpent's Dance

Glossary

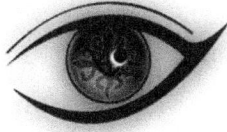

Malayalam terms:
Malayalam is the native language spoken in Kerala, south-west India.

Malayali/Keralite – someone from Kerala/someone who speaks Malayalam.

Aadivasees – local Indian tribes

Amma – mother

Asura – mythological demons that inhabit the Underworld, usually depicted as being evil. Also called rakshasa

Ayurveda – literally means the "science of life", an ancient form of healing

Biryani – mixed rice dish, with spices and/or meat

Chechi – elder sister

Chetan – elder brother

Churidar - Indian clothing consisting of long flowing top, leggings and shawl

Gudgunu, jadamanji, karimbadam, kannumkombu, muringa – Ayurvedic herbs, plants with medicinal properties

Kaivisham – literally "hand-poison", a form of black magic

Khavi – saffron-coloured religious wear

Kumkumam – saffron

Lakhsham – hundred thousand (rupees in this context)

Makri – (little) frog
Mandapam – altar/shrine
Manthram - magic
Mritasanjeevani – magical herb that can restore the dead
Puja room – prayer room
Purdah – religious clothing for Muslim women
Rakshasa – see asura
Sari – traditional Indian attire for women, composed of six metres of cloth wrapped artistically around the body
Thulasi – holy basil
Unmaadham – a blanket term meaning insanity/fury
Vaidhyan – a physician who practices Ayurveda (the term is not confined to Ayurveda practitioners, can refer to related schools of medicine)
Yagna – a Hindu ritual worship done in front of a sacred fire, often with mantras

NB: Karuppuraja (Karuppu Raja) = Black King/Prince ≈ Prince of Darkness

Acknowledgements

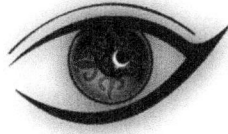

As ever, thank you to my parents for their eternal support and encouragement. I can't tell you how much I appreciate the solid foundation you've given me.

Iqbal Uncle – thank you for having our backs. We really appreciate it.

Unnikrishnan Uncle – you are a constant source of comfort. Thank you.

Mummy's Daddy, Mummy's Mummy, Suresh Uncle and Salim Uncle – love you all. Thank you.

PRISM OF TRUTH
DOVES IN FLIGHT

Shivon Mirza Sudesh

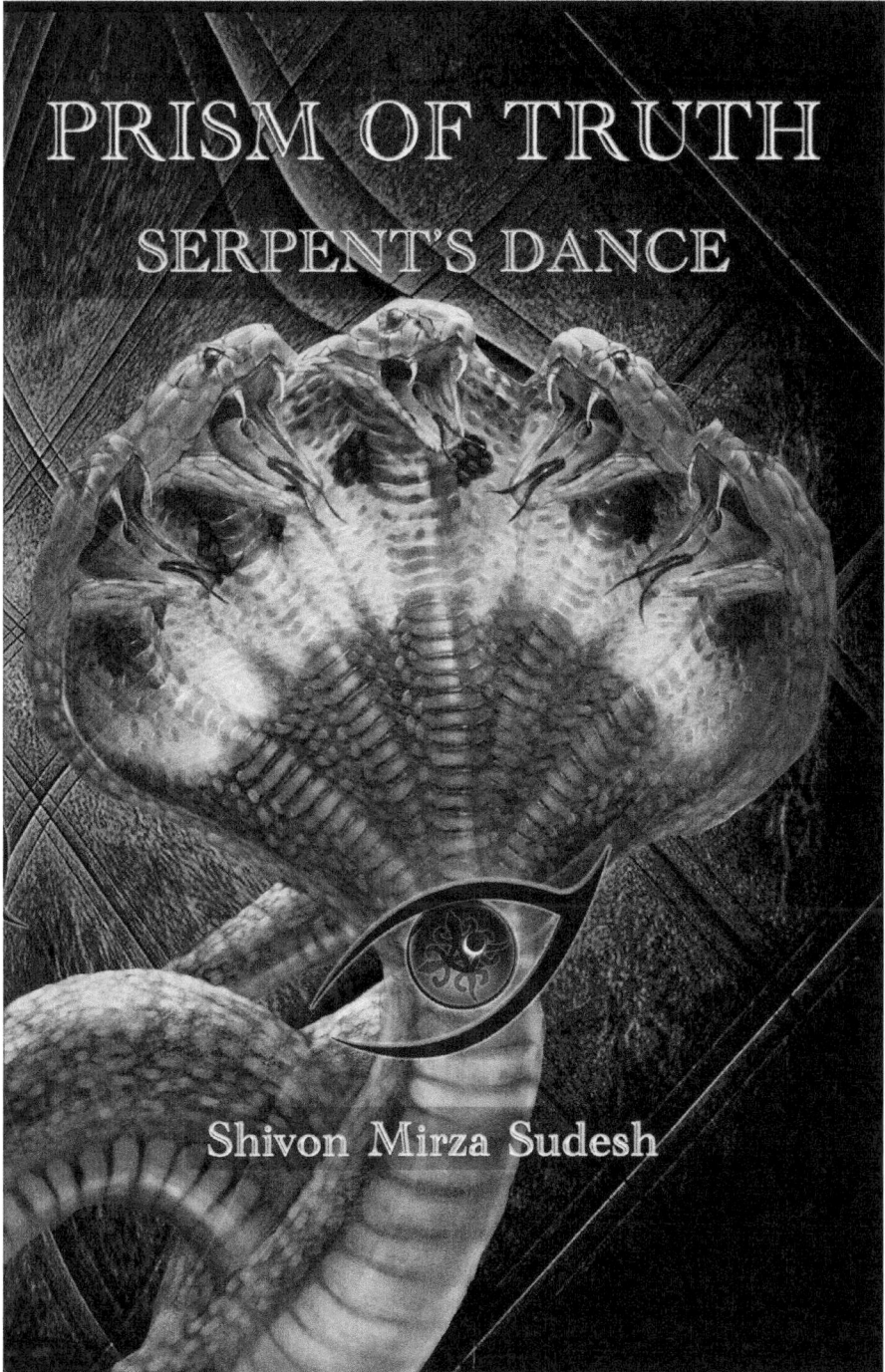

PRISM OF TRUTH

SERPENT'S DANCE

Shivon Mirza Sudesh

Printed in Dunstable, United Kingdom